Carl Hiaasen was born and raised in Florida. His previous novels include the bestselling *Nature Girl*, *Star Island*, *Bad Monkey* and *Razor Girl*, and three bestselling children's books, *Hoot*, *Flush* and *Scat*. They have been translated into 34 languages, 33 more than he can read or write. Carl Hiaasen also writes an award-winning weekly column for the *Miami Herald*.

Also by Carl Hiaasen

Tourist Season
Double Whammy
Skin Tight
Native Tongue
Strip Tease
Stormy Weather
Lucky You

Sick Puppy
Basket Case
Skinny Dip
Nature Girl
Star Island
Bad Monkey
Razor Girl

With William Montalbano

A Death in China
Trap Line

Powder Burn

For young readers

Hoot
Flush
Scat

Chomp
Skink
Squirm

Non-fiction

Paradise Screwed:
Selected Columns (edited
by Diane Stevenson)
Kick Ass: Selected Columns
(edited by Diane Stevenson)
Team Rodent: How Disney
Devours the World

The Downhill Lie: A
Hacker's Return to
a Ruinous Sport
Dance of the Reptiles (edited
by Diane Stephenson)
Accept the Worst
(with Roz Chast)

Native Tongue

CARL HIAASEN

SPHERE

SPHERE

First published in the United States in 1991 by Alfred A. Knopf, Inc.,
an imprint of Penguin Random House LLC
This paperback edition published in Great Britain in 2023 by Sphere

1 3 5 7 9 10 8 6 4 2

A CIP catalogue record for this book
is available from the British Library.

ISBN 978-1-4087-2921-2

Printed and bound in Great Britain by Clays Ltd, Elcograf S.p.A.

Papers used by Sphere are from well-managed forests
and other responsible sources.

FSC
www.fsc.org

MIX
Supporting
responsible forestry
FSC® C104740

Sphere
An imprint of
Little, Brown Book Group
Carmelite House
50 Victoria Embankment
London EC4Y 0DZ

An Hachette UK Company
www.hachette.co.uk

www.littlebrown.co.uk

For my brother Rob

One

On July 16, in the aching torpid heat of the South Florida summer, Terry Whelper stood at the Avis counter at Miami International Airport and rented a bright red Chrysler LeBaron convertible. He had originally signed up for a Dodge Colt, a sensible low-mileage compact, but his wife had told him go on, be sporty for once in your life. So Terry Whelper got the red LeBaron plus the extra collision coverage, in anticipation of Miami drivers. Into the convertible he inserted the family—his wife Gerri, his son Jason, his daughter Jennifer—and bravely set out for the turnpike.

The children, who liked to play car games, began counting all the other LeBarons on the highway. By the time the Whelpers got to Snapper Creek, the total was up to seventeen. "And they're all rentals," Terry muttered. He felt like a fool; every tourist in Miami was driving a red LeBaron convertible.

"But look at all this legroom," said his wife.

From the back seat came Jennifer's voice: "Like, what if it rains?"

"Like, we put up the top," Terry said.

His wife scolded him for being sarcastic with their daughter. "She's only eleven, for heaven's sake."

"Sorry," said Terry Whelper. Then louder, over his shoulder: "Jenny, I'm sorry."

"For what?"

Terry shook his head. "Nothing, hon."

It started raining near Florida City, and of course the convertible top wouldn't go up; something was stuck, or maybe Terry wasn't pushing the right button on the dash. The Whelpers sought shelter at an Amoco station, parked near the full-service pumps and waited for the cloudburst to stop. Terry was dying to tell his wife I-told-you-so, sporty my ass, but she wouldn't look up from the paperback that she was pretending to read.

Jennifer asked, "Like what if it rains all day and all night?"

"It won't," said Terry, trying hard to be civil.

The shower stopped in less than an hour, and the Whelpers were off again. While the kids used beach towels to dry off the interior of the convertible, Gerri passed around cans of Pepsi-Cola and snacks from the gas station vending machine. In vain Terry fiddled with the buttons on the car radio, trying to find a station that played soft rock.

The Whelpers were halfway down Card Sound Road when a blue pickup truck passed them the other way doing at least eighty. Without warning, something flew out of the truck driver's window and landed in the back seat of the LeBaron. Terry heard Jason yell; then Jennifer started to wail.

"Pull over!" Gerri cried.

"Easy does it," said her husband.

The convertible skidded to a halt in a spray of grass and gravel. The Whelpers scrambled from the car, checked themselves for injuries and reassembled by the side of the road.

"It was two guys," Jason declared, pointing down the road. "White guys, too."

"Are you sure?" asked his mother. The family had been

on guard for possible trouble from blacks and Hispanics; a neighbor in Dearborn had given them the scoop on South Florida.

"They looked white to me," Jason said of the assailants.

Terry Whelper frowned. "I don't care if they were purple. Just tell me, what did they throw?"

Jennifer stopped crying long enough to say: "I dunno, but it's alive."

Terry said, "For Christ's sake." He walked over to the convertible and leaned inside for a look. "I don't see anything."

Jennifer cried even harder, a grating subhuman bray. "You . . . don't . . . believe . . . me!" she said, sobbing emphatically with each word.

"Of course we believe you," said her mother.

"I saw it, too," said Jason, who rarely took his sister's side on anything. "Try down on the floor, Dad."

Terry Whelper got into the back seat of the LeBaron, squeezed down to his knees and peered beneath the seat. The children heard him say, "Holy shit," then he leapt out of the car.

"What is it?" asked his wife.

"It's a rat," said Terry Whelper. "The ugliest goddamn rat I ever saw."

"They threw a rat in our car?"

"Apparently."

Jason said, "Too bad we didn't bring Grandpa's gun."

Gerri Whelper looked shaken and confused. "Why would they throw a rat in our car? Is it alive?"

"Very much so," Terry reported. "It's eating from a bag of Raisinets."

"Those are mine!" Jennifer cried.

The Whelpers stood there discussing the situation for fifteen minutes before a highway patrol car pulled up, and a young state trooper asked what was the matter. He listened sympathetically to the story about the rat in the rented LeBaron.

"You want me to call the Avis people?" he asked. "Maybe they'll send another car."

"Actually, we're on a pretty tight schedule," explained Gerri Whelper. "We've got reservations at a motor lodge in Key Largo. They said we had to be there by five or else we lose the rooms."

Jennifer, who had almost stopped crying, said: "I don't care about the motel, I want a different car."

Terry Whelper said to the trooper, "If you could just help me get rid of it."

"The rat?"

"It's a big one," Terry said. "Well, I can probably shoot it."

"Could you?" Gerri said. "Please?"

The trooper said, "Technically, it's against regulations. But since you're from out of town . . . "

He stepped out of the patrol car and unsnapped the holster strap on his .357.

"Wow!" said Jason.

Jennifer put her arms around her mother's waist. Terry Whelper manfully directed his brood to move safely out of the line of fire. The state trooper approached the LeBaron with the calm air of a seasoned lawman.

"He's under the seat," Terry advised. "Yeah, I see him."

The trooper fired three times. Then he holstered the gun, reached into the convertible and picked up what remained of the creature by what remained of its tail. He tossed the misshapen brown lump into some holly bushes.

"Thank you so much," said Gerri Whelper.

"You say it was a blue pickup. You didn't happen to see the license plate?"

"No," said Terry. He was wondering what to tell Avis about the bullet holes in the floorboard. When the kids climbed

4

back in the rental car, their mother said, "Don't touch any of those raisins! We'll get more candy when we get to the Amazing Kingdom."

"Good, I want a Petey Possum Popsicle," Jennifer said, nearly recovered from the trauma. Jason asked if he could keep one of the empty shell casings out of the state trooper's revolver, and the trooper said sure.

Terry Whelper grimly contemplated the upcoming journey in the red, rat-befouled LeBaron. He felt fog-headed and emotionally drained. To think, just that morning he'd been safe and sound in his bed back in Michigan.

"Don't forget to buckle up," said the trooper, holding the door open.

Terry said, "This ever happen before?"

"What do you mean?"

"This rat business."

"I'm sure it has. We don't hear about everything." The trooper smiled as he closed Terry Whelper's door. "Now, you all have a nice vacation."

In the blue pickup truck, still heading north, Danny Pogue said, "That was the damnedest thing I ever saw."

Bud Schwartz, who was driving, said, "Yeah, that was some shot. If I do say so."

"There was kids in that car."

"It was just a mouse, for Chrissakes."

"It wasn't a mouse, it was a rat." Danny Pogue poked his partner in the shoulder. "What if those was your kids? You like it, somebody throws a fucking rat in their laps?"

Bud Schwartz glanced at the place on his shoulder where Danny Pogue had touched him. Then he looked back at the highway. His bare bony arms got rigid on the steering wheel. "I wasn't exactly aiming for the kids."

"Were too."

After a few strained moments, Bud Schwartz said, "You don't see that many convertibles anymore."

"So when you finally see one, you throw a rat in it? Is that the deal?" Danny Pogue picked at a pair of ripe pimples on the peak of his Adam's apple.

"Let's just drop it," said Bud Schwartz.

But Danny Pogue remained agitated all the way to Florida City. He told Bud Schwartz to let him off in front of the Long John Silver's.

"No way," said Bud Schwartz.

"Then I'll jump outta the goddamn truck."

Danny Pogue would damn sure try it, too, Bud thought. Jump out of the damn truck purely on principles.

Bud Schwartz said, "Hey, you don't want to do that. We've gotta go get your money."

"I'll find my own ride."

"It'll look hinky, we don't show up together."

Danny Pogue said, "I'm not riding nowhere with a guy that throws rats on little kids. Understand?"

"What if I said I was sorry," Bud Schwartz said. "I'm sorry, all right? It was a shitty thing to do. I feel terrible, Danny, honest to God. I feel like a shit."

Danny Pogue gave him a sideways look.

"I mean it," said Bud Schwartz. "You got me feeling so bad I got half a mind to cry. Swear to God, look here—my eyes are all watered up. For a second I was thinking of Bud Jr., about what I'd do, some asshole threw a rat or any other damn animal at my boy. Probably kill him, that's what I'd do."

As he spun through this routine, Bud Schwartz was thinking: The things I do to keep him steady.

And it seemed to work. In no time Danny Pogue said, "It's all right, Bud. Least nobody got hurt."

"That's true."

"But don't scare no more little kids, understand?"

Bud Schwartz said, "I won't, Danny. That's a promise."

Ten minutes later, stopped at a traffic light in Cutler Ridge, Danny Pogue turned in the passenger seat and said, "Hey, it just hit me."

He was grinning so wide that you could count all the spaces where teeth used to be.

"What?" said Bud Schwartz.

"I remember you told me that Bud Schwartz wasn't your real name. You said your real name was Mickey Reilly."

"Mike. Mike Reilly," said Bud Schwartz, thinking, Here we go. "Okay, then how could you have a kid named Bud Jr.?"

"Well—"

"If your name's Mike."

"Simple. I changed the boy's name when I changed mine."

Danny Pogue looked skeptical. Bud Schwartz said, "A boy oughta have the same name as his daddy, don't you agree?"

"So his real name was—"

"Mike Jr. Now it's Bud Jr."

"You say so," said Danny Pogue, grinning again, a jack-o'-lantern with volcanic acne.

"What, you don't believe me?"

"No, I don't believe you," said Danny Pogue, "but it was a damn good story. Whatever your fucking name is."

"Bud is just fine. Bud Schwartz. And let's not fight no more, we're gonna be rich."

Danny Pogue got two beers out of the Styrofoam cooler in the back of the cab. He popped one of the cans for his partner and handed it to him. "I still can't believe they're payin' us ten grand apiece to steal a boxful of rats."

"This is Miami," said Bud Schwartz. "Maybe they're voodoo rats. Or maybe they're fulla dope. I heard where they smuggle coke in French rubbers, so why not rats."

Danny Pogue lifted the box from behind the front seat and

placed it carefully on his lap. He leaned down and put his ear to the lid. "Wonder how many's in there," he said.

Bud Schwartz shrugged. "Didn't ask."

The den box was eighteen inches deep, and twice the size of a briefcase. It was made of plywood, painted dark green, with small hinged doors on each end. Air holes had been drilled through the side panels; the holes were no bigger than a dime, but somehow one of the animals had managed to squeeze out. Then it had scaled the front seat and perched on Danny Pogue's headrest, where it had balanced on its hind legs and wiggled its velvety snout in the air. Laughing, Bud Schwartz had deftly snatched it by the tail and dangled it in his partner's face. Over Danny Pogue's objections, Bud Schwartz had toyed with the rodent for six or seven miles, until he'd spotted the red convertible coming the other way down the road. Then he had said, "Watch this," and had tossed the animal out the window, into the passing car.

Now Danny Pogue lifted the green box off his lap and said, "Sure don't weigh much."

Bud Schwartz chuckled. "You want a turn, is that it? Well, go ahead then, grab one."

"But I don't wanna get bit."

"You got to do it real fast, way I did. Hurry now, here comes one of them Winnebagos. I'll slow down when we go by."

Danny Pogue said, "The top of this box ain't even locked."

"So what're you waiting for?" said his partner. "Pop goes the weasel."

After the rat attack, the Whelper family rode in edgy silence until they arrived at the Amazing Kingdom of Thrills. They parked the red LeBaron in the Mr. Bump-a-Rump lot, Section Jellybean, and took the tram to the main gate. There they came upon a chaotic scene: police cars, an ambulance, TV trucks, news photographers. The ticket turnstiles were all blocked.

"Swell," said Terry Whelper. "Beautiful."

"Maybe they're filming a movie," his wife suggested. "Maybe it's not real."

But it was. The center of attention was a supremely tanned young man in a blue oxford shirt with a dark red club tie, loosened fashionably at the throat. Once all the TV lights were on, the man started to read from a typed sheet of paper. He said he was a spokesperson for the company.

"This is a message for all our friends and visitors to the Amazing Kingdom of Thrills," the man began. "We deeply regret the incident that disturbed today's Summerfest celebration. We are proud of our security arrangements here at the park, and proud of our safety record. Up until today, there had been—and I say this unequivocally—no serious crimes committed within our friendly gates."

In the swell of the crowd, Terry Whelper felt his wife's chin digging into his shoulder blade. "What do you suppose he's talking about?" she said.

The man in the oxford shirt continued: "We believe there was no way to anticipate, much less prevent, what happened this afternoon in the Rare Animal Pavilion."

Terry Whelper said, "This oughta be good." A large woman wearing a damp cotton blouse and a Nikkormat around her neck turned and shot him a dirty look.

The man at the TV microphones was saying, "At approximately 2:15 p.m., two men entered the compound and attacked one of the wildlife exhibits with a sledgehammer, breaking the glass. One of our park employees courageously tried to stop the intruders, but was overpowered and beaten. The two men then grabbed a box of specimens from the exhibit arena and ran. In the confusion, the suspects managed to escape from the park, appar ently by mingling with ordinary tourists aboard the Jungle Jerry Amazon Boat Cruise."

Jason Whelper said, "Specimens? What kinda specimens?"

Jennifer announced, "I don't want to go on the Jungle Jerry anymore."

Terry Whelper told the children to be quiet and listen. The tanned man in the blue shirt was saying that the park employee who had so bravely tried to stop the crime was being rushed to the hospital for X-rays.

"Hey, look!" said Jason, pointing.

Somebody in an oversized polyester animal outfit was being loaded into the ambulance.

"That's Robbie Raccoon!" cried Jennifer Whelper. "He must be the one who got hurt."

All around them in the crowd, other tourist children began to whimper and sniffle at the sight of Robbie Raccoon on the stretcher. Jason swore he saw some blood on Robbie Raccoon's nose.

"No, he's going to be fine," said Gerry Whelper. "See there, he's waving at us!"

And, indeed, whoever was inside the Robbie Raccoon costume managed a weak salute to the crowd before the ambulance door swung closed.

"It's gotta be ninety-eight degrees out here," marveled Terry Whelper. "You'd think they'd get the poor guy out of that raccoon getup."

Terry Whelper's wife whispered urgently to the nape of his neck, "Not in front of Jennifer. She thinks he's real."

"Oh, you're kidding," Terry said.

Under the TV lights, the tan young spokesperson finally was revealing what had been stolen in the daring robbery.

"As many of you know," he said, "the Amazing Kingdom of Thrills is home to several endangered varieties of wildlife. Unfortunately, the animals that were stolen this afternoon are among the rarest, and most treasured, in our live-animal collection. In fact, they were believed to be the last two surviving specimens of the blue-tongued mango vole." Here the handsome spokesman paused dramatically. Then: "The animals were being kept here in a specially climatized habitat, in the hope that they might breed and keep the species alive. Tragically, that dream came to an end this afternoon."

"Mango voles!" exclaimed Jason Whelper. "Dad, did you hear? Maybe that's what landed in our car. Maybe those guys in the pickup truck were the crooks!"

Terry Whelper took his son by the arm and led him back toward the tram, away from the tourist crowd. Gerry and Jennifer followed steadfastly.

Gerri whispered to her husband: "What do you think? Maybe Jason is right."

"I don't know what to think. You were the one who wanted to come to Florida."

Jason cut in: "Dad, there was only two of those mangos left in the whole wide world. And we shot one!"

"No, we didn't. The policeman did."

"But we told him to!"

Terry Whelper said, "Be quiet, son. We didn't know."

"Your father's right," added Gerri. "How were we to know?"

Jennifer hugged her mother fiercely around the waist. "I'm so scared—can we drive to Epcot instead?"

"Excellent idea," said Terry Whelper. Like a cavalry commander, he raised his right arm and cocked two fingers toward the parking lot. "Everybody back to the car."

Two

As soon as Charles Chelsea got back to the Publicity Department, he took a poll of the secretaries. "How was I?" he asked. "How'd I do? What about the necktie?"

The secretaries told Chelsea that he looked terrific on television, that loosening the necktie was a nifty touch, that overall it was quite a solid performance. Chelsea asked if Mr. Kingsbury had called, but the secretaries said he hadn't.

"Wonder why not," said Chelsea.

"He's playing golf up at Ocean Reef."

"Yeah, but he's got a cellular. He could've called." Chelsea told one of the secretaries to get Joe Winder, and then went into his private office and closed the door.

Ten minutes later, when Joe Winder got there, Charles Chelsea was watching himself on the VCR, reliving the press conference. "Whadja think?" he asked, motioning at the television screen in the cabinet.

"I missed it," said Joe Winder.

"You missed it? It was your bloody speech—how'd you miss it?"

"I heard you were dynamite."

Charles Chelsea broke into a grin. "Yeah? Who said?"

"Everybody," lied Joe Winder. "They said you're another Mario Cuomo."

"Well, your speech had something to do with it."

It wasn't a speech, Winder thought; it was a *statement*. Forty lines, big deal.

"It was a great speech, Joe," Chelsea went on, "except for one part. *Specially climatized habitat*. That's a mouthful. Maybe we should've tried something else." With pursed lips he repeated the culprit phrase: "'Climatized habitat'—when I was trying to say it, I accidentally spit on that girl from Channel 10. The cute one. Next time be more careful, okay? Don't sneak in any zingers without me knowing."

Joe Winder said, "I was in a hurry." The backs of his eyeballs were starting to throb. Sinus headache: Chelsea always gave him one. But Winder had to admit, the guy looked like a million bucks in an oxford shirt. He looked like a vice president in charge of public relations, which he was.

Chelsea was saying, "I don't even know what it means, climatized habitat."

"That's the beauty of it," Winder said.

"Now, now." Chelsea wagged a well-tanned finger. "None of that, Joey. There's no place for cynics here at the Amazing Kingdom. You know what Kingsbury says."

"Yeah. We're all little kids." Winder kneaded his skull with both hands, trying to squeeze out the pain.

"Children," Charles Chelsea said. He turned off the VCR and spun his chair to face Joe Winder. "The moment we walk through that gate, we're all children. We see the world through children's eyes; we cry children's tears, we laugh children's laughter. We're all innocent again, Joe, and where there's innocence there can't be cynicism. Not here in the Amazing Kingdom."

Joe Winder said, "You're giving me a fucking headache. I hope you're happy."

Charles Chelsea's blue eyes narrowed and darkened. "Look, we hired you because you're good and you're fast. But this isn't a big city newsroom, you can't use that type of coarse language. Children don't talk like that, Joe. That's gutter language."

"Sorry," said Winder, concealing his amusement. Gutter language, that was a good one.

"When's the last time you heard a child say that word?"

"Which word, Charlie?"

"You know. The 'F' word."

"I've heard children say it. Plenty of times."

"Not here, you haven't." Charles Chelsea sat up straight, trying to radiate authority. "This is a major event for us, Joey. We've had a robbery on the premises. Felons invaded the theme park. Somebody could've been hurt."

"Rat-nappers," Winder remarked. "Not exactly Ted Bundy."

"Hey," Chelsea said, tapping a lacquered fingernail on the desk. "Hey, this is serious. Mr. X is watching very closely to see how we do. All of us, Joe, all of us in Publicity are on red alert until this thing blows over. We mishandle it, and it blows up into a story about crime at the Amazing Kingdom. If we can spin it around, it's a story about a crime against Nature. Nature with a capital 'N.' The annihilation of an entire species. Where's your notebook?"

"Downstairs, on my desk."

"Listen, you're my ace in the hole. Whatever gets dumped in my lap gets dumped in yours."

Joe Winder's sinuses hurt so much he thought his eyeballs must be leaking from the inside. He didn't want to be Chelsea's ace in the hole.

Chelsea said, "And, Joe, while we're at it, what'd I tell you about the hair? No braids."

"But it's all the rage," Winder said.

"Get it cut before Kingsbury sees you. Please, Joe, you look like a Navajo nightmare."

"Nice talk, Charlie."

"Sit down," said Chelsea, "and put on your writing cap."

"I'd love to look as spiffy as you, but you bought up all the oxford shirts in Miami. Either that or you wear the same one every day."

Chelsea wasn't listening. "Before we begin, there's some stuff you need to know."

"Like what?"

"Like their names."

"Whose names?"

"The voles," Charles Chelsea said. "Vance and Violet—two helpless, adorable, fuzzy little furballs. Mated for life. The last of their species, Joey."

With a straight face, Winder repeated the names of the missing creatures. "Vance and Violet Vole. That's lovely." He glanced at his wristwatch, and saw that it was half past five. "Charlie," he said, "you don't happen to have any Darvons?"

Chelsea said, "I wish you were writing this stuff down."

"What the hell for?"

"For the story. The story of how Francis X. Kingsbury tried everything in his power to save the blue-tongued mango voles from extinction."

"Only to be thwarted by robbers?"

"You got it," said Charles Chelsea. "Stay late if necessary and take a comp day next week—I need a thousand words by tomorrow morning. I promised Corporate a press kit." He stood up and waited for Joe Winder to do the same. "Get with Koocher for more background on the missing animals. He's got reams of pictures, too, in case you need inspiration. By the way, did you ever get to see them?"

Winder felt oddly detached. "The voles? No, not in person," he said. "I wasn't even aware they had actual names."

"They do now."

At the door, Charles Chelsea winked and shook Joe Winder's hand. "You know, Joe, some people in the organization weren't too thrilled when we brought you aboard. I mean, after what happened up at Disney."

Winder nodded politely. Chelsea's hand felt moist and lifeless, like a slab of cold grouper.

"But, by God, I knew you'd be fine. That speech today was masterful, Joey, a classic."

"A classic."

"I need you on this one. The other kids are fine, they can turn a phrase. But they're right out of school, most of them, and they're not ready for something so big. For this I need somebody with scars. Combat experience."

With effort, Joe Winder said, "Guess I'm your man."

Charles Chelsea chucked him on the arm and opened the door.

"What about a reward?" Winder asked. "In the press release, should I say we're offering a reward?"

Thinking about it, Chelsea nearly rubbed the tan off his chin. "I guess it couldn't hurt," he said finally. "What do you think?"

"For two rats? Ten grand is good."

"Voles, Joe. Don't ever say rats. And five grand is plenty."

Winder shrugged. "The park netted forty-two million dollars last year. I know a few reporters who'd be happy to remind us."

"All right, go for ten," said Charles Chelsea. "But don't overplay it. Otherwise every geek in Miami is going to show up at the gate with shoe boxes full of God knows what."

The thought of it made Joe Winder smile for the first time all day.

One of the few things Winder liked about his new job was the golf cart he got to drive around the Amazing Kingdom of Thrills. It was a souped-up Cushman with an extra set of twelve-volts, and headlights scavenged off a real Jeep.

It was the closest thing to a company car that Joe Winder ever had, and sometimes (especially on that long downhill stretch between Magic Mansion and the Wet Willy) he could stomp on the tiny accelerator and forget what exactly he did for a living.

At night Joe Winder tried to drive more carefully, because it was harder to watch out for the tourists. The tourists at the Amazing Kingdom seldom paid attention to where they were going; they wandered and weaved, peered and pointed. And who could blame them? There were so many colorful and entertaining distractions. Before Charles Chelsea had given Joe Winder the keys to the Cushman, he had warned him to be wary when driving near the tourists. "Whatever you do, don't hit one," Chelsea had said. "If you're going to crash, aim for a building," he had advised, "or even a park employee. Anything but a paying customer."

So Joe Winder drove with extra caution in the golf cart at night. He arrived at the Rare Animal Pavilion shortly after eight, and parked in the back. Dr. Will Koocher, the vole man, was waiting inside with handouts and glossy photographs. Winder sat on a lab stool and skimmed the material.

Koocher said, "We kept the information fairly general. They tell me the pictures usually go over big."

As Winder studied the photographs, he said, "Cute little buggers."

"They're just rodents," the doctor noted, without malice.

"You don't understand," Winder said. "Cuteness is vital for a story like this." He explained how newspapers and television stations got much more excited about animal stories when the animal came across as cuddly and lovable. "I'm not saying it's good or bad, but that's the way it is."

Will Koocher nodded. "Like with the manatees—everybody wants to save the manatees, but nobody gives a hoot about the poor crocodiles."

"Because they're not particularly cute," Winder said. "Who wants to hug a reptile?"

"I see your point." Will Koocher was a gaunt young man with the longest neck that Joe Winder had ever seen. He seemed painfully earnest and shy, and Winder liked him immediately.

"I'll tell you what I can," Koocher said, "but I've only been here a month."

Like everything else at the Amazing Kingdom, the Vole Project had begun as a scheme to compete with Walt Disney World. Years earlier, Disney had tried to save the dusky seaside sparrow, a small marsh bird whose habitat was being wiped out by overdevelopment along Florida's coastline. With much fanfare, Disney had unveiled a captive-breeding program for the last two surviving specimens of the dusky. Unfortunately, the last two surviving specimens were both males, and even the wizards of Disney could not induce the scientific miracle of homosexual procreation. Eventually the sparrow fell to extinction, but the Disney organization won gobs of fawning publicity for its conservation efforts.

Not to be outdone (although he invariably was), Francis X. Kingsbury had selected another endangered species and commanded his staff save it, ASAP. And so the Vole Project was born.

Koocher had gotten the phone call while finishing his thesis at Cornell. "I'd published two field studies on the genus *Microtus*, so I suppose that's where they got my name. Anyway, this guy Chelsea calls and asks if I'd heard of *Microtus mango*, and I said no, all my work was on the northern species. He sent me a scientific paper that had been published, and offered me a job. Forty grand a year."

"That's good money right out of school."

"Tell me about it. I burned up the interstate getting down here."

"And that's when you met Violet and Vance."

"Who's that?"

"The voles," Winder said. "They've got names now."

"Really?" Will Koocher looked doubtful. "I always called them Male One and Female One."

"Not anymore. Kingsbury's got big plans, PR-wise. The little mango cuties are going to be famous—don't be surprised if the networks show up tomorrow."

"Is that so," Koocher said, with not the wildest enthusiasm. Winder sensed that the scientist disapproved of anthropomorphizing rodents, so he decided to lay off the Vance-and-Violet routine. Instead he asked about the tongue.

"Well, it really is blue," Koocher said stiffly. "Remarkably blue."

"Could I say indigo?" Joe Winder was taking notes.

"Yeah," said Koocher, "that's about right." He started to say something more, but caught himself.

Joe Winder asked: "So what killed off the rest of them? Was it disease?"

"No, same old story. The encroachment of mankind." Koocher unfolded a map that illustrated how the mango vole had once ranged from the Middle Keys up to Palm Beach. As the coastline surrendered to hotels, subdivisions and condominiums, the voles' territory shrank. "They tell me the last known colony was here, on North Key Largo. One of Kingsbury's foremen found it in 1988, but so did a hungry barn owl. They were lucky to save the two that they did."

"And they mated for life?" said Winder.

Koocher seemed amused. "Who told you that?"

"Chelsea."

"That figures. Voles don't mate for life. They mate for fun, and they mate with just about anything that resembles another vole."

Winder said, "Then here's another dumb question: Why

19

were there only two in our exhibit? They'd been together, what, a year? So where're all the bouncing baby voles?"

Edgily, Koocher said, "That's been our biggest disappointment."

"I did some reading up on it," Winder said. "With your typical *Microtus*, the female gives birth every two months. Each litter's got eight or nine babies—at that rate, you could replenish the whole species in a year."

Will Koocher shifted uncomfortably. "Female One was not receptive," he said. "Do you understand what that means?"

"Do I ever."

"This was an extreme case. The female nearly killed the male on several occasions. We had to hire a Wackenhut to watch the cage."

"A guard?" said Joe Winder.

"To make sure she didn't hurt him."

Winder swallowed a laugh. Apparently, Koocher saw no humor in the story. He said, "I felt sorry for the little guy. The female was much larger, and extremely hostile. Every time the male would attempt to mount her, she would attack."

Joe Winder put his notebook away. He'd think of a way to write around the reproduction question.

Koocher said: "The female vole wasn't quite right."

"In what way?"

But Koocher was staring past him. Winder turned and saw Charles Chelsea on the other side of the glass door. Chelsea gave a chipper, three-fingered salute and disappeared.

The doctor said, "Now's not a terrific time to get into all this. Can we talk later?"

"You bet. I'll be in the publicity office."

"No, not here. Can I call you at home in a day or two?"

Winder said sure. "But I've got to write the press release tonight. If there's something I ought to know, please tell me before I make an ass of myself."

20

Koocher stood up and smoothed the breast of his lab coat. "That business about the networks coming—were you serious?"

"Cute sells," Winder said. "You take an offbeat animal story on a slow news day, we're talking front page."

"Christ." Koocher sighed.

"Hey, I'm sorry," Winder said. He hadn't meant to come off as such a coldhearted prick. "I know what these little critters meant to you."

Will Koocher smiled ruefully. He folded the habitat map and put it away. He looked tired and sad, and Winder felt bad for him. "It's all right," the young scientist said. "They were doomed, no matter what."

"We're all doomed," said Joe Winder, "if you really think about it." Which he tried not to.

Bud Schwartz parked the pickup truck under an immense ficus tree. He told Danny Pogue not to open the doors right away, because of all the mosquitoes. The insects had descended in a sibilant cloud, bouncing off the windows and the hood and the headlights.

"I bet we don't have no bug spray," said Danny Pogue.

Bud Schwartz pointed at the house. "On the count of three, make a run for it."

Danny Pogue remarked that the old place was dark. "She saving on the electricity, or what? I bet she's not even home. I bet she was hoping we got caught, so she wouldn't have to pay us."

"You got no faith," said Bud Schwartz. "You're the most negative fucking person I ever met. That's why your skin's broke out all the time—all those negative thoughts is like a poison in your bloodstream."

"Wait a minute, now. Everybody gets pimples."

Bud Schwartz said, "You're thirty-one years old. Tell me that's normal."

"Do we got bug spray or not?"

"No." Bud Schwartz unlocked the door. "Now let's go—one, two, three!"

They burst out of the pickup and bolted for the house, flailing at mosquitoes as they ran. When they got inside the screened porch, the two men took turns swatting the insects off each other. A light came on, and Molly McNamara poked out of the door. Her white hair was up in curlers, her cheeks were slathered in oily yellow cream and her broad, pointy-shouldered frame was draped in a blue terry-cloth bathrobe.

"Get inside," she said to the two men.

Immediately Bud Schwartz noticed how grim the woman looked. The curlers, cream and bathrobe didn't help.

The house was all mustiness and shadows, made darker and damper by the ubiquitous wood paneling. The living room smelled of jasmine, or some other old-woman scent. It reminded Bud Schwartz of his grandmother's sewing room.

Molly McNamara sat down in a rocker. Bud Schwartz and Danny Pogue just stood there like the hired help they were.

"Where are they?" Molly demanded. "Where's the box?"

Danny Pogue looked at Bud Schwartz, who said, "They got away."

Molly folded her hands across her lap. She said, "You're lying to me."

"No, ma'am."

"Then tell me what happened."

Before Bud Schwartz could stop him, Danny Pogue said, "There was holes in the box. That's how they got out."

Molly McNamara's right hand slipped beneath her bathrobe and came out holding a small black pistol. Without saying a word she shot Danny Pogue twice in the left foot. He fell down, screaming, on the smooth pine floor. Bud Schwartz couldn't believe it; he tried to speak, but there was no air in his lungs.

"You boys are lying," Molly said. She got up from the

rocker and left the room. She came back with a towel, chipped ice, bandages and a roll of medical adhesive tape. She told Bud Schwartz to patch up his partner before the blood got all over everything. Bud Schwartz knelt on the floor next to Danny Pogue and tried to calm him. Molly sat down and started rocking.

"The towel is for his mouth," she said, "so I don't have to listen to all that yammering."

And it was true, Danny Pogue's wailing was unbearable, even allowing for the pain. It reminded Bud Schwartz of the way his first wife had sounded during the thrashings of childbirth.

Molly said, "It's been all over the news, so at least I know that you went ahead and did it. I suppose I'm obliged to pay up."

Bud Schwartz was greatly relieved; she wouldn't pay somebody she was about to kill. The thought of being murdered by a seventy-year-old woman in pink curlers was harrowing on many levels.

"Tell me if I'm wrong," Molly said. "Curiosity got the best of you, right? You opened the box, the animals escaped."

"That's about the size of it," said Bud Schwartz, wrapping a bandage around Danny Pogue's foot. He had removed the sneaker and the sock, and examined the wounds. Miraculously (or maybe by design) both bullets had missed the bones, so Danny Pogue was able to wiggle all his toes. When he stopped whimpering, Bud Schwartz removed the towel from his mouth.

"So you think they're still alive," Molly said. "Why not? Who'd be mean enough to hurt 'em?"

"This is important," said Molly. The pistol lay loose on her lap, looking as harmless as a macramé.

Danny Pogue said, "We didn't kill them things, I swear to God. They just scooted out of the damn truck."

23

"We didn't know there was only two," he said. "We thought there must be a whole bunch in a box that size. That's how come we wasn't so worried when they got away—see, we thought there was more."

Molly started rocking a little faster. The rocking chair didn't squeak a bit on the varnished pine. She said, "I'm very disappointed in the both of you."

Bud Schwartz helped his partner limp to an ottoman. All he wanted was to get the money and get the hell out of this spooky old house, away from this crazy witch.

"Here's the really bad news," said Molly McNamara. "It's your truck—only about a thousand people saw you drive away. Now, I don't know if they got the license tag, but they sure as hell got a good description. It's all over the TV."

"Shit," said Bud Schwartz.

"So you're going to have to keep a low profile for a while."

Still breathing heavily, Danny Pogue said, "What's that mean?"

Molly stopped rocking and sat forward. "For starters, say goodbye to the pickup truck. Also, you can forget about going home. If the police got your tag, they'll be waiting."

"I'll take my chances," said Bud Schwartz.

"No, you won't," said Molly. "I'll give you a thousand dollars each. You'll get the rest in two weeks, if things die down. Meanwhile, I've arranged a place for you boys to stay."

"Here?" asked Danny Pogue in a fretful, pain-racked voice.

"No, not here," Molly said. "Not on your life."

She stood up from the rocker. The pistol disappeared again into a fuzzy pocket of the blue robe. "Your foot's going to be fine," she announced to Danny Pogue. "I hope I made my point."

The bafflement on the two men's faces suggested otherwise.

Molly McNamara said, "I chose you for a reason."

"Come on," said Bud Schwartz, "we're just burglars."

"And don't you ever forget it," Molly said.

Danny Pogue couldn't believe she was talking to them this way. He couldn't believe he was being terrorized by an old lady in a rocking chair.

"There's something else you should know," said Molly McNamara. "There are others."

Momentarily Bud Schwartz's mind had stuck on that thousand dollars she'd mentioned. He had been thinking: Screw the other eight, just grab the grand and get lost. Now she was saying something about others—what others?

"Anything happens to me," Molly said, "there's others that know who you are. Where you live. Where you hang out. Everything."

"I don't get it," muttered Danny Pogue.

"Burglars get shot sometimes," Molly McNamara said. "Nobody says boo about it, either. Nobody gets arrested or investigated or anything else. In this country, you kill a burglar and the Kiwanis gives you a plaque. That's the point I was trying to make."

Danny Pogue turned to Bud Schwartz, who was staring down at his partner's swollen foot and wondering if it was too late to make a run for it. Finally he said, "Lady, we're very sorry about your animals."

"They're not my animals," said Molly, "any more than you are."

Three

At half past ten Joe Winder went down to The Catacombs, the underground network of service roads that ran beneath the Amazing Kingdom of Thrills. It was along these winding cart paths, discreetly out of view from visitors, that the food, merchandise, money and garbage were moved throughout the sprawling amusement park. It was also along these secret subterranean passageways that the kiddie characters traveled, popping up suddenly at strategic locations throughout the Amazing Kingdom and imploring tourists to snap their picture. No customers ("guests" was the designated term) ever were allowed to venture into The Catacombs, lest they catch a glimpse of something that might tarnish their image of the Amazing Kingdom—a dog rooting through a dumpster, for example. Or one of Uncle Ely's Elves smoking a joint.

Which is what Joe Winder saw when he got to the bottom of the stairs.

"I'm looking for Robbie Raccoon," he said to the elf, who wasn't particularly jolly or gnomelike.

The elf belched blue smoke and asked which Robbie Raccoon he was looking for, since there were three.

"The one who was on duty this afternoon," Winder said. "The one who fought with the rat robbers."

26

The big elf pointed with the smoldering end of the joint.

"Okay, there's a locker room on the west side. Just follow the orange signs." He took another drag. "I'd offer you a hit, but I got this nasty chest virus. Hate to pass it along."

"Sure," said Joe Winder. "No problem."

The lockers were at the end of a damp concrete tunnel that smelled of stale laundry and ammonia. Robbie Raccoon was straddling the bench, trying to unzip his head. Winder introduced himself, and explained that he was from the Publicity Department.

"I'm writing a press release about what happened earlier today," he said. "A few quick questions is all."

"Fire away," said Robbie Raccoon. The words came out muffled, from a small opening in the neck of the costume.

Winder said, "I can barely hear you."

With a grunt Robbie Raccoon removed his head, which was as large as a beach ball. Joe Winder was startled by what he saw beneath it: long shimmering blond hair, green eyes and mascara. Robbie Raccoon was a woman.

She said, "If you're going to make a joke, get it over with."

"No, I wasn't."

"Don't think this is my life ambition or anything."

"Of course not," said Joe Winder.

The woman said her name was Carrie Lanier. "And I got my SAG card," she said, still somewhat defensive. "That's the only reason I took this stupid job. I'm going to be an actress."

Mindlessly Winder said, "You've got to start somewhere."

"Darn right."

He waited for Carrie Lanier to remove the rest of the raccoon outfit, but she didn't. He took out his notebook and asked her to describe what had happened at the Rare Animal Pavilion.

Carrie shrugged in an exaggerated way, as if she were still in character. "It was two men, we're talking white trash. One of

27

them has a sledgehammer, and they're both walking real fast. I start to follow, don't ask me why—I just had a hunch. All of a sudden the one with the hammer smashes out the glass in one of the exhibits."

"And you tried to stop him?"

"Yeah, I jumped the guy. Climbed on his back. He turned around and clobbered me pretty solid. Thank God for this." Carrie knocked on the crown of the raccoon head, which was propped face-up on the bench. Her fist made a sharp hollow sound. "Chicken wire, plaster and Kevlar," she explained. "They say it's bulletproof."

Joe Winder wrote this down, even though Charles Chelsea would never let him use it in the press release. At the Amazing Kingdom, each publicity announcement was carefully purged of all intriguing details. Winder was having a tough time kicking the habit of taking good notes.

Carrie Lanier said, "He knocked me down pretty hard, but that's about it. There was a tour group from Taiwan, Korea, someplace like that. They helped me off the ground, but by then the two dirtbags were long gone. I could've done without the ambulance ride, but Risk Management said I had to."

"Can I say you suffered a slight head injury?" Joe Winder asked, pen poised.

"No," said Carrie Lanier. "As soon as the X-rays came out negative, they hauled me back to work. I'm fine."

That wouldn't go over well with Charles Chelsea; the vole story was infinitely more dramatic if a park employee had been wounded in the rescue attempt.

"Not even a headache?" Winder persisted.

"Yeah, I've got a headache," Carrie said. "I've always got a headache. Take a whiff of this place." She stood up and yanked on the fluffy striped raccoon tail, which was attached to the rump of the costume by a Velcro patch. The tail made a ripping sound when Carrie took it off. She tossed it in her locker and said, "Why would anyone steal rats?"

"Voles," said Joe Winder.

"The guys who did it, boy, what a pair. Scum of the earth."

Again Winder didn't bother to write this down.

"It's crazy," said Carrie Lanier. She reached beneath her left armpit and found, deep in the fur, another zipper. Carefully she unzipped the costume lengthwise down to her ankle. She did the same on the other side. As she stepped out of the animal outfit, Winder saw that she was wearing only a bra and panties. He tried not to stare.

Carrie hung the costume on a pair of hooks in the locker. She said, "This damn thing weighs a ton, I wish you'd write that down. It's about a hundred twenty degrees inside, too. OSHA made them put in air conditioners, but they're always broken."

Winder stepped closer to examine the raccoon costume, not Carrie Lanier in her bra (which was the type that unhooked in the front; pink with lacy cups). Winder held up the animal suit and said, "Where's the AC?"

"In the back. Here, look." Carrie showed him. "The batteries last about two hours max, then forget about it. We tried to call the feds and complain—what a joke. They haven't been out here since the day Petey Possum died."

"Do I want to hear this story?"

"Heart attack," Carrie Lanier went on. "This was Sessums. Billy Sessums. The very first Petey Possum. He'd been twenty-two years with Disneyland—Goofy, Pluto, you name it. Billy was a pro. He taught me plenty."

"So what happened?"

"One of those days. Ninety-two in the shade, one twelve inside the possum suit. The AC went out, and so did Billy." Carrie Lanier paused reflectively. "He was an older fella but still . . ."

29

"I'm sorry," said Joe Winder. He put his notebook away. He was starting to feel prickly and claustrophobic.

Carrie said, "You're gonna put my name in the press release?"

"I'm afraid not. It's company policy not to identify the actors who portray the animal characters. Mr. Kingsbury says it would spoil the illusion for the children."

Carrie laughed. "Some illusion. I've had kids grab my boobs, right through the costume. One time there was a Shriner, tried to goose me in the Magic Mansion."

Winder said, "How'd they know you were a woman?"

"That's the scary part." Her eyes flashed mischievously. "What if they didn't know I was a woman? What if they thought I was a real raccoon? What would Mr. Francis X. Kingsbury say about that?" She took a pair of blue jeans out of the locker and squirmed into them. "Anyhow, I don't want my name in any stupid press release," she said. "Not for this place."

"Maybe not, but you did a brave thing," said Winder.

As Carrie buttoned her blouse, she said, "I don't want my folks knowing what I do. You blame me?"

"You make lots of little children happy. What's wrong with that?"

She looked at him evenly. "You're new here, aren't you?"

"Yeah," Joe Winder said.

"My job's crummy, but you know what? I think your job is worse."

Joe Winder wrote the press release in forty minutes. "Theft of Rare Animals Stuns Amazing Kingdom." Ten paragraphs on the crime itself, with a nod to the heroics of Robbie Raccoon ("who barely escaped serious injury"). Three paragraphs of official reaction ("a sad and shocking event") from Francis X. Kingsbury, chairman and president of the park. Three grafs more of scientific background on the blue-tongued mango vole, with a suitable quote from Dr. Will Koocher. A hundred words about the $10,000 reward, and a hundred more announcing new beefed-up security precautions at the park.

Winder put the press release on Charles Chelsea's desk and went home. By the time he called Nina, it was nearly one in the morning. He dialed the number and hoped she would be the one to answer.

"Hello, sugar," Nina said.

"It's me."

"God, I need to talk to a real man," she said. "I had a fantasy that got me so hot. We were on the bow of a sailboat. Making love in the sun. I was on top. Suddenly a terrible storm came—"

"Nina, it's me!"

"—but instead of hiding in the cabin, we lashed each other to the deck and kept on doing it in the lightning and thunder. Afterwards the warm rain washed the salt off our bodies . . . "

"For Christ's sake."

"Joe?"

"Yeah, it's me. Why don't you ever listen?"

"Because they don't pay me to listen," Nina said. "They pay me to talk."

"I wish you'd get a normal job."

"Joe, don't start."

Nina was a voice for one of those live dial-a-fantasy telephone services. She worked nights, which put a strain on her personal relationships. Also, every time Joe Winder called, it cost him four bucks. At least the number was easy to remember: 976-COME.

Nina said, "What do you think about the lightning-and-thunder business? I added it to the script myself."

"What was it before—something about whales, right?"

"Porpoises, Joe. *A school of friendly porpoises leaped and frolicked in the water while we made love. Our animal cries only seemed to arouse them.*"

Nina had a wonderful voice, Winder had to admit. "I like the new stuff better," he agreed. "The storm idea is good—you wrote that yourself?"

"Don't sound so surprised." She asked him how his day had gone, and he told her about the stolen voles.

Nina said, "See? And you thought you were going to be bored."

"I am bored. Most of the time."

"Joe, it's never going to be like the old days."

He wasn't in the mood to hear it. He said, "How's it going with you?"

"Slow," Nina said. "Beverly went home early. It's just me and Miriam."

"Any creeps call in?" Of course creeps had called—who else would bother?

"The usual jack-off artists," Nina reported. "They're harmless, Joe, don't worry. I just give a straight read, no moans or groans, and still they get off in about thirty seconds. I had one guy fall asleep afterwards. Snoring like a baby."

Sometimes she talked about her job as if it were a social service, like UNICEF or Meals on Wheels.

"When will you be home?" Winder asked.

The usual, Nina said, meaning four in the morning. "Want me to wake you up?"

"Sure." She had loads of energy, this girl. Winder needed somebody with energy, to help him use up his own. One of the drawbacks of his high-paying bullshit PR job was that it took absolutely nothing out of him, except his pride.

Hurriedly Nina said, "Joe, I got another call waiting."

"Make it short and sweet."

"I'll deal with you later, sailor boy."

And then she hung up.

*

32

Winder couldn't sleep, so he put a Warren Zevon tape in the stereo and made himself a runny cheese omelet. He ate in the living room, near the speakers, and sat on a box because there were no chairs in the apartment. The box was filled with old newspaper clippings, his own, as well as plaques and certificates from various journalism awards that he had received over the years. The only important journalism award that wasn't in the box was the single one that impressed anybody—the Pulitzer Prize, which Joe Winder had never won.

When he was first interviewed for the publicity-writing job at the Amazing Kingdom of Thrills, Joe Winder had been asked if he'd ever gotten a Pulitzer. When he answered no, Charles Chelsea had threatened to put him on the polygraph machine.

"I never won," Winder insisted. "You can look it up."

And Charles Chelsea did. A Pulitzer on the wall would have disqualified Joe Winder from the PR job just as surely as flunking a urinalysis for drugs.

"We're not in the market for aggressive, hard-bitten newshounds," Chelsea had warned him. "We're looking for writers with a pleasing, easygoing style. We're looking for a certain attitude."

"I'm flexible," Joe Winder had said. "Especially my attitude."

Chelsea had grilled him about the other journalism awards, then about the length of his hair, then about the thin pink scar along his jawline.

Eyeing Winder's face at close range, the publicity man had said, "You look like a bar fighter. Did you get that scar in a fight?"

"Car accident," Joe Winder had lied, figuring what the hell, Chelsea must've known the truth. One phone call to the newspaper, and any number of people would've been happy to drop the dime.

But Chelsea never said another word about the scar, never gave a hint that he'd even picked up the rumor. It was Joe Winder's journalism achievements that seemed to disturb the publicity man, although these concerns were ultimately outweighed by the discovery that Winder had been born and raised in Florida. The Publicity Department at the Amazing Kingdom was desperate for native talent, somebody who understood the mentality of tourists and crackers alike.

The Disney stint hadn't hurt Joe Winder's chances, either; he had worked among the enemy, and learned many of their professional secrets. So Charles Chelsea had set aside his doubts and hired him.

That was two weeks ago. It was still too early for Winder to compare the new job with the one at Disney World. Certainly Disney was slicker and more efficient than the Amazing Kingdom, but it was also more regimented and impersonal. The Disney bureaucracy, and its reach, was awesome. In retrospect Joe Winder wasn't sure how he had lasted as long as he did, six months, before he was caught having sex on Mr. Toad's Wild Ride and fired for not wearing his ID card. Winder felt especially bad that the young woman with whom he'd been dallying, a promising understudy to Cinderella, had also been dismissed over the incident; she for leaving Main Street during Mickey's Birthday Parade.

During the job interview at the Amazing Kingdom, Charles Chelsea had told him: "You work for us, you'd better keep it in your pants, understand?"

"I've got a girlfriend now," Joe Winder had said.

"Don't think you won't be tempted around here."

Winder hadn't been tempted once, until today. Now he was thinking about Carrie Lanier, the fearless beauty inside a seven-foot raccoon suit.

This is what happens when you turn thirty-seven, Winder

thought; the libido goes blind with fever. What else could explain his attraction to Nina? Or her attraction to him?

Being a newspaper reporter had left Joe Winder no time for such reckless attachments. Being a flack left him all the time in the world. Now that he was forbidden to write about trouble, he seemed determined to experience it.

He finished his omelet and opened a beer and slumped down on the floor, between the stereo speakers. Something had been nagging at him all afternoon, ever since the insufferable Chelsea had drafted him to help with the robbery crisis. In the push toward his deadline, it was clear to Joe Winder that none of his writing skills had eroded—his speed at the keyboard, his facile vocabulary, his smooth sense of pacing and transition. Yet something from the old days was missing.

Curiosity. The most essential and feral of reporters' instincts, the urge to pursue. It was dead. Or dying.

Two strangers had invaded a family theme park in broad daylight and kidnapped a couple of obscure rodents from an animal exhibit. Winder had thoroughly and competently reported the incident, but had made no effort to explore the fascinating possibilities. Having established the *what*, he had simply ignored the *why*.

Even by South Florida standards the crime was perverse, and the old Joe Winder would have reveled energetically in its mysteries. The new Joe Winder had merely typed up his thousand words, and gone home.

Just as he was supposed to do.

So this is how it feels, he thought. This is how it feels to sell out. On the stereo, Warren Zevon was singing about going to the Louvre museum and throwing himself against the wall. To Joe Winder it sounded like a pretty good idea.

He closed his eyes tightly and thought: Don't tell me I'm getting used to this goddamn zombie job. Then he thought: Don't tell me I'm getting drunk on one lousy beer.

He crawled across the carpet to the phone, and tried to call Nina at the service. The woman named Miriam answered instead, and launched into a complicated fantasy involving trampolines and silver ankle bracelets. Miriam was struggling so valiantly in broken English ("Ooooh, bebee, chew make me comb so many time!") that Joe Winder didn't have the heart to interrupt.

What the hell, it was only four bucks. He could certainly afford it.

Four

On the morning of July 17, Danny Pogue awoke in a cold sweat, his T-shirt soaked from neck to navel. He kicked the covers off the bed and saw the lump of gauze around his foot. It wasn't a dream. He limped to the window and from there he could see everything: the Olympic-sized swimming pool, the freshly painted tennis courts, the shady shuffleboard gazebo. Everywhere he looked there were old people with snowy heads and pale legs and fruit-colored Bermuda shorts. All the men wore socks with their sandals, and all the women wore golf visors and oversized sunglasses.

"Mother of Christ," said Danny Pogue. He hollered for his partner to come quick.

Bud Schwartz ambled in, looking settled and well rested. He was spooning out half a grapefruit, cupped in the palm of one hand. "Do you believe this fucking place?" he said to Danny Pogue. "What a gas."

"We gotta get out."

"How come?"

"Just look." Danny Pogue pointed out the window.

"So now you got a problem with senior citizens? What—they don't have the right to have fun? Besides, there's some young people that live here, too. I saw a couple of hot ones out by the swimming pool. Major titties."

"I don't care," mumbled Danny Pogue.

"Hey," Bud Schwartz said. "She shot your foot, not your weenie."

"Where is she?"

"Long gone. You want some lunch? She loaded up at the Publix, you should see. Steaks, chops, beer—we're set for a couple of weeks, easy."

Danny Pogue hopped back to the bed and peeled off the damp shirt. He spotted a brand-new pair of crutches propped in the corner. He said, "Bud, I'm gonna split. Seriously, I'm taking off."

"I can give you ten thousand reasons not to."

"Speaking of which."

"She's bringing a grand for each of us, just like she promised," said Bud Schwartz. "Good faith money is what she called it."

"Invisible is what I call it."

"Hey, lighten the fuck up. She's an old lady, Danny. Old ladies never lie." Bud Schwartz lobbed the grapefruit skin into some kind of designer wastebasket. "What's wrong with you, man? This is like a vacation, all expenses paid. Look at this freaking condo—two bedrooms, two bathrooms. Microwave in the kitchen, Cinemax on the cable. Say what you will, the old geezer knows how to live."

"Who is she?" Danny Pogue asked. "Who cares?"

"I care. She shot me."

Bud Schwartz said, "Just some crazy, rich old broad. Don't worry about it."

"It's not you that got shot."

"She won't do it again, Danny. She got it out of her system." Bud Schwartz wiped his hands on the butt of his jeans to get the grapefruit juice off. He said, "She was pissed, that's all. On account of us losing the rats."

Danny Pogue said, "Well, screw that deal. I'm leaving." He made a move for the crutches but faltered, hot and dizzy. Molly McNamara had fed him some pain pills late last night; that much he remembered.

"I don't know where you think you're going," said Bud Schwartz. "The truck's history."

"I'll hitch," said Danny Pogue woozily.

"Look in the mirror. Your own mother wouldn't pick you up. The Hell's Fucking Angels wouldn't pick you up."

"Somebody'll stop," Danny Pogue said. "Especially with me on them crutches."

"Oh, sure."

"Maybe even some girls." Danny Pogue eased himself back on the pillow. He took deep breaths and tried to blink away the haze in his brain.

"Have another codeine," said Bud Schwartz. "Here, she got a whole bottle." He went to the kitchen and came back with a cold Busch.

Danny Pogue swallowed two more pills and slurped at the beer can noisily. He closed his eyes and said, "She ain't never gonna pay us, Bud."

"Sure she is," said his partner. "She's loaded, just look at this place. You should see the size of the TV."

"We better get away while we can."

"Go back to sleep," said Bud Schwartz. "I'll be down at the pool."

The Mothers of Wilderness met every other Tuesday at a public library in Cutler Ridge. This week the main item on the agenda was the proposed bulldozing of seventy-three acres of mangroves to make room for the back nine of a championship golf course on the shore of North Key Largo. The Mothers of Wilderness strenuously opposed the project, and had begun to map a political strategy to obstruct it. They pursued such crusades with unflagging optimism, despite the fact that they had never succeeded in stopping a single development. Not one. The builders ignored them. Zoning boards ignored them. County commissioners listened politely, nodded intently, then ignored them, too. Of all the environmental groups fighting to preserve what little remained of Florida, the Mothers of Wilderness was regarded as the most radical and shrill and intractable. It was also, unfortunately, the smallest of the groups and thus the easiest to brush off.

Still, the members were nothing if not committed. Molly McNamara steadfastly had refused all offers to merge her organization with the Audubon Society or the Sierra Club or the Friends of the Everglades. She wanted no part of coalitions because coalitions compromised. She enjoyed being alone on the fringe, enjoyed being the loose cannon that establishment environmentalists feared. The fact that the Mothers of Wilderness was politically impotent did not diminish Molly McNamara's passion, though occasionally it ate at her pride.

She ran the meetings with brusque efficiency, presiding over a membership that tended to be retired and liberal and well-to-do. For its size, the Mothers of Wilderness was exceedingly well financed; Molly knew this was why the other environmental groups wooed her, in hopes of a merger. The Mothers had bucks.

They had hired a hotshot Miami land-use lawyer to fight the golf course project, which was called Falcon Trace. The lawyer, whose name was Spacci, stood up at the meeting to update the Mothers on the progress of the lawsuit, which, typically, was about to be thrown out of court. The case was being heard in Monroe County—specifically, Key West—where many of the judges were linked by conspiracy or simple inbreeding to the crookedest politicians. Moreover, the zoning lawyer admitted he was having a terrible time ascertaining the true owners of the Falcon Trace property; he had gotten as far as a blind trust in Dallas, then stalled.

Molly McNamara thanked Spacci for his report and made a motion to authorize another twenty thousand dollars for legal fees and investigative expenses. It passed unanimously.

After the meeting, Molly took the lawyer aside and said, "Next time I want to see some results. I want the names of these bastards."

"What about the lawsuit?"

"File a new one," Molly said. "You ever considered going federal?"

"How?" asked Spacci. "On what grounds?"

Pinching his elbow, Molly led him to an easel behind the rostrum. Propped on the easel was an aerial map of North Key Largo. Molly pointed and said, "See? There's where they want the golf course. And right here is a national wildlife refuge. That's your federal jurisdiction, Counselor."

The lawyer plucked a gold pen from his breast pocket and did some pointing of his own. "And right here, Ms. McNamara, is a two-thousand-acre amusement park that draws three million tourists every year. We'd be hard pressed to argue that one lousy golf course would be more disruptive to the habitat than what's already there—a major vacation resort."

Molly snapped, "You're the damn attorney. Think of something."

Bitterly she remembered the years she had fought the Kingsbury project; the Mothers of Wilderness had been the only group that had never given up. Audubon and the others had realized immediately that protest was futile; the prospect of a major theme park to compete with Disney World carried an orgasmic musk to local chambers of commerce. The most powerful of powerful civic leaders clung to the myth that Mickey Mouse was responsible for killing the family tourist trade in

41

South Florida, strangling the peninsula so that all southbound station wagons stopped in Orlando. What did Miami have to offer as competition? Porpoises that could pitch a baseball with their blowholes? Wise-cracking parrots on unicycles? Enjoyable diversions, but scarcely in the same high-tech league with Disney. The Mouse's sprawling self-contained empire sucked tourists' pockets inside out; they came, they spent until there was nothing left to spend; then they went home *happy*. To lifelong Floridians it was a dream concept: fleecing a snowbird in such a way that he came back for more. Astounding! So when Francis X. Kingsbury unveiled his impressive miniature replica of the Amazing Kingdom of Thrills—the Wet Willy water flume, the Magic Mansion, Orky the Killer Whale, Jungle Jerry, and so on—roars of exultation were heard from Palm Beach to Big Pine. The only cry of dismay came from the Mothers of Wilderness, who were (as usual) ignored.

"No golf course," Molly told Spacci the lawyer, "and no more chickenshit excuses from you." She sent him away with the wave of a blue-veined hand.

After the rank and file had gone home, Molly gathered the board of directors in the back of the library. Five women and two men, all nearly as gray as Molly, they sat in molded plastic chairs and sipped herbal tea while Molly told them what had happened.

It was a bizarre and impossible scheme, but no one asked Molly why she had done it. They knew why. In a fussy tone, one of the Mothers said: "This time you went too far."

"It's under control," Molly insisted.

"Except for the voles. They're not under control."

Another Mother asked: "Any chance of finding them?"

"You never know," said Molly.

"Horseshit," said the first Mother. "They're gone for good. Dead, alive, it doesn't matter if we can't locate the damn things."

Molly said, "Please. Keep your voice down."

The second Mother: "What about these two men? Where are they now?"

"My condo," Molly replied. "Up at Eagle Ridge."

"Lord have mercy."

"That's enough," said Molly sharply. "I said it's under control, and it's under control."

A silence fell over the small group. No one wished to challenge her authority, but this time things had really gotten out of hand. This time there was a chance they could all go to jail. "I'll have some more tea," the first Mother said finally, "and then I'd love to hear your new plan. You do have one?"

"Of course I do," said Molly McNamara. "For heaven's sake."

When Joe Winder got to work, Charles Chelsea was waiting in yet another blue oxford shirt. He was sitting on the edge of Winder's desk in a pose of casual superiority. A newspaper was freshly folded under one arm. "Fine job on the press release," Chelsea said. "I changed a word or two, but otherwise it went out just like you wrote it."

Calmly Joe Winder said, "Which word or two did you change?"

"Oh, I improved Mr. Kingsbury's comments. Couple of adverbs here and there."

"Fine." Winder wasn't so surprised. It was well known that Chelsea invented all of Francis X. Kingsbury's quotes. Kingsbury was one of those men who rarely spoke in complete sentences. Didn't have to. For publicity purposes this made him perfectly useless and unquotable.

Chelsea said, "I also updated the info on Robbie Raccoon. Turns out he got a mild concussion from that blow to the head."

Winder forced a smile and set his briefcase on the desk. "It's a she, Charlie. And she was fine when I spoke to her last night. Not even a bruise."

Chelsea's voice took on a scolding tone. "Joey, you know the gender rule. If it's a male character, we always refer to it with masculine pronouns—regardless of who's inside the costume. I explained all this the day you were hired. It comes straight from Mr. X. Speaking of which, weren't you supposed to get a haircut?"

"Don't be a dork, Charlie."

"What's a dork?"

"You're not serious."

Charles Chelsea said, "Really, tell me. You called me a dork, I'd like to know what exactly that is."

"It's a Disney character," said Joe Winder. "Daffy Dork." He opened the briefcase and fumbled urgently for his sinus medicine. "Anyway, Charlie, the lady in the coon suit didn't have a concussion. That's a lie, and it's a stupid lie because it's so easy to check. Some newspaper reporter is going to make a few calls and we're going to look sleazy and dishonest, all because you had to exaggerate."

"No exaggeration," Charles Chelsea said, stiffening. "I spoke with Robbie Raccoon myself, first thing this morning. He said he got dizzy and sick overnight. Doctor said it's probably a concussion."

Winder popped two pills into his mouth and said, "You're amazing."

"We'll have a neurologist's report this afternoon, in case anybody wants to see. Notarized, too." Chelsea looked pleased with himself. "Mild concussion, Joe. Don't believe me, just ask Robbie."

"What'd you do, threaten to fire her? Bust her down to the elf patrol?"

Charles Chelsea stood up, shot his cuffs, gave Joe Winder his coldest, hardest look. "I came down here to thank you for doing such outstanding work, and look what I get. More of your cynicism. Just because you had a rotten night, Joey, it's no reason to rain on everyone else's parade."

Did the man really say that? Winder wondered. Did he really accuse me of raining on his parade? "That's the only reason you're here?" Winder said. "To thank me?"

"Well, not entirely." Charles Chelsea removed the newspaper from under his arm, unfolded it and handed it to Joe Winder. "Check the last three paragraphs."

It was the story about the theft of the blue-tongued mango voles. The *Herald* had stripped it across the top of the Local News page, a feature play. "Hey," Winder said brightly, "they even used one of our pictures."

"Never mind that, just read the last three grafs."

The newspaper story ended like this:

An anonymous caller identifying himself as an animal-rights activist telephoned the Miami office of the Associated Press late Monday and took credit for the incident at the popular theme park. The caller claimed to be a member of the radical Wildlife Rescue Corps.

"We freed the voles because they were being exploited," he said. "Francis Kingsbury doesn't care about saving the species, he just wanted another stupid tourist attraction."

Officials at the Amazing Kingdom of Thrills were unavailable for comment late Monday night.

Joe Winder gave the newspaper back to Charles Chelsea and said, "What a kick in the nuts. I'll bet the boss man is going batshit."

"You find this amusing?"

"Don't you?" Winder asked. "I guess not."

"No," said Chelsea. He refolded the newspaper and returned it to his armpit. "What do you suggest in the way of a response?"

"I suggest we forget the fucking voles and get on with our lives."

"This is serious."

Winder said, "So I was right, Kingsbury's on a tear. Then I would suggest you tell him that we're waiting to see if there's any truth to this claim. Tell him that if we say anything now, it might turn around and bite us in the rat hole."

Chelsea started rubbing his chin, a sign of possible cognition. "Go on," he told Winder. "I'm listening."

"For instance, suppose the real Wildlife Rescue Corps calls up and denies any involvement. Hell, Charlie, there's a good chance the caller was a crank. Had nothing to do with the group. To play it safe, we don't respond for now. We say absolutely nothing."

"But if it turns out to be true?"

"Then," said Joe Winder, "we express outrage that any organization, no matter how worthy its cause, would commit a violent felony and endanger the lives of innocent bystanders."

Chelsea nodded enthusiastically; he liked what he was hearing. "Not just any bystanders," he said. "Tourists."

Winder went on: "We would also recount Mr. Kingsbury's many philanthropic gifts to the ASPCA, the World Wildlife Fund, Save the Beavers, whatever. And we would supply plenty of testimonial quotes from eminent naturalists supporting our efforts on behalf of the endangered mango vole."

"Excellent," Charles Chelsea said. "Joe, that's perfect."

"Pure unalloyed genius," Winder said.

"Let's hope it doesn't come to that," Chelsea said. "You don't want to spend the rest of the week writing about rodents. Too much like covering City Hall, right?"

Joe Winder chuckled politely. He could tell Chelsea was worried about pitching it to Kingsbury.

In a hopeful voice, Chelsea said, "You think the guy was really just a nut? This guy who called the AP?"

"Who knows," Winder said. "We've certainly got our share."

Charlie Chelsea nodded hopefully. A simple nut would be fine with him, PR-wise; it's the zealots you had to worry about.

"The only thing to do is wait," said Joe Winder. Already he could feel his sinuses drying up. He felt suddenly clear-headed, chipper, even optimistic. Maybe it was the medicine flushing his head, or maybe it was something else.

Like having a real honest-to-God story, for a change. A story getting good and hot.

Just like the old days.

Five

Chelsea had a stark, irrational fear of Francis X. Kingsbury. It was not Kingsbury's physical appearance (for he was gnomish and flabby) but his volcanically profane temper that caused Chelsea so much anxiety. Kingsbury long ago had practically ceased speaking in complete sentences, but his broken exclamations could be daunting and acerbic. The words struck venomously at Charles Chelsea's insecurities, and made him tremble.

On the afternoon of July 17, Chelsea finished his lunch, threw up, flossed his teeth and walked briskly to Kingsbury's office. Kingsbury was leaning over the desk; the great man's sleeves were rolled up to reveal the famous lewd tattoo on his doughy left forearm. The other arm sparkled with a gold Robbie Raccoon wristwatch, with emerald insets. Today's surfer-blond hairpiece was longish and curly.

Kingsbury grunted at Charles Chelsea and said: "Wildlife Rescue Corps?" He raised his hands. "Well?"

Chelsea said, "The group exists, but the phone calls could be a crank. We're checking it out."

"What's this exploitation—shit, we're talking about, what, some kind of rodent or such goddamn thing."

Not even close to a quotable sentence, Chelsea thought. It was astounding—the man spoke in overtorqued, expletive-laden fragments that somehow made perfect sense. At all times, Charles Chelsea knew exactly what Francis X. Kingsbury was talking about.

The publicity man said, "Don't worry, sir, the situation is being contained. We're ready for any contingency."

Kingsbury made a small fist. "Damage control," he said.

"Our top gun," Chelsea said. "His name is Joe Winder, and he's a real pro. Offering the reward money was his idea, sir. The AP led with it this morning, too."

Kingsbury sat down. He fingered the florid tip of his bulbous nose. "These animals, there's still a chance maybe?"

Chelsea could feel a chilly dampness spreading in deadly crescents from his armpits. "It's unlikely, sir. One of them is dead for sure. Shot by the highway patrol. Some tourists apparently mistook it for a rat."

"Terrific," said Kingsbury.

"The other one, likewise. The bandits threw it in the window of a Winnebago camper."

Kingsbury peered from beneath dromedary lids. "Don't," he said, exhaling noisily. "This is like . . . no, don't bother."

"You might as well know," said Chelsea. "It was a church group from Boca Raton in the Winnebago. They beat the poor thing to death with a golf umbrella. Then they threw it off the Card Sound Bridge."

There, Chelsea thought. He had done it. Stood up and delivered the bad news. Stood up like a man.

Francis X. Kingsbury entwined his hands and said: "Who knows about this? Knows that *we* know? Anybody?"

"You mean anybody on the outside? No." Charles Chelsea paused. "Well, except the highway patrol. And I took care of them with some free passes to the Kingdom."

"But civilians?"

"No, sir. Nobody knows that we know the voles are dead."

"Fine," said Francis X. Kingsbury. "Good time to up the reward."

"Sir?"

"Make it a million bucks. Six zeros, if I'm not mistaken."

Chelsea took out a notebook and a Cross pen, and began to write. "That's one million dollars for the safe return of the missing voles."

"Which are dead."

"Yes, sir."

"Simple, hell. Very simple."

"It's a most generous offer," said Charles Chelsea.

"Bullshit," Kingsbury said. "It's PR, whatever. Stuff for the fucking AP."

"But your heart's in the right place."

Impatiently Kingsbury pointed toward the door. "Fast," he said. "Before I get sick."

Chelsea was startled. Backing away from Kingsbury's desk, he said, "I'm sorry, sir. Is it something I said?"

"No, something you are." Kingsbury spoke flatly, with just a trace of disgust.

On the way back to his office, Charles Chelsea stopped in the executive washroom and threw up again.

Like many wildly successful Floridians, Francis X. Kingsbury was a transplant. He had moved to the Sunshine State in balding middle age, alone and uprooted, never expecting that he would become a multimillionaire.

And, like so many new Floridans, Kingsbury was a felon on the run. Before arriving in Miami, he was known by his real name of Frankie King. Not Frank, but Frankie; his mother had named him after the singer Frankie Lane. All his life Frankie King had yearned to change his name to something more distinguished, something with weight and social bearing. A racketeering indictment (twenty-seven counts) out of Brooklyn was as good an excuse as any.

Once he was arrested, Frankie King exuberantly began ratting on his co-conspirators, which included numerous high-ranking members of the John Gotti crime organization. Frankie's testimony conveniently glossed over the fact that it was he, not the surly Zuboni brothers, who had personally flown to San Juan and picked up the twenty-seven crateloads of bootleg "educational" videotapes that were eventually sold to the New York City school system for $119.95 apiece. Under oath, Frankie King indignantly blamed the Zubonis and, indirectly, John Gotti himself for failing to inspect the shipment once it had arrived at JFK. On the witness stand, Frankie expressed tearful remorse that, in TV classrooms from Queens to Staten Island, students expecting to see "Kermit's Wild West Adventure" were instead exposed to a mattress-level montage of Latin porn star Pina Kolada deepthroating a semi-pro soccer team.

The Zuboni brothers and a cluster of dull-eyed kneecappers were swiftly convicted by a horrified jury. The reward for Frankie King's cooperation was a suspended sentence, ten years' probation and a new identity of his choosing: Francis X. Kingsbury. Frankie felt the "X" was a classy touch; he decided it should stand for Xavier.

When the man from the Witness Relocation Program told him that Miami would be his new home, Frankie King thought he had died and gone to heaven. *Miami!* Frankie couldn't believe his good fortune; he had no idea the U.S. government could be so generous. What Frankie did not know was that Miami was the prime relocation site for scores of scuzzy federal snitches (on the theory that South Florida was a place where just about any dirtbag would blend in smoothly with the existing riffraff). Frankie King continued to entertain the false notion that he was somebody special in

51

the witness program, a regular Joe Valachi, until he saw the accommodations provided by his government benefactors: a one-bedroom apartment near the railroad tracks in beautiful downtown Naranja.

When Frankie complained about the place, FBI agents reminded him that the alternative was to return to New York and take his chances that John Gotti was a compassionate and forgiving fellow. With this on his mind, Francis X. Kingsbury began a new life.

Like all Floridians with time on their hands, he went to night school and got his real-estate license. It was an entirely new racket, and Frankie worked at it tirelessly; first he specialized in small commercial properties, then citrus groves and farmlands. Doggedly he worked his way east toward the good stuff—oceanfront, the Big O. He went from condos to prime residential estates in no time flat.

Francis X. Kingsbury had found a new niche. He was, undeniably, a whiz at selling Florida real estate. In five short years he had accumulated more money than in an entire lifetime of mob bunko, jukebox skimming and mail fraud. He had a home down on Old Cutler, a beautiful young wife and a closetful of mustard blazers. But he wanted more.

One day he walked into the boardroom of Kingsbury Realty and announced that he was selling the business. "I'm ready to move up in the world," he told his startled partners. "I'm ready to become a developer."

Six months later, Kingsbury stood before a luncheon meeting of the Greater Miami Chamber of Commerce and unveiled his model of the Amazing Kingdom of Thrills. It was the first time in his life that Frankie had gotten a standing ovation. He blushed and said: "Florida is truly the land of opportunity."

His probation officer, standing near the salad bar, had to bite back tears.

*

"This is a very bad idea, Charlie." Joe Winder was talking about the phony million-dollar reward. "A very bad idea. And cynical, I might add."

Over the phone, Chelsea said: "Don't give me any lectures. I need five hundred words by tomorrow morning."

"This is nuts."

"And don't overdo it."

"This is not just dumb," continued Joe Winder, "it's dishonest. The blue-tongued mango voles are dead, Charlie. Everybody at the park is talking about it."

Chelsea said, "Mr. X is adamant. He considers the money a symbolic gesture of his commitment to preserving the environment."

"Did you write that yourself?" Winder asked. "That's fucking awful, Charlie. *Symbolic gesture!* You ought to be shot."

"Joey, don't talk to me that way. This thing was your idea, offering a reward."

"I was wrong," Winder said. "It was a big mistake."

"No, it was genius. The AP had it all over the wires."

"Look, I'm trying to save your ass," Winder said. "And mine, too. Listen to me. This morning, a man with a cardboard box showed up at the front gate of the Amazing Kingdom. Said he'd found the missing voles. Said he'd come to collect his ten-thousand-dollar reward. Listen to me, Charlie. Know what was in the box? Rabbits. Two baby rabbits."

"So what? They don't look anything like a vole."

"They do when you cut their ears off, Charlie. That's what the sonofabitch had done. Cut the ears off a couple of little tiny bunny rabbits."

Charles Chelsea gasped.

"I know, I know," Winder said. "Think about what's going to happen we dangle a million bucks out there. Think of the freaks and sadists and degenerates stampeding this place."

"Holy Christ," said Chelsea.

"Now," said Joe Winder, "think of the headlines."

"I'll talk to Kingsbury."

"Good."

"Maybe I'll bring you along."

"No thank you."

"You owe me," said Chelsea. "Please. I've been good to you, Joe. Remember who hired you in the first place."

Thanks for reminding me, Winder thought, for the two-thousandth time. "I'm not the right man to deal with Mr. X," he said. "I make a lousy first impression."

"You're right," said Chelsea, rethinking his plan. "Tell me one thing—that sicko with the bunny rabbits ... what happened?"

"Don't worry," said Winder. "We paid him to go away."

"How much? Not the whole ten grand?"

"No, not ten grand." Winder sighed. "Try fifty bucks. And he was delighted, Charlie. Positively thrilled."

"Thank God for that." There was a brittle pause on Chelsea's end. "Joe?"

"What?"

"This is turning into something real bad, isn't it?"

Late in the afternoon, Joe Winder decided to drive down to the Rare Animal Pavilion and find out more about the voles. He needed someone to take his mind off the rabbit episode, which made him heartsick. He should've seen it coming—naturally some greedy psychopath would mutilate helpless bunny rabbits for ten lousy thousand fucking dollars. It's South Florida, isn't it? Winder should've anticipated the worst. That's why Chelsea had hired him, for his native instinct.

The door to the vole lab was locked but the lights were on. Winder knocked twice and got no answer. He could hear a telephone ringing on the other side of the door. It stopped briefly, then began ringing again. He used his car keys to rap sharply on the glass, but there was no sign of Koocher. Winder figured the doctor was taking a late lunch.

He strolled out to the pavilion, where he found a group of tourists milling around the empty mango-vole exhibit. A tarpaulin had been hung to cover the mess, but somebody had lifted a corner to peek inside the enclosure, which was littered with glass and smudged with fingerprint dust. A yellow police ribbon lay crumpled like a dead snake on the porch of the vole hutch. Some of the tourists were snapping pictures of the scene of the crime.

A voice behind Joe Winder said, "You work here?"

It was an old woman wearing a floppy pink Easter hat and a purse the size of a saddlebag. She eyed Joe Winder's ID badge, which was clipped to his belt.

"You a security man?" the woman asked.

Winder tried to remember what Chelsea had told him about speaking to park visitors; some gooey greeting that all employees were supposed to say. *Welcome to the Amazing Kingdom. How can I help you?* Or was it: *How may I help you?* No, that wasn't it. *How can we help you?*

Eventually Joe Winder said, "I work in Publicity. Is something wrong?"

The old lady made a clucking noise and foraged in her enormous purse. "I've a little something for you."

In a helpful tone Winder said, "The Lost and Found is down by the killer-whale tank."

"This isn't lost and it isn't found." The old lady produced an envelope. "Here," she said, pressing it into Joe Winder's midsection. "And don't try to follow me."

She turned and scuttled off, one hand atop her head, holding the Easter hat in place. Winder stuffed the envelope into his pocket and started after her. "Hey! Wait a second."

He had taken only three steps when a fist came out of

55

somewhere and smashed him behind the right ear. He pitched forward on the walkway, skidding briefly on his face. When he awoke, Joe Winder was staring at shoes: Reeboks, loafers, sandals, Keds, orthopedics, Hush Puppies, flip-flops. The tourists had gathered in a murmuring semicircle around him. A young man knelt at his side, asking questions in German.

Winder sat up. "Did anybody see who hit me?" His cheek stung, and he tasted blood on his lower lip.

"Beeg orange!" sputtered a woman wearing two cameras around her neck. "Beeg orange man!"

"Swell," Winder said. "Did he have a cape? A ray gun?"

The young German tourist patted him on the shoulder and said, "You okay, *ja*?"

"Yah," Winder muttered. "Fall down go boom."

He picked himself up, waved idiotically at his audience and retreated to the men's room. There he tore open the old lady's envelope and studied the message, which was typed double-spaced on ordinary notebook paper. It said: "WE DID IT. WE'RE GLAD. LONG LIVE THE VOLES."

It was signed by the Wildlife Rescue Corps.

With copies, Joe Winder noted glumly, to every major news organization on the planet.

Bud Schwartz shook Danny Pogue awake and said, "Look who's here. I told you not to worry."

Molly McNamara was in the kitchen, fussing around. Danny Pogue was on the sofa in the living room. He had fallen asleep watching *Lady Chatterley IV* on Cinemax.

Bud Schwartz sat down, grinning. "She brought the money, too," he said.

"All of it?"

"No, just the grand. Like she said before."

"You mean the two grand," Danny Pogue said. "One for each of us." He didn't entirely trust his partner.

Bud Schwartz said, "Yeah, that's what I meant. A thousand bucks each."

"Then let's see it."

Molly came in, drying her hands on a flowered towel. She looked at Danny Pogue as if he were a dog that was supposed to stay off the good furniture. She said, "How's that foot?"

"Hurts." Danny Pogue frowned. "Hurts like a bitch."

"He's all out of them pills," added Bud Schwartz.

"Already?" Molly sounded concerned. "You finished the whole bottle?"

"Danny's got what you call a high resistance to pharmaceuticals," Bud Schwartz said. "We had to double the dose."

"Bull," said Danny Pogue. "Bud here just helped hisself."

"Is that true?" asked Molly McNamara. "Did you take some of your friend's pills?"

"Aw, come on," said Bud Schwartz. "Jesus Christ, there's nothing else to do around here. I was bored stiff."

"That was prescription medicine," Molly said sternly.

She went back to the kitchen and got her handbag. It was the largest handbag that Bud Schwartz or Danny Pogue had ever seen. Molly took out another plastic bottle of codeine pills and handed them to Danny Pogue. Then she took out her gun and shot Bud Schwartz once in the left hand.

He fell down, shaking his arm as if it were on fire.

In a whisper Danny Pogue said, "Oh Lord Jesus." He felt the blood flooding out of his brain, and saw the corners of the room get fuzzy.

Molly said, "Am I getting through to you fellows?" She returned the gun to her purse. "There will be no illegal drug activity in this condominium, is that clear? The owners' association has very strict rules. Here, take this." She handed Danny Pogue two packets of cash. Each packet was held together with a fresh bank wrapper.

"That's one thousand each, just like I promised," she said.

Then, turning to Bud Schwartz: "Does it hurt?"

"The fuck do you think?" He was squeezing the wounded purple hand between his knees. "Damn right it hurts!"

"In that case, you may borrow your friend's pills. But only as needed." Then Molly McNamara put on her floppy pink Easter hat and said good night.

Nina was naked, kneeling on Joe Winder's back and rubbing his shoulders. "See, isn't this better than sex?"

"No," he said, into the pillow. "Good, but not better."

"It's my night off," Nina said. "All week long, all I do is talk about it."

"We don't have to talk," Joe Winder mumbled. "Let's just do."

"Joe, I need a break from it." She kneaded his neck so ferociously that he let out a cry. "You understand, don't you?"

"Sure," he said. It was the second time in a week that they'd had this conversation. Winder had a feeling that Nina was burning out on her job; practically nothing aroused her lately. All she wanted to do was sleep, and of course she talked in her sleep, said the most tantalizing things.

It was driving Joe Winder crazy. "I had a particularly lousy day," he said. "I was counting on you to wear me out."

Nina climbed off his back. "I love you," she said, slipping her long legs under the sheets, "but at this moment I don't have a single muscle that's the least bit interested."

This, from the same wonderful woman who once left fingernail grooves in the blades of a ceiling fan. Winder groaned in self-pity.

From the other side of the bed came Nina's delicious voice: "Tell me the weirdest thing that happened to you today."

It was a bedtime ritual, exchanging anecdotes about work. Joe Winder said: "Some creep claimed he found the

58

missing voles, except they weren't voles. They were baby rabbits. He was trying to con us." Winder left out the grisly details.

"That's a tough one to beat," Nina remarked.

"Also, I got slugged in the head."

"Really?" she said. "Last night I had a caller jerk himself off in eleven seconds flat. Miriam said it might be a new world's record."

"You timed it?"

"Sort of." Playfully she reached between his legs and tweaked him. "Miriam has an official Olympic stopwatch."

"Nina, I want you to get another job. I'm serious."

She said, "That reminds me—some strange guy phoned for you this afternoon. A doctor from the park. He called twice."

"Koocher?"

"Yeah," said Nina. "Interesting name. Anyway, he made it sound important. I told him to try you at the office, but he said no. He wouldn't leave a message, either, just said he'd call back. The second time he said to tell you a man from Security was in the lab."

Joe Winder lifted his head off the pillow. "A man from Security."

"That's what he said."

"Anything else?" Winder was thinking about the empty laboratory: lights on, phone ringing. Maybe he should've tried the door.

"I told him you'd be home soon, but he said he couldn't call back. He said he was leaving with the guy from Security." Nina propped herself on one elbow. "Joe, what's going on over there?"

"I thought I knew," said Winder, "but obviously I don't."

With a fingertip she traced a feathery line down his cheek. "Do me a favor," she said.

"I know what you're going to say."

She scooted closer, under the covers, and pressed against him. "But things are going so great."

Winder kissed her on the tip of the nose, and started to roll out of bed.

"Joe, don't go crazy on me," Nina said. "Please."

He rolled back, into her arms. "All right," he said. "Not just yet."

Six

The next morning, in the hallway by the water fountain, Charles Chelsea seized Joe Winder by the sleeve and tugged him into the office. Two men shared opposite ends of Chelsea's leather sofa—one was the immense Pedro Luz, chief of security for the Animal Kingdom, and the other was a serious-looking fellow with a square haircut and a charcoal suit.

"Joe," Chelsea said, "this gentleman is from the FBI."

"I can see that."

Chelsea cleared his throat. "This is Agent Hawkins."

Joe Winder stuck out his hand. "Billy, isn't it? You worked a Coral Gables Savings job about four years back."

The agent smiled cautiously. "And you were with the *Herald*."

"Right."

"Dated one of the tellers."

"Right again."

Charles Chelsea was trying to set some sort of record for clearing his throat. "What a coincidence that you two guys know each other."

Joe Winder sat down and stretched his legs. "Bank robbery. Billy here was the lead agent. Funny story, too—it was the Groucho guy."

"Yeah," said Hawkins, loosening up. "Wore the big nose and the eyebrows, even carried a cigar. We finally caught up with him in Clearwater."

"No kidding?" Winder said, knowing that it was driving Chelsea crazy, all this friendly conversation with a real FBI man. "All the way up in Clearwater?"

"Gentlemen," Chelsea cut in, "if you don't mind."

"What is it, Charlie?"

"Agent Hawkins is here at Mr. Kingsbury's personal request." Chelsea lowered his voice. "Joe, there were three notes delivered to employees in the park. Each was signed by this Wildlife Rescue Corps."

Winder reached in his pocket. "You mean like this?" He handed his copy to Billy Hawkins. He told him what had happened at the Rare Animal Pavilion—the old lady in the Easter bonnet, the phantom punch. Hawkins took it all down in a notebook.

Chelsea tried to contain his irritation. "Why didn't you report this to Security?" he asked Joe Winder.

"Because I didn't want to interrupt Pedro's nap."

Pedro Luz darkened. Every now and then he dozed off in the security office. "All you had to do was ring the buzzer," he snapped at Winder. He glanced at the FBI man, whose expression remained impassive and nonjudgmental. "I've had a touch of the flu," Pedro Luz added defensively. "The medicine makes me sleepy." For a large man he had a high tinny voice.

"Never mind," said Charles Chelsea. "The point is, everybody's calling up for comment. The networks. The wires. We're under siege, Joe."

Winder felt his headache coming back. Agent Billy Hawkins admitted that the federal government didn't know much about the Wildlife Rescue Corps.

"Most of these groups seem to specialize in rodents," the

agent said. "Laboratory rats, mostly. Universities, pharmaceutical houses—those are the common targets. What usually happens, they break in at night and free the animals."

"But we weren't doing experiments." Chelsea was exasperated. "We treated Vance and Violet as royalty."

"Who?" the agent said.

"The voles," Joe Winder explained cheerfully.

Charles Chelsea continued to whine. "Why have they singled out the Amazing Kingdom? We didn't abuse these creatures. Quite the opposite."

"You do any vivisections here?" asked Agent Hawkins. "These groups are quite vocal against vivisection."

Chelsea paled. "Vivisection? Christ, we gave the little bastards fresh corn on the cob every morning. Sometimes even citrus!"

"Well, this is what we've got." Hawkins flipped backwards in his notebook. "Two white males, aged twenty-five to thirty-five, fleeing the scene in a 1979 blue Ford pickup, license GPP-B06. The registration comes back to a convicted burglar whose current alias is Buddy Michael Schwartz. I might add that Mr. Schwartz's rap sheet shows no history of a social conscience with regard to animal rights, or any other."

"Somebody hired him," Joe Winder said.

"Most likely," agreed the FBI man. "Anyway, they dragged the truck out of a rock pit this morning. No bodies."

"Any sign of the voles?"

Billy Hawkins allowed himself a slight frown. "We believe the animals are dead." He handed Winder copies of the highway patrol reports, which described the incident with the tourist family in the red LeBaron, as well as the subsequent Winnebago attack. As Winder scanned the reports, Charles Chelsea reminded him to keep the news under his hat.

Agent Hawkins said, "I heard something on the radio about a million-dollar reward."

"Right!" Winder said.

"How can you do that," the FBI man said, "when you know these animals are dead?"

Joe Winder was having a wonderful time. "Go ahead," he said to Charles Chelsea. "Explain to the gentleman."

"Where's Koocher?" Chelsea grumbled. "I left about a dozen messages."

"Let's ask Pedro," said Joe Winder. "He sent one of his boys over to the lab yesterday. Must've had a reason."

Charles Chelsea folded his hands on the desk, waiting. Agent Billy Hawkins turned slightly on the couch to get a better angle on the security chief. Joe Winder arched his eyebrows and said, "How about it, Pedro? Something else happen at the Rare Animal Pavilion?"

Pedro Luz scowled, his tiny black eyes receding under the ledge of his forehead. "I don't know what you're talking about," he said. "Nothing happened nowhere." He fumbled with his clipboard. "See? There is no report."

The Security Department at the Amazing Kingdom of Thrills was staffed exclusively by corrupt ex-policemen, of which there was a steady supply in South Florida. The chief of Security, Pedro Luz, was a black-haired pinheaded giant of a young man who had been fired from the Miami Police for stealing cash and cocaine from drug dealers, then pushing them out of a Beechcraft high over the Everglades. Pedro Luz's conviction had been overturned by an appeals court, and the charges ultimately dropped when the government's key witness failed to appear for the new trial. The witness's absence was later explained when bits and pieces of his body were found in a shrimper's net off Key West, although there was no evidence linking this sad turn of events to Pedro Luz himself.

Once the corruption and murder charges had been

dismissed, Pedro Luz promptly sued the police department to reclaim his old job, plus back wages and vacation time. Meanwhile, to keep his hand in law enforcement, Pedro Luz went to work at Francis X. Kingsbury's vacation theme park. The pay was only $8.50 an hour, but as a perk Pedro was given free access to the executive gym, where he spent hours of company time lifting weights and taking anabolic steroids. This leisurely regimen was interrupted by the embarrassing daylight theft of the prized voles—and a personal communication of urgency from Francis X. Kingsbury himself. Chief Pedro Luz immediately put the security staff on double shifts, and rented a cot for himself in the office.

Which is where he snoozed at one-thirty in the afternoon when he heard a knock on the bulletproof glass.

Pedro Luz sat up slowly and swung his thick legs off the bed. He stood up, strapped on his gun, straightened the shoulders of his uniform shirt. The knocking continued.

Through the glass, Pedro Luz saw a wiry brown man in a sweaty tank top. The man battled a spastic tic on one side of his face; it looked as if a wasp were loose in one cheek.

Pedro Luz opened the door and said, "What do you want?"

"I'm here for the money," the man said, twitching. He clutched a grocery bag to his chest. "The million dollars."

"Go away," said Pedro Luz.

"Don't you even want to see?"

"The voles are dead."

The wiry man said, "But I heard on the news—"

"Go away," said Pedro Luz, "before I break your fucking legs."

"But I found the mango voles. I want my money."

Pedro Luz stepped out of the office and closed the door. He stood a full foot taller than the man with the grocery bag, and outweighed him by a hundred pounds.

"You don't listen so hot," Pedro Luz said.

The man's face twitched uncontrollably as he tried to open the bag. "Just one look," he said, "please."

Pedro Luz seized the man by the throat and shook him like a doll. The grocery bag fell to the ground and tore open. Pedro Luz was so involved in assaulting the derelict that he didn't notice what came out of the bag: two half-starved, swaybacked ferrets, eyes glazed and bluish, lips flecked with foam. Instantly they settled in chewing on Pedro Luz's right ankle, and did not stop until he tore them off, bare-handed, and threw them with all his might against the nearest wall.

One hour later, the Publicity Department of the Amazing Kingdom of Thrills faxed the following statement to all media, under the caption "Rare Voles Now Believed Dead":

Police authorities reported today that the blue-tongued mango voles stolen this week from the Amazing Kingdom of Thrills are probably dead. According to the Florida Highway Patrol and the Federal Bureau of Investigation, the rare mammals— believed to be the last of the species— were killed while crossing a highway after being abandoned by the robbers who took them.

Francis X. Kingsbury, founder and chairman of the Amazing Kingdom, expressed shock and sorrow at the news. "This is a tragedy for all of us at the park," he said Wednesday. "We had come to love and admire Vance and Violet. They were as much a part of our family as Robbie Raccoon or Petey Possum."

Mr. Kingsbury, who had offered $1 million for the safe return of the missing animals, said he will use part of the money as a reward for information leading to the arrest and conviction of those responsible for the crime.

A radical outlaw group calling itself the Wildlife Rescue Corps has claimed responsibility for the robbery at the popular amusement resort. Mr. Kingsbury said he was "shocked and dismayed that anyone claiming to support such a cause would commit crimes of violence—crimes that ultimately led not only to the animals' deaths, but to the extinction of an entire species."

Charles Chelsea, vice president in charge of public relations, said that the blue-tongued mango voles were provided with the best possible care while in captivity at the Amazing Kingdom. Only last year, the Florida Audubon Society praised the Vole Project as "a shining example of private enterprise using its vast financial resources to save a small but precious resource of nature."

Next week, the Amazing Kingdom of Thrills will present a multi-media retrospective featuring slides and videotapes of the voles during their time at the park. Entitled "Vance and Violet: The Final Days," the presentation will be shown three times daily at the Rare Animal Pavilion.

Tickets will be $4 for adults, $2.75 for children and senior citizens.

In the cafeteria, Charles Chelsea handed Joe Winder the fax and said, "Nice job, big guy."

Winder stopped on the last sentence. "You're charging money? For a goddamn slide show?"

"Joey, we're running a business here. We're not the *National Geographic*, okay? We're not a charity."

"A rodent slide show." Joe Winder wadded up the press release. "The amazing thing is not that you'd do it, because I'd think you'd charge tourists twenty bucks to watch the pelicans fuck, if they'd let you. The amazing thing is, people will actually come and pay."

He clapped his hands once, loudly. "I love this business, Charlie. Every day I learn something new."

Chelsea tightened his necktie. "Christ, here we go again. I try to pay you a compliment, and you twist it into some sort of cynical ... *commentary.*"

"Sorry," said Winder. He could feel his sinuses filling up like a bathtub.

"For your information," said Chelsea, "I got people calling all the way from Alaska, wanting to buy Vance-and-Violet T-shirts." Chelsea sighed, to show how disappointed he was in Joe Winder's attitude. Then he said, with an edge of reluctance, "You did some nice writing on this piece, Joe. Got us all off the hook."

"Thanks, boss. And you're right—it was a piece."

Chelsea sat down, eyeing the fast-food debris on Joe Winder's tray. One of Uncle Ely's Elves, sitting at the other end of the table, belched sonorously. Charles Chelsea pretended not to notice. He said, "Not to brag, Joey, but I think I did a pretty fair job with this ditty myself. Mr. X loved his quotes. He said I made him sound like a real human being."

With the tips of his fingers, Joe Winder began to rub both his temples in a ferocious circular motion.

Chelsea asked, "Now what's the matter?"

"Headache." Winder squinted as tightly as he could, to wring the pain out of his eyeballs. "Listen, I called Dr. Koocher's house. He didn't go home last night. His wife is scared out of her mind."

"Maybe he just got depressed and tied one on. Or maybe he's got a girlfriend."

Joe Winder decided not to tell Chelsea that Koocher had tried to reach him. "His wife's eight months pregnant, Charlie. She says he usually calls about nineteen times an hour, but she hasn't heard a word since yesterday."

"What would you like me to do?"

"Worry like hell," said Winder. He stood up. "Also, I'd

like your permission to talk to Pedro Luz. I think he's hiding something."

Charles Chelsea said, "You can't talk to him, Joe. He's in the hospital." He paused wearily and shook his head. "Don't ask."

"Come on, Charlie."

"For rabies shots."

"I should've guessed," Winder said. "My condolences to the dog."

"It wasn't a dog," Chelsea said. "Can't this wait till tomorrow?

Pedro's in a lot of pain."

"No," said Joe Winder, "that's perfect."

Pedro Luz had been taken to the closest emergency room, which was Mariners' Hospital down on Plantation Key. The nurse on duty remembered Pedro Luz very well, and directed Joe Winder to a private room on the second floor.

He didn't bother to knock, just eased the door open. The impressive bulk of Pedro Luz was propped up in bed, watching a Spanish-language soap opera on Channel 23. He was sucking on one end of the plastic IV tube, which he had yanked out of his arm.

"That doesn't go in your mouth," Winder told him.

"Yeah, well, I'm thirsty."

"You're bleeding all over the place."

"What do you care?" said Pedro Luz. With a corner of the sheet he swabbed the blood from his arm. "You better get out of here. I mean right now."

Joe Winder pulled a chair close to the bed and sat down. Pedro Luz smelled like a fifty-five-gallon drum of rubbing alcohol. His luxuriant hair stood in oily black spikes, and his massive neck was covered with angry purple acne, a side effect of the fruit-and-steroid bodybuilding diet.

"You like your job?" Winder asked him.

"What do you mean—at the Kingdom? Sure, I guess." The security man pulled the covers off his legs, so Joe Winder could see the bandages on his ferret-gnawed ankle. "Except for shit like this," said Pedro Luz. "Otherwise, it's an okay job most of the time."

Winder said, "So you really wouldn't want to get fired."

"The hell are you talking about?"

"For lying. I think you're lying."

"What about?"

Joe Winder said, "Don't play dumb with me." As if the guy had a choice. "Tell me why you sent a man to Koocher's lab yesterday. I know you did, because he called me about it."

Pedro Luz got red in the cheeks. The cords in his neck stood out like a rutting bull's. "I already told you," he said. "I don't have no report on that guy."

"He's missing from the park."

"Then I'll do up a report," Pedro Luz said. He breathed deeply, as if trying to calm himself. "Soon as I get outta here, I'll make a report." He took the IV tube out of his mouth. "This stuff's not so bad," he said thoughtfully. "Tastes like sugar syrup." He replaced the tube between his lips and sucked on it loudly.

Joe Winder said, "You're a moron."

"What did you say?"

"Make that a submoron."

Pedro Luz shrugged. "I'd beat the piss out of you, if I didn't feel so bad. They gave me about a million shots." He leered woozily and opened his gown. "See, they broke two needles on my stomach."

Joe Winder couldn't help but admire Pedro Luz's physique. He could see the bright crimson spots where the hypodermics had bent against the muscle.

"Least I won't get the rabies," said Pedro Luz, drawing merrily on the tube. "You oughta take off, before I start feeling better."

Winder stood up and slid the chair back to its corner. "Last chance, Hercules. Tell me why you sent a man to the lab yesterday."

"Or else what?"

"Or we play '*This Is Your Life, Pedro Dipshit.*' I tell Kingsbury's people all about your sterling employment record with the Miami Police Department. I might even give them a copy of the indictment. A spine-chilling saga, Pedro. Not for the meek and mild." Pedro Luz removed the tube and wiped his lips on the sleeve of his gown. He looked genuinely puzzled. "But they know," he said. "They know all about it."

"And they hired you anyway?"

"'Course," said Pedro Luz. "It was Kingsbury himself. He said every man deserves a second chance."

"I admire that philosophy," Joe Winder said, "most of the time."

"Yeah, well, Mr. X took a personal liking to me. That's why I'm not too worried about all your bullshit."

"Yes," said Joe Winder, "I'm beginning to understand."

"Because you couldn't get me fired no matter what," said Pedro Luz. "And you know what else? Don't never call me a moron again, if you know what's good for you."

"I guess I don't," said Joe Winder. "Obviously."

Seven

The ticket taker at the Wet Willy attraction was trying to control his temper. *Firm, but friendly.* That's how you deal with difficult customers; that's what they taught in ticket-taker training. The young man, who was new on the job, said, "I'm sorry, sir, but you can't cut to the front of the line. These other people have been waiting for a long time."

"These other people," the man said, "tell me, do they own this fucking joint?"

The ticket taker did not recognize Francis X. Kingsbury, who wore thong sandals, baggy pastel swim trunks and no shirt. He also had a stopwatch hanging from a red lanyard around his neck.

"Now, you don't want me to call Security," the ticket taker said.

"Nothing but idiots," Kingsbury muttered, pushing his pallid belly through the turnstile. He shuffled up two flights of stairs to the launching ramp, and dropped to all fours.

The Wet Willy ride was one of the Amazing Kingdom's most popular thrill attractions, and one of the cheapest to operate. A marvel of engineering simplicity, it was nothing but a long translucent latex tube. The inside was painted in outrageous psychedelic hues, and kept slippery with drain water diverted at no cost from nearby drinking fountains. The narrow tube descended from a height of approximately six stories, with riders plunging downhill at an average angle of twenty-seven exhilarating degrees.

Francis X. Kingsbury was exceptionally proud of the Wet Willy because the whole contraption had been his idea, his concept. The design engineers at the Amazing Kingdom had wanted something to compete with Disney's hugely successful Space Mountain ride. Kingsbury had collected all the press clippings about Space Mountain and used a bright yellow marker to emphasize his contempt for the project, particularly the development cost. "Seventeen million bucks," he had scoffed, "for a frigging roller ride in the dark."

The engineers had earnestly presented several options for the Amazing Kingdom—Jungle Coaster, Moon Coaster, Alpine Death Coaster—but Kingsbury rejected each for the obvious reason that roller-coaster cars and roller-coaster tracks cost money. So did the electricity needed to run them.

"Gravity!" Kingsbury had grumped. "The most underused energy source on the planet."

"So you're suggesting a slide," ventured one of the engineers. "Maybe a water slide."

Kingsbury had shaken his head disdainfully. Slides *look* cheap, he'd complained, we're not running a goddamn State Fair. A tube would be better, a sleek space-age tube.

"Think condom," he had advised the engineers. "A three-hundred-foot condom."

And so the Wet Willy was erected. Instantly it had become a sensation among tourists at the park, a fact that edified Kingsbury's belief that the illusion of quality is more valuable than quality itself.

Lately, though, ridership figures for the Wet Willy had shown a slight but troubling decline. Francis X. Kingsbury decided to investigate personally, without notifying the engineers, the ticket takers, the Security Department or anyone else at the park. He wanted to test his theory that the ride had become less popular because it had gotten slower. The stopwatch would tell the story.

The way the Wet Willy was designed, a 110-pound teenager would be able to slide headlong from the ramp to the gelatin-filled landing sac in exactly 22.7 seconds. Marketing specialists had calibrated the time down to the decimal point—the ride needed to be long enough to make customers think they were getting their money's worth, yet fast enough to seem dangerous and exciting.

Francis X. Kingsbury weighed considerably more than 110 pounds as he crawled into the slippery chute. Ahead of him, he saw the wrinkled bare soles of a child disappear swiftly into the tube, as if flushed down a rubber commode. Kingsbury pressed the button on the stopwatch, eased to his belly and pushed off. He held his arms at his sides, like an otter going down a riverbank. In this case, an overweight otter in a ridiculous Jack Kemp hairpiece.

Kingsbury grimaced as he swooshed downward, skimming on a thin plane of clammy water. He thought: This is supposed to be fun? The stopwatch felt cold and hard against his breastbone. The bright colors on the walls of the tube did little to lift his spirits; he noticed that some of the reds had faded to pink, and the blues were runny. Not only that, sections of the chute seemed irregular and saggy, as if the latex were giving way.

He took his eyes off the fabric long enough to notice, with alarm, that he was gaining on the youngster who had entered the Wet Willy ahead of him. Suddenly Kingsbury was close enough to hear the child laughing, oblivious to the danger— no! Close enough to make out the grinning, bewhiskered visage of Petey Possum waving from the rump of the youngster's swimming trunks.

"Shit," said Kingsbury. Feverishly he tried to brake, digging into the rubber with his toes and fingernails. It was no use: gravity ruled the Wet Willy.

Kingsbury overtook the surprised child and they became one, hurtling down the slick pipe in a clumsy union of tangled torsos.

"Hey!" the kid cried. "You're smushing me!" It was a boy, maybe nine or ten, with bright red hair and freckles all over his neck. Francis X. Kingsbury now steered the kid as if he were a toboggan.

They hit the gelatin sac at full speed and disengaged. The boy came out of the goo bawling, followed by Kingsbury, who was studying the dial of the stopwatch and frowning. He seemed not to notice the solemn group waiting outside the exit: the earnest young ticket taker, plus three uniformed security men. All were breathing heavily, as if they had run the whole way.

The ticket taker pointed at Kingsbury and said, "That's him. Except he wasn't bald before."

The security men, all former crooked cops recruited by Pedro Luz, didn't move. They recognized Mr. X right away.

The ticket taker said, "Get him, why don't you!"

"Yeah," said the red-haired tourist kid. "He hurt me."

"Mildew," said Francis X. Kingsbury, still preoccupied. "Fucking mildew under my fingernails." He looked up and, to no one in particular, said: "Call Maintenance and have them Lysol the Willy, A-S-A-P."

The tourist kid raised the pitch of his whining so that it was impossible to ignore. "That's the man who tried to smush me. On my bottom!"

"Give the little turd a free pass to the Wild Bill Hiccup," said Francis X. Kingsbury. "And *him*," pointing at the ticket taker, "throw his ass, I mean it, off the property."

The boy with the Petey Possum swimsuit ran off, sniffling

melodramatically. As the security men surrounded the ticket taker, Kingsbury said, "What, like it takes three of you monkeys?"

The men hesitated. All were reluctant to speak.

"You," Kingsbury said, nodding at the smallest of the guards. "Go back up and slide this goddamn tube. Yeah, you heard me. See if you can beat twenty-seven-point-two."

The security man nodded doubtfully. "All right, sir."

"Yeah, and my hair," said Kingsbury, "it's up there somewhere. Grab it on the way down."

Bud Schwartz paused at the door and looked back. "It don't seem right," he said. "Maybe just the VCR."

"Forget it." Danny Pogue was rocking on his crutches down by the elevator. "Where we gonna hide anything? Come on, Bud, let's just go."

The elevator came and Danny Pogue clumped in. With one crutch he held the elevator door and waited for his partner. Bud Schwartz was trying to tear himself away from Molly McNamara's fancy condo. "Look at all this shit we're leaving behind," he said longingly. "We could probably get five hundred easy for the Dolbys."

Danny Pogue leaned out of the elevator. "And how the fuck we supposed to carry 'em? Me with these toothpicks and you with one good arm. Would you get your ass moving, please, before the bitch comes back?"

As they rode to the first floor, Danny Pogue said, "Besides, we got no car."

Bud Schwartz grunted sourly, wondering what became of the blue pickup. "I feel like she owes us."

"She does owe us. She owes us eight grand, to be exact. But we agreed it wasn't worth waiting, right?"

"I mean, owes us for this." Bud Schwartz brandished a gauze-wrapped hand. "Shooting us, for no good reason."

"She's a nut case. She don't need a reason." They got off the elevator and for once Danny Pogue led the way, swinging on his crutches.

They could see the gatehouse at the main entrance, on the other side of the condominium complex. Rather than follow the sidewalks, they decided to shorten the trip by cutting across the grounds, which were sparsely landscaped and dimly lit. In the still of the evening, the high-rise community of Eagle Ridge was at rest, except for a noisy bridge tournament being held in the rec room. On the screened porches of ground-floor apartments, couples could be seen watering their plants or feeding their cats.

As the two outsiders made their way across the darkened shuffleboard courts, Danny Pogue's left crutch gave out and he went down with a cry.

"Goddamn," he said, splayed on the concrete. "Look here, somebody left a puck on the court."

Bud Schwartz said, "It's not a puck. Pucks are for hockey."

Danny Pogue held the plastic disk like a Danish. "Then what do you call it?"

"I don't know what you call it," said Bud Schwartz, "but people are staring, so why don't you get up before some fucking Good Samaritan calls 911."

"I ought to sue the assholes for leaving this damn thing lying around."

"Good idea, Danny. We'll go see a lawyer first thing in the morning. We'll sue the bastards for a jillion trillion dollars. Then we'll retire down to Club Med." With great effort, Bud Schwartz helped Danny Pogue off the cement and steadied him on the crutches.

"So who's watching us?"

"There." Bud Schwartz raised his eyes toward a third-floor balcony, where three women stood and peered, arms on their hips, like cranky old cormorants drying their wings.

"Hey!" Danny Pogue yelled. "Get a life!"

The women retreated into the apartment, and Danny Pogue laughed. Bud Schwartz didn't think it was all that funny; he'd been in a rotten frame of mind ever since Molly McNamara had shot him in the hand.

As they approached the gatehouse, Danny Pogue said, "So where's the taxi?"

"First things first," said Bud Schwartz. Then, in a whisper: "Remember what we talked about. The girl's name is Annie. Annie Lefkowitz."

He had met her that afternoon by the swimming pool and gotten nowhere—but that's who they were visiting, if anybody asked. No way would they mention Molly McNamara; never heard of her.

A rent-a-cop came out of the gatehouse and nodded neutrally at the two men. He was a young muscular black man with a freshly pressed uniform and shiny shoes. Over his left breast pocket was a patch that said, in navy-blue stitching: "Eagle Ridge Security." Danny Pogue and Bud Schwartz were surprised to see what appeared to be a real Smith & Wesson on his hip.

The rent-a-cop said: "Looks like you guys had a rough night."

"Barbecue blew up," said Bud Schwartz. "Ribs all over the place."

Danny Pogue extended his wounded foot, as if offering it for examination. "Burns is all," he said. "We'll be okay."

The rent-a-cop didn't seem in a hurry to move out of the way. He asked for their names, and Bud Schwartz made up a couple of beauts. Ron Smith and Dick Jones.

"Where are you staying?" the rent-a-cop said. "Which building?"

"With Amy Leibowitz," answered Danny Pogue.

"Lefkowitz," said Bud Schwartz, grinding his molars. "Annie *Lefkowitz*. Building K."

"Which unit?" asked the rent-a-cop.

"We're visiting from up North," said Bud Schwartz. "We're not related or anything. She's just a friend, if you know what I mean."

"But which unit?"

Bud Schwartz made a sheepish face. "You know, I don't even remember. But her last name's Lefkowitz, you can look it up."

The rent-a-cop said: "There are four different Lefkowitzes that live here. Hold tight, I'll be right back."

The guard went back inside, and Danny Pogue leaned closer to his partner. The gatehouse cast just enough light to reveal a change in Bud Schwartz's expression.

"So help me God," said Danny Pogue, "if you leave me here, I'll go to the cops."

"What're you talking about?"

"You're gonna run, goddamn you."

"No, I'm not," said Bud Schwartz, although that was precisely what he was considering. He had spotted the yellow taxi, parked near a mailbox across the street.

"Don't even think about it," said Danny Pogue. "You're still on probation."

"And you're on parole," Bud Schwartz snapped. Then he thought: Hell, what are we worried about? We're not even arrested. And this jerk-off's not even a real cop.

"This guy, he can't stop us from leaving," said Bud Schwartz. "He can stop us from trying to get in, but he can't stop us from getting out."

Danny Pogue thought about this. "You're right," he said. "Why don't we just take off?"

"Taking off is not how I'd describe it, considering the shape we're in. Limping off is more like it."

"I wonder if that gun's loaded," said Danny Pogue. "Or if he's allowed to use it."

Bud Schwartz told him not to worry, they could still talk their way out of it. When the rent-a-cop came out of the gatehouse, he held a clipboard in one hand and a big ugly Maglite in the other.

"Miss Lefkowitz says she's had no visitors."

Bud Schwartz looked stunned. "Annie? Are you sure you got the right one?" He stuck with it, digging them in even deeper. "She's probably just pissed off 'cause we're leaving, that's all. Got a good taste and doesn't want to let go."

The rent-a-cop pointed the white beam of the Maglite at Bud Schwartz's face and said, "Why don't you fuckheads come with me."

Danny Pogue retreated a couple of steps. "We didn't do nothin' wrong."

"You lied," said the rent-a-cop. "That's wrong."

Half-blind from the flashlight, Bud Schwartz shielded his eyes and said, "Look, I can explain about Annie." He was ummming and awwwwing, trying to come up with something, when he heard a shuffling noise off to his left. The rent-a-cop aimed the flashlight toward Danny Pogue, but Danny Pogue was gone.

Bud Schwartz said, "I'm not believing this."

The rent-a-cop seemed mildly annoyed. They could hear the frantic thwuck-thwuck of the crutches, heading down the unlit road.

"Bastard," said Bud Schwartz. He felt sharp fingers— impressively strong—seize the loose span of flesh where his neck met his shoulder.

"Before I go get the gimper," said the rent-a-cop, pinching harder, "how about you telling me some portion of the truth."

"Really I can't," said Bud Schwartz. "I'd like to, but it's just not possible."

Then the Maglite came down against the top of his forehead, and the shutters of his brain slammed all at once, leaving the interior of his skull very cool, black, empty.

*

Joe Winder parked at the end of the gravel road and changed out of his work clothes. The necktie was the first thing to come off. He put on a pair of cutoffs, slipped into some toeless sneakers, slathered on some Cutter's and grabbed his spinning rod out of the car. He found the path through the mangroves—his path, to the water's edge. He came here almost every day after work, depending on how badly the wind was blowing. Sometimes he fished, sometimes he sat and watched.

Today he made his way quickly, worried about missing the best of the tide. When he got to the shoreline, he put on the Polaroids and swept the shallow flats with his eyes. He spotted a school of small bonefish working against the current, puffing mud about forty yards out. He grinned and waded out purposefully, sliding his feet silently across the marly bottom. A small plane flew over and the rumble of the engine flushed the fish. Joe Winder cursed, but kept his gaze on the nervous wake, just in case. Sure enough, the bonefish settled down and started feeding again. As he edged closer, he counted five in all, small black torpedoes.

As Joe Winder lifted his arm to cast, he heard a woman call out his name. The distraction was sufficient to ruin his aim; the small pink jig landed smack in the middle of the school, causing the fish to depart at breakneck speed for Andros Island and beyond. An absolutely terrible cast.

He turned and saw Nina waving from the shore. She was climbing out of her blue jeans, which was no easy task.

"I'm coming out," she called. "I can see that."

And out she came, in an aqua T-shirt, an orange Dolphins cap, black panties and white Keds. Under these circumstances, it was impossible for Joe Winder to stay angry about the bonefish.

Nina was laughing like a child when she reached him. "The water's so warm," she said. "Makes me want to dive in."

He gave her a left-handed hug. "Did you put on some bug spray?" he asked.

"Designer goo," said Nina. "Some sort of weird enzyme. The bugs gag on it."

Joe Winder pointed with the tip of the fishing rod. "See that? They're mocking me." Another school of bonefish cavorted, tails flashing, far out of human casting range.

"I'll take your word for it," said Nina, squinting. "Joe, what'd you do to your hair?"

"Cut it."

"With what?"

"A steak knife. I couldn't find the scissors."

Nina reached up and touched what was left. "For God's sake, why?"

"Chelsea said I looked like one of the Manson family."

Nina frowned. "Since when do you give a hoot what Charlie Chelsea thinks."

"It's part of the damn dress code. Kingsbury's cracking down, or so Charlie says. I was trying to be a team player, like you wanted." Joe Winder spotted a small bonnet shark cruising the shallows, and cast the jig for the hell of it. The shark took one look and swam away arrogantly.

Joe Winder said, "So now I look like a Nazi."

"No," said Nina, "the Nazis had combs."

"How's the new routine coming? I assume that's why you're here." It was the time of the week when the girls on the sex-phone line had to update their shtick.

"Tell me what you think." Nina reached into the breast pocket of the T-shirt and pulled out a folded piece of notebook paper. Carefully she unfolded it. "Now be honest," she said to Winder.

"Always."

"'Kay, here goes." She cleared her throat. "You say, 'Hello.'"

"Hello!" Joe Winder sang out.

"Hi, there," said Nina, reading. "*I was just thinking about you. I was thinking it would be so nice to go on a train, just you and me. A long, romantic train ride. I love the way trains rock back and forth. At first they start out so slow and hard, but then*"—here Nina had scripted a pause—"*but then they get faster and stronger. I love the motion of a big locomotive, it gets me so hot.*"

"Gets me going," suggested Joe Winder. "Hot is a cliché."

Nina nodded in agreement. "That's better, yeah. *I love the motion of a big locomotive, it really gets me going.*"

Joe Winder noticed that the tide was slowing. These fish would be gone soon.

But there was Nina in her black panties. Knee deep in the Atlantic. Blond hair tied back under her cap with a pink ribbon. Reading some damn nonsense about sex on the Amtrak, in that killer voice of hers. The words didn't matter, it was all music to Joe Winder; he was stirred by the sight of her in the water with the sun dropping behind the Keys. At times like this he sure loved Florida.

Nina told him to quit staring at her all sappy and listen, so he did.

"*Sometimes, late at night, I dream that you're a locomotive. And I'm riding you on top, stretched out with my legs around your middle. First we go uphill, real slow and hard and rough. Then all of a sudden I'm riding the engine down, faster and harder and hotter until . . .*"

"Until what?" Joe Winder said.

"Until whatever," said Nina with a shrug. "I figure I'd just leave the rest to their imagination."

"No," said Winder. "A metaphor like that, you need a big ending." He slapped a mosquito that had penetrated the sheen of Cutter's on his neck. "How about: *We're going downhill, out of control, faster and hotter. I scream for you to stop but you keep pumping and pumping until I explode, melting against you.*"

From someplace—her bra?—Nina produced a ballpoint

pen and began to scribble. "The pumping business is a bit much," she said, "but I like the melting part. That's good imagery, Joe, thanks."

"Any time."

"Miriam's writing up another hot-tub blowjob."

"Not again," said Joe Winder.

"She says it's going to be a series." Nina folded the notebook paper and slipped it back in the pocket of her shirt. "I'm going to be late to work if I don't get a move on. You coming in?"

"No, there's another school working that deep edge. I'm gonna try not to brain 'em with this feather."

Nina said good luck and sloshed back toward shore. Halfway there, she turned and said, "My God, I almost forgot. I got one of those phone calls at home."

Winder stopped tracking the fish. He closed the bail on his spinning reel, and tucked the rod in the crook of an elbow. "Was it Koocher?" he asked, across the flat.

Nina shook her head. "It was a different voice from last time." She took a half-dozen splashy steps toward him, so she wouldn't have to yell so far. "But that's what I wanted to tell you. The guy today said he was Dr. Koocher, only he wasn't. It was the wrong voice from before."

Joe Winder said, "You're sure?"

"It's my business, Joe. It's what I do all night, listen to grown men lie."

"What exactly did he say, Nina? The guy who called. Besides that he was Koocher."

"He said all hell was breaking loose at the park."

"All hell," repeated Winder.

"And he said he wanted to meet you tonight at the Card Sound Bridge."

"When?"

"Midnight sharp." Nina shifted her weight from one leg

to the other, rippling the water. "You're not going," she said. "Please?"

Joe Winder looked back across the flats, lifeless in the empty auburn dusk. "No sign of those fish," he said. "I believe this tide is officially dead."

Eight

Bud Schwartz didn't have to open his eyes to know where he was; the scent of jasmine room freshener assailed his nostrils. He was in Molly McNamara's place, lying on the living-room sofa. He could feel her stare, unblinking, like a stuffed owl.

"I know you're awake," she said.

He elected not to open his eyes right away.

"Son, I know you're there."

It was the same tone she had used the first time they met, at one of the low points in Bud Schwartz's burglary career; he had been arrested after his 1979 Chrysler Cordoba stalled in the middle of 163rd Street, less than a block from the duplex apartment he had just burglarized with his new partner, Danny Pogue. The victim of the crime had been driving home when he saw the stalled car, stopped to help and immediately recognized the Sony television, Panasonic clock radio, Amana microwave and Tandy laptop computer stacked neatly in the Cordoba's back seat. The reason the stuff was lying in the back seat was because the trunk was full of stolen Neil Diamond cassettes that the burglars could not, literally, give away.

Bud Schwartz had been smoking in a holding cell of the Dade County Jail when Molly McNamara arrived. At the time, she was a volunteer worker for Jackson Memorial

Hospital and the University of Miami Medical School; her job was recruiting jail inmates as subjects for medical testing, a task that suited her talent for maternal prodding. She had entered the holding cell wearing white rubber-soled shoes, a polyester nurse's uniform and latex gloves.

"I'm insulted," Bud Schwartz had said.

Molly McNamara had eyed him over the top of her glasses and said, "I understand you're looking at eighteen months."

"Twelve, tops," Bud Schwartz had said.

"Well, I'm here to offer you a splendid opportunity."

"And I'm here to listen."

Molly had asked if Bud Schwartz was interested in testing a new ulcer drug for the medical school.

"I don't have no ulcers."

"It doesn't matter," Molly had said. "You'd be in the control group." A pill a day for three months, she had explained. Sign up now, the prosecutor asks the judge to chop your time in half.

"Your friend's already agreed to it."

"That figures," Bud Schwartz had said. "I end up with ulcers, he'll be the cause of it."

When he'd asked about possible side effects, Molly read from a printed page: headaches, high blood pressure, urinary-tract infections.

"Run that last one by me again."

"It's unlikely you'll experience any problems," Molly had assured him. "They've been testing this medication for almost two years."

"Thanks, just the same."

"I know you're smarter than this," Molly had told him in a chiding tone.

"If I was really smart," Bud Schwartz had said, "I'd a put new plugs in the car."

A week later she had returned, this time without the rubber

gloves. Pulled his rap sheet out of her purse, held it up like the Dead Sea Scrolls.

"I've been looking for a burglar," she had said. "What for?"

"Ten thousand dollars."

"Very funny," Bud Schwartz had said.

"Call me when you get out. You and your friend."

"You serious?"

"It's not what you think," Molly had said.

"I can't think of anything. Except maybe you're some kinda snitch for the cops."

"Be serious, young man." Again with the needle in her voice, worse than his mother. "Don't mention this to anyone."

"Who the hell would believe it? Ten grand, I swear."

"Call me when you get out."

"Be a while," he said. "Hey, is it too late to get me in on that ulcer deal?"

That was six months ago.

Bud Schwartz touched the place on his brow where the rent-a-cop's flashlight had clobbered him. He could feel a scabby eruption the size of a golf ball. "Damn," he said, opening his eyes slowly.

Molly McNamara moved closer and stood over him. She was wearing her reading glasses with the pink roses on the frames. She said, "Your friend is in the bedroom."

"Danny's back?"

"I was on my way here when I spotted him at the Farm Stores. He tried to get away, but—"

"You didn't shoot him again?" Bud Schwartz was asking more out of curiosity than concern.

"No need to," said Molly. "I had the Cadillac. I think your friend realized there's no point in getting run over."

With a wheeze, Bud Schwartz sat up. His ears pounded and stomach juices bubbled up sourly in his throat. As always, Molly was prompt with the first aid. She handed him a towel filled with chipped ice and told him to pack it against his wound.

Danny Pogue clumped into the living room and sat on the other end of the sofa. "You look like shit," he said to Bud Schwartz.

"Thank you, Tom Selleck." From under the towel Bud Schwartz glared with one crimson eye.

Molly McNamara said, "That's enough, the both of you. I can't begin to tell you how much trouble you've caused."

"We was trying to get out of your hair is all," said Danny Pogue. "Why're you keeping us prisoners?"

Molly said, "Aren't we being a bit melodramatic? You are not prisoners. You're simply two young men in my employ until I decide otherwise."

"In case you didn't hear," said Bud Schwartz, "Lincoln freed the slaves a long time ago."

Molly McNamara ignored the remark. "At the gatehouse I had to tell Officer Andrews a lie. I told him you were my nephews visiting from Georgia. I told him we'd had a fight and that's why you were trying to sneak out of Eagle Ridge. I told him your parents died in a plane crash when you were little, and I was left responsible for taking care of you."

"Pitiful," said Bud Schwartz.

"I told him you both had emotional problems."

"We're heading that direction," Bud Schwartz said.

"I don't like to lie," Molly added sternly. "Normally I don't believe in it."

"But shooting people is okay?" Danny Pogue cackled bitterly. "Lady, pardon me for saying, but I think you're goddamn fucking nutso."

Molly's eyes flickered. In a frozen voice she said, "Please don't use that word in my presence."

Danny Pogue mumbled that he was sorry. He wasn't sure which word she meant.

"I'm not certain Officer Andrews believed any of it," Molly went on. "I wouldn't be surprised if he reported the entire episode to the condominium association. You think you've got problems now! Oh, brother, just wait."

Bud Schwartz removed the towel from his forehead and examined it for bloodstains. Molly said, "Are you listening to me?"

"Hanging on every word."

"Because I've got some very bad news. For all of us."

Bud Schwartz grunted wearily. What now? What the hell now?

"It was on the television tonight," Molly McNamara said. "The mango voles are dead. Killed on the highway."

Nervously Danny Pogue glanced at his partner, whose eyes were fixed hard on the old woman. Waiting, no doubt, to see if she pulled that damn pistol from her sweater.

Molly said, "I don't know all the details, but I suppose it's not important. I feel absolutely sick about this."

Good, thought Bud Schwartz, maybe she's not blaming us.

But she was. "If only I'd known how careless and irresponsible you were, I would never have recruited you for this job." Molly took off her rose-framed glasses and folded them meticulously. Her gray eyes were misting.

"The blue-tongued mango voles are extinct because of me," she said, blinking, "and because of you."

Bud Schwartz said, "We're real sorry."

"Yeah," agreed Danny Pogue. "It's too bad they died."

Molly was downcast. "This is an unspeakable sin against Nature. The death of these dear animals. I can't tell you—it goes against everything I've worked for, everything I believe in. I was so stupid to entrust this project to a couple of reckless, clumsy criminals."

"That's us," said Bud Schwartz.

Danny Pogue didn't like his partner's casual tone. He said

to Molly, "We didn't know they was so important. They looked like regular old rats."

The old woman absently fondled the buttons of her sweater. "There's no point belaboring it. The damage is done. Now we've got to atone."

"Atone," said Bud Schwartz suspiciously.

"What does that mean?" asked Danny Pogue. "I don't know that word."

Molly said, "Tell him, Bud."

"It means we gotta do something to make up for all this."

Molly nodded. "That's right. Somehow we must redeem ourselves."

Bud Schwartz sighed. He wondered what crazy lie she'd told the rent-a-cop about their gunshot wounds. And this condo association—what's she so worried about?

"Have you ever heard of the Mothers of Wilderness?" asked Molly McNamara.

"No," said Bud Schwartz, "can't say that I have." Danny Pogue said he'd never heard of them, either.

"No matter," said Molly, brightening, "because as of tonight, you're our newest members. Congratulations, gentlemen!"

Restlessly Danny Pogue squeezed a pimple on his neck. "Is it like a nature club?" he said. "Do we get T-shirts and stuff?"

"Oh, you'll enjoy it," said Molly. "I've got some pamphlets in my briefcase."

Bud Schwartz clutched at the damp towel. This time he pressed it against his face. "Cut to the chase," he muttered irritably. "What the hell is it you want us to do?"

"I'm coming to that," said Molly McNamara. "By the way, did I mention that Mr. Kingsbury is offering a reward to anyone who turns in the vole robbers?"

"Oh, no," said Danny Pogue.

"Quite an enormous reward, according to the papers."

"How nice," said Bud Schwartz, his voice cold.

"Oh, don't worry," Molly said. "I wouldn't dream of saying anything to the authorities."

"How could you?" Danny Pogue exclaimed. "You're the one asked us to rob the place!"

Molly's face crinkled in thought. "That'd be awfully hard to swallow, that an old retired woman like myself would get involved in such a distasteful crime. I suppose the FBI would have to decide whom to believe—two young fellows with your extensive criminal pasts, or an older woman like myself who's never even had a parking ticket."

Danny Pogue angrily pounded the floor with one of his crutches. "For someone who don't like to lie, you sure do make a sport of it."

Bud Schwartz stretched out on the sofa, closed his eyes and smiled in resignation. "You're a piece of work," he said to Molly McNamara. "I gotta admit."

The Card Sound Bridge is a steep two-lane span that connects the northern tip of Key Largo with the South Florida mainland. Joe Winder got there two hours early, at ten o'clock. He parked half a mile down the road and walked the rest of the way. He staked out a spot on some limestone boulders, which formed a jetty under the eastern incline of the bridge. From there Winder could watch for the car that would bring the mystery caller to this meeting.

He knew it wouldn't be Dr. Will Koocher; Nina was never wrong about phone voices. Joe Winder had no intention of confronting the impostor, but at least he wanted to get a good look, maybe even a tag number.

Not much was biting under the bridge. Effortlessly Winder cast the same pink wiggle-jig he'd been using on the bonefish flats. He let it sink into the fringe of the sea grass, then reeled in slowly, bouncing the lure with the tip of his rod. In this fashion he picked up a couple of blue runners and a large spiny pinfish, which he tossed back. The other fishermen were using dead shrimp with similar unexciting results. By eleven most of them had packed up their buckets and rods and gone home, leaving the jetty deserted except for Joe Winder and two other diehards.

The other men stood side by side, conversing quietly in Spanish. As Joe Winder watched them more closely, it seemed that the men were doing more serious talking than fishing. They were using Cuban yo-yo rigs, twirling the lines overhead and launching the baits with a loud plop into the water. Once in a while they'd pull in the lines and cast out again, usually without even checking the hooks.

One of the men was a husky no-neck in long canvas pants. The other was short and wiry, and as dark as coffee. Both wore baseball caps and light jackets, which was odd, considering the heat. Every few minutes a pair of headlights would appear down Card Sound Road, and Joe Winder would check to see if the car stopped at the foot of the bridge. After a while, he noticed that the two other fishermen were doing the same. This was not a good sign.

As midnight approached, the other men stopped pretending to fish and concentrated on the road. Joe Winder realized that he was stranded on the jetty with two goons who probably were waiting to ambush him. Worse, they stood squarely between Winder and the relative safety of the island. The most obvious means of escape would be jumping into Card Sound; while exceptionally dramatic, such a dive would prove both stupid and futile. The bay was shallow and provided no cover; if the goons had guns, they could simply shoot him like a turtle.

Joe Winder's only hope was that they wouldn't recognize him in the dark with his hair hacked off. It was a gray overcast night, and he was doing a creditable impersonation of a preoccupied angler. Most likely the goons would be expecting him at twelve sharp, some dumb shmuck hollering Koocher's name under the bridge.

The strategy of staying invisible might have worked if only a powerful fish had not seized Joe Winder's lure. The strike jolted his arms, and reflexively he yanked back hard to set the hook. The fish streaked toward the rocks, then back out again toward open water. The buzz of Winder's reel cut like a saw through the stillness of the bay. The two goons stopped talking and looked up to see what was happening.

Joe Winder knew. It was a snook, a damn big one. Any other night he would have been thrilled to hook such a fish, but not now. From the corner of his eye he could see the goons rock-hopping down the jetty so they could better view the battle. Near a piling the fish broke to the surface, shaking its gills furiously before diving in a frothy silver gash. The goons pointed excitedly at the commotion, and Winder couldn't blame them; it was a grand fish.

Joe Winder knew what to do, but he couldn't bring himself to do it. Palm the spool. Break the damn thing off, before the two guys got any closer. Instead Joe Winder was playing the fish like a pro, horsing it away from the rocks and pilings, letting it spend itself in short hard bursts. What am I, crazy? Winder thought. From up here I could never land this fish alone. The goons would want to help, sure they would, and then they'd see who I was and that would be it. One dead snook and one dead flack.

Again the fish thrust its underslung snout from the water and splashed. Even in the tea-colored water the black lateral stripe was visible along its side. Twelve pounds easy, thought Winder. A fine one.

One of the goons clapped his hands and Joe Winder looked up. "Nize goying," the man said. "Dat's some fugging fish." It was the short wiry one.

"Thanks," said Winder. Maybe he was wrong. Maybe these weren't the bad guys, after all. Or maybe they hadn't come to hurt him; maybe they just wanted to talk. Maybe they had Koocher and were scheming for a ransom.

After five minutes of back-and-forth, the snook was tiring. Twenty yards from the jetty it glided to the surface and flopped its tail once, twice. Not yet, Winder thought; don't give up yet, you marvelous bastard.

He heard their heavy footsteps on the rocks. Now they were behind him. He heard their breathing. One of them was chewing gum. Joe Winder smelled hot spear-mint and beer.

"What're you waiting for?" asked the big one.

"He's not ready," Winder said, afraid to turn and give them a look at his face. "He's still got some gas."

"No, look at the fugging thin," said the little one. "He juice about dead, mang."

The snook was dogging it on top, barely putting a bend in Joe Winder's fishing rod.

"That's some good eating," the big no-neck goon remarked.

Winder swallowed dryly and said, "Too bad they're out of season."

He heard both of the men laugh. "Hey, you don't want him, we'll take it off your hands. Fry his ass up in a minute. Right, Angel?"

The little one, Angel, said, "Yeah, I go down and grab hole the fugging thin." He took off his baseball cap and scrabbled noisily down the rocks.

Joe Winder got a mental picture of these two submorons in yellowed undershirts—swilling beer, watching "Wheel" on the tube—cooking up the snook on a cheap gas stove in some rathole Hialeah duplex. The thought of it was more than he could stand. He placed his hand on the spool of the reel and pulled once, savagely.

The snook had one good powerful surge left in its heart, and the fishing line snapped like a rifle shot. Joe Winder fell back, then steadied himself. "Goddammit," he said, trying to sound disappointed.

"That was really stupid," said the big goon. "You don't know shit about fighting a fish."

"I guess not."

The wiry one had been waiting by the water when the fish got off. Cursing in Spanish, he monkeyed back up the rocks. To guide himself, he held a small flashlight in one hand. The beam caught Joe Winder flush in the face; there was nothing he could do.

Instantly the big goon grabbed him by the shoulder. "Hey! You work at the park."

"What park?"

The wiry one said, "Doan tell me he's the guy."

"Yup," said the big one, tightening his grip.

The men edged closer. Joe Winder could sense they were angry about not recognizing him sooner.

"Mr. Fisherman," said the big one acidly.

"That's me," said Winder. "You must be the one who wanted to talk about Dr. Koocher."

The goon named Angel turned off the flashlight and buried it in his jacket. "Two hours with these damn mosquitoes and you standing right here, the whole fugging tine!" He punched Joe Winder ferociously in the kidney.

As Winder fell, he thought: So they're not here to chat.

His head bounced against limestone and he began to lose consciousness. Then he felt himself being lifted by the armpits, which hurt like hell. They were carrying him somewhere in a hurry.

The husky one, Spearmint Breath, was talking in Joe Winder's ear. "What'd he say on the phone?"

"Who?"

"The rat doctor."

"Nothing." Winder was panting.

"Aw, bullshit."

"I swear. He left a message, that's all." Winder tried to walk but felt his legs pedaling air, being swept along. "Just a message was all," he said again. "He wanted to see me but he didn't say why."

In his other ear, Joe Winder heard the wiry one call him a stinken fugging liar.

"No, I swear."

They had him up against the side of a truck. Bronco. White. Rusty as hell. Ford Bronco, Winder thought. In case I live through this.

In case anybody might be interested.

The big goon spun Joe Winder around and pinned his arms while the one named Angel slugged him on the point of the jaw. Then he hit him once in each eye. Winder felt his face start to bloat and soften, like a melon going bad. With any luck, total numbness would soon follow.

Angel was working up a sweat. Every time he threw a punch, he let out a sharp yip, like a poodle. It would have been hilarious except for the pain that went with it.

Finally, Spearmint Breath said, "I don't think he knows jack shit." Then he said something in Spanish.

Angel said, "Chur he does, the cokesucker." This time he hit Joe Winder in the gut.

Perfect. Can't breathe. Can't see. Can't talk.

The big goon let go, and Winder fell limp across the hood of the truck.

The man named Angel said, "Hey, what the fug." There was something new in his voice; he sounded very confused. Even in a fog, Joe Winder could tell that the little creep wasn't talking to him—or to Spearmint Breath, either.

Suddenly a great turmoil erupted around the truck, and

the man named Angel gave out a scream that didn't sound anything like a little dog. The scream made Joe Winder raise his head off the fender and open what was left of his eyelids.

Through misty slits he saw the husky no-neck goon running toward the bridge. Running away as fast as he could.

Where was Angel?

Something lifted Joe Winder off the truck and laid him on the gravel. He struggled to focus on the face. Face? Naw, had to be a mask. A silvery beard of biblical proportions. Mismatched eyes: one as green as mountain pines, the other brown and dead. Above that, a halo of pink flowers. Weird. The mask leaned closer and whispered in Joe Winder's ear.

The words tumbled around like dice in his brainpan. Made no damn sense. The stranger bent down and said it again.

"I'll get the other one later."

Joe Winder tried to speak but all that came out was a gulping noise. He heard a car coming down the old road and turned his head to see. Soon he became mesmerized by the twin beams of yellow light, growing larger and larger; lasers shooting out of the mangroves. Or was it a spaceship?

When Winder turned back, he was alone. The man who had saved his life was gone.

The car went by in a rush of noise. Joe Winder watched the taillights vanish over the crest of the bridge. It was an hour before he could get to his feet, another twenty minutes before he could make them move in any sensible way.

As he staggered along the pavement, he counted the cars to keep his mind off the pain. Seven sped past without stopping to help. Winder was thinking, Maybe I feel worse than I look. Maybe the blood doesn't show up so well in the dark. Two or three drivers actually touched the brakes. One honked and hurled a Heineken bottle at him.

The eighth car went by doing seventy at least, heading eastbound to the island. Joe Winder saw the brake lights wink and heard the tires squeal. Slowly the car backed up. The door on the passenger side swung open.

A voice said: "My God, are you all right?"

"Not really," said Joe Winder. Half-blind, he was trying to fit himself into the car when he encountered something large and fuzzy on the upholstery.

It was an animal head. He hoped it was not real.

Carrie Lanier picked it up by the snout and tossed it into the back seat. She took Joe Winder's elbow and helped him sit down. Reaching across his lap, she slammed the car door and locked it. "I can't believe this," she said, and stepped on the accelerator.

To Joe Winder it felt as if they were going five hundred miles an hour, straight for the ocean.

Carrie Lanier kept glancing over at him, probably to make sure he was still breathing. After a while she said, "I'm sorry, what was your name again?"

"Joe. Joe Winder."

"Joe, I can't believe they did this to you."

Winder raised his head. "Who?" he said. "Who did this to me?"

Nine

Carrie Lanier pulled off Joe Winder's shoes and said, "You want me to call your girlfriend?"

Winder said no, don't bother. "She'll be home in a couple hours."

"What does she do? What kind of work?"

"She talks dirty," said Joe Winder, "on the phone."

Carrie sat on the edge of the bed. She put a hand on his forehead and felt for fever.

He said, "Thanks for cleaning me up."

"It's all right. You want more ginger ale?"

"No, but there's some Darvocets in the medicine cabinet."

"I think Advils will do just fine."

Winder grunted unhappily. "Look at me. You ever see a face like this on an Advil commercial?"

She brought him one lousy Darvocet and he swallowed it dry. He felt worse than he could remember ever feeling, and it wasn't only the pain. It was anger, too.

"So who beat me up?" he said.

"I don't know," said Carrie Lanier. "I imagine it was somebody from the park. I imagine you stuck your nose where it doesn't belong."

"I didn't," Joe Winder said, "not yet."

He felt her rise from the bed, and soon heard her moving around the apartment. He called her name and she came back to the bedroom, sitting in the same indentation on the mattress.

"I was looking for something to bandage those ribs."

"That's okay," said Winder. "It only hurts when I breathe."

Carrie said, "Maybe I don't need to tell you this, but the Amazing Kingdom is not what it seems. It's not fun and games, there's a ton of money at stake."

"You mean it's a scam?"

"Hey, everything's a scam when you get down to it." Her voice softened. "All I'm saying is, stick to your job. I know it's boring as hell, but stick to it anyway. You shouldn't go poking around."

Joe Winder said, "My poking days are over."

"Then what were you doing out there tonight?"

"Meeting someone at the bridge. What about you?"

"I had a free-lance gig," Carrie said. "A birthday party up in South Miami. Mummy and Daddy wanted Junior to meet Robbie Raccoon in person. What the heck, it was an easy five hundred. And you should've seen the house. Or should I say mansion."

Floating, Joe Winder said: "What do you have to do at these parties?"

"Dance with the kiddies. Waggle my coon tail. Juggle marshmallows, whatever. And pose for pictures, of course. Everybody wants a picture."

She touched his brow again. "You're still hot. Maybe I ought to call your girlfriend at work."

"Don't do that," said Joe Winder, "please." He didn't want Carrie to hook up with Miriam by accident. Miriam and her hot-tub "blow-yobs."

"This is important," he said. "Did you see anyone else on the road out there? Like maybe a circus-type person."

"You're not well," said Carrie Lanier.

"No, I mean it. Big guy with a beard. Flowers on his head." It sounded so ridiculous, maybe he'd hallucinated the whole thing.

"That's not a circus person you're describing. That's Jesus. Or maybe Jerry García."

"Whatever," Joe Winder said. "Did you see anybody on the road? That's all I'm asking."

"Nope," Carrie said. "I really ought to be on my way. What'd you decide about calling the cops?"

"Not a good idea," said Winder. "Especially with Dr. Koocher still missing. Maybe the bad guys'll call back."

"The creeps who did this to you?" Carrie sounded incredulous. "I don't think so, Joe."

She didn't say anything for several moments. Joe Winder tried to read her expression but she had turned away.

"How much does she make, your girlfriend, talking sexy on the phone?"

"Not much. Two hundred a week, sometimes two fifty. They get a bonus for selling videos. And panties, too. Twenty bucks a pair. They buy 'em wholesale from Zayre's."

"Two fifty, that stinks," said Carrie Lanier. "But, hey, I've been there. You do what you have to."

"Nina's got no complaints," said Joe Winder. "She says there's a creative component to every job; the trick is finding it."

Carrie turned around, glowing. "She's absolutely right, your girlfriend is. You know what I did before I got my SAG card? I worked in a cough-drop factory. Wrapping the lozenges in foil, one at a time. The only way I kept from going crazy—each cough drop, I'd made a point to wrap it differently from the others. One I'd do in squares, the next I'd do in a triangle, the one after that I'd fold into a rhombus or something. Believe me, it got to be a challenge, especially at thirty lozenges per

102

minute. That was our quota, or else we got docked."

Joe Winder said the first dumb thing that popped into his brain. "I wonder if Nina has a quota."

"She sounds like she's doing just fine," Carrie said. "Listen, Joe, I think you ought to know. There's a rumor going around about the rat doctor. Supposedly they found a note."

"Yeah?"

"You know what kind of note I mean. The bad kind. Goodbye, cruel world, and all that. Supposedly they found it in his desk at the lab."

Joe Winder said, "What exactly did it say, this supposed note?"

"I don't know all the details." Carrie Lanier stood up to go. "Get some rest. It's just a rumor."

"Give me another pill, and sit down for a second."

"Nope, I can't."

"Get me another goddamn pill!"

"Go to sleep, Joe."

By eight the next morning, a crowd had gathered beneath the Card Sound Bridge to see the dead man hanging from the center span. From a distance it looked like a wax dummy with an elongated neck. Up close it looked much different.

The crowd was made up mostly of tourist families on their way down to the Florida Keys. They parked haphazardly on the shoulder of the road and clambered down to where the police cars and marine patrols were positioned, blue lights flashing in that insistent syncopation of emergency. A few of the tourist husbands took out portable video cameras to record the excitement, but the best vantage was from the decks of the yachts and sleek sailboats that had dropped anchor in the channel near the bridge. The mast of one of the sloops had snagged on the hanging dead man and torn off his trousers as the vessel had passed through the bridge at dawn. By now everyone had noticed that the corpse wore no underwear.

A man from the Dade County Medical Examiner's Office stood on the jetty and looked up at the dead body swinging in the breeze, forty feet over the water. Standing next to the man from the medical examiner's was FBI Agent Billy Hawkins, who was asking lots of questions that the man from the medical examiner's didn't answer. He was keenly aware that the FBI held absolutely no authority in this matter.

"I was on my way to the park," Agent Hawkins was saying, "and I couldn't help but notice."

With cool politeness, the man from the medical examiner's office said: "Not much we can tell you at the moment. Except he's definitely dead, that much is obvious." The coroner knew that most FBI agents went their whole careers without ever setting eyes on an actual corpse. The way Billy Hawkins was staring, he hadn't seen many.

"The poor bastard has no pants," the agent observed. "What do you make of that?"

"Sunburned testicles is what I make of that. If we don't haul him down soon."

Agent Hawkins nodded seriously. He gave the coroner a card. The feds, they loved to hand out cards.

The man from the medical examiner's played along. "I'll call if anything turns up," he lied. The FBI man said thanks and headed back toward his car; he was easy to track—a blocky gray suit moving through a bright sea of Hawaiian prints and Day-Glo surfer shorts. A dog in a flower bed.

The amused coroner soon was joined by an equally amused trooper from the Florida Highway Patrol.

"Nice day for a hangin'," drawled the trooper. His name was Jim Tile. He wore the standard mirrored sunglasses with gold wire frames.

"I don't see a rope," said the coroner, gesturing at the dead man high above them. "What the hell's he hanging with?"

"That would be fishing line," Jim Tile said.

The coroner thought about it for several moments. Then he said, "All right, Jim, what do you think?"

"I think it's a pretty poor excuse for a suicide," said the trooper.

A tanned young man in a crisp blue shirt and a red necktie worked his way out of the crowd. The man walked up to the coroner and somberly extended his right hand. He wore some kind of plastic ID badge clipped to his belt. The coroner knew that the tanned young man wasn't a cop, because his ID badge was in the shape of an animal head, possibly a raccoon or a small bear.

Charles Chelsea gestured toward the dead man without looking. In a voice dripping with disgust, he said, "Can't you guys do something about that?"

"We're working on it," replied the coroner.

"Well, work a little faster."

The man from the medical examiner's looked down at Charles Chelsea's animal-head ID and smiled. "These things can't be hurried," he said.

A jurisdictional dispute had delayed the removal of the offending body for most of the morning. It was a tricky geographic dilemma. The middle of the Card Sound Bridge marked the boundary line between Dade and Monroe counties. The Monroe County medical examiner's man had arrived first on the scene, and decided that the dead man was hanging in Dade County airspace and therefore was not his responsibility. The Dade County medical examiner's man had argued vigorously that the victim had most certainly plummeted from the Monroe County side of the bridge. Besides which the Dade County morgue was already packed to the rafters with homicides, and it wouldn't kill Monroe County to take just one. Neither coroner would budge, so the dead body just hung there for four hours until the Monroe County medical examiner announced that he was needed at a fatal traffic accident in Marathon, and scurried away, leaving his colleague stuck with the corpse—and now some whiny pain-in-the-ass PR man.

The coroner said to Charles Chelsea: "We've got to get some pictures. Take some measurements. Preserve the scene, just in case."

"In case of what? The poor jerk killed himself." Chelsea sounded annoyed. Preserving the scene was the opposite of what he wanted.

Trooper Jim Tile removed his sunglasses and folded them into a breast pocket. "I guess I can go home. Now that we got an expert on the case."

Charles Chelsea started to rebuke this impertinent flatfoot, but changed his mind when he took a good look. The trooper was very tall and very muscular and very black, all of which made Chelsea edgy. He sensed that Jim Tile was not the sort to be impressed by titles, but nonetheless he introduced himself as a vice president at the Amazing Kingdom of Thrills.

"How nifty," said the trooper.

"Yes, it is," Chelsea said pleasantly. Then, lowering his voice: "But, to be frank, we could do without this kind of spectacle." His golden chin pointed up at the hapless corpse. Then he jerked a thumb over his shoulder at the chattering throng of onlookers.

"All these people," Chelsea said urgently, "were on their way to our theme park."

"How do you know?" asked Jim Tile.

"Look around here—where else would they be going? What else is there to see?"

"In other words, you would like us to remove the deceased as quickly as possible."

"Yes, exactly," said Charles Chelsea.

"Because it's competition."

The publicity man's eyes narrowed. Frostily he said, "That's not at all what I meant." Giving up on the black policeman, he appealed to the coroner's sense of propriety: "All the young children hanging around—they shouldn't be witness to something like this. Vacations are for fun and fantasy, not for looking at dead bodies."

Jim Tile said, "They seem to be enjoying it."

"We didn't ask for an audience," the coroner added. He was accustomed to gawkers in Miami. Shopping malls were the worst; drug dealers were always leaving murdered rivals in the trunks of luxury automobiles at shopping malls. The crowds were unbelievable, pushing and shoving, everybody wanting a peek at the stiff.

The coroner told Charles Chelsea: "This always happens. It's just a sick fact of human nature."

"Well, can't you hurry up and get him—it—down? The longer it stays up there, the more people will stop." Chelsea paused to survey the size of the crowd. "This is horrible," he said, "right in the middle of Summerfest. It's giving all these folks the wrong idea."

Jim Tile couldn't wait to hear more. "The wrong idea about what?"

"About Florida," said Charles Chelsea. The indignation in his tone was authentic. "This is not the image we're trying to promote. Surely you can understand."

Grimly he turned and disappeared into the gallery of onlookers.

The coroner once again fixed his attention on what was hanging from the Card Sound Bridge. He asked Jim Tile, "So what do you think about getting him down from there?"

"Easy," said the trooper. "I'll go up and cut the line."

"You really think that's safe?"

Jim Tile looked at him curiously.

"With all these people milling around," said the coroner. "What if he hits somebody? Look at all these damn boats." He frowned and shook his head. "I think we've got a serious liability risk here. Somebody could be injured or killed."

"By a falling corpse," said Jim Tile thoughtfully.

"You betcha. Look at all these damn tourists."

Jim Tile took out a bullhorn and ordered the boats to weigh anchor. He also instructed the bystanders to get off the jetty under threat of arrest. Then he went to the top of the bridge and quickly found what he was looking for: a nest of heavy monofilament fishing line tangled around the base of a concrete column. One end of the monofilament was attached to the type of flat plastic spool used by Cuban handline fishermen. The other end of the line led over the side of the bridge, and was attached to the dead man's neck.

The trooper got a 35-millimeter camera out of the patrol car and took pictures of the column and the knot. Then he got down on his belly and extended his head over the side of the bridge and snapped several aerial-type photographs of the hanging corpse.

After Jim Tile put the camera away, he waved twice at the coroner, still standing on the rocks below. Then, when the coroner gave the signal, the trooper unfolded his pocketknife and cut through the monofilament fishing line.

He heard the crowd go *ooooohhhh* before he heard the splash. A marine patrol boat idled up to the dead man and fished him out of the water with a short-handled gaff.

They were loading the body into the van when the coroner told his theory to Jim Tile. "I don't think it's suicide," he said.

"What, somebody was using him for bait?"

"No, this is what I think happened," said the coroner, demonstrating with his arms. "You know how these Cuban guys twirl the fishlines over their heads real fast to make a long cast? It looks to me like he messed up and wrapped the damn thing tight around his neck, like a bolo. That's what I think." He picked up a clipboard and began to write. "What was the color of his eyes? Brown, I think."

"I didn't look," said Jim Tile. He wasn't crazy about dead bodies.

The man from the medical examiner's reached into the van and tugged at the woolen blanket, revealing the dead man's features.

"I was right," said the coroner, scribbling again. "Brown they are."

Jim Tile stared at the rictus face and said, "Damn, I know that guy." He wasn't a fisherman.

"A name would be nice," the coroner said. "He lost his wallet when he lost his pants."

"Angel," the trooper said. "Angel Gaviria. Don't ask me how to spell it."

"Where do you know him from?"

"He used to be a cop." Jim Tile yanked the blanket up to cover the dead man's face. "Before he got convicted."

"Convicted of what?"

"Everything short of first-degree murder."

"Jesus Christ. And here he is, out of the slammer already."

"Yeah," said Jim Tile. "Modeling neckwear."

Bud Schwartz had been a two-bit burglar since he was seventeen years old. He was neither proud of it nor ashamed. It was what he did, period. It suited his talents. Whenever his mother gave him a hard time about getting an honest job, Bud Schwartz reminded her that he was the only one of her three children who was not in psychoanalysis. His sister was a lawyer and his brother was a stockbroker, and both of them were miserably fucked up. Bud Schwartz was a crook, sure, but at least he was at peace with himself.

He considered himself a competent burglar who was swift, thorough and usually cautious. The times he'd been caught—five in all—these were flukes. A Rottweiler that wasn't in the yard the night before. A nosy neighbor, watering her begonias at three in the goddamn morning. A getaway car with bad plugs. That sort of thing. Occupational hazards, in Bud Schwartz's opinion—plain old lousy luck.

Normally he was a conservative guy who played the odds and didn't like unnecessary risks. Why he ever accepted the ratnapping job from Molly McNamara, he couldn't figure. Broad daylight, thousands of people, the middle of a fucking theme park. Jesus! Maybe he did it just to break the monotony. Or maybe because ten grand was ten grand.

Definitely a score. In his entire professional burgling career, Bud Schwartz had never stolen anything worth ten thousand dollars. The one time he'd pinched a Rolex Oyster, it turned out to be fake. Another time he got three diamond rings from a hotel room on Key Biscayne—a big-time movie actress, too—and the fence informed him it was all zircon. Fucking paste. Or so said the fence.

Who could blame him for saying yes to Molly McNamara, or at least checking it out? So when he gets out of jail, he rounds up Danny Pogue—Danny, who's really nothing but a pair of hands; somebody you drag along to help carry the shit to the car. But reliable, as far as that goes. Not really smart enough to pull anything.

So together they meet the old lady once, twice. Get directions, instructions. Go over the whole damn thing until they're bored to tears, except for the part about what to do with the voles. Bud Schwartz had assumed the whole point was to free the damn things, the way Molly talked. "Liberate" was the word she'd used. Of course, if he'd known then what he knew now, he wouldn't have chucked that one little rat into the red convertible. If he'd known there were only two of the damn things left on the whole entire planet, he wouldn't ever have let Danny take a throw at the Winnebago.

110

Now the voles were gone, and Bud Schwartz and Danny Pogue were nursing their respective gunshot wounds in the old lady's apartment.

Watching a slide show about endangered species.

"This formidable fellow," Molly McNamara was saying, "is the North American crocodile."

Danny Pogue said, "Looks like a gator."

"No, it's a different animal entirely," said Molly. "There's only a few dozen left in the wild."

"So what?" said Danny Pogue. "You got tons of gators. So many they went and opened a hunting season. I can't see gettin' all worked up about crocodiles dyin' off, not when they got a season on gators. It don't make sense."

Molly said, "You're missing the point."

"He can't help it," said Bud Schwartz. "Just go on to the next slide."

Molly clicked the remote. "This is the Schaus' swallow-tail butterfly."

"Now that's pretty," said Danny Pogue. "I can see wanting to save somethin' like that. Isn't that a pretty butterfly, Bud?"

"Beautiful," said Bud Schwartz. "Really gorgeous. Next?"

Molly asked why he was in such a hurry.

"No reason," he replied.

Danny Pogue snickered. "Maybe 'cause there's a movie he wants to see on cable."

"Really?" Molly said. "Bud, you should've told me. We can always continue the orientation tomorrow."

"That's okay," Bud Schwartz said. "Go on with the program."

"*Amazon Cheerleaders*," said Danny Pogue. "We seen the ending the other night."

Molly said, "I don't believe I've heard of that one."

"Get on with the slides," said Bud Schwartz gloomily. Of

all the partners he'd ever had, Danny Pogue was turning out to be the dumbest by a mile.

A picture of something called a Key Largo wood rat appeared on the slide screen, and Danny exclaimed: "Hey, it looks just like one of them voles!"

"Not really," said Molly McNamara patiently. "This hardy little fellow is one of five endangered species native to the North Key Largo habitat." She went on to explain the uniqueness of the island—hardwood hammocks, brackish lakes and acres of precious mangroves. And, only a few miles offshore, the only living coral reef in North America. "Truly a tropical paradise," said Molly McNamara, "which is why it's worth fighting for."

As she clicked through the rest of the slides, Bud Schwartz was thinking: How hard would it be to overpower the old bat and escape? Two grown men with six functional limbs, come on. Just grab the frigging purse, take the gun—what could she do?

The trouble was, Bud Schwartz wasn't fond of guns. He didn't mind stealing them, but he'd never pointed one at anybody, never fired one, even at a tin can. Getting shot by Molly McNamara had only reinforced his view that guns were a tool for the deranged. He knew the law, and the law smiled on harmless unarmed house burglars. A burglar with a gun wasn't a burglar anymore, he was a robber. Not only did robbers get harder time, but the accommodations were markedly inferior. Bud Schwartz had never been up to Raiford but he had a feeling he wouldn't like it. He also had a hunch that if push came to shove, Danny Pogue would roll over like a big dumb puppy. Do whatever the cops wanted, including testify.

Bud Schwartz decided he needed more time to think.

A new slide came up on the screen and he told Molly McNamara to wait a second. "Is that an endangered species, too?" he asked.

"Unfortunately not," Molly said. "That's Francis X. Kingsbury, the man who's destroying the island."

Danny Pogue lifted his chin out of his hands and said, "Yeah? How?"

"Mr. Kingsbury is the founder and chief executive officer of the Amazing Kingdom of Thrills—the so-called amusement park you boys raided the other day. It's a tourist trap, plain and simple. It brings traffic, garbage, litter, air pollution, effluent—Kingsbury cares nothing about preserving the habitat. He's a developer."

The word came out as an epithet.

Bud Schwartz studied the jowly middle-aged face on the screen. Kingsbury was smiling, and you could tell it was killing him. His nose was so large that it seemed three-dimensional, a huge mottled tuber of some kind, looming out of the wall.

"Public enemy number one," said Molly. She glared at the picture on the screen. "Yes, indeed. The park is only a smokescreen. We've got reason to believe that Mr. Kingsbury holds the majority interest in a new golfing resort called Falcon Trace, which abuts the Amazing Kingdom. We have reason to believe that Kingsbury's intention is to eventually bulldoze every square inch of ocean waterfront. You know what that means?"

Danny Pogue pursed his lips. Bud Schwartz said nothing; he was trying to guess where the old coot was heading with this.

Molly said, "It means no more crocodiles, no more wood rats, no more swallowtail butterflies."

"No more butterflies?" Danny Pogue looked at her with genuine alarm. "What kinda bastard would do something like that?"

"This kind," said Molly, aiming a stern papery finger at the screen.

"But we can stop him, right?" Bud Schwartz was smiling.

"You can help, yes."

"How?" Danny Pogue demanded. "What do we do?"

Molly said, "I need to know the full extent of Mr. Kingsbury's financial involvement—you see, there are legal avenues we could pursue, if only we knew." She flicked off the slide projector and turned on a pair of brass table lamps. "Unfortunately," she said, "Mr. Kingsbury is a very secretive man. Every document we've gotten, we've had to sue for. He is extremely wealthy and hires only the finest attorneys."

From his expression it was clear that Danny Pogue was struggling to keep up. "Go on," he said.

Bud Schwartz inhaled audibly, a reverse sigh. "Danny, we're burglars, remember? What do burglars do?"

Danny Pogue glanced at Molly McNamara, who said, "Your partner's got the right idea."

"Wait a second," Bud Schwartz said. "No more voles."

By now he was planning ahead again, feeling better about his prospects. He was wondering about Francis X. Kingsbury's money, and thinking what a shame that a bunch of greedy lawyers should get so much of it, all for themselves.

Ten

Nina didn't believe him, not for a second.

"You were drinking. You opened your big fat mouth and somebody smacked you."

"No," Joe Winder said. "That's not what happened."

Well, the truth would only frighten her. He sat up and squinted brutally at the sunlight.

"I'm so disappointed in you," Nina said. She studied the bruises on his face, and not out of concern; she was looking for clues.

"I wasn't drinking," said Joe Winder. That much he had to assert, out of pride. "They were muggers, that's all."

Nina pointed to his wallet, which was on the dresser. "Muggers, Joe? Some muggers."

"A car scared them off."

She rolled her eyes. "You're only making it worse."

"What happened to trust?" Winder said. "What happened to true goddamn love?" He got out of bed and tested his legs. Nina watched reproachfully.

"I smell perfume," she said. "Did you bring a woman home last night?"

"No, a woman brought *me*. She saw me on Card Sound

Road and wanted to go to the police. I told her to bring me here so I could be with the love of my life."

"Did you screw her?"

"Only six or seven times." He went to the bathroom and stuck his face under the shower and screamed at the top of his lungs, it hurt so bad. He screamed until his ears reverberated. Then he came out, dripping, and said: "Nina, be reasonable. Who'd make love with me, looking like this?"

"Not me."

"Not anybody. Besides, I was half blind. I probably would've stuck it in her ear by mistake."

Nina smiled. Finally.

Winder asked her who'd called so damn early. The phone is what woke him up.

"Your employer, Mr. Charles Chelsea. He wanted you to know there was a dead person hanging from the bridge this morning."

Joe Winder shuffled back to the shower. This time he stepped all the way in and braced his forehead against the tile. He made the water as hot as he could bear. Maybe the dead man was Angel, he thought, or maybe it was the big guy who'd saved him from Angel.

When Winder got out, Nina stood poised with a towel in her hand. She wore a white halter top and no panties. Winder took the towel and draped it over his head.

"Why do you do this to me," he mumbled.

"Did you hear what I said? About the dead man?" She peeled off the halter and climbed in the shower. "Did you save me some hot water? I've got to shave my legs." She turned the faucet handles and cursed the cold.

"Sorry," said Joe Winder. Raising his voice over the beating of the water: "So why is Chelsea calling me, just because there's some dead guy? The bridge is five miles from the Kingdom."

Nina didn't answer, just filed the question away and

kept on shaving. Joe Winder sat down on the toilet and watched the fixtures fog up. Plenty of hot water, he thought; no problem.

When she came out, he remarked how beautiful she looked. "Like a sleek arctic seal."

"Oh stop it."

"Don't dry off, please. Don't ever dry off."

"Get your hand away from there." Nina slapped him sharply. "Put your clothes on. Chelsea's waiting at the office."

Joe Winder said, "I'm phoning in sick."

"No, you're not. You can't." She wrapped the towel around her hair and left the rest bare. "He wasn't calling about the dead person on the bridge, he was calling about the whale."

"Orky?"

Nina opened the bathroom door to let out the steamy humidity. Joe Winder impulsively clutched her around the waist. He pressed his cheek against her damp thigh, and began to hum the tune of "Poor Pitiful Me." Nina pried him loose and said, "I'm glad you don't get beat up every day."

Something was out of alignment in Winder's brain. He blinked three or four times, slowly, but even as the steam cleared it didn't go away. Double vision! The bastards had pounded him that badly. Nina's bare bottom appeared to him as four gleaming porcelain orbs.

Distractedly, he said, "Go on. Something about the whale?"

"Yes," said Nina. She stood before the mirror, checking her armpits for stubble. "Chelsea said the whale is dead."

"Hmmm," said Joe Winder. Orky the Killer Whale.

"And?" he said.

"And, I don't know." Nina stepped into her panties. "He said for you to come right away. He said it was an emergency."

"First let's go to bed." Winder came up behind her. In the mirror he saw two pairs of hands cupping two pairs of nipples.

He saw two faces that looked just like his—lumpy, lacerated, empurpled—nuzzling the tan silky slopes of two feminine necks.

"All right, Joe," Nina said, turning around. "But I've got to be honest: I'm very disappointed in you—"

"It wasn't what you think."

"—and I'm only doing this because you're in pain." Mechanically Nina took his hand and led him toward the bed. She kicked off her underwear and unwrapped the towel from her hair. Winder was grinning like an idiot.

"I'm warning you," Nina said, "this isn't an act of passion, it's an act of pity."

"I'll take it," said Joe Winder. "But, please, no more talking for a while."

"All right," she said. "No more talking."

Orky the Killer Whale had come to the Amazing Kingdom of Thrills under clouded circumstances. His true name (or the name bestowed by his human captors off the coast of British Columbia) was Samson. Delivered in a drugged stupor to a north California marine park, he was measured at twenty-nine feet and seven inches, a robust male example of the species *orca*. Samson was larger than the other tame killer whales in the tank, and proved considerably more recalcitrant and unpredictable. In his first six months of captivity he mauled two trained porpoises and chomped the tail off a popular sea lion named Mr. Mugsy. Trainers worked overtime trying to teach their new star the most rudimentary of whale tricks—leaping through a plastic hoop, or snatching a dead mackerel from the fingers of a pretty model— with minimal success. One day he would perform like a champ, the next he would sink to the bottom of the tank and fart belligerently, launching balloon-sized bubbles of fishy gas to the surface. The audience seldom found this entertaining. Eventually most of the seasoned whale trainers refused to enter the water with Samson. Those who tried to ride his immense black dorsal were either whiplashed or pretzeled or corkscrewed into semiconsciousness.

Quite by accident, it was discovered that Samson was enraged by the color green. This became evident on the day that the human trainers switched to vivid Kelly-green tank suits without telling the other performing mammals. Samson was supposed to open the first show by fetching an inflatable topless mermaid and gaily delivering it to a young man on a ladder, in exchange for a fistful of smelts. On this particular morning, Samson retrieved the toy, carried it across the water on his snout, flipped it into the bleachers, snatched the green-clad trainer off the ladder, flipped *him* into the bleachers, then dived to the bottom of the tank and began to pass gas relentlessly. Each time somebody tried to lure him up, Samson shot from the depths with his mouth open, the great black-and-white jaws clacking like a truck door. The crowd loved it. They thought it was part of the act.

Reluctantly the curators of the California marine park concluded that this whale was one dangerous rogue. They attempted to peddle him to another marine park, far away on the western coast of Florida, but first they changed his name to Ramu. The transaction took place at a time when ocean-theme parks around the country were reporting various troubles with trained killer whales, and animal-rights groups were seeking legislation to prevent capturing them for exhibit. Word of Samson's behavioral quirks had spread throughout the marine-park industry, which is why it was necessary to change his name before trying to sell him.

The day the deal was done, Samson was tranquilized, lashed to a canvas litter and placed aboard a chartered Sikorsky helicopter. There workers took turns sponging him with saltwater during the arduous cross-country flight, which lasted seventeen hours, including stops for refueling. By the time Samson arrived in Sarasota, he was in a vile and vindictive mood. During his first fifteen minutes in the new tank, he savagely foreshortened a pectoral fin on another male *orca* and destroyed the floating basket through which he was supposed to slam-dunk beach balls. Weeks passed with little improvement in the new whale's temperament. One fateful Sunday, the animal abruptly awakened from its funk, tail-walked across the tank and did a dazzling double somersault before hundreds of delighted tourists. When a stubby woman in a green plaid sundress leaned too close with her Nikon, the whale seized her in his teeth, dragged her once around the tank, then spit her out like an olive pit.

It was then that Samson's new owners realized that they had been duped; they'd bought themselves a bum whale. Ramu was in fact the infamous and incorrigible Samson. Immediately the beast was quarantined as a repeat offender, while the Sarasota theme park made plans to resell him under the misleadingly gentle name of Orky.

Francis X. Kingsbury was the ideal chump. The soon-to-be-opened Amazing Kingdom of Thrills was shopping for a major ocean attraction to compete with Disney World's "living reef." Kingsbury saw the Orky offer as a bargain of a lifetime—a trained killer whale for only nine hundred bucks, plus freight! Kingsbury snapped at it.

Orky was more than a disappointment, he was a dud. No one at the Amazing Kingdom could train the whale to do a single trick on cue; capable of wondrous gymnastic feats, the animal remained oblivious of regimen and performed only when he damn well felt like it. Often he did his best work in the middle of the night, when the stadium was empty. But on those nocturnal occasions, when the park was closed and there was no one to reward him with buckets of dead mullet, Orky furiously would ram the sides of the whale tank until the Plexiglas cracked and the plaster buckled.

Because it was impossible to predict his moods, Orky's

shows were not posted in a regular schedule. Tourists paid their money, took their seats and hoped for the best. Once in a great while, the killer whale would explode in exuberant ballet, but more often he just sulked or blew water aimlessly.

One time Francis X. Kingsbury had suggested punishing the mammoth creature by withholding supper. Orky retaliated by breaking into the pelican pool and wolfing down nine of the slow-moving birds. After that, Kingsbury said to hell with the goddamn whale and gave up on training the beast. He knew he'd been scammed but was too proud to admit it. Kingsbury's corporate underlings sensed that Orky was a sore spot with the boss, and avoided mentioning the whale exhibit in his presence.

Until today.

With Orky unexpectedly dead, the subject was bound to come up. Charles Chelsea decided on a pre-emptive strike. He broke the news as Francis Kingsbury was munching his regular breakfast bagel. "Good," Kingsbury said, spraying crumbs. "Hated that fucking load."

"Sir, it's not good," said Charles Chelsea, "publicity-wise."

"How do you figure," Kingsbury said. "I mean, shit, what's a lousy whale to these people. You know who I mean—the media."

Charles Chelsea said he would try to explain it on the way to the autopsy.

Joe Winder's vision returned to normal after making love to Nina; he regarded this as providential. He took a cab to Card Sound Road and retrieved his car. When he got back to the apartment, he changed to a long-sleeved shirt, charcoal trousers and a navy necktie, in the hope that high fashion would divert attention from his pulverized face. When he got to the Amazing Kingdom, he saw he had nothing to worry about. Everybody was staring at the dead killer whale.

They had hauled the remains to one of the parking lots, and roped a perimeter to keep out nosy customers. To conceal Orky's corpse, which was as large as a boxcar, Charles Chelsea had rented an immense tent from an auto dealership in Homestead. The tent was brilliantly striped and decorated with the legend "SOUTH FLORIDA TOYOTA-THON." A dozen or so electric fans had been requisitioned to circulate the air, which had grown heavy with the tang of dead whale. The staff veterinarian, a man named Kukor, was up to his knees in Orky's abdomen when Joe Winder arrived.

"Joe, thank God," said Chelsea, with an air of grave urgency. He led Winder to a corner and said, "Mr. X is here, to give you some idea."

"Some idea of what?"

"Of how serious this is."

Joe Winder said, "Charlie, I don't mean to be disrespectful but I'm not sure why I'm needed." Over his shoulder, he heard somebody crank up a chain saw.

"Joey, think! First the damn mango voles and now Orky. It's gonna look like we're neglecting the wildlife. And this whole killer-whale thing, it's gotten very controversial. There was a piece in *Newsweek* three weeks ago." Charles Chelsea was sweating extravagantly, and Winder assumed it had something to do with the presence of Francis X. Kingsbury.

Chelsea went on, "I know it's unpleasant, Joe, but you can leave as soon as Doc Kukor gives us a cause of death."

Joe Winder nodded. "How many words?"

"Three hundred. And I need it for the early news."

"Fine, Charlie. Later you and I need to talk."

Chelsea was peering through the flaps in the tent, making sure that no gawkers had sneaked past the security men.

"Listen to me," Joe Winder said. "There's some big trouble in this park. I got the shit kicked out of me last night because of it."

For the first time Chelsea noticed the battered condition of Joe Winder's face. He said, "What the hell happened? No, wait, not now. Not with Mr. X around. We'll chat later, I promise."

Winder grabbed his elbow. "I need to know everything about the dead man at the bridge."

Chelsea shook free and said, "Later, Joe, for heaven's sake. Let's tackle the crisis at hand, shall we?"

Together they returned to the autopsy. Instead of concentrating on Orky's entrails, Joe Winder scanned the small group of official observers: a state wildlife officer, taking notes; the tow-truck drivers who had hauled the whale corpse to the tent; three of Uncle Ely's Elves, apparently recruited as extra manpower; and Francis X. Kingsbury himself, mouthing obscenities over the gruesome ceremony.

Nervously Chelsea directed Joe Winder to Kingsbury's side and introduced him. "This is the fellow I told you about," said the PR man. "Our ace in the hole."

Kingsbury chuckled darkly. "Blame us for this? Some fucking fish croaks, how can they blame us?"

Joe Winder shrugged. "Why not?" he said.

Cutting in quickly, Chelsea said: "Don't worry, sir, it'll die down. It's just the crazy pro-animal types, that's all." He planted a moist hand on Winder's shoulder. "Joe's got the perfect touch for this."

"Hope so," said Francis X. Kingsbury. "Meanwhile, the stink, holy Christ! Don't we have some Glade? I mean, this is fucking rank."

"Right away," said Chelsea, dashing off in search of air freshener.

Kingsbury gestured at the billowing tent, the murmuring onlookers, the husk of deceased behemoth. "You believe this shit?" he said to Joe Winder. "I'm a goddamn real-estate man is all. I don't know from animals."

"It's a tricky business," Winder agreed.

"Who'd believe it, I mean, looking at this thing."

It was quite a strange scene, Joe Winder had to admit. "I'm sure they can find a new whale for the show."

"This time mechanical," Kingsbury said, jabbing a finger at Orky's lifeless form. "No more real ones. Computerized, that'd be the way to go. That's how Disney would handle it, eh?"

"Either that or a hologram," said Joe Winder with a wink. "Think of all the money you'd save on whale food."

Just then Dr. Kukor, the veterinarian, tripped on something and fell down inside Orky's closet-sized stomach cavity. Two of Uncle Ely's Elves bravely charged forward to help, hoisting the doctor to his feet.

"Oh my," Kukor said, pointing. The elves ran away frantically, their huge curly-toed shoes slapping noisily on the blood-slickened asphalt.

"What?" barked Francis X. Kingsbury. "What is it?"

"I don't believe this," said the veterinarian.

Kingsbury stepped forward to see for himself and Joe Winder followed, though he was sorry he did.

"Call somebody," wheezed Dr. Kukor.

"Looks like a human," Kingsbury remarked. He turned to stare at Winder because Winder was clinging to his arm. "Don't puke on me or you're fired," said Kingsbury.

Joe Winder was trying not to pass out. The corpse wasn't in perfect condition, but you could tell who it was.

A wan and shaky Dr. Kukor stepped out of Orky's excavated carcass. "Asphyxiation," he declared numbly. "The whale choked to death."

"Well, damn," said Francis X. Kingsbury.

Joe Winder thought: Choked to death on Will Koocher. Koocher, in a mint-green golf shirt.

"Somebody call somebody," Kukor said. "This is way out of my field."

Winder reeled away from the scene. In a croaky voice he said, "That's the worst thing I ever saw."

"You?" Kingsbury laughed harshly. "Three fucking tons of whale meat, talk about a nightmare."

"Yes," Joe Winder said, gasping for fresh air.

"I'm thinking South Korea or maybe the Sudan," Kingsbury was saying. "Stamp it 'Tuna,' who the hell would ever know? Those little fuckers are starving."

"What?" said Winder. "What did you say?"

"Providing I can get some goddamn ice, pronto."

Eleven

Charles Chelsea decreed that there should be no mention of Dr. Will Koocher in the press release. "Stick to Orky," he advised Joe Winder. "Three hundred words max."

"You're asking me to lie."

"No, I'm asking you to omit a few superfluous details. The whale died suddenly overnight, scientists are investigating, blah, blah, blah. Oh, and be sure to include a line that Mr. Francis X. Kingsbury is shocked and saddened." Chelsea paused, put a finger to his chin. "Scratch the 'shocked,'" he said. "'Saddened' is plenty. 'Shocked' makes it sound like something, I don't know, something—"

"Out of the ordinary?" said Joe Winder.

"Right. Exactly."

"Charlie, you are one sorry bucket of pus."

Chelsea steepled his hands on his chest. Then he unfolded them. Then he folded them once more and said, "Joe, this is a question of privacy, not censorship. Until Dr. Koocher's wife is officially notified, the least we can do is spare her the agony of hearing about it on the evening news."

For a moment, Winder saw two Charles Chelseas instead of one. Somewhere in the cacophonous gearbox of his brain, he heard the hiss of a peacock, blowing off steam. "Charlie," he said blankly, "the man was eaten by a fucking thirty-foot leviathan. This isn't going to remain our little secret very long."

Chelsea's brow wrinkled. "Eventually, yes, I suppose we'll have to make some sort of public statement. Seeing as it was our whale."

Joe Winder leaned forward on one elbow. "Charlie, I'm going to be honest."

"I appreciate that."

"Very soon I intend to kick the living shit out of you."

Chelsea stiffened. He shifted in his chair. "I don't know what to make of a remark like that."

Joe Winder imagined his eyeballs pulsating in the sockets, as if jolted by a hot wire.

Charles Chelsea said, "You mean, punch me? Actually punch me?"

"Repeatedly," said Winder, "until you are no longer conscious."

The publicity man's voice was plaintive, but it held no fear. "Do you know what kind of day I've had? I've dealt with two dead bodies—first the man on the bridge, and now the vole doctor. Plus I've been up to my knees in whale guts. I'm drained, Joe, physically and emotionally drained. But if it makes you feel better to beat me up, go ahead."

Joe Winder said he was a reasonable man. He said he would reconsider the beating if Charles Chelsea would show him the suicide note allegedly written by Dr. Will Koocher.

Chelsea unlocked a file drawer and took out a sheet of paper with block printing on it. "It's only a Xerox," he said, handing it to Winder, "but still it breaks your heart."

It was one of the lamest suicide notes that Joe Winder had ever seen. In large letters it said: "TO MY FRIENDS AND FAMILY, I SORRY BUT I CAN'T GO ON. NOW THAT MY WORK IS OVER, SO AM I."

The name signed at the bottom was "*William Bennett Koocher, PhD.*"

Winder stuffed the Xerox copy in his pocket and said, "This is a fake."

"I know what you're thinking, Joey, but it wasn't only the voles that got him down. There were problems at home, if you know what I mean."

"My goodness." Winder whistled. "Problems at home. I had no idea."

Chelsea continued: "And I know what else you're thinking. Why would anybody kill himself in this ... *extreme* fashion? Jumping in a whale tank and all."

"It struck me as a bit unorthodox, yes."

"Well, me too," said Chelsea, regaining some of his starch, "until I remembered that Koocher couldn't swim a lick. More to the point, he was deathly afraid of sharks. It's not so surprising that he chose to drown himself here, indoors, rather than the ocean."

"And the green shirt?"

"Obviously he wasn't aware of Orky's, ah, problem."

Joe Winder blinked vigorously in an effort to clear his vision. He said, "The man's spine was snapped like a twig."

"I am told," said Charles Chelsea, "that it's not as bad as it appears. Very quick, and nearly painless." He took out a handkerchief and discreetly dried the palms of his hands. "Not everyone has the stomach for using a gun," he said. "Myself, I'd swallow a bottle of roach dust before I'd resort to violence. But, anyway, I was thinking: Maybe this was Koocher's way of joining the lost voles. A symbolic surrender to Nature, if you will. Sacrificing himself to the whale."

Chelsea squared the corners of the handkerchief and tucked it into a pants pocket. He looked pleased with his theory. Sagely he added, "In a sense, what happened that night in Orky's tank was a purely natural event: Dr. Koocher became part of the food chain. Who's to say he didn't plan it that way?"

Joe Winder stood up, clutching the corners of Charles Chelsea's desk. "It wasn't a suicide," he said, "and it wasn't an accident."

"Then what, Joe?"

"I believe Koocher was murdered."

"Oh, for God's sake. At the Amazing Kingdom?"

Again Winder felt the sibilant whisper from a valve letting off pressure somewhere deep inside his skull. He reached across the desk and got two crisp fistfuls of Chelsea's blue oxford shirt. *"I sorry but I can't go on?"*

Perplexed, Chelsea shook his head.

Joe Winder said, "The man was a PhD, Charlie. *I sorry but I can't go on?* Tonto might write a suicide note like that, but not Dr. Koocher."

Chelsea pulled himself free of Winder's grip and said: "It was probably just a typo, Joe. Hell, the man was terribly depressed and upset. Who proofreads their own damn suicide note?"

Pressing his knuckles to his forehead, Winder said, "A typo? With a Magic Marker, Charlie? *I sorry* is not a bummed-out scientist making a mistake; it's an illiterate moron trying to fake a suicide note."

"I've heard just about enough." Chelsea circled the desk and made for the door. He stepped around Winder as if he were a rattlesnake.

Chelsea didn't leave the office. He held the door open for Joe Winder, and waited.

"I see," said Winder. On his way out, he stopped to smooth the shoulders of Chelsea's shirt, where he had grabbed him.

"No more talk of murder," Charles Chelsea said. "I want you to promise me."

"All right, but on the more acceptable subject of suicide—who was the dead guy hanging from the Card Sound Bridge?"

"I've no idea, Joe. It doesn't concern us."

"It concerns me."

"Look, I'm starting to worry. First you threaten me with physical harm, now you're blabbing all these crazy theories. It's alarming, Joe. I hope I didn't misjudge your stability."

"I suspect you did."

Warily, Chelsea put a hand on Winder's arm. "We've got a tough week ahead. I'd like to be able to count on you."

"I'm a pro, Charlie."

"That's my boy. So you'll give me Orky by four o'clock?"

"No sweat," Winder said. "Three hundred words."

"Max," reminded Charles Chelsea, "and keep it low key."

"My middle name," said Joe Winder.

In the first draft of the press release, he wrote: *Orky the Killer Whale, a popular but unpredictable performer at the Amazing Kingdom of Thrills, died suddenly last night after asphyxiating on a foreign object.*

Chelsea sent the press release back, marked energetically in red ink.

In the second draft, Joe Winder wrote: *Orky the Whale, one of the most colorful animal stars at the Amazing Kingdom of Thrills, passed away last night of sudden respiratory complications.*

Chelsea returned it with a few editing suggestions in blue ink.

In the third draft, Winder began: *Lovable Orky the Whale, one of the most colorful and free-spirited animal stars at the Amazing Kingdom of Thrills, was found dead in his tank this morning.*

While pathologists conducted tests to determine the cause of death, Francis X. Kingsbury, founder of the popular family theme park, expressed deep sorrow over the sudden loss of this majestic creature.

"We had come to love and admire Orky," Kingsbury said. "He was as much a part of our family as Robbie Raccoon or Petey Possum."

Joe Winder sent the press release up to Charles Chelsea's office and decided not to wait for more revisions. He announced that he was going home early to have his testicles reattached.

Before leaving the park, Winder stopped at a pay phone near the Magic Mansion and made a few calls. One of the calls was to an old newspaper source who worked at the Dade County Medical Examiner's Office. Another call was to the home of Mrs. Will Koocher, where a friend said she'd already gone back to Ithaca to await her husband's coffin. A third phone call went to Nina at home, who listened to Joe Winder's sad story of the dead vole doctor, and said: "So the new job isn't working out, is that what you're saying?"

"In a nutshell, yes."

"If you ask me, your attitude is contributing to the problem."

Joe Winder spotted the acne-spackled face of Pedro Luz, peering suspiciously from behind a Snappy-the-Troll photo gazebo, where tourists were lined up to buy Japanese film and cameras. Pedro Luz was again sucking on the business end of an intravenous tube; the tube snaked up to a bottle that hung from a movable metal sling. Whenever Pedro Luz took a step, the IV rig would roll after him. The liquid dripping from the bottle was the color of weak chicken soup.

Joe Winder said to Nina: "My attitude is not a factor."

"Joe, you sound . . . "

"Yes?"

"Different. You sound different."

"Charlie made me lie in the press release."

"And this comes as a shock? Joe, it's a whole different business from before. We talked about this at length when you took the job."

"I can fudge the attendance figures and not lose a minute of sleep. Covering up a murder is something else."

On Nina's end he heard the rustling of paper. "I want to read you something," she said.

"Not now, please."

"Joe, it's the best thing I've ever done."

Winder glanced over toward the Snappy photo gazebo, but Pedro Luz had slipped out of sight.

Nina began to read: *Last night I dreamed I fell asleep on a diving board; the highest one, fifty meters. It was a hot steamy day, so I took my top off and lay down. I was so high up that no one but the sea gulls could see me. The sun felt wonderful. I closed my eyes and drifted off to sleep—*

"Not '*meters*,'" Winders cut in. "'Meters' is not a sexy word."

Nina kept going: *When I awoke, you were standing over me, naked and brown from the sun. I tried to move but I couldn't—you had used the top of my bikini to tie my hands to the board. I was helpless, yet afraid to struggle . . . we were up so high. But then you knelt between my legs and told me not to worry. Before long, I forgot where we were . . .*

"Not bad." Joe Winder tried to sound encouraging, but the thought of trying to have sex on a high-diving board made his stomach pitch.

Nina said: "I want to leave something to the imagination. Not like Miriam, she's unbelievable. *I took chew in my mouth and sock like a typhoon.*"

Winder conceded that this was truly dreadful.

"I've got to listen to that pulp all night long," Nina said. "While she's clipping her toenails!"

"And I thought I had problems."

She said, "Was that sarcasm? Because if it was—"

The telephone receiver was getting heavy in Joe Winder's hand. He wedged it in the crook of his shoulder and said, "Can I tell you what I was thinking just now? I was thinking about the gastric secretions inside a killer whale's stomach. I was thinking how unbelievably powerful the digestive juices

132

must be in order for a whale to be able to eat swordfish beaks and seal bones and giant squid gizzards and the like."

In a flat voice, Nina said, "I have to go now, Joe. You're getting morbid again."

"I guess I am."

The click on the other end seemed an appropriate punctuation.

On the way home he decided to stop and try some bonefishing at his secret spot. He turned off County Road 905 and came to the familiar gravel path that led through the hardwoods to the mangrove shore.

Except the woods were gone. The buttonwoods, the mahogany, the gumbo-limbos—all obliterated. So were the mangroves.

Joe Winder got out of his car and stared. The hammock had been flattened; he could see all the way to the water. It looked as if a twenty-megaton bomb had gone off. Bulldozers had piled the dead trees in mountainous tangles at each corner of the property.

Several hundred yards from Joe Winder's car, in the center of what was now a vast tundra of scrabbled dirt, a plywood stage had been erected. The stage was filled with men and women, all dressed up in the dead of summer. A small crowd sat in folding chairs laid out in rows in front of the stage. Joe Winder could hear the brassy strains of "America the Beautiful" being played by a high-school band, its lone tuba glinting in the afternoon sun. The song was followed by uneven applause. Then a man stood up at a microphone and began to speak, but Joe Winder was too far away to hear what was being said.

In a daze, Winder kicked out of his trousers and changed into his cutoffs. He got his fly rod out of the trunk of the car and assembled it. To the end of the monofilament leader he attached a small brown epoxy fly that was intended to resemble a crustacean. The tail of the fly was made from deer hair; Winder examined it to make sure it was bushy enough to attract fish.

Then he tucked the fly rod under his left arm, put on his Polaroid sunglasses and marched across the freshly flattened field toward the stage. Absolutely nothing of logic went through his mind.

The man at the microphone turned out to be the mayor of Monroe County, Florida. It was largely a ceremonial title that was passed in odd-numbered years from one county commissioner to another, a tradition interrupted only by death or indictment. The current mayor was a compact fellow with silvery hair, olive skin and the lean fissured face of a chain-smoker.

"This is a grand day for the Florida Keys," the mayor was saying. "Nine months from today, this will be a gorgeous fairway." A burst of masculine clapping. "The sixteenth fairway, if I'm not mistaken. A four-hundred-and-twenty-yard par-four dogleg toward the ocean. Is that about right, Jake?"

A heavyset man sitting behind the mayor grinned enormously in acknowledgment. He had squinty eyes and a face as brown as burned walnut. He waved at the audience; the hearty and well-practiced wave of a sports celebrity. Joe Winder recognized the squinty-eyed man as Jake Harp, the famous professional golfer. He looked indefensibly ridiculous in a bright lemon blazer, brown beltless slacks, shiny white loafers and no socks.

At the microphone, the mayor was going on about the championship golf course, the lighted tennis courts, the his-and-her spas, the posh clubhouse with its ocean view and, of course, the exclusive luxury waterfront homesites. The mayor was effervescent in his presentation, and the small overdressed audience seemed to share his enthusiasm. The new development was to be called Falcon Trace.

"And the first phase," said the mayor, "is already sold out. We're talking two hundred and two units!"

Joe Winder found an empty chair and sat down. He propped the fly rod in his lap so that it rose like a nine-foot CB antenna out of his crotch. He wondered why he hadn't heard about this project, considering that the property abutted the southern boundary of the Amazing Kingdom of Thrills. He didn't remember seeing anything in the newspapers about a new country club. He felt a homicidal churning in his belly.

Not again, he thought. Not again, not again, not again.

The mayor introduced Jake Harp—"one of the greatest cross-handed putters of all time"—and the audience actually rose to its feet and cheered.

Jake Harp stood at the podium and waved ebulliently. Waved and waved, as if he were the bloody pope.

"Welcome to Falcon Trace," he began, reading off an index card. "Welcome to my new home."

More clapping as everyone settled back in their chairs.

"You know, I've won the PGA three times," said Jake Harp, "and finished third in the Masters twice. But I can honestly say that I was never so honored as when y'all selected me as the touring pro for beautiful Falcon Trace."

A voice piped up near the stage: "You rot in hell!"

A strong empassioned voice—a woman. The crowd murmured uncomfortably. Jake Harp nervously cleared his throat, a tubercular grunt into the microphone.

Again the woman's voice rose: "We don't need another damn golf course. Why don't you go back to Palm Springs with the rest of the gangsters!"

Now she was standing. Joe Winder craned to get a good look.

The famous golfer tried to make a joke. Painfully he said, "I guess we got ourselves a golf widow in the audience."

"No," the woman called back, "a real widow."

On stage, Jake Harp bent over and whispered something to the mayor, who was smoking fiercely. Someone signaled to the conductor of the high-school band, which adroitly struck up a Michael Jackson dance number. Meanwhile three uniformed sheriff's deputies materialized and edged toward the rude protester. The woman stood up, shook a fist above the silvery puff that was her head and said something that Joe Winder couldn't quite hear, except for the word "bastard."

Then she put on a floppy pink Eastern bonnet and permitted herself to be arrested.

Well, hello, thought Winder. The lady from the Wildlife Rescue Corps, the one who'd slipped him the note at the Amazing Kingdom.

Joe Winder watched the deputies lead the old woman away. He wanted to follow and ask what in the hell was going on, but she was quickly deposited in the back of a squad car, which sped off toward Key Largo. As Jake Harp resumed his speech, Winder got up and walked past the stage toward the ocean. In a few minutes he found the familiar trench of shoreline where he usually searched for bonefish, but the water was too milky to see over the tops of his own sneakers. As he waded into the flats, he could hear the high-school band begin to play "The Star Spangled Banner," signaling the climax of the groundbreaking ceremony.

As he slid his feet across the rocks and sea grass, Joe Winder started false-casting his fly, stripping out the line as he moved forward. The water was murky, roiled, just a mess. There would be no fish here, Winder knew, but still he drove the meat of the line seventy feet hard into the wind, and watched the tiny plop of the fly when it landed.

Joe Winder fished in manic motion because he knew time was running out. Before long, this fine little bay would be a stagnant ruin and the only fish worth catching would be gone, spooked by jet skis, sail-boarders, motorboats and plumes of rank sewage blossoming from submerged drainage pipes.

Welcome to Falcon Trace.

He took another step and felt something seize his right ankle. When he tried to pull free, he lost his balance and fell down noisily in the water. He landed on his ass but quickly rolled to his knees, careful to hold the expensive Seamaster fly reel high and dry. Irritably Winder groped beneath the surface for the thing that had tripped him.

His fingers closed around the slick branch of a freshly cut tree. He lifted it out of the water, examined it, then let it drop again. A red mangrove, bulldozed, ripped out by the roots and dumped on the flats. Illegal as hell, but who besides the fish would ever know?

Joe Winder knelt in the shallows and thought about what to do next. Back on the soon-to-be-sixteenth hole, the band played on. After a while, the music stopped and voices could be heard, collegial chamber-of-commerce good-old-boy voices, dissipating in the afternoon breeze. Not long afterward came the sounds of luxury cars being started.

Eventually the place got quiet, and Joe Winder knew he was alone again in his favorite fishing spot. He stayed on his knees in the water until the sun went down.

In the evening he drove out to the Card Sound Bridge and parked. He got a flashlight from the trunk and began to walk along the road, keeping close to the fringe of the trees and playing the light along the ground. Soon he found the place where he had been beaten by the two goons, Angel and Spearmint Breath. Here Joe Winder slowed his pace and forced himself to concentrate.

He knew what he was looking for: a trail.

He'd spent most of his childhood outdoors, cutting paths

to secret hideaways in the hammocks, glades and swamps. At a young age he had become an expert woodsman, a master of disappearing into impenetrable pockets where no one else wanted to go. Every time his father bought a new piece of property, Joe Winder set out to explore each acre. If there was a big pine, he would climb it; if there was a lake or a creek, he'd fish it. If there was a bobcat, he'd track it; a snake, he'd catch it.

He would pursue these solitary adventures relentlessly until the inevitable day when the heavy machinery appeared, and the guys in the hard hats would tell him to beat it, not knowing he was the boss's kid.

On those nights, lying in his bed at home, he would wait for his mother to come in and console him. Often she would suggest a new place for his expeditions, a mossy parcel off Old Cutler Road, or twenty acres in the Gables, right on the bay. Pieces his father's company had bought, or was buying, or was considering.

Raw, tangled, hushed, pungent with animals, buzzing with insects, glistening with extravagant webs, pulsing, rustling and doomed. And always the portal to these mysterious places was a trail.

Which is what Winder needed on this night.

Soon he found it: an ancient path of scavengers, flattened by raccoons and opossums but widened recently by something much larger. As Winder slipped into the woods, he felt ten years old again. He followed the trail methodically but not too fast, though his heart was pounding absurdly in his ears. He tried to travel quietly, meticulously ducking boughs and stepping over rotted branches. Every thirty or so steps, he would turn off the flashlight, hold his breath and wait. Before long, he could no longer hear the cars passing on Card Sound Road. He was so deep in the wetlands that a shout or a scream would be swallowed at once, eternally.

He walked for fifteen minutes before he came upon the remains of a small campfire. Joe Winder knelt and sniffed at the half-burned wood; somebody had doused it with coffee. He poked at the acrid remains of something wild that had been cooked in a small rusty pan. He swung the flashlight in a semi-circle and spotted a dirty cooler, some lobster traps and a large cardboard box with the letters "EDTIAR" stamped on the side. On the ground, crumpled into a bright pile, was a fluorescent-orange rainsuit. Winder unfolded it, held it up to gauge the size. Then he put it back the way he found it.

Behind him, a branch snapped and a voice said, "How do you like the new pants?"

Winder wheeled around and pointed the flashlight as if it were a pistol.

The man was eating—and there was no mistaking it—a fried snake on a stick.

"Cottonmouth," he said, crunching off a piece. "Want some?"

"No thanks."

"Then we've got nothing to talk about."

Joe Winder politely took a bite of snake. "Like chicken," he said.

The man was cleaning his teeth with a fishhook. He looked almost exactly as Joe Winder remembered, except that the beard was now braided into numerous silvery sprouts that drooped here and there from the man's jaw. He was probably in his early fifties, although it was impossible to tell. The mismatched eyes unbalanced his face and made his expression difficult to read; the snarled eyebrows sat at an angle of permanent scowl. He wore a flowered pink shower cap, sunglasses on a lanyard, a heavy red plastic collar and no shirt. At first Joe Winder thought that the man's chest was grossly freckled, but in the flashlight's trembling beam the freckles began to hover and dance: mosquitoes, hundreds of them, feasting on his blood.

In a strained voice Joe Winder said, "I can't help but notice that thing on your neck."

"Radio collar." The man lifted his chin so Winder could see it. "Made by Telonics. A hundred fifty megahertz. I got it off a dead panther."

"Does it work?" Winder asked.

"Like a charm." The man snorted. "Why else would I be wearing it?"

Joe Winder decided this was something they could chat about later. He said, "I didn't mean to bother you. I just wanted to thank you for what you did the other night."

The stranger nodded. "No problem. Like I said, I got a pair of pants out of the deal." He slapped himself on the thigh. "Canvas, too."

"Listen, that little guy—Angel Gaviria was his name. They found him hanging under the bridge." Winder's friend at the medical examiner's office had confirmed the identity.

"What do you know," the stranger said absently.

"I was wondering about the other one, too," said Winder, "since they were trying to kill me."

"Don't blame you for being curious. By the way, they call me Skink. And I already know who you are. And your daddy, too, goddamn his soul."

He motioned for Joe Winder to follow, and crashed down a trail that led away from the campfire. "I went through your wallet the other night," Skink was saying, "to make sure you were worth saving."

"These days I'm not so sure."

"Shit," said Skink. "Don't start with that."

After five minutes they broke out of the hardwoods into a substantial clearing. A dump, Joe Winder noticed.

"Yeah, it's lovely," muttered Skink. He led Winder to the oxidized husk of an abandoned Cadillac, and lifted the trunk hatch off its hinges. The nude body of Spearmint Breath had been fitted inside, folded as neatly as a beach chair.

"Left over from the other night," Skink explained. "He ran out of steam halfway up the big bridge. Then we had ourselves a talk."

"Oh Jesus."

"A bad person," Skink said. "He would've brought more trouble."

An invisible cloud of foul air rose from the trunk. Joe Winder attempted to breathe through his mouth.

Skink played the beam of the flashlight along the dead goon's swollen limbs. "Notice the skeeters don't go near him," he said, "so in one sense, he's better off."

Joe Winder backed away, speechless. Skink handed him the light and said, "Don't worry, this is only temporary." Winder hoped he wasn't talking to the corpse.

Skink replaced the trunk hatch on the junked Cadillac. "Asshole used to work Security at the Kingdom. He and Angel baby. But I suppose you already knew that."

"All I know," said Winder, "is that everything's going bad and I'm not sure what to do."

"Tell me about it. I still can't believe they shot John Lennon and it's been—what, ten years?" He sat down heavily on the trunk of the car. "You ever been to the Dakota?"

"Once," Joe Winder said.

"What's it like?"

"Sad."

Skink twirled the fishhook in his mouth, bit off the barb, and spit it out savagely. "Some crazy shithead with a .38—it's the story of America, isn't it?"

"We live in violent times. That's what they say."

"Guys like that, they give violence a bad name." Skink

stretched out on the trunk, and stared at the stars. "Sometimes I think about that bastard in jail, how he loves all the publicity. Went from being nobody to The Man Who Shot John Lennon. I think some pretty ugly thoughts about that."

"It was a bad day," Joe Winder agreed. He couldn't tell if the man was about to sleep or explode.

Suddenly Skink sat up. With a blackened fingernail he tapped the radio collar on his neck. "See, it's best to keep moving. If you don't move every so often, a special signal goes out. Then they think the panther's dead and they all come searching."

"Who's they?"

"Rangers," Skink replied. "Game and Fish."

"But the panther *is* dead."

"You're missing the whole damn point."

As usual. Joe Winder wondered which way to take it, and decided he had nothing to lose. "What exactly are you doing out here?" he asked.

Skink grinned, a stunning, luminous movie-star grin. "Waiting," he said.

Twelve

On the morning of July 21, a Saturday, Molly McNamara drove Bud Schwartz and Danny Pogue to the Amazing Kingdom of Thrills for the purpose of burglarizing the office of Francis X. Kingsbury.

"All you want is files?" asked Bud Schwartz.

"As many as you can fit in the camera bag," Molly said. "Anything to do with Falcon Trace."

Danny Pogue, who was sitting in the back seat of the El Dorado, leaned forward and said, "Suppose there's some other good stuff. A tape deck or a VCR, maybe some crystal. Is it okay we grab it?"

"No, it is not," Molly replied. "Not on my time."

She parked in the Cindy-the-Sun-Queen lot and left the engine running. The radio was tuned to the classical station, and Bud Schwartz asked if Molly could turn it down a notch or two. She went searching through her immense handbag and came out with a Polaroid camera. Without saying a word, she snapped a photograph of Bud Schwartz, turned halfway in the seat and snapped one of Danny Pogue. The flashbulb caused him to flinch and make a face. Molly plucked the moist negatives from the slot in the bottom of the camera and slipped them into the handbag.

"What's that all about?" said Danny Pogue.

"In case you get the itch to run away," Molly McNamara said, "I'd feel compelled to send your photographs to the authorities. They are still, I understand, quite actively investigating the theft of the mango voles."

"Pictures," said Bud Schwartz. "That's cute."

Molly smiled pleasantly and told both men to listen closely. "I rented you a blue Cutlass. It's parked over by the tram station. Here are the keys."

Bud Schwartz put them in his pocket. "Something tells me we won't be cruising down to Key West."

"Not if you know what's good for you," Molly said.

Danny Pogue began to whine again. "Ma'am, I don't know nothin' about stealing files," he said. "Now I'm a regular bear for tape decks and Camcorders and shit like that, but frankly I don't do much in the way of, like, *reading*. It's just not my area."

Molly said, "You'll do fine. Get in, grab what you can and get out."

"And hope that nobody recognizes us from before." Bud Schwartz arched his eyebrows. "What happens then? Or didn't you think of that?"

Molly chuckled lightly. "Don't be silly. No one will recognize you dressed the way you are."

She had bought them complete golfing outfits, polyester down to the matching socks. Danny Pogue's ensemble was raspberry red and Bud Schwartz's was baby blue. The pants were thin and baggy; the shirts had short sleeves and loud horizontal stripes and a tiny fox stitched on the left breast.

Bud Schwartz said, "You realize we look like total dipshits."

"No, you look like tourists."

"It's not that bad," agreed Danny Pogue.

"Listen," Molly said again. "When you're done with the job, get in the Cutlass and come straight back to my place. The phone will ring at one sharp. If you're not there, I'm going directly to the post office and mail these snapshots to the police, along with your names. Do you believe me?"

"Yeah, sure," said Bud Schwartz.

She got out of the Cadillac and opened the doors for the burglars. "How is your hand?" she asked Bud Schwartz. "Better let your friend carry the camera bag."

She held Danny Pogue's crutch (mending quickly, he was down to one) while he slipped the camera bag over his right shoulder. "The tram's coming," she announced. "Better get moving."

As the men hobbled away, Molly called out cheerfully and waved good-bye, as if she were their mother, or a loving old aunt.

With a trace of fondness, Danny Pogue said, "Look at her."

"Look at *us*," said Bud Schwartz. "Real fucking pros."

"Well, at least it's for a good cause. You know, saving them butterflies."

Bud Schwartz eyed his partner in a clinical way. "Danny, you ever had a CAT scan?"

"A what?"

The burglars were huffing pretty heavily by the time they made it to the tram. They climbed on the last car, along with a family of nine from Minneapolis. Every one of them had sandy hair and Nordic-blue eyes and eyebrows so blond they looked white in the sunlight.

A little girl of about seven turned to Danny Pogue and asked what had happened to his foot.

"I got shot," he said candidly.

The little girl flashed a glance at her mother, whose eyes widened.

"A tetanus shot," said Bud Schwartz. "He stepped on a rusty nail."

The mother's eyes softened with relief. "Where are you from?" she asked the men.

"Portugal," said Danny Pogue, trying to live up to the tourist act.

"Portugal, Ohio," Bud Schwartz said, thinking: There is no hope for this guy; he simply can't be allowed to speak.

The tiny blond girl piped up: "We heard on the radio that the whale died yesterday. Orky the Whale."

"Oh no," said Danny Pogue. "You sure?"

The tram rolled to a stop in front of the main gate, where the burglars got off. Nodding good-bye to the blond Minneapolitans, Bud Schwartz and Danny Pogue slipped into the throng and located the shortest line at the ticket turnstiles.

In a gruff tone, Bud Schwartz said, "*Portugal?* What kind of fuckhead answer is that?"

"I don't know, Bud. I don't know a damn thing about tourists or where they come from."

"Then don't say anything, you understand?" Bud Schwartz got out the money that Molly had given them to buy the admission tickets. He counted out thirty-six dollars and handed the cash to his partner.

"Just hold up one finger, that's all you gotta do," said Bud Schwartz. "One finger means one ticket. Don't say a goddamn thing."

"All right," Danny Pogue said. "Man, I can't believe the whale croaked, can you?"

"Shut up," said Bud Schwartz. "I'm not kidding."

Danny Pogue didn't seem the least bit nervous about returning to the scene of their crime. To him the Amazing Kingdom of Thrills was a terrific place, and he strutted around with a permanent grin. Bud Schwartz thought: He's worse than these damn kids.

Outside the Magic Mansion, Danny Pogue stopped to shake hands with Petey Possum. A tourist lady from Atlanta took a photograph, and Danny Pogue begged her to send him a copy. At this point Bud Schwartz considered ditching the dumb shit altogether and pulling the job alone.

Golf duds and all, Bud Schwartz was antsy about being back on the premises so soon after the rat-napping; it went against his long-standing aversion to dumb risk. He wanted to hurry up and get the hell out.

It wasn't easy locating Francis X. Kingsbury's office because it didn't appear on any of the colorful maps or diagrams posted throughout the amusement park. Bud Schwartz and Danny Pogue checked closely; there was the Cimarron Trail Ride, Orky's Undersea Paradise, the Wet Willy, the Jungle Jerry Amazon Boat Cruise, Bigfoot Mountain, Excitement Boulevard, and so on, with no mention of the administration building. Bud Schwartz decided Kingsbury's headquarters must be somewhere in the geographic center of the Amazing Kingdom of Thrills, and for security reasons probably wasn't marked.

"Why don't we ask somebody?" Danny Pogue suggested.

"Very smart," said Bud Schwartz. "I got a better idea. Why don't we just paint the word 'thief ' in big red letters on our goddamn foreheads?"

Danny Pogue wasn't sure why his partner was in such a lousy mood. The Kingdom was awesome, fantastic, sensational. Everywhere they went, elves and fairy princesses and happy animal characters waved or shook hands or gave a hug.

"I never seen so much friendliness," he remarked.

"It's the crutch," said Bud Schwartz.

"No way."

"It's the damn crutch, I'm tellin' you. They're only being nice because they got to, Danny. Anytime there's a customer on crutches, they make a special point. You know, in case he's dying a some fatal disease."

Danny Pogue said, "You go to hell."

"Ten bucks says it's right in the training manual."

"Bud, I swear to God."

"Gimme the crutch and I'll prove it."

Danny Pogue said, "You're the one's always on my ass about attitude. And now just listen to yourself—all because people're actin' nice to me and not to you."

"That's not it," said Bud Schwartz, but when he turned around his partner was gone. He found him on line at the Wild Bill Hiccup rodeo ride; Danny Pogue had stashed his crutch in the men's room and was determined to give Wild Bill Hiccup a go. Bud Schwartz was tired of bickering.

The ride was set up in an indoor corral that had been laboriously fabricated, from the brown-dyed dirt to the balsa fence posts to the polyethylene cowshit that lay in neat regular mounds, free of flies. Twenty-five mechanical bulls (only the horns were real) jumped and bucked on hidden tracks while a phony rodeo announcer described the action through a realistically tinny megaphone.

During this particular season, the twenty-five bulls were mounted by twenty-three tourists and two professional crooks. Before the ride began, Bud Schwartz leaned over to Danny Pogue and told him to be sure and fall off.

"What?"

"You heard me. And make it look good."

When the bell rang, Bud Schwartz hung on with his good hand and bounced back and forth for maybe a minute without feeling anything close to excitement. Danny Pogue, however, was launched almost instantly from the sponge hump of his motorized Brahma—a tumble so spectacular that it brought three Company Cowpokes out of the bronco chute at a dead run. They surrounded Danny Pogue, measured his blood pressure, palpated his ribs and abdomen, listened to his heart, shined a light in his eyeballs and finally shoved a piece of paper under his nose.

"Why don't you put your name on this, li'l pardner?" said one of the Cowpokes.

Danny Pogue examined the document, shook his head and handed it to Bud Schwartz for interpretation.

"Release of liability," Bud Schwartz said. He looked up with a dry smile. "This means we can't sue, right?"

"Naw," said the solicitous Cowpoke. "All it means is your buddy's not hurt."

"Says who?" said Bud Schwartz. "Bunch a dumb cowboy shit-kickers. Thanks, but I think we'll try our luck with an actual doctor."

The Cowpokes didn't look so amiable anymore, or so Western. In fact, they were starting to look like pissed-off Miami insurance men. Danny Pogue got to his feet, dusted off his butt and said, "Hell, Bud, it's my fault anyhow—"

"Not another word." Bud Schwartz seized his partner by the elbow, as if to prop him up. Then he announced to the Cowpokes: "We'd like to file a complaint about this ride. Where exactly is the administration office?"

The Cowpoke in charge of the blood-pressure cuff said, "It's closed today."

"Then we'll come back Monday," said Bud Schwartz. "Where is the office, please?"

"Over Sally's Saloon," the Cowpoke answered. "Upstairs, ask for Mr. Dexter in Risk Management."

"And he'll be in Monday?"

"Nine sharp," muttered the Cowpoke.

The other tourists watched curiously as Bud Schwartz led Danny Pogue haltingly out of the corral. By this time the Wild Bill Hiccup attraction had come to a complete and embarrassing stop (a man with a sprocket wrench had beheaded Danny Pogue's bull), and Bud Schwartz wanted to depart the arena before his partner spoiled the plan by saying something irretrievably stupid.

Into Danny Pogue's ear he said, "You're doing fine."

"It wasn't on purpose."

"Yeah, I had a feeling."

As they watched Danny Pogue's genuine hobble, the three Cowpokes from Risk Management began to worry that they might have missed something during their quickie medical exam.

One of them called out: "Hey, how about a wheelchair?"

Without turning around, Bud Schwartz declined the offer with the wave of an arm.

"No thanks, li'l pardner," he called back.

The same tool that picked the lock on Francis X. Kingsbury's office did the job on the rosewood file cabinet.

"So now what?" Danny Pogue said.

"We read." Bud Schwartz divided the files into two stacks. He showed his partner how to save time by checking the index labels.

"Anything to do with banks and property, put it in the bag. Also, anything that looks personal."

"What about Falcon Trace?" asked Danny Pogue. "That's what Mrs. McNamara said to get."

"That, too."

They used pocket flashlights to examine the files because Bud Schwartz didn't want to turn on the lights in Kingsbury's office. They were on the third floor of the administration building, above Sally's Cimarron Saloon. Through the curtains Bud Schwartz could watch the Wild West show on the dusty street below. Tourists shrieked as two scruffy bank robbers suddenly opened fire on the sheriff; bloodied, the sheriff managed to shoot both bandits off their horses as they tried to escape. The tourists cheered wildly. Bud Schwartz grunted and said, "Now there's a job for you. Fallin' off horses."

Sitting on the floor amid Kingsbury's files, Danny Pogue

looked orphaned. He said, "I know lawyers that couldn't make sense a this shit." He couldn't take his eyes off a portable Canon photocopier: seventy-five bucks, staring him in the face.

"We'll give it an hour," said Bud Schwartz, but it didn't take him that long to realize that his partner was right. The files were impenetrable, stuffed with graphs and pie charts and computer printouts that meant nothing to your average break-in artist. The index tabs were marked with hopelessly stilted titles like "Bermuda Intercontinental Services, Inc.," and "Ramex Global Trust, N.A.," and "Jersey Premium Market Research."

Bud Schwartz arbitrarily selected the three thickest files and stuffed them in the camera bag. This would keep the old bat busy for a while.

"Look here," said Danny Pogue, holding up a thin file. "Credit cards."

The index tab was marked "Personal Miscellany." Inside was a folder from the American Express Company that listed all the activity on Francis X. Kingsbury's Platinum Card for the previous twelve months. Bud Schwartz's expression warmed as he skimmed the entries.

Reading over his shoulder, Danny Pogue said, "The guy sure knows how to eat."

"He knows how to buy jewelry, too." Bud Schwartz pointed at some large numbers. "Look here."

"Yeah," said Danny Pogue, catching on. "I wonder where he keeps it, all that jewelry."

Bud Schwartz slipped Kingsbury's American Express folder into the camera bag. "This one's for us," he told his partner. "Don't show the old lady unless I say so."

Danny Pogue said, "I heard a that place in New York. Cartier's." He pronounced it "Car-teer's."

"That's some expensive shit they sell."

"You bet," said Bud Schwartz. Another thin file had caught his attention. He opened it on his lap, using his good hand to hold the flashlight while he read. The file contained Xeroxed copies of numerous old newspaper clippings, and three or four letters from somebody at the U.S. Department of Justice. The letterhead was embossed, and it felt important.

"Jesus," said Bud Schwartz, sizing things up.

"What is it?"

He thrust the file at Danny Pogue. "Put this in the damn bag, and let's get going."

Danny Pogue peered at the index tab and said, "So what does it mean?"

"It means we're gonna be rich, li'l pardner."

Danny Pogue contemplated the name on the file folder. "So how do you pronounce it anyway?"

"Gotti," said Bud Schwartz. "Rhymes with body."

Thirteen

Rummaging through a dead man's belongings at midnight was not Joe Winder's idea of fun. The lab was as cold and quiet as a morgue. Intimate traces of the late Will Koocher were everywhere: a wrinkled lab coat hung on the back of a door; a wedding picture in a brass frame on a corner of his desk; a half-eaten roll of cherry-flavored Tums in the drawer; Koocher's final paycheck, endorsed but never cashed.

Winder shivered and went to work. Methodically he pored through the vole files, and quickly learned to decipher Koocher's daily charts: size, weight, feeding patterns, sleeping patterns, stool patterns. Some days there was blood work, some days there were urine samples. The doctor's notes were clinical, brief and altogether unenlightening. Whatever had bothered Koocher about the mango-vole program, he hadn't put it in the charts.

It was an hour before Joe Winder found something that caught his eye: a series of color photographs of the voles. These were different from the glossy publicity pictures—these were extreme close-ups taken from various angles to highlight anatomical characteristics. Typed labels identified the animals as either "Male One" or "Female One." Several pictures of the female had been marked up in red wax pencil, presumably by Will Koocher. In one photograph, an arrow had been drawn to the rump of the mango vole, accompanied by the notation "CK. TAIL LENGTH." On another, Koocher had written: "CK. MICROTUS FUR COLOR—IS THERE BLOND PHASE?" In a third photograph, the animal's mouth had carefully been propped open with a Popsicle stick, which allowed a splendid frontal view of two large yellow incisors and a tiny indigo tongue.

Obviously the female vole had troubled Koocher, but why? Winder slipped the photos into his briefcase, and turned to the next file. It contained a muddy Xerox of a research paper titled, "Habitat Loss and the Decline of *Microtus mango* in Southeastern Florida." The author of the article was listed as Dr. Sarah Hunt, PhD, of Rollins College. In red ink Koocher had circled the woman's name, and put a question mark next to it. The research paper was only five pages long, but the margins were full of Koocher's scribbles. Winder was trying to make sense of them when he heard a squeaking noise behind him.

In the doorway stood Pedro Luz—pocked, bloated, puffy-eyed Pedro. "The fuck are you doing?" he said.

Joe Winder explained that a janitor had been kind enough to loan him a key to the lab.

"What for?" Pedro Luz demanded.

"I need some more information on the voles."

"Haw," said Pedro Luz, and stepped inside the lab. The squeaking came from the wheels of his mobile steroid dispenser, the IV rig he had swiped from the hospital. A clear tube curled from a hanging plastic bag to a scabby junction in the crook of Pedro Luz's left arm; the needle was held in place by several cross-wraps of cellophane tape.

The idea had come to him while he was hospitalized with the ferret bites. He had been so impressed with the wonders of intravenous refueling that he'd decided to try it with his anabolic steroids. Whether this method was effective, or even safe, were questions that Pedro Luz hadn't considered because the basic theory seemed unassailable: straight from bottle to vein, just like a gasoline pump. No sooner had he hung the first bag than he had felt the surge, the heat, the tingling glory of muscles in rapture. Even at ease, his prodigious biceps twitched and rippled as if prodded by invisible electrodes.

Joe Winder wondered why Pedro Luz kept staring down at himself, smiling as he admired the dimensions of his own broad chest and log-sized arms.

"Are you feeling all right?" Winder asked.

Pedro Luz looked up from his reverie and blinked toadlike.

Affably, Winder remarked, "You're working mighty late tonight."

Pedro Luz grunted: "I feel fine." He walked up to the desk and grabbed the briefcase. "You got no authorization to be here after hours."

"Mr. Chelsea won't mind."

Invoking Charlie's name made no impression on Pedro Luz, who plucked a leaf out of Joe Winder's hair. "Look at this shit on your head!"

"I spent some time in the mangroves," Winder said. "Ate snake-on-a-stick."

Pedro Luz announced: "I'm keeping your damn briefcase." He tucked it under his right arm. "Until I see some fucking authorization."

"What's in the IV bag?" Joe Winder asked.

"Vitamins," said Pedro Luz. "Now get the hell out."

"You know what I think? I think Will Koocher was murdered."

Pedro Luz scrunched his face as if something toxic were burning his eyes. His jaw was set so rigidly that Joe Winder expected to hear the teeth start exploding one by one, like popcorn.

Winder said, "Well, I guess I'll be going."

Pedro Luz followed him out the door, the IV rig squeaking behind them. To the back of Winder's neck, he growled, "You dumb little shit, now I gotta do a whole report."

"Pedro, you need some rest."

"The doctor wasn't murdered. He killed hisself."

"I don't think so."

"Man, I used to be a cop. I know the difference between murder and suicide."

Pedro Luz turned to lock the laboratory door. Joe Winder thought it would be an excellent moment to snatch his brief-case from the security man and make a run for it. He figured Pedro Luz could never catch him as long as he was attached to the cumbersome IV rig.

Winder pondered the daring maneuver too long. Pedro Luz glanced over his shoulder and caught him staring at the briefcase.

"Go ahead," the big man taunted. "Just go ahead and try."

Francis X. Kingsbury and Jake Harp had an early starting time at the Ocean Reef Club, up the road a few miles from the Amazing Kingdom of Thrills. Kingsbury played golf two or three times a week at Ocean Reef, even though he was not a member and would never be a member. A most exclusive outfit, the Ocean Reef board had voted consistently to black-ball Kingsbury because it could not verify several important details of his biography, beginning with his name. Infuriated by the rejection, Kingsbury made himself an unwelcome presence by wheedling regular golf invitations from all acquaintances who happened to be members, including the famous Jake Harp.

Reluctantly Jake Harp had agreed to play nine holes. He didn't like golf with rich duffers but it was part of the deal; playing with Francis X. Kingsbury, though, was a special form of torture. All he talked about was Disney this and Disney that. If the stock had dropped a point or two, Kingsbury was euphoric; if the stock was up, he was bellicose and depressed. He referred to the Disney mascot as Mickey Ratface, or sometimes simply The Rat. "The Rat's updating his pathetic excuse for a jungle cruise," Kingsbury would report with a sneer. "The fake hippos must be rusting out." Another time, while Jake Harp was lining up a long putt for an eagle, Kingsbury began to cackle. "The Rat's got a major problem at the Hall of the Presidents! Heard they had to yank the Nixon robot because his jowls were molting!"

Jake Harp, a lifelong Republican, had suppressed the urge to take a Ping putter and clobber Francis X. Kingsbury into a deep coma. Jake Harp had to remain civil because of the Falcon Trace gig. It was his second chance at designing a golf course and he didn't want to screw up again; over on Sanibel they were still searching for that mysterious fourteenth tee, the one Jake Harp's architects had mistakenly located in the middle of San Carlos Bay.

As for his title of Falcon Trace "touring pro," it was spending money, that's all—tape a couple of television spots, get your face on a billboard, play a couple of charity tournaments in the winter. Hell, no one seriously expected you to actually show up and give golf lessons. Not the great Jake Harp.

In the coffee shop Francis X. Kingsbury announced that he was in a hurry because he was leaving town later in the day. The sooner the better, thought Jake Harp.

Standing on the first tee, Kingsbury spotted two of the Ocean Reef board members waiting in a foursome behind them. The men smiled thinly and nodded at him. Kingsbury placidly flipped them the finger. Jake Harp grimaced and reached for his driver.

"Love it," said Kingsbury. "Think they're such hot snots."

Jake Harp knocked the ball two hundred and sixty yards

down the left side of the fairway. Kingsbury hit it about half as far and shrugged as if he didn't care. Once he got in the golf cart, he drove like a maniac and cursed bitterly.

"Our club'll make this place look like a buffalo latrine." The cart jounced heedlessly along the asphalt path. "Like fucking Goony Golf—I can't wait."

Jake Harp, who was badly hung over, said: "Let's take it easy, Frank."

"They're dying to know how I did it," Kingsbury went on, full tilt. "This island, it's practically a goddamn nature preserve. I mean, you can't mow your lawn without a permit from the fucking EPA."

He stomped the brake, got out and lined up his second shot. Jake Harp asked: "You gonna use the driver again?"

Kingsbury swung like a canecutter, topping the ball noisily. It skidded maybe eighty yards, cutting a bluish vector through the dew-covered grass.

"Keep your head down," advised Jake Harp.

Kingsbury hopped back in the cart and said: "Grandfathering, that's how I did it. The guy I bought from, he'd had his permits since '74. I'm talking Army Corps, Fish and Wildlife, even Interior. The state—well, yeah, that was a problem. For that I had to spread a little here and there. And Monroe County, forget it."

He shut up long enough to get out and hit again. This time he switched to a four-wood, which he skied into a liver-shaped bunker. "Fuck me," muttered Francis Kingsbury. He remained silent as Jake Harp casually knocked his second shot thirty feet from the pin.

"What was that, a five-iron? A six?"

"A six," replied Jake Harp, pinching the bridge of his nose. He figured if he could just cut off circulation, it would starve the pain behind his eyeballs and make his hangover go away.

Kingsbury punched the accelerator and they were off again.

"You know how I got the county boys? The ones giving me a bad time, I promised 'em units. Not raw lots, no fucking way—town houses is all, the one-bedrooms with no garage."

"Oh," said Jake Harp, feeling privileged. He'd been given a double lot, oceanfront, plus first option on one of the spec homes.

"Town houses," Kingsbury repeated with a laugh. "And they were happy as clams. All I got to do, it's easy, is sit on the titles until Phase One is built. You know, keep it off the tax rolls for a few months. 'Case some damn reporter shows up at the courthouse and starts looking up names."

Jake Harp didn't understand the nuances of Francis Kingsbury's scheme. The man was proud of himself, that much was obvious.

When they pulled up to the sand trap, they saw that Kingsbury's golf ball was practically buried under the lip. It appeared to have landed at the approximate speed and trajectory of a mortar round.

Kingsbury stood over the ball for a long time, as if waiting for it to make a move. Finally he said to Jake Harp: "You're the pro. What the hell now, a wedge? A nine, maybe?"

"Your only prayer," said Jake Harp, forcing a rheumy chuckle, "is a stick of dynamite." Miraculously, Kingsbury needed only three swings to blast out of the bunker, and two putts to get down.

While waiting on the next tee, Jake Harp said he thought it would be better if he didn't do any more speaking engagements on behalf of Falcon Trace.

Kingsbury scowled. "Yeah, I heard what happened, some broad."

"I'm not comfortable in those situations, Frank."

"Well, who the hell is? We got her name, the old bitch." Kingsbury took out a wood and started whisking the air with violent practice swings. Jake Harp could scarcely stand to look.

"One of those damn bunny huggers," Kingsbury was saying. "Anti this and anti that. Got some group, the Mothers of some fucking thing."

"It doesn't really matter," said Jake Harp.

"The hell it doesn't." Francis X. Kingsbury stopped swinging and pointed the polished head of the driver at Jake Harp's chest. "Now that we know who she is, don't you worry. This shit'll stop—it's been taken care of. You'll be fine from now on."

"I'm a golfer is all. I don't do speeches."

Kingsbury wasn't listening. "Maybe these assholes'll let us play through." He hollered down the fairway toward the other golfers, but they seemed not to hear. Kingsbury teed up a ball. He said, "Fine, they want to be snots."

"Don't," pleaded Jake Harp. The slow-playing foursome was well within the limited range of Kingsbury's driver. "Frank, what's the hurry?"

Kingsbury had already coiled into his backswing. "Yuppie snots," he said, following through with a ferocious grunt. The ball took off like a missile, low and true.

Terrific, thought Jake Harp. The one time he keeps his left arm straight.

The other golfers scattered and watched the ball streak past. They reassembled in the middle of the fairway, shook their fists at Kingsbury and began a swift march back toward the tee.

"Shit," said Jake Harp. He didn't have the energy for a fistfight; he didn't have the energy to watch.

Francis X. Kingsbury put the wood in his bag, and sat down behind the steering wheel of the golf cart. The angry players were advancing in an infantry line that was the color of lollipops. Where Kingsbury came from, it would be hard to regard such men as dangerous.

"Aw, let's go," said Jake Harp.

Kingsbury nodded and turned the golf cart around. "Trying to make a point is all," he said. "Etiquette, am I right? Have some fucking common courtesy for other players."

Jake Harp said, "I think they got the message." He could hear the golfers shouting and cursing as they drove away. He hoped none of them had recognized him.

On the drive back to the clubhouse, Francis Kingsbury asked Jake Harp for the name of the restaurant manager at Ocean Reef.

"I've got no idea," Jake Harp said.

"But you're a member here."

"Frank, I'm a member of seventy-four country clubs all over the damn country. Some I've never even played."

Kingsbury went on: "The reason I asked, I got a line on a big shipment of fish. Maybe they'd want to buy some."

"I'll ask around. What kind of fish?"

"Tuna, I think. Maybe king mackerel."

"You don't know?"

"Hell, Jake, I'm a real-estate man, not a goddamn chef. It's a trailer full of fish is all I know. Maybe six thousand pounds."

Jake Harp said, "Holy Jesus."

Francis Kingsbury wasn't about to get into the whole messy story. He'd been having a devil of a time penetrating the Sudanese bureaucracy; UNICEF was no better. *Yes, of course we'd welcome any famine relief, but first you'll have to fill out some forms and answer some questions . . .* Meanwhile, no one at the Amazing Kingdom seemed to know how long whale meat would stay fresh.

From the back of the golf cart came a high-pitched electronic beeping. Kingsbury quickly pulled off the path and parked in a stand of Australian pines. He unzipped his golf bag and removed a cellular telephone.

When he heard who was on the other end, he lowered his voice and turned away. Jake Harp took the hint; he slipped

161

into the trees to get rid of the two Bloody Marys he'd had for breakfast. It was several seconds before he realized he was pissing all over somebody's brand-new Titleist. He carefully wiped it dry with a handkerchief, and dropped it in his pocket.

Francis X. Kingsbury was punching a new number into the phone when Jake Harp returned to the golf cart.

"Get me that dildo Chelsea," he was saying. "No . . . who? I don't care—where did you say he is? Twenty minutes, he's not in my office and that's it. And get that fucking Pedro, he's in his car. Keep him on the line till—right—I get back."

He touched a button and the cellular phone made a burp. Kingsbury put it away. He was steaming mad.

Jake Harp said, "More problems?"

"Yeah, a major goddamn problem," said Kingsbury. "Only this one works for me."

"So fire him."

"Oh, I am," Kingsbury said, "and that's just for starters."

Fourteen

Molly McNamara came out of the kitchen carrying a silver teapot on a silver tray.

"No thank you," said Agent Billy Hawkins.

"It's herbal," Molly said, pouring a cup. "Now I want you to try this."

Hawkins politely took a drink. It tasted like cider.

"There now," said Molly. "Isn't that good?"

Hiding behind the door of the guest bedroom, Bud Schwartz and Danny Pogue strained to hear what was going on. They couldn't believe she was serving tea to an FBI man.

"I'd like to ask you a few questions," Billy Hawkins was saying.

Molly cocked her head pleasantly. "Of course. Fire away."

"Let's begin with the Mothers of Wilderness. You're the president?"

"And founder, yes. We're just a small group of older folks who are deeply concerned about the future of the environment." She held her teacup steady. "I'm sure you know all this."

Agent Hawkins went on: "What about the Wildlife Rescue Corps? What can you tell me about it?"

Molly McNamara was impressed by the FBI man's grammar; most people would have used "them" instead of "it."

"Just what I've read in the papers," she said, sipping. "That's the organization that is taking credit for freeing the mango voles, is that correct?"

"Right."

"I'm assuming this is what gives you jurisdiction in this matter—the fact that the voles are a federally protected endangered species."

"Right again," said Hawkins. She was a sharp one.

Behind the bedroom door, Bud Schwartz was ready to yank his hair out. The crazy old twat was screwing with the FBI, and enjoying it!

Danny Pogue looked as confused as ever. He leaned close and whispered: "I thought sure he was after you and me."

"Shut up," Bud Schwartz said. He was having a hard enough time hearing the conversation in the living room.

The FBI man was saying: "We have reason to suspect a connection between the Wildlife Rescue Corps and the Mothers of Wilderness—"

"That's outlandish," said Molly McNamara.

Agent Hawkins let the idea hang. He just sat there with his square shoulders and his square haircut, looking impassive and not the least bit accusatory.

Molly asked: "What evidence do you have?"

"No evidence, just indications."

"I see." Her tone was one of pleasant curiosity.

Billy Hawkins opened his briefcase and took out two shiny pieces of paper. Xeroxes. "Last month the Mothers of Wilderness put out a press release. Do you remember?"

"Certainly," said Molly. "I wrote it myself. We were calling for an investigation of zoning irregularities at Falcon Trace. We thought the grand jury should call a few witnesses."

The FBI agent handed her the papers. "That one's a copy of your press release. The other is a note delivered to the

164

Amazing Kingdom of Thrills soon after the theft of the blue-tongued mango voles."

Molly held both documents in her lap. "It looks like they were done on the same typewriter," she remarked.

In the bedroom, Bud Schwartz slumped to his knees when he heard what Molly said. He thought: She's insane. She's crazy as a goddamn bedbug. *We're all going to jail!*

Back in the living room, Molly was saying: "I'm no expert, but the typing looks very similar."

If Agent Billy Hawkins was caught off guard, he masked it well.

"You're right," he said without expression. "Both of these papers were typed on a Smith-Corona model XD 5500 electronic. We don't know yet if they came out of the same machine, but they were definitely done on the same model."

Molly cheerfully took the half-empty teapot back to the kitchen. Hawkins heard a faucet running, the sound of silverware clanking in the sink. In the bedroom, Danny Pogue put his mouth to Bud Schwartz's ear and said: "What if she shoots him?"

Bud Schwartz hadn't thought of that. Christ, she couldn't be that loony, to kill an FBI man in her own apartment! Unless she planned to pin it on a couple of dirtbag burglars in the bedroom . . .

When Molly came bustling out again, Billy Hawkins said: "We've sent the originals to Washington. Hopefully they'll be able to say conclusively if it was the same typewriter."

Molly sat down. "It's quite difficult to tell, isn't it? With these new electronic typewriters, I mean. The key strokes are not as distinct. I read that someplace."

The FBI man smiled confidently. "Our lab is very, very good. Probably the best in the world."

Molly McNamara took out a pale blue tissue and began to

clean her eyeglasses: neat, circular swipes. "I suppose it's possible," she said, "that somebody in our little group has gotten carried away."

"It's an emotional issue," agreed Billy Hawkins, "this animal-rights thing."

"Still I cannot believe any of the Mothers would commit a crime. I simply cannot believe they would steal those creatures."

"Perhaps they hired somebody to do it."

Hawkins went into the briefcase again and came out with a standard police mug shot. He handed it to Molly and said; "Buddy Michael Schwartz, a convicted felon. His pickup truck was seen leaving the Amazing Kingdom shortly after the theft. Two white males inside."

Behind the bedroom door, Bud Schwartz steadied himself. His gut churned, his throat turned to chalk. Danny Pogue looked frozen and glassy-eyed, like a rabbit trapped in the diamond lane of I-95. "Bud," he said. "Oh shit." Bud Schwartz clapped a hand over his partner's mouth.

They could hear Molly saying, "He looks familiar, but I just can't be sure."

The hair prickled on Bud Schwartz's arms. The old witch was going to drop the dime. Unbelievable.

Agent Hawkins was saying, "Do you know him personally?"

There was a pause that seemed to last five minutes. Molly nudged her eyeglasses up the bridge of her nose. She held the photograph near a lamp, and examined it from several angles.

"No," she said finally. "He looks vaguely familiar, but I really can't place the face."

"Do me a favor. Think about it."

"Certainly," she said. "May I keep the picture?"

"Sure. And think about the Wildlife Rescue Corps, too."

Molly liked the way this fellow conducted an interview. He

knew precisely how much to say without giving away the good stuff—and he certainly knew how to listen. He was a pro.

"Talk to your friends," said Billy Hawkins. "See if they have any ideas."

"You're putting me in a difficult position. These are fine people."

"I'm sure they are." The FBI man stood up, straight as a flagpole. He said, "It would be helpful if I could borrow that Smith-Corona—the one that was used for your press announcements. And the ribbon cartridge as well."

Molly said, "Oh dear."

"I can get a warrant, Mrs. McNamara."

"That's not it," she said. "You see, the typewriter's been stolen."

Billy Hawkins didn't say anything.

"Out of my car."

"That's too bad," the agent said.

"The trunk of my car," Molly added. "While I was grocery-shopping."

She walked the FBI man to the front door. "Can I ask you something, Agent Hawkins? Are you fellows investigating the death of the killer whale, as well?"

"Should we?"

"I think so. It looks like a pattern, doesn't it? Terrible things are happening at that park." Molly looked at him over the tops of her glasses. He felt as if he were back in elementary school. She said, "I know the mango voles are important, but if I may make a suggestion?"

"Sure," said Hawkins.

"Your valuable time and talents would be better spent on a thorough investigation of the Falcon Trace resort. It's a cesspool down there, and Mr. Francis X. Kingsbury is the root of the cess. I trust the FBI is still interested in bribery and public corruption."

"We consider it a priority."

"Then you'll keep this in mind." Molly's eyes lost some of their sparkle. "They've up and bulldozed the whole place," she said. "The trees, everything. It's a crime what they did. I drove by it this morning."

For the first time Billy Hawkins heard a trembling in her voice. He handed her a card. "Anything solid, we'll look into it. And thank you very much for the tea."

She held the door open. "You're a very polite young man," she said. "You renew my faith in authority."

"We'll be talking soon," said Agent Hawkins.

As soon as he was gone, Molly McNamara heard a whoop from the bedroom. She found Danny Pogue dancing a one-legged jig, ecstatic that he was not in federal custody. Bud Schwartz sat on the edge of the bed, nervously pounding his fist in a pillow.

Danny Pogue took Molly by the arms and said: "You did good. You stayed cool!"

Bud Schwartz said, "Cool's not the word for it."

Molly handed him the mug shot. "Next time comb your hair," she said. "Now then—let's have a look at those files you boys borrowed from Mr. Kingsbury."

Joe Winder took Nina's hand and led her down the trail. "You're gonna love this guy," he said.

"What happened to the movie?"

"Later," Winder said. "There's a ten-o'clock show." He hated going to the movies. Hated driving all the way up to Homestead.

Nina said, "Don't you have a flashlight?"

"We've got a good hour till dusk. Come on."

"It's my night off," she said. "I wanted to go someplace."

Winder pulled her along through the trees. "Just you wait," he said.

They found Skink shirtless, skinning a raccoon at the campsite. He grunted when Joe Winder said hello. Nina wondered if the plastic collar around his neck was from a prison or some other institution. She stepped closer to get a look at the dead raccoon.

"Import got him," Skink said, feeling her stare. "Up on 905 about two hours ago. Little guy's still warm."

Winder cleared a spot for Nina to sit down. "How do you know it was a foreign car?" he asked. He truly was curious.

"Low bumper broke his neck, that's how I know. Usually it's the tires that do the trick. That's because the rental companies prefer mid-sized American models. Fords and Chevys. We got a ton of rentals up and down this stretch."

He stripped the skin off the animal and laid it on one side. To Nina he said: "They call me Skink."

She took a small breath. "I'm Nina. Joe said you were the governor of Florida."

"Long time ago." Skink frowned at Winder. "No need to bring it up."

The man's voice was a deep, gentle rumble. Nina wondered why the guys who phoned the sex line never sounded like that. She shivered and said: "Joe told me you just vanished. Got up and walked away from the job. It was in all the papers."

"I'm sure. Did he also tell you that I knew his daddy?"

"Ancient history," Winder cut in. "Nina, I wanted you to meet this guy because he saved my life the other night."

Skink sliced the hindquarters off the dead raccoon and placed them side by side in a large fry pan. He said to Nina: "Don't believe a word of it, darling. The only reason he wanted you to meet me was so you'd understand."

"Understand what?"

"What's about to happen."

Nina looked uncomfortable. With one hand she began twisting the ends of her hair into tiny braids.

"Don't be nervous," Joe Winder said, touching her knee.

"Well, what's he talking about?"

Skink finished with the raccoon carcass and slopped the innards into a grocery bag, which he buried. After he got a fire going, he wiped his palms on the seat of his new canvas trousers, the ones he'd taken off Spearmint Breath. He watched, satisfied as the gray meat began to sizzle and darken in the fry pan.

"I don't suppose you're hungry," Skink said.

"We've got other plans." Nina was cordial but firm.

Skink foraged through a rubble of old crates and lobster traps, mumbled, stomped into the woods. He came back carrying a dirty blue Igloo cooler. He took out three beers, opened one and gave the other two to Nina and Joe Winder.

Before taking a drink, Nina wiped the top of the can on the sleeve of Winder's shirt. She touched a hand to her neck and said, "So what's with the collar?"

"Telemetry." Skink pointed a finger at the sky. "Every week or so, a plane comes around."

"They think he's a panther," Joe Winder explained. "See, it's a radio collar. He took it off a dead panther."

Skink quickly added: "But I'm not the one who killed it. It was a liquor truck out of Marathon. Didn't even stop."

Nina wasn't plugging in. After a pause she said, "Joe, don't forget about our movie."

Winder nodded. Sometimes he felt they were oceans apart. "The panther's all but extinct," he said. "Maybe two dozen left alive. The Game and Fish Department uses radio collars to keep track of where they are."

Skink drained his beer. "Two nights later, here comes the liquor truck again. Only this time he blows a tire on some barbed wire."

"In the middle of the road?" Nina said.

"Don't ask me how it got there. Anyway, I had a good long talk with the boy."

Winder said, "Jesus, don't tell me."

"Cat's blood was still on the headlights. Fur, too." Skink spat into the fire. "Cracker bastard didn't seem to care."

"You didn't . . ."

"No, nothing permanent. Nothing his insurance wouldn't cover."

In her smoothest voice Nina asked, "Did you eat the panther, too?"

"No, ma'am," said Skink. "I did not."

The big cat was buried a half-mile up the trail, under brilliant bougainvilleas that Skink himself had planted. Joe Winder thought about showing Nina the place, but she didn't act interested. Darkness was settling in, and the mosquitoes had arrived by the billions. Nina slapped furiously at her bare arms and legs, while Joe Winder shook his head to keep the little bloodsuckers out of his ears.

Skink said, "I got some goop if you want it. Great stuff." He held his arms out in the firelight. The left one was engulfed by black mosquitoes; the right one was untouched.

"It's called EDTIAR," Skink said. "Extended Duration Topical Insect/Arthropod Repellent. I'm a field tester for the U.S. Marines; they pay me and everything." Studiously he began counting the bites on his left arm.

Nina, on the shrill edge of misery, whacked a big fat arthropod on Joe Winder's cheek. "We've got to get going," she said.

"They're nasty tonight," Skink said sympathetically. "I just took seventeen hits in thirty seconds."

Winder himself was getting devoured. He stood up, flailing his own torso. The bugs were humming in his eyes, his mouth, his nostrils.

"Joe, what's the point of all this?" Nina asked.

"I'm waiting for him to tell me who killed Will Koocher."

"Oh, for God's sake."

Skink said, "We're in dangerous territory now."

"I don't care," Winder said. "Tell me what happened. It had something to do with the mango voles, I'm sure."

"Yes," said Skink.

Nina announced that she was leaving. "I'm getting eaten alive, and we're going to miss the movie."

"Screw the movie," said Joe Winder, perhaps too curtly.

For Nina was suddenly gone—down the trail, through the woods. Snapping twigs and muffled imprecations divulged her path.

"Call me Mr. Charm," Winder said.

Skink chuckled. "You'd better go. This can wait."

"I want to know more."

"It's the voles, like you said." He reached into his second-hand trousers and took out a bottle so small it couldn't have held more than four ounces. He pressed it into the palm of Joe Winder's right hand.

"Ah, the magic bug goop!"

"No," Skink said. "Now take off, before Snow White gets lost in the big bad forest."

Blindly Winder jogged down the trail after his girlfriend. He held one arm across his face to block the branches from slashing him, and weaved through the low viny trees like a halfback slipping trackers.

Nina had given up her solo expedition forty yards from Skink's campsite, and that's where Winder found her, leaning against the slick red trunk of a gumbo-limbo.

"Get us out of here," she said, brushing a squadron of plump mosquitoes from her forehead.

Out of breath, Winder gave her a hug. She didn't exactly melt in his arms. "You were doing fine," he said. "You stayed right on the trail."

They were in the car, halfway to Homestead, when she spoke again: "Why can't you leave it alone? The guy's nothing but trouble."

"He's not crazy, Nina."

"Oh right."

"A man was murdered. I can't let it slide."

She picked a buttonwood leaf from her sleeve, rolled down the window and flicked the leaf away. She said, "If he's not crazy, then how come he lives the way he does? How come he wears that electric collar?"

"He says it keeps him on his toes." Joe Winder plugged a Zevon tape in the stereo. "Look, I'm not saying he's normal. I'm just saying he's not crazy."

"Like you would know," Nina said.

Fifteen

On Sunday, July 22, Charles Chelsea got up at eight-thirty, showered, shaved, dressed (navy slacks, Cordovan loafers, blue oxford shirt, burgundy necktie), trimmed his nose hairs, splashed on about three gallons of Aramis and drove off to work in his red Mazda Miata, for which he had paid thirty-five hundred dollars over dealer invoice.

Chelsea had two important appointments at the Amazing Kingdom of Thrills. One of them would be routine, and one promised to be unpleasant. He had not slept well, but he didn't feel exceptionally tired. In fact, he felt surprisingly confident, composed, tough; if only he could remain that way until his meeting with Joe Winder.

A crew from Channel 7 was waiting outside the main gate. The reporter was an attractive young Latin woman wearing oversized sunglasses. Chelsea greeted her warmly and told her she was right on time. They all got in a van, which was driven by a man wearing a costume of bright neoprene plumes. The man introduced himself as Baldy the Eagle, and said he was happy to be their host. He began a long spiel about the Amazing Kingdom of Thrills until Charles Chelsea flashed his ID badge, at which point the bird man shrugged and shut up. Chelsea slapped his arm when he tried to bum a Marlboro off the Channel 7 cameraman.

When they arrived at the killer-whale tank, Chelsea stepped from the van and held the door for the reporter, whose first name was Maria. Chelsea led the way inside the marine stadium, where the TV crew unpacked and began to set up the equipment. Chelsea sat next to Maria in the front row, facing the empty blue pool. Above them, men on scaffolds were sandblasting the word "Orky" from the coral-colored wall.

Chelsea said, "I guess the others will be along soon."

Maria removed her sunglasses and brushed her hair. She took out a spiral notebook and flipped to a blank page.

"The other stations," Chelsea said, "they must be running a little late."

Five others had received the same fax as Channel 7 had. Surely more crews would show up—it was Sunday, after all, the slowest news day of the week.

Maria said, "Before we go on the air—"

"You want some background," Chelsea said helpfully. "Well, to be perfectly frank, Orky's death left us with a rather large vacancy. Here we have this beautiful saltwater tank, as you see, and a scenic outdoor stadium. A facility like this is too special to waste. We thought about getting another whale, but Mr. Kingsbury felt it would be inappropriate. He felt Orky was irreplaceable."

Charles Chelsea glanced over Maria's shoulder to see the Minicam pointed at him. Its red light winked innocuously as the tape rolled. The cameraman was on his knees. Squinting through the viewfinder, he signaled for Chelsea to keep talking.

"Are we on?" the PR man said. "What about the mike? I don't have a mike."

The cameraman pointed straight up. Chelsea raised his

175

eyes. A gray boom microphone, the size of a fungo bat, hung over his head. The boom was controlled by a sound man standing to Chelsea's right. The man wore earphones and a Miami Dolphins warm-up jacket.

Maria said, "You mentioned Orky. Could you tell us what your staff has learned about the whale's death? What exactly killed it?" Chelsea fought to keep his Adam's apple from bobbing spasmodically, as it often did when he lied. "The tests," he said, "are still incomplete."

Maria's warm brown eyes blinked inquisitively. "There's a rumor that the whale died during an encounter with an employee of the Amazing Kingdom."

"Oh, that's a good one." Chelsea laughed stiffly. "Where did you hear that?"

"Is it true?"

The camera's blinking red light no longer seemed harmless. Charles Chelsea said, "I'm not going to dignify such a question by responding."

The reporter said nothing, just let the tape roll. Let him choke on the silence. It worked.

"We did have a death that night," Chelsea admitted, toying with his cuffs. "An employee of the park apparently took his own life. It was very, very tragic—"

"What was the name of this employee?"

Chelsea's tone became cold, reproachful. "It is our strict policy not to discuss such matters publicly. There is an issue of privacy, and respect for the family."

Maria said, "The rumor is—"

"We don't respond to rumors, Ms. Rodríguez." Now Chelsea was leaning forward, lecturing. The boom mike followed him. "Would you like to hear about our newest attraction, or not?"

She smiled like a moray eel. "That's why we're here."

Oh no it isn't, thought Chelsea, trying not to glare, trying not to perspire, trying not to look like the unvarnished shill he was.

"I brought a bathing suit," Maria said, "as you suggested."

"Maybe we should wait for the others."

"I think we're it, Mr. Chelsea. I don't think any of the other stations are coming."

"Fine." He tried not to sound disappointed.

The cameraman stopped taping. Chelsea dabbed his forehead in relief; he needed to collect himself, recover from the ambush. Everybody wants to be Mike Wallace, he thought bitterly. Everybody's a hardass.

Maria picked up a tote bag and asked directions to the ladies' room. When she returned, she was wearing a tight melon-colored tonga that required continual adjustment. At the sight of her, Charles Chelsea inadvertently licked the corners of his mouth. It wasn't so bad after all, coming to work on a Sunday.

"Should I get in?" Maria asked.

"Sure." Chelsea signaled across the pool to a young man dressed in khaki shorts. This was one of the trainers.

Maria slipped into the whale pool, dipped her head underwater, and smoothed her hair straight back. The tape was rolling again.

Eyes twinkling, she smiled up at the camera. The guy with the boom mike leaned over the wall of the tank to capture her words.

"Hi, this is Maria Rodríguez. Today we're visiting the Amazing Kingdom of Thrills in North Key Largo. As you can see, it's a gorgeous summer day—"

Chelsea was thinking: Good girl, stick to the fluff.

"—and we're about to meet the newest star of the Kingdom's outdoor marine show. His name is Dickie the Dolphin . . . cut! Hold it, Jimmy."

The cameraman stopped the tape. Bobbing in the whale

pool, Maria groped beneath the surface, frowned and spun away. Chelsea could see that she was struggling to realign the bathing suit.

"Damn thing's riding up my crack."

"Take your time," said the cameraman. "We got plenty of light."

Moments later, Maria was ready again; fresh, sleek, languid. She splashed herself lightly in the face so that droplets glistened in her eyelashes; Charles Chelsea was transfixed.

"Hi, this is Maria Rodríguez reporting from the Amazing Kingdom of Thrills in North Key Largo. As you can see, it's a gorgeous summer day in South Florida—perfect for a swim with the newest star of the Amazing Kingdom's marine show. His name is Dickie the Dolphin and, starting tomorrow, you can swim with him, too!"

Chelsea cued the trainer, who pulled the pin on the gate to the whale pool. Pushing a V-shaped wake, the dolphin charged from the holding tank and sounded.

The TV reporter continued: "It's the latest concept in marine theme parks—customer participation. Instead of sitting in the bleachers and watching these remarkable mammals do tricks, you can actually get in the water and play with them. It costs a little more, but—believe me—it's worth it."

A few yards behind her, Dickie the Dolphin rolled, blowing air noisily. Maria kept her poise, glancing over one shoulder with a breezy, affectionate smile. Chelsea was impressed; she had the whole script memorized.

Turning back to the camera, Maria said: "To be in the water with these gentle, intelligent creatures is an experience you'll never forget. Scientists say the dolphin's brain is actually larger than ours, and much of their complex social behavior remains a mystery . . . "

Dickie the Dolphin surfaced lazily near Maria, who grabbed its dorsal fin with both hands. Chelsea stood up quickly and waved a warning, but it was too late. The dolphin carried the TV reporter across the top of the water; she closed her eyes and squealed with childlike excitement.

"Great fucking video," remarked Jimmy the cameraman, panning expertly with the action.

The boom man said, "She's getting out of range."

Charles Chelsea cupped his hands and shouted. "Let go! No rides allowed!"

Maria couldn't hear a word. She was holding her breath underwater while the dolphin imitated a torpedo. Every few seconds her long brown legs would slice the surface as she was dragged along, like the tail of a kite. Chelsea bit his lip and watched in queasy silence. Finally Maria splashed to the surface—and she was laughing, thank God! She thought it was all in fun, and maybe it was.

The sound man scurried along the rim of the tank and repositioned the boom. Giggling, short of breath, Maria's eyes found the camera. She said, "Folks, this is unbelievable. Bring the family, you're gonna love it!" Dickie the Dolphin appeared at her side, and she stroked its sleek flank. Wondrously, it seemed to nuzzle her bosom with its snout.

"He's so *adorable*!" Maria exclaimed.

From the feeding platform on the side of the tank, the trainer called out, "Hey, be careful!" Then he started peeling off his khakis.

"Such friendly animals," Maria was saying. "Notice how they always look like they're smiling!"

Dickie the Dolphin slapped its tail on the surface and pushed even closer. Maria threw both arms around the slippery mammal, which obligingly rolled on its back.

Chelsea saw the trainer dive in. He saw Maria's expression change from tenderness to awe. Then he saw the dolphin hook her with its flippers and drag her down.

When she broke to the top, Maria's giggle had become

a low fearful moan. As the dolphin's dark form appeared beneath her, she seemed to rise from the water. Then, just as slowly, the creature drew her under.

The cameraman muttered that he was running out of tape. A voice behind him said: "You'll miss the best part."

It was Joe Winder. He stood next to Charles Chelsea, who was clutching the rail with knuckles as pink as shrimp. In the water, the trainer was trying without much success to separate the dolphin from the TV reporter.

Chelsea said to Winder: "Maybe it's a new trick—"

"It's no trick. He's trying to boink her."

"That's not funny, Joe."

Winder pointed, "What do you think *that* is? See?"

"I—I don't know."

"It's a dolphin shlong, Charlie. One of Nature's marvels."

Chelsea began to stammer.

"They get in moods," Joe explained. "Same as dogs."

"My God."

"Don't worry, Charlie, it'll pass."

With the trainer's help, Maria Rodríguez finally broke free from Dickie the Dolphin's embrace. Cursing, tugging at her tonga, she paddled furiously toward the ladder on the wall of the tank.

"Faster!" Charles Chelsea hollered. "Here he comes again!"

Two hours later, he was still trying to apologize without admitting the truth. "Sometimes they play too rough, that's all."

"Playing?" Maria sniffed sarcastically. "Excuse me, Mr. Chelsea, but I know a dick when I see one." She had changed back to TV clothes, although her hair was still wrapped in a towel. "I ought to sue your ass," she said.

They were sitting in Chelsea's office—the reporter, Charles Chelsea, and Joe Winder. The crew had returned to the truck to put the dish up, just in case.

180

"Come on," Winder said to Maria, "be a sport."

"What?" She gave him an acid glare. "What did you say?" She whipped the towel off her head and tossed it on the floor.

Very impolite, Winder thought, and unprofessional. "Take it easy," he said. "Nothing unspeakable happened."

Maria pointed a finger in his face and said, "Someone could get killed out there."

Charles Chelsea was miserable. "How can we make it up to you?" he asked Maria Rodríguez. "How about we comp you some passes to the Wild Bill Hiccup show?"

She was gone before he could come up with something better. On her way out, she kicked at the towel.

Joe Winder said, "Don't worry, she won't sue."

"How do you know?"

"It's too embarrassing. Hell, she'll probably destroy the tape on the way back to Miami."

Defensively Chelsea said, "She wasn't supposed to grab the dolphin. No touching is allowed—swimming only."

"This was a terrible idea, Charlie. Who thought of it?"

"Fifty bucks a head. They've got a bunch of these places in the Keys."

Joe Winder asked where Kingsbury had purchased the new dolphin.

"How should I know?" Chelsea snapped. "A dolphin's a dolphin, for Christ's sake. They don't come with a pedigree."

"This one needs a female," Winder said, "before you let tourists in the water."

"Thank you, Professor Cousteau." The publicity man got up and closed the door. He looked gravely serious when he returned to the desk.

Joe Winder said, "I hope you're not going to make me write a press release about this. I've got more important things to do."

"Me too." To steel himself, Charles Chelsea tightened his stomach muscles. "Joe, we're going to have to let you go."

"I see."

Chelsea studied his fingernails, trying not to make eye contact with Winder. "It's a combination of things."

"My attitude, I suppose."

"That's a factor, yes. I tried to give some latitude. The hair. The casual clothing."

Winder said, "Anything else?"

"I understand you broke into the vole lab."

"Would you like to hear what I found?"

"Not particularly," Chelsea said.

"A paper written about the blue-tongued mango voles. The one you sent to Will Koocher when you were recruiting him."

Chelsea gave Winder a so-what look. "That it?"

"Funny thing, Charlie. The person who supposedly wrote that paper, this Dr. Sarah Hunt? Rollins College never heard of her." Winder raised his palms in mock puzzlement. "Never on the faculty, never graduated, never even attended—what do you make of that, Charlie?"

"Pedro told me of your ridiculous theory." Chelsea's lips barely moved when he spoke; he looked like a goldfish burping. "Dr. Koocher wasn't murdered, Joe, but in your twisted brain I'm sure you've made some connection between his unfortunate death and this ... this typographical error."

Winder laughed. "A typo? You're beautiful, Charlie. The paper's a goddamn fake."

Chelsea rolled his eyes. "And I suppose a simpler explanation is impossible—that perhaps the author's name was misspelled by the publisher, or that the university was misidentified ... "

"No way."

"You're not a well person," Chelsea said. "And now I learn

that you've telephoned Koocher's widow in New York. That's simply inexcusable." The way he spit out the word was meant to have a lacerating effect.

"What's inexcusable," said Winder, "is the way you lied."

"It was a judgment call." Chelsea's cheek twitched. "We were trying to spare the woman some grief."

"I told her to get a lawyer."

Chelsea's tan seemed to fade.

Joe Winder went on: "The newspapers are bound to find out the truth. 'Man Gobbled by Whale. Modern-Day Jonah Perishes in Freak Theme Park Mishap.' Think about it, Charlie."

"The coroner said he drowned. We've never denied it."

"But they didn't say *how* he drowned. Or why."

Charles Chelsea began to rock back and forth. "This is all academic, Joey. As of this moment, you no longer work here."

"And here I thought I was your ace in the hole."

Chelsea extended a hand, palm up. "The keys to the Cushman, please."

Winder obliged. He said, "Charlie, even though you're an obsequious dork, I'd like to believe you're not a part of this. I'd like to believe that you're just incredibly dim."

"Go clean out your desk."

"I don't have to. There's nothing in it."

Chelsea looked momentarily confused.

Winder waved his arms. "Desks are places to keep facts, Charlie. Who needs a desk when the words simply fly off the tops of our head! Hell, I've done my finest work for you while sitting on the toilet."

"If you're trying to insult me, it won't work." Chelsea lowered his eyelids in lizardly disinterest. "We all fudge the truth when it suits our purposes, don't we? Like when you told me you got that scar in a car accident."

So he knew all along, just as Joe Winder had suspected.

"I heard it was a fight in the newsroom," Chelsea said, "a fistfight with one of your editors."

"He had it coming," said Winder. "He screwed up a perfectly good news story."

The story concerned Joe Winder's father bribing a county commissioner in exchange for a favorable vote on a zoning variance. Winder had written the story himself after digging through a stack of his father's canceled checks and finding five made out to the commissioner's favorite bagman.

Though admiring of Winder's resourcefulness, the editor had said it created an ethical dilemma; he decided that someone else would have to write the piece. You're too emotionally involved, the editor had told him.

So Winder had gotten a firm grip on the editor's head and rammed it through the screen of the word processor, cutting himself spectacularly in the struggle that followed.

"I'm sorry, Charlie," he said. "Maybe you shouldn't have hired me."

"The understatement of the year."

"Before I go, may I show you something?" He took out the small bottle that Skink had given him and placed it in the center of Chelsea's desk blotter.

The publicity man examined it and said, "It's food coloring, so what?"

"Look closer."

"Betty Crocker food coloring. What's the point, Joe?"

"And what color?"

"Blue." Chelsea was impatient. "The label says blue."

Winder twisted the cap off the bottle. He said, "I believe this came from the vole lab, too. You might ask Pedro about it."

Baffled, Charles Chelsea watched Joe Winder toss back his

head and empty the contents of the bottle into his mouth. He sloshed the liquid from cheek to cheek, then swallowed.

"Ready?" Winder said. He stuck out his tongue, which now was the color of indigo dye.

"That's a very cute trick." Chelsea sounded nervous.

Joe Winder climbed onto the desk on his hands and knees. "The voles were phony, Charlie. Did you know that?" He extended his tongue two inches from Chelsea's nose, then sucked it back in. He said, "There's no such thing as a blue-tongued mango vole. Kingsbury faked the whole deal. Invented an entire species!"

"You're cracking up," Chelsea said thinly.

Winder grabbed him by the collar. "You fucker, did you know all along?"

"Get out, I'm calling Security."

"That's why Will Koocher was killed. He'd figured out everything. He was going to rat, so to speak, on the upstanding Mr. Kingsbury."

Chelsea's upper lip was a constellation of tiny droplets. He tried to pull away. "Let me go, Joe. If you know what's good for you."

"They painted their tongues, Charlie. Think of it. They took these itty-bitty animals and dyed their tongues blue, all in the name of tourism."

Straining against Winder's grasp, Chelsea said, "You're talking crazy."

Joe Winder licked him across the face. "Stop it!"

Winder slurped him again. "It's your color, Charlie. Very snappy."

His tongue waggled in mockery; Chelsea eyed the fat blue thing as if it were a poisonous slug.

"You can fire me," Winder announced, "but I won't go away."

He climbed off the desk, careful not to drop the bottle of

food coloring. Chelsea swiftly began plucking tissues from a silver box and wiping his face, examining each crumpled remnant for traces of the dye. His fingers were shaking.

"I should have you arrested," he hissed.

"But you won't," Winder said. "Think of the headlines."

He was halfway to the door when Chelsea said, "Wait a minute, Joey. What is it you want?"

Winder kept walking, and began to laugh. He laughed all the way down the hall, a creepy melodic warble that made Charles Chelsea shudder and curse.

Sixteen

As a reward for the successful theft of Francis X. Kingsbury's files, Molly McNamara allowed Bud Schwartz and Danny Pogue to keep the rented Cutlass for a few days.

On the evening of July 22, they drove down Old Cutler Road, where many of Miami's wealthiest citizens lived. The homes were large and comfortable-looking, and set back impressively from the tree-shaded street. Danny Pogue couldn't get over the size of the yards, the tall old pines and colorful tropical shrubbery; it was beautiful, yet intimidating.

"They got those Spanish bayonets under the windows," he reported. "God, I hate them things." Wicked needles on the end of every stalk—absolute murder, even with gloves.

Bud Schwartz said, "Don't sweat it, we'll find us a back door."

"For sure they got alarms."

"Yeah."

"And a goddamn dog, too."

"Probably so," said Bud Schwartz, thinking: Already the guy's a nervous wreck.

"You ever done a house like this?"

"Sure." Bud Schwartz was lying. Mansions, that's what

these were, just like the ones on "Miami Vice." The bandage on his bad hand was damp with perspiration. Hunched over the steering wheel, he thought: Thank God for the rental—at least we got a car that'll move.

To cut the tension, he said: "Ten bucks it's a Dobie."

"No way," said Danny Pogue. "I say Rottweiler, that's the dog nowadays."

"For the Yuppies, sure, but not this guy. I'm betting on a Dobie."

Danny Pogue fingered a pimple on his neck. "Okay, but give me ten on the side."

"For what?"

"Give me ten on the color." Danny Pogue slugged him softly on the shoulder. "Black or brown?"

Bud Schwartz said, "I'll give you ten if it's brown."

"Deal."

"You're a sucker. Nobody in this neighborhood's got a brown Doberman."

"We'll see," said Danny Pogue. He pointed as they passed a crimson Porsche convertible parked on a cobbler drive. A beautiful dark-haired girl, all of seventeen, was washing the sports car under a quartet of halogen spotlights. The girl wore a dazzling green bikini and round reflector sunglasses. The sun had been down for two hours.

Danny Pogue clapped his hands. "Jesus, you see that?"

"Yeah, hosing down her Targa. And here we are in the middle of a drought." Bud Schwartz braked softly to peer at the name on a cypress mailbox. "Danny, what's that house number? I can't see it from here."

"Four-oh-seven."

"Good. We're almost there."

"I was wondering," said Danny Pogue.

"Yeah, what else is new."

"Do I get twenty bucks if it's a brown Rottweiler?"

"They don't come in brown," said Bud Schwartz. "I thought you knew."

It wasn't a Doberman pinscher or a Rottweiler.

"Maybe some type of weasel," whispered Danny Pogue. "Except it's got a collar on it."

They were kneeling in the shelter of a sea-grape tree. "One of them beady-eyed dogs from Asia," said Bud Schwartz, "or maybe it's Africa." Dozing under the electric bug lamp, the animal showed no reaction to the sizzle and zap of dying moths.

Carefully Bud Schwartz inserted four Tylenol No. 3 tablets into a ten-ounce patty of prime ground sirloin. With his good hand he lobbed the meat over the fence. It landed with a wet slap on the patio near the pool. The weasel-dog lifted its head, barked once sharply and got up.

Danny Pogue said, "That's the ugliest goddamn thing I ever saw."

"Like you're Mel Gibson, right?"

"No, but just look."

The dog found the hamburger and gulped it in two bites. When its front legs began to wobble, Danny Pogue said, "Jesus, what'd you use?"

"About a hundred milligrams of codeine."

Soon the animal lay down, snuffling into a stupor. Bud Schwartz hopped the fence and helped his crutchless partner across. The two burglars crab-walked along a low cherry hedge until they reached the house. Through a glass door they saw that all the kitchen lights were on; in fact, lamps glowed in every window. Bud Schwartz heard himself take a short breath; he was acting against every instinct, every fundamental rule of the trade. Never *ever* break into an occupied dwelling—especially an occupied dwelling protected by four thousand dollars' worth of electronic burglar alarm.

189

Bud Schwartz knew the screens would be wired, so busting the windows was out of the question. He knew he couldn't jimmy the sliding door because that would trip the contact, also setting off the alarm. The best hope was cutting the glass door in such a way that it wouldn't trigger the noise detectors; he could see one of the matchbook-sized boxes mounted on a roof beam in the kitchen. Its tiny blue eye winked insidiously at him.

"What's the plan?" asked Danny Pogue.

Bud Schwartz took the glass cutter out of his pocket and showed it to his partner, who hadn't the faintest idea what it was. Bud Schwartz got to his knees. "I'm going to cut a square," he said, "big enough to crawl through."

"Like hell." Danny Pogue was quite certain they would be arrested any moment.

Bud Schwartz dug the blades of the glass cutter into the door and pressed with the full strength of his good arm. The door began to slide on its rollers. "Damn," said Bud Schwartz. Cold air rushed from the house and put goose bumps on his arms.

Danny Pogue said: "Must not be locked."

The door coasted open. No bells or sirens went off. The only sound came from a television, probably upstairs.

They slipped into the house. Bud Schwartz's sneakers squeaked on the kitchen tile; hopping on one leg, Danny Pogue followed his partner through the living room, which was decorated hideously in black and red. The furniture was leather, the carpeting a deep stringy shag. On a phony brick wall over the fireplace hung a painting that was, by Bud Schwartz's astonished calculation, larger than life-sized. The subject of the painting was a nude blond with a Pepsodent smile and breasts the size of soccer balls. She wore a yellow visored cap, and held a flagstick over her shoulder. A small brass plate announced the title of the work: "My Nineteenth Hole."

It was unspeakably crude, even to two men who had spent most of their adult lives in redneck bars and minimum-security prisons. Bud Schwartz gazed at the painting and said: "I'll bet it's the wife."

"No way," said Danny Pogue. He couldn't imagine being married to someone who would do such a thing.

As they moved cautiously through the house, Bud Schwartz couldn't help but notice there wasn't much worth stealing, even if they'd wanted to. Oh, the stuff was expensive enough, but tacky as hell. A Waterford armadillo—how could million-aires have such lousy taste?

The burglars followed the sound of the television down a hallway toward a bedroom. Bud Schwartz had never been so jittery. *What if the asshole has a gun?* This had been Danny Pogue's question, and for once Bud Schwartz couldn't answer. The asshole probably *did* have a gun; it was Miami, after all. Probably something in a semi-automatic, a Mini-14 or a MAC-11. Christ, there's a pleasant thought. Ten, fifteen rounds a second. Hardly time to piss in your pants.

Danny Pogue's whiny breathing seemed to fill the hallway. Bud Schwartz glared, held a finger to his lips. The door to the bedroom was wide open; somebody was switching the chan-nels on the television. Momentously, Bud Schwartz smoothed his hair; Danny Pogue did the same. Bud Schwartz nodded and motioned with an index finger; Danny Pogue gave a con-stipated nod in return.

When they stepped into the room, they saw the blond woman from the golf painting. She was lying naked on the bed. Two peach-colored pillows were tucked under her head, and the remote control was propped on her golden belly. At the sight of the burglars, the woman covered her chest. Excitedly she tried to speak—no sounds emerged, though her jaws moved vigorously, as if she were chewing a wad of bubble gum.

Inanely, Bud Schwartz said, "Don't be afraid."

The woman forced out a low guttural cry that lasted several seconds. She sounded like a wildcat in labor.

"Enough a that," said Danny Pogue tensely.

Suddenly a door opened and a porky man in powder-blue boxer shorts stepped out of the bathroom. He was short and jowly, with skin like yellow lard. Tattooed on his left forearm was a striking tableau: Minnie Mouse performing oral sex on Mickey Mouse. At least that's what it looked like to Danny Pogue and Bud Schwartz, who couldn't help but stare. Mickey was wearing his sorcerer's hat from *Fantasia*, and appeared to be whistling a happy tune.

Danny Pogue said, "That'd make a great T-shirt."

With fierce reddish eyes, the man in the boxer shorts studied the two intruders.

"Honey!" cried the woman on the bed.

The man scowled impatiently. "Well, shit, get it over with. Take, you know, whatever the hell."

Bud Schwartz said, "We didn't mean to scare you, Mr. Kingsbury."

"Don't fucking flatter yourself. And, Penny, watch it with that goddamn thing!"

Still recumbent, the naked Mrs. Kingsbury now was aiming a small chrome-plated pistol at Danny Pogue's midsection.

"I knew it," muttered Bud Schwartz. He hated the thought of getting shot twice in the same week, especially by women. This one must've had it under the damn pillows, or maybe in the sheets.

Danny Pogue's lips were quivering, as if he were about to cry. He held out his arms beseechingly.

Quickly Bud Schwartz said: "We're not here to rob you. We're here to talk business."

Kingsbury hooked his nubby thumbs into the elastic

waistband of his underpants. "Make me laugh," he said. "Break into my house like a couple of putzes."

"We're pros," said Bud Schwartz.

Kingsbury cackled, snapping the elastic. "Two hands, babe," he reminded his wife.

Danny Pogue said, "Bud, make her drop it!"

"It's only a .25," said Kingsbury. "She's been out to the range— what?—a half-dozen times. Got the nerves for it, apparently."

Bud Schwartz tried to keep his voice level and calm. He said to Kingsbury: "Your office got hit yesterday, right?"

"As a matter of fact, yeah."

"You're missing some files."

The naked Mrs. Kingsbury said, "Frankie, you didn't tell me." Her arms were impressively steady with the gun.

Kingsbury took his hands out of his underwear and folded them in a superior way across his breasts, which were larger than those of a few women whom Danny Pogue had known.

"Not exactly the Brink's job," Kingsbury remarked. "Well, we got your damn files," said Bud Schwartz.

"That was you? Bullshit."

"Maybe you need some proof. Maybe you need to see some credit-card slips."

Kingsbury hesitated. "Selling them back, is that the idea?"

Some genius businessman, thought Bud Schwartz. The guy was a bum, a con. You could tell right away.

"Tell your wife to drop the piece."

"Penny, you heard the man."

"And tell her to go lock herself in the john."

"What?"

The wife said, "Frankie, I don't like this." Carefully she placed the gun on the nightstand next to a bottle of Lavoris mouthwash. A tremor of relief passed through Danny Pogue, starting at the shoulders. He hopped across the room and sat down on the corner of the bed.

"It's better if she's in the john," Bud Schwartz said to Francis X. Kingsbury. "Or maybe you don't care."

Kingsbury gnawed his upper lip. He was thinking about the files, and what was in them.

His wife wrapped herself in a sheet. "Frank?"

"Do what he said," Kingsbury told her. "Take a magazine or something. A book if you can find one."

"Fuck you," said Penny Kingsbury. On her way to the bathroom, she waved a copy of *GQ* in his face.

"At Doral is where I met her. Selling golf shoes."

"How nice," said Bud Schwartz.

"Fuzzy Zoeller, Tom Kite, I'm not kidding. Penny's customers." Kingsbury had put on a red bathrobe and turned up the television, in case his wife was at the door trying to eavesdrop. Bud Schwartz lifted the handgun from the nightstand and slipped it into his pocket; the cold weight of the thing in his pants, so close to his privates, made him shudder. God, how he hated guns.

Kingsbury said, "The painting in the big room—you guys get a look at it?"

"Yeah, boy," answered Danny Pogue.

"We did that up on the Biltmore. Number seven or ten, I can't remember. Some par three. Anyway, I had to lease the whole fucking course for a day, that's how long it took. Must've been two hundred guys standing around, staring at her boobs. Penny didn't mind, she's proud of 'em."

"And who wouldn't be," said Bud Schwartz, tight as a knot. "Can we get to it, please? We got plenty to talk about."

Francis X. Kingsbury said, "I'm trying to remember. You got the Ramex Global file. Jersey Premium. What else?"

"You know what else."

Kingsbury nodded. "Start with the American Express. Give me a number."

Bud Schwartz sat down in a high-backed colonial chair. From memory he gave Kingsbury an inventory: "We got a diamond tennis necklace in New York, earrings in Chicago. Yeah, and an emerald stickpin in Nassau of all places, for like three grand." He motioned to Danny Pogue, who hobbled over to Mrs. Kingsbury's dresser and began to look through the boxes.

Dispiritedly, Kingsbury said, "Forget it, you won't find it there."

"So who got it all?"

"Friends. It's not important."

"Not to us, maybe." Bud Schwartz nodded toward the bathroom. "I got a feeling your old lady might be interested."

Kingsbury lowered his voice. "The reason I use the credit card, hell, who carries that much cash?"

"Plus the insurance," said Danny Pogue, pawing through Mrs. Kingsbury's jewelry. "Stuff gets broke or stolen, they replace it, no questions. It's a new thing."

Great, Bud Schwartz thought; now he's doing commercials.

"There's some excellent shit here. Very nice." Danny Pogue held up a diamond solitaire and played it off the light. "I'm guessin' two carats."

"Try one-point-five," said Kingsbury.

"There were some dinners on your card," Bud Schwartz said. "And plane tickets, too. It's handy how they put it all together at the end of the year where you can check it."

Kingsbury asked him how much.

"Five grand," Bud Schwartz said, "and we won't say a word to the wife."

"The file, Jesus, I need it back."

"No problem. Now let's talk about serious money."

Kingsbury frowned. He pulled on the tip of his nose with a thumb and forefinger, as if he were straightening it.

Bud Schwartz said, "The Gotti file, Mr. King."

"Mother of Christ."

"'Frankie, The Ferret, King.' That's what the indictment said."

"You got me by surprise," Kingsbury said.

Danny Pogue looked up from an opal bracelet he was admiring. "So who's this Gotti dude again? Some kinda gangster is what Bud said."

"How much?" said Kingsbury. He leaned forward and put his hands on his bare knees. "Don't make it, like ... a game."

Bud Schwartz detected visceral fear in the man's voice; it gave him an unfamiliar feeling of power. On the other side of the bathroom door, Francis Kingsbury's wife shouted something about wanting to get out. Kingsbury ignored her.

"The banks that made the loans on Falcon Trace, do they know who you are?" Bud Schwartz affected a curious tone. "Do they know you're a government witness? A mob guy?"

Kingsbury didn't bother to reply.

"I imagine they gave you shitloads a money," Bud Schwartz went on, "and I imagine they could call it back."

Francis Kingsbury went to the bathroom door and told Penny to shut up and sit her sweet ass on the can. He turned back to the burglars and said: "So what's the number, the grand total? For Gotti, I mean."

Danny Pogue resisted the urge to enter the negotiation; expectantly he looked at his partner. Bud Schwartz smoothed his hair, pursed his mouth. He wanted to hear what kind of bullshit offer Kingsbury would make on his own.

"I'm trying to think what's fair."

"Give me a fucking number," said Kingsbury, "and I'll goddamn tell you if it's fair."

What the hell, thought Bud Schwartz. "Fifty grand," he said calmly. "And we toss in Ramex and the rest for free."

Excitedly Danny Pogue began excavating a new pimple.

Kingsbury eyed the men suspiciously. "Fifty, you said? As in five-oh?"

"Right." Bud Schwartz gave half a grin. "That's fifty to give back the Gotti file . . . "

"And?"

"Two hundred more to forget what was in it."

Kingsbury chuckled bitterly. "So I was wrong," he said. "You're not such a putz."

Danny Pogue was so overjoyed that he could barely control himself on the ride back to Molly's condominium. "We're gonna be rich," he said, pounding both hands on the upholstery. "You're a genius, man, that's what you are."

"It went good," Bud Schwartz agreed. Better than he had ever imagined. As he drove, he did the arithmetic in his head. Five thousand for the American Express file, fifty for the Gotti stuff, another two hundred in hush money . . . rich was the word for it. "Early retirement," he said to Danny Pogue. "No more damn b-and-e's."

"You don't think he'll call the cops?"

"That's the last place he'd call. Guy's a scammer, Danny."

They stopped at a U-Tote-Em and bought two six-packs of Coors and a box of jelly doughnuts. In the parking lot they rolled down the windows and turned up the radio and stuffed themselves in jubilation. It was an hour until curfew; if they weren't back by midnight, Molly had said, she would call the FBI and say her memory had returned.

"I bet she'll cut us some slack," said Danny Pogue, "if we're a little late."

"Maybe." Bud Schwartz opened the door and rolled an empty beer can under the car. He said, "I'm sure gettin' tired of being her pet burglar."

"Well, then, let's go to a tittie bar and celebrate." Danny

Pogue said he knew of a place where the girls danced naked on the tables, and let you grab their ankles for five bucks.

Bud Schwartz said not tonight. There would be no celebration until they broke free from the old lady. Tonight he would make a pitch for the rest of the ten grand that she'd promised. Surely they were square by now; Molly had been so thrilled by the contents of the Ramex file that she'd given him a hug. Then she'd gone out and had eight copies made. What more could she want of them?

Back on the road, Bud Schwartz said: "Remember, don't say a damn thing about what we done tonight."

"You told me a hundred times."

"Well, it'll screw up everything. I mean it, don't tell her where we been."

"No reason," said Danny Pogue. "It's got nothin' to do with the butterflies, right?"

"No, it sure does not."

Danny Pogue said he was hungry again, so they stopped to pick up some chicken nuggets. Again they ate in the parking lot, listening to a country station. Bud Schwartz had never before driven an automobile with a working clock, so he was surprised to glance at the dashboard of the Cutlass and find that it was half past twelve, and counting.

"Better roll," Danny Pogue said, "just in case."

"I got a better idea—gimme a quarter." Bud Schwartz got out and walked to a pay telephone under a streetlight. He dialed the number of Molly McNamara's condominium and let it ring five times. He hung up, retrieved the quarter and dialed again. This time he let it ring twice as long.

In the car, speeding down U.S. 1, Danny Pogue said, "I can't believe she'd do it—maybe she went someplace else. Maybe she left us a note."

Bud Schwartz gripped the wheel with both hands; the bullet wound was numb because he had forgotten about it.

Escape was on his mind—what if the old bitch had run to the feds? Worse, what if she'd found the Gotti file? What if she'd gone snooping through the bedroom and found it hidden between the mattress and the box spring, which in retrospect was probably not the cleverest place of concealment.

"Shit," he said, thinking of the bleak possibilities.

"Don't jump the gun," said Danny Pogue, for once the optimist.

They made it back to the condo in twenty-two minutes, parked the rental car and went upstairs. The door to Molly's apartment was unlocked. Bud Schwartz knocked twice anyway. "It's just us," he announced lightly, "Butch and Sundance."

When he went in, he saw that the place had been torn apart. "Oh Jesus," he said.

Danny Pogue pushed him with the crutch. "I can't fucking believe it," he said. "Somebody hit the place."

"No," said Bud Schwartz, "it's more than that."

The sofas had been slit, chairs broken, mirrors shattered. A ceramic Siamese cat had been smashed face-first through the big-screen television. While Danny Pogue hopscotched through the rubble, Bud Schwartz went directly to the bedroom, which also had been ransacked and vandalized. He reached under the mattress and found the Kingsbury files exactly where he had left them. Whoever did the place hadn't been looking very hard, if at all.

A hoarse shout came from the kitchen.

Bud Schwartz found Danny Pogue on his knees next to Molly McNamara. She lay on her back, with one leg folded crookedly under the other. Her housecoat, torn and stained with something dark, was bunched around her hips. Her face had been beaten to pulp; beads of blood glistened like holly berries in her snowy hair. Her eyes were closed and her lips were gray, but she was breathing—raspy, irregular gulps.

Danny Pogue took Molly's wrist. "God Almighty," he said, voice quavering. "What—who do we call?"

"Nobody." Bud Schwartz shook his head ruefully. "Don't you understand, we can't call nobody." He bent down and put his bandaged hand on Molly's forehead. "Who the hell would do this to an old lady?"

"I hope she don't die."

"Me too," said Bud Schwartz. "Honest to God, this ain't right."

Seventeen

Joe Winder's trousers were soaked from the thighs down. Nina took a long look and said, "You've been fishing."

"Yes."

"In the middle of the day."

"The fish are all gone," Winder said dismally. "Ever since they bulldozed the place."

Nina sat cross-legged on the floor. She wore blue-jean shorts and a pink cotton halter; the same outfit she'd been wearing the day he'd met her, calling out numbers at the Seminole bingo hall. Joe Winder had gone there to meet an Indian named Sammy Deer, who purportedly was selling an airboat, but Sammy Deer had hopped over to Freeport for the weekend, leaving Joe Winder stuck with three hundred chain-smoking white women in the bingo hall. Halfway out the door, he'd heard Nina's voice ("Q 34; Q, as in 'quicksilver,' 34!"), spun around and went back to see if she looked as lovely as she sounded, and she had. Nina informed him that she was part-timing as a bingo caller until the telephone gig came through, and he confided to her that he was buying an airboat so he could disappear into the Everglades at will. He changed his plans after their first date.

Now, analyzing her body language, Joe Winder knew that

201

he was in danger of losing Nina's affections. A yellow legal pad was propped on her lap. She tapped on a bare knee with her felt-tipped pen, which she held as a drummer would.

"What happened to your big meeting?" she said. "Why aren't you at the Kingdom?"

He pretended not to hear. He said, "They dumped a ton of fill in the cove. The bottom's mucky and full of cut trees." He removed his trousers and arranged them crookedly on a wire hanger. "All against the law, of course. Dumping in a marine sanctuary."

Nina said, "You got canned, is that it?"

"A mutual parting of the ways, and not a particularly amicable one." Joe Winder sat down beside her. He sensed a lecture coming on.

"Put on some pants," she said.

"What's the point?"

Nina asked why his tongue was blue, and he told her the story of the bogus mango voles. She said she didn't believe a word.

"Charlie practically admitted everything."

"I don't really care," Nina said. She stopped drumming on her kneecap and turned away.

"What is it?"

"Look, I can't afford to support you." When she looked back at him, her eyes were moist and angry. "Things were going so well," she said.

Winder was stunned. Was she seriously worried about the money? "Nina, there's a man dead. Don't you understand? I can't work for a murderer."

"Stop it!" She shook the legal pad in front of his nose. "You know what I've been working on? Extra scripts. The other girls like my stuff so much they offered to buy, like, two or three a week. Twenty-five bucks each, it could really add up."

"That's great." He was proud of her, that was the hell of it. She'd never believe that he could be proud of her.

Pen in mouth, Nina said: "I wrote about an out-of-body experience. Like when you're about to die and you can actually see yourself lying there—but then you get saved at the very last minute. Only my script was about making love, about floating out of yourself just as you're about to come. *Suspended in air, I looked down at the bed and saw myself shudder violently, my fingernails raking across your broad tan shoulders.* I gave it to the new girl, Addie, and she tried it Friday night. One guy, she said, he called back eleven times."

"Is that a new record?"

"It just so happens, yes. But the point is, I'm looking at a major opportunity. If I start selling enough scripts, maybe I can get off the phones. Just stay home and write—wouldn't that be better?"

"Sure would." Winder put his arm around her. "You can still do that, honey. It would be great."

"Not with you sitting here every day. Playing your damn Warren Zevon."

"I'll get another job."

"No, Joe, it'll be the same old shit." She pulled away and got up from the floor. "I can't write when my life is in turmoil. I need a stabilizer. Peacefulness. Quiet."

Winder felt wounded. "For God's sake, Nina, I know a little something about writing. This place is plenty quiet."

"There is tension," she said grimly, "and don't deny it."

"Writers thrive on domestic tension. Look at Poe, Hemingway—and Mailer in his younger days, you talk about tense." He hoped Nina would appreciate being included on such an eminent roster, but she didn't. Impatiently he said, "It isn't exactly epic literature, anyway. It's phone porn."

Her expression clouded. "Phone porn? Thanks, Joe."

"Well, Christ, that's what it is."

Coldly she folded her arms and leaned against one of the tall speakers. "It's still writing, and writing is hard work. If I'm going to make a go of it, I need some space. And some security."

"If you're talking about groceries, don't worry. I intend to pull my own weight."

Nina raised her hands in exasperation. "Where can you find another job that pays so much?"

Joe Winder couldn't believe what he was hearing. Why the sudden anxiety? The laying on of guilt? If he'd known he was in for a full-blown argument, he indeed would have put on some pants.

Nina said, "It's not just the money. I need someone reliable, someone who will be here for me."

"Have I ever let you down?"

"No, but you will."

Winder didn't say anything because she was absolutely correct; nothing in his immediate plans would please her.

"I know you," Nina added, in a sad voice. "You aren't going to let go of this thing."

"Probably not."

"Then I think we're definitely heading in different directions. I think you're going to end up in jail, or maybe dead."

"Have some faith," Joe Winder said.

"It's not that easy." Nina stalked to the closet, flung open the door and stared at the clutter. "Where'd you put my suitcase?"

In the mid-1970s, Florida elected a crusading young governor named Clinton Tyree, an ex-football star and Vietnam War veteran. At six feet six, he was the tallest chief executive in the history of the state. In all likelihood he was also the most honest. When a ravenous and politically connected land-development company attempted to bribe Clinton Tyree, he tape-recorded their offers, turned the evidence over to the

FBI and volunteered to testify at the trial. By taking a public stand against such omnipotent forces, Clinton Tyree became something of a folk hero in the Sunshine State, and beyond. The faint scent of integrity attracted the national media, which roared into Florida and anointed the young governor a star of the new political vanguard.

It was, unfortunately, a vanguard of one. Clinton Tyree spoke with a blistering candor that terrified his fellow politicians. While others reveled in Florida's boom times, Clinton Tyree warned that the state was on the brink of an environmental cataclysm. The Everglades were drying up, the coral reefs were dying, Lake Okeechobee was choking on man-made poisons and the bluegills were loaded with mercury. While other officeholders touted Florida as a tropical dreamland, the governor called it a toxic dump with palm trees. On a popular call-in radio show, he asked visitors to stay away for a couple of years. He spoke not of managing the state's breakneck growth, but of halting it altogether. This, he declared, was the only way to save the place.

The day Clinton Tyree got his picture on the cover of a national newsmagazine, some of the most powerful special interests in Florida—bankers, builders, highway contractors, sugar barons, phosphate-mining executives—congealed in an informal conspiracy to thwart the new governor's reforms by stepping around him, as if he were a small lump of dogshit on an otherwise luxuriant carpet.

Bypassing Clinton Tyree was relatively easy to do; all it took was money. In a matter of months, everyone who could be compromised, intimidated or bought off was. The governor found himself isolated from even his own political party, which had no stake in his radical bluster because it was alienating all the big campaign contributors. Save Florida? Why? And from what? The support that Clinton Tyree enjoyed among voters didn't help him one bit in the back rooms of Tallahassee; every bill he wanted passed got gutted, buried or rebuffed. The fact that he was popular with the media didn't deter his enemies; it merely softened their strategy. Rather than attack the governor's agenda, they did something worse—they ignored it. Only the most gentlemanly words were publicly spoken about young Clint, the handsome war hero, and about his idealism and courage to speak out. Any reporter who came to town could fill two or three notebooks with admiring quotes—so many (and so effusive) that someone new to the state might have assumed that Clinton Tyree had already died, which he had, in a way.

On the morning the Florida Cabinet decided to shut down a coastal wildlife preserve and sell it dirt cheap to a powerful land-sales firm, the lone dissenting vote trudged from the Capitol Building in disgust and vanished from the political landscape in the back of a limousine.

At first authorities presumed that the governor was the victim of a kidnapping or other foul play. A nationwide manhunt was suspended only after a notarized resignation letter was analyzed by the FBI and found to be authentic. It was true; the crazy bastard had up and quit.

Journalists, authors and screenwriters flocked to Florida with hopes of securing exclusive rights to the renegade governor's story, but none could find him. Consequently, nothing was written that even bordered on the truth.

Which was this: Clinton Tyree now went by the name of Skink, and lived in those steamy clawing places where he was least likely to be bothered by human life-forms. For fifteen years the governor had been submerged in an expatriation that was deliberately remote and anonymous, if not entirely tranquil.

Joe Winder wanted to talk about what happened in Tallahassee. "I read all the stories," he said. "I went back and looked up the microfiche."

"Then you know all there is to know." Skink was on his haunches, poking the embers with a stick. Winder refused to look at what was frying in the pan.

He said, "All this time and they never found you."

"They quit searching," Skink said. A hot ash caught in a wisp of his beard. He snuffed it with two fingers. "I don't normally eat soft-shell turtle," he allowed.

"Me neither," said Joe Winder.

"The flavor makes up for the texture."

"I bet." Winder knelt on the other side of the fire.

Out of the blue Skink said, "Your old man wasn't a bad guy, but he was in a bad business."

Winder heard himself agree. "He never understood what was so wrong about it. Or why I was so goddamn mad. He died not having a clue."

Skink lifted the turtle by the tail and stuck a fork in it. "Ten more minutes," he said, "at least."

It wasn't easy trying to talk with him this way, but Winder wouldn't give up: "It's been an interesting day. In the space of two hours I lost my job and my girlfriend."

"Christ, you sound like Dobie Gillis."

"The job was shit, I admit. But I was hoping Nina would stay strong. She's one in a million."

"Love," said Skink, "it's just a kiss away."

Dejectedly, Winder thought: I'm wasting my time. The man couldn't care less. "I came to ask about a plan," Winder said. "I've been racking my brain."

"Come on, I want to show you something." Skink rose slowly and stretched, and the blaze-orange rainsuit made a crackling noise. He pulled the shower cap tight on his skull and, in high steps, marched off through the trees. To the west, the sky boiled with fierce purple thunderheads.

"Keep it moving," Skink advised, over his shoulder.

Joe Winder followed him to the same dumpsite where the

corpse of Spearmint Breath had been hidden. When they walked past the junker Cadillac, Winder noted that the trunk was open, and empty. He didn't ask about the body. He didn't want to know.

Skink led him through a hazardous obstacle course of discarded household junk—shells of refrigerators, ripped sofas, punctured mattresses, crippled Barcaloungers, rusty barbecue grills, disemboweled air conditioners—until they came to a very old Plymouth station wagon, an immense egg-colored barge with no wheels and no windshield. A yellow beach umbrella sprouted like a giant marigold from the dashboard, and offered minimal protection from blowing rain or the noonday sun. Skink got in the car and ordered Joe Winder to do the same.

The Plymouth was full of books—hundreds of volumes arranged lovingly from the tailgate to the front. With considerable effort, Skink turned completely in the front seat; he propped his rear end on the warped steering wheel. "This is where I come to read," he said. "Believe it or not, the dome light in this heap still works."

Joe Winder ran a finger along the spines of the books, and found himself smiling at the exhilarating variety of writers: Churchill, Hesse, Sandburg, Steinbeck, Camus, Paine, Wilde, Vonnegut, de Tocqueville, Salinger, García Márquez, even Harry Crews.

"I put a new battery in this thing," Skink was saying. "This time of year I've got to run the AC at least two, three hours a day. To stop the damn mildew."

"So there's gas in this car?" Winder asked.

"Sure."

"But no wheels."

Skink shrugged. "Where the hell would I be driving?"

A cool stream of wind rushed through the open windshield, and overhead the yellow beach umbrella began to flap noisily.

A fat drop of rain splatted on the hood, followed by another and another.

"Damn," said Skink. He put a shoulder to the door and launched himself out of the station wagon. "Hey, Flack, you coming or not?"

The storm came hard and they sat through it, huddled like Sherpas. The campfire washed out, but the soft-shelled turtle was cooked to perfection. Skink chewed intently on its tail and blinked the raindrops from his good eye; the other one fogged up like a broken headlight. Water trickled down his bronze cheeks, drenching his beard. Lightning cracked so close they could smell it—Winder ducked, but Skink showed no reaction, even when thunder rattled the coffeepot.

He adjusted the blaze weather suit to cover the electronic panther collar on his neck. "They say it's waterproof, but I don't know."

Winder could scarcely hear him over the drum of the rain against the trees. Lightning flashed again, and reflexively he shut his eyes.

Skink raised his voice: "You know about that new golf resort?"

"I saw where they're putting it."

"No!" Skink was shouting now. "You know who's behind it? That fucking Kingsbury!"

The wind was getting worse, if that was possible. With his free hand, Skink wrung out the tendrils of his beard. "Goddammit, man, are you listening? It all ties together."

"What—with Koocher's death?"

"Everything—" Skink paused for another white sizzle of lightning. "Every damn thing."

It made sense to Winder. A scandal at the Amazing Kingdom wouldn't only be bad for business, it might jeopardize Francis Kingsbury's plans for developing Falcon Trace.

If anyone revealed that he'd lied about the "endangered" voles, the feds might roll in and halt the whole show. The EPA, the Army Corps of Engineers, the Department of Interior—they could jerk Kingsbury around until he died of old age.

"Look at the big picture," Skink said. With a tin fork he cleaned out the insides of the turtle shell. The wind was dying quickly, and the rain was turning soft on the leaves. The clouds broke out west, revealing raspberry patches of summer sunset. The coolness disappeared and the air turned muggy again.

Skink put down the fry pan and wiped his mouth on the sleeve of his rainsuit. "It's beautiful out here," he remarked. "That squall felt damn good."

"It might be too late," Joe Winder said. "Hell, they've started clearing the place."

"I know." The muscles in Skink's neck tightened. "They tore down an eagle nest the other day. Two little ones, dead. That's the kind of bastards we're talking about."

"Did you see—"

"I got there after the fact," Skink said. "Believe me, if I could've stopped them ... "

"What if we're too late?"

"Are you in or not? That's all I need to know."

"I'm in," said Winder. "Of course I am. I'm just not terribly optimistic."

Skink smiled his matinee smile, the one that had gotten him elected so many years before. "Lower your sights, boy," he said to Joe Winder. "I agree, justice is probably out of the question. But we can damn sure ruin their day."

He reached under the flap of his rainsuit, grunted, fumbled inside his clothing. Finally his hand came out holding a steel-blue semiautomatic pistol.

"Don't worry," he said. "I've got an extra one for you."

*

The woman who called herself Rachel Lark was receiving a vigorous massage when Francis X. Kingsbury phoned. She'd been expecting to hear from him ever since she'd read in the *Washington Post* about the theft of the blue-tongued mango voles in Florida. Her first thought, a natural one, was that Kingsbury would try to talk her into giving some of the money back. Rachel Lark braced for the worst as she sat up, naked, and told the masseur to give her the damn telephone.

On the other end, Kingsbury said: "Is this my favorite redhead?"

"Forget it," said the woman who called herself Rachel Lark, though it was not her true name.

Kingsbury said, "Can you believe it, babe? My luck, the goddamn things get swiped."

"I've already spent the money," Rachel Lark said, "and even if I didn't, a deal's a deal."

Instead of protesting, Kingsbury said, "Same here. I spent mine, too."

"Then it's a social call, is it?"

"Not exactly. Are you alone, babe?"

"Me and a nice young man named Sven."

The image gave Kingsbury a tingle. Rachel was an attractive woman, a bit on the heavy side, but a very hot dresser. They had met years before in the lobby of a prosecutor's office in Camden, where both of them were waiting to cut deals allowing them to avert unpleasant prison terms. Frankie King had chosen to drop the dime on the Zubonis, while the woman who now called herself Rachel Lark (it was Sarah Hunt at that time) was preparing to squeal on an ex-boyfriend who had illegally imported four hundred pounds of elephant ivory. In the lobby that day, the two informants had amiably traded tales about life on the lam. Later they'd exchanged phone numbers and a complete list of aliases, and promised to keep in touch.

211

Rachel's specialty was wildlife, and Kingsbury phoned her soon after opening the Amazing Kingdom of Thrills. Before then, he had never heard of the Endangered Species Act, never dreamed that an obscure agency of the federal government would casually fork over two hundred thousand dollars in grant money for the purpose of preserving a couple of lousy rodents. Rachel Lark had offered to provide the animals and the documentation, and Kingsbury was so intrigued by the plan—not just the dough, but the radiant publicity for the Amazing Kingdom—that he didn't bother to inquire if the blue-tongued mango voles were real.

The government check had arrived on time, they'd split it fifty-fifty and that was that. Francis Kingsbury paid no further attention to the creatures until customers started noticing that the voles' tongues were no longer very blue. Once children openly began grilling the Amazing Kingdom tour guides about how the animals got their name, Kingsbury ordered Pedro Luz to get some food coloring and touch the damn things up. Unfortunately, Pedro had neither the patience nor the gentle touch required to be an animal handler, and one of the voles—the female—was crushed accidentally during a tongue-painting session. Afraid for his job, Pedro Luz had told no one of the mishap. To replace the deceased vole, he had purchased a dwarf hamster for nine dollars from a pet store in Perrine. After minor modifications, the hamster had fooled both the customers and the male vole, which repeatedly attempted to mount its chubby new companion. Not only had the hamster rejected these advances, it had counter-attacked with such ferocity that Pedro Luz had been forced to hire a night security guard to prevent a bloodbath.

Matters were further complicated by the appearance of an ill-mannered pinhead from U.S. Fish and Wildlife, who had barged into the theme park and demanded follow-up data from the "project manager." Of course there was no such person because there was no project to manage; research consisted basically of making sure that the rodents were still breathing every morning before the gates were opened. With the feds suddenly asking questions, Charles Chelsea had quietly put out an all-points bulletin for a legitimate biologist—a recruiting effort that eventually induced Dr. Will Koocher to come to the Amazing Kingdom of Thrills.

Kingsbury decided not to burden Rachel Lark with the details of the doctor's grisly demise; it was irrelevant to the purpose of his call.

"Forget the money," Kingsbury told her.

"I must be hearing things."

"No, I mean it."

"Then what do you want?"

"More voles."

"You're joking."

"My customers, hell, they go nuts for the damn things. Now I got spin-offs, merchandise—a major warehouse situation, if you follow me."

"Sorry," Rachel Lark said, "it was a one-time deal." She'd pulled off the endangered-species racket on two other occasions—once for a small Midwestern zoo, and once for a disreputable reptile farm in South Carolina. Neither deal made as much money as the mango-vole scam, but neither had wound up in the headlines of the *Washington Post*, either.

Kingsbury said, "Look, I know there's no more mango voles—"

"Hey, sport, there never *were* any mango voles."

"So what you're saying, we defrauded the government."

"God, you're quick."

"I'm wondering," said Kingsbury, "those fucking furballs I paid for—what were they? Just out of curiosity."

Rachel Lark said, "Give me some credit, Frankie. They were voles. *Microtus pitymys.* Common pine voles."

"Not endangered?"

"There's billions of the darn things."

It figures, Kingsbury thought. The blue tongues were a neat touch. "So get me some more," he said. "We'll call 'em something else—banana voles or whatever. The name's not important, long as they're cute."

The woman who called herself Rachel Lark said: "Look, I can get you other animals—rare, not endangered—but my advice is to stay away from the feds for a while. You put in for another big grant, it's a swell way to get audited."

Again Kingsbury agreed without objection. "So what else have you got, I mean, in the way of a species?"

"Lizards are your best bet." Rachel Lark stretched on her belly and motioned the masseur, whose real name was Ray, to do her spine.

"Christ on a Harley, who wants goddamn lizards!" Kingsbury cringed at the idea; he had been thinking more along the lines of a panda or a koala bear. "I need something, you know, soft and furry and all that. Something the kiddies'll want to take home."

Rachel Lark explained that the Florida Keys were home to a very limited number of native mammals, and the sudden discovery of a new species (so soon after the mango-vole announcement) would attract more scientific scrutiny than the Amazing Kingdom could withstand.

"You're saying, I take it, forget about pandas."

"Frank, they'd die of heatstroke in about five minutes."

Exasperated, Kingsbury said, "I got problems down here you wouldn't believe." He nearly told her about the blackmailing burglars.

"A new lizard you can get away with," she said, "especially in the tropics."

"Rachel, what'd I just say? Fuck the lizards. I can't market lizards."

Rachel Lark moaned blissfully as the masseur kneaded the muscles of her neck. "My advice," she said into the phone, "is stay away from mammals and birds—it's too risky. Insects are another story. Dozens of species of insects are discovered every year. Grasshoppers, doodlebugs, you name it."

There was a grumpy pause on the other end. Finally, Francis X. Kingsbury said, "Getting back to the lizards. I mean, for the sake of argument . . . "

"They're very colorful," said the woman who called herself Rachel Lark.

"Ugly is out of the question," Kingsbury stated firmly. "Ugly scares the kiddies."

"Not all reptiles are ugly, Frankie. In fact, some are very beautiful."

"All right," he said. "See what you can do."

The woman who called herself Rachel Lark hung up the phone and closed her eyes. When she awoke, the masseur was gone and the man from Singapore was knocking on the door. In one hand was a small bouquet of yellow roses, and in the other was a tan briefcase holding a large down payment for a shipment of rare albino scorpions. Real ones.

Eighteen

On the morning of July 23, a semi-tractor truck leaving North Key Largo lost its brakes on the Card Sound Bridge. The truck plowed through the tollbooth, jackknifed and over-turned, blocking both lanes of traffic and effectively severing the northern arm of the island from the Florida mainland. The gelatinous contents of the container were strewn for ninety-five yards along the road, and within minutes the milky-blue sky filled with turkey buzzards—hundreds of them, wheeling counterclockwise lower and lower; only the noisy throng of gawkers kept the hungry scavengers from landing on the crash site. The first policeman to arrive was Highway Patrol Trooper Jim Tile, who nearly flipped his Crown Victoria cruiser when he tried to stop on the freshly slickened pavement. The trooper tugged the truck driver from the wreckage and, while splinting the man's arm, demanded to know what godforsaken cargo he'd been hauling.

"A dead whale," moaned the driver, "and that's all I'm saying."

Charles Chelsea was summoned to Francis X. Kingsbury's office at the unholy hour of seven in the morning. Kingsbury looked as if he hadn't slept since Easter. He asked Chelsea how long it would take to get the TV stations out to the Amazing Kingdom of Thrills.

"Two hours," Chelsea said confidently.

"Do it." Kingsbury blew his nose. "On the horn, now."

"What's the occasion, if I might ask."

Kingsbury held up five fingers. "Today's the big day. Our five-millionth visitor. Arrange something, a fucking parade, I don't care."

Charles Chelsea felt his stomach yaw. "Five million visitors," he said. "Sir, I didn't realize we'd reached that milestone."

"We haven't." Kingsbury hacked ferociously into a monogrammed handkerchief. "Damn this hay fever, I think it's the mangroves. Every morning my head's fulla snot." He pushed a copy of the *Wall Street Journal* at Chelsea. A column on the front page announced that Walt Disney World was expanding its empire to build a mammoth retail shopping center, one of the largest in the Southeastern United States.

"See, we can't just sit here," Kingsbury said. "Got to come back strong. Big media counterpunch."

Chelsea skimmed the *Journal* article and laid it on his lap. Tentatively he said, "It's hard to compete with something like this. I mean, it goes so far beyond the realm of a family theme park—"

"Bullshit," said Kingsbury. "The Miami-Lauderdale TV market is—what, three times the size of Orlando. Plus CNN, don't they have a bureau down here?" Kingsbury spun his chair and gazed out the window. "Hell, that new dolphin I bought—can't you work him into the piece? Say he rescued somebody who fell in the tank. A pregnant lady or maybe an orphan. Rescued them from drowning—that's your story! 'Miracle Dolphin Saves Drowning Orphan.'"

"I don't know if that's such a good idea," said Chelsea, though inwardly he had to admit it would have been one helluva headline.

"This celebration, make it for noon," Kingsbury said. "Whoever comes through the turnstiles, strike up the band. But make sure it's a tourist, no goddamn locals. Number five million, okay? In giant letters."

His gut tightening, Chelsea said, "Sir, it might be wiser to go with two million. It's closer to the real number . . . just in case somebody makes an issue of it."

"No, two is—chickenshit, really. Five's better. And the parade, too, I'm serious." Kingsbury stood up. He was dressed for golf. "A parade, that's good video," he said. "Plenty of time to get it for the six-o'clock news. That's our best demographic, am I right? Fucking kids, they don't watch the eleven."

Chelsea nodded. "What do we give the winner? Mr. Five Million, I mean."

"A car, Jesus Christ." Kingsbury looked at him as if he were an idiot. A few years earlier, Disney World had given away an automobile every day for an entire summer. Kingsbury had never gotten over it. "Make it a Corvette," he told Chelsea.

"All right, but you're looking at forty thousand dollars. Maybe more."

Kingsbury extended his lower lip so far that it seemed to touch his nose; for a moment he wore the pensive look of a caged orangutan. "Forty grand," he repeated quietly. "That's brand new, I suppose."

"When you give one away, yes. Ordinarily the cars should be new."

"Unless they're classics." Kingsbury winked. "Make it a classic. Say, a 1964 Ford Falcon. You don't see many of those babies."

"Sure don't."

"A Falcon convertible, geez, we could probably pick one up for twenty-five hundred."

"Probably," agreed Chelsea, not even pretending enthusiasm.

"Well, move on it." Francis X. Kingsbury thumbed him out of the office. "And tell Pedro, get his ass in here."

Pedro Luz was in the executive gym, bench-pressing a bottle of stanozolol tablets. He was letting the tiny pink pills drop one by one into his mouth.

A man named Churrito, lounging on a Nautilus, said: "Hiss very bad for liver."

"Very good for muscles," said Pedro Luz, mimicking the accent.

Churrito was his latest hire to the security squad at the Amazing Kingdom of Thrills. He had accompanied Pedro Luz on his mission to Miami, but had declined to participate in the beating. Pedro Luz was still miffed about what had happened—the old lady chomping off the top joint of his right index finger.

"You're useless," he had told Churrito afterward.

"I am a soldier," Churrito had replied. "I dun hit no wooman."

Unlike the other security guards hired by Pedro Luz, Churrito had not been a crooked cop. He was a Nicaraguan *contra* who had moved to Florida when things were bleak, and had not gotten around to moving back. While Churrito was pleased at the prospect of democracy taking seed in his homeland, he suspected that true economic prosperity was many years away. Elections notwithstanding, Churrito's buddies were still stuck in the border hills, frying green bananas and dynamiting the rivers for fish. Meanwhile his uncle, formerly a sergeant in Somoza's National Guard, now lived with a twenty-two-year-old stewardess in a high-rise condo on Key Biscayne. To Churrito, this seemed like a pretty good advertisement for staying right where he was.

Pedro Luz had hired him because he looked mean, and because he'd said he had killed people.

"*Comunistas*," Churrito had specified, that night at the old lady's apartment. "I only kill commoonists. And I dun hit no wooman."

And now here he was, lecturing Pedro Luz about the perils of anabolic steroids.

"Make you face like balloon."

"Shut up," said Pedro Luz. He was wondering if the hospital in Key Largo would sell him extra bags of dextrose water for the IV. Grind up the stanozolols, drop them in the mix and everything would be fine again.

"Make you bulls shrink, too."

"That's enough," Pedro Luz said.

Churrito held up two fingers. "Dis big. Like BBs."

"Quiet," said Pedro Luz, "or I call a friend a mine at INS." He couldn't decide whether to fire the guy or beat him up. He knew which would give more pleasure.

"They got, like, three flights a day to Managua," he said to Churrito. "You getting homesick?"

The Nicaraguan grimaced.

"I didn't think so," said Pedro Luz. "So shut up about my medicines."

Charles Chelsea appeared at the foot of the weight bench. He had never seen Pedro Luz without a shirt, and couldn't conceal his awe at the freakish physique—the hairless bronze trunk of a chest, cantaloupe biceps, veins as thick as a garden hose. Chelsea didn't recognize the other fellow—shorter and sinewy, with skin the color of nutmeg.

"I'm working out," said Pedro Luz.

"Mr. Kingsbury needs to see you."

"Who ees that?" Churrito said.

Pedro Luz sat up. "That be the boss."

"Right away," said Charles Chelsea.

"Can I go?" asked Churrito. He didn't want to miss an opportunity to meet the boss; according to his uncle, that's what success in America was all about. Kissing ass.

"I'm sorry," Chelsea said, "but Mr. Kingsbury wants to see Chief Luz alone."

"Yeah," said Pedro Luz. As he rolled off the bench, he made a point of clipping Churrito with a casual forearm. Churrito didn't move, didn't make a sound. His eyes grew very small and he stared at Pedro Luz until Pedro Luz spun away, pretending to hunt for his sweatshirt.

Churrito pointed at the scarlet blemishes on Pedro Luz's shoulder blades and said: "You all broke out, man."

"Shut up before I yank your nuts off."

Backing away, Charles Chelsea thought: Where do they get these guys?

Francis X. Kingsbury offered a Bloody Mary to Pedro Luz, who guzzled it like Gatorade.

"So, Pedro, the job's going all right?"

The security chief was startled at Kingsbury's genial tone. A ration of shit was what he'd expected; the old man had been livid since the burglary of his private office. The crime had utterly baffled Pedro Luz, who hadn't the first notion of how to solve it. He had hoped that the mission to Eagle Ridge would absolve him.

"I took care of that other problem," he announced to Kingsbury.

"Fine. Excellent." Kingsbury was swiveling back and forth in his chair. He didn't look so good: nervous, ragged, droopy-eyed, his fancy golf shirt all wrinkled. Pedro Luz wondered if the old fart was doing coke. The very idea was downright hilarious.

"She won't bother you no more," he said to Kingsbury.

"You made it look, what—like muggers? Crack fiends?"

"Sure, that's what the cops would think. If she calls them, which I don't think she will. I made it clear what could happen."

"Fine. Excellent." Kingsbury propped his elbows on the

desk in a way that offered Pedro Luz an unobstructed view of the lurid mouse tattoo.

"Two things—" Kingsbury paused when he spotted the bandage on Pedro Luz's finger.

"Hangnail," said the security chief.

"Whatever," Kingsbury said. "Two things—some assholes, the guys who stole my files, they're blackmailing me. You know, shaking me down."

Pedro Luz asked how much money he had promised them.

"Never mind," Kingsbury replied. "Five grand so far is what I paid. But the files, see, I can't just blow 'em off. I need the files."

"Who are these men?"

Francis Kingsbury threw up his hands. "That's the thing—just ordinary shitheads. White trash. I can't fucking believe it."

Pedro Luz had never understood the concept of white trash, or how it differed from black trash or Hispanic trash or any other kind of criminal dirtbag. He said, "You want the files but you don't want to pay."

"Exacto!" said Kingsbury. "In fact, the five grand—I wouldn't mind getting it back."

Pedro Luz laughed sharply. Months go by and the job's a snooze—now suddenly all this dirty work. Oh well, Pedro thought, it beats painting rat tongues. He hadn't shed a tear when the mango voles were stolen.

Kingsbury was saying, "The other thing, I fired a guy from Publicity."

"Yeah?" Watching that damn tattoo, it was driving Pedro silly. Minnie on her knees, polishing Mickey's knob—whoever did the drawing was damn good, almost Disney caliber.

"You need to go see this guy I fired," Kingsbury was saying. "Find out some things."

Pedro Luz asked what kind of things.

Kingsbury moved his lips around, like a camel getting ready to spit. Eventually he said, "The problem we had before? This is worse, okay. The guy I mentioned, we're talking major pain in the rectum."

"Okay."

"As long as he worked for us, we had some control. On the outside, hell, he's a major pain. I just got a feeling."

Pedro Luz gave him a thumbs-up. "Don't worry."

"Carefully," Kingsbury added. "Same as before would be excellent. Except no dead whales this time."

God, thought Pedro Luz, what a fuckup *that* was.

"Do I know him?" he asked Kingsbury.

"From Publicity. Joe Winder's his name."

"Oh." Pedro Luz perked up. Winder was the smartass who'd been hassling him about Dr. Koocher. The same guy he'd sent Angel and Big Paulie to teach a lesson, only something went sour and Angel ended up dead and Paulie must've took off. Next thing Pedro knows, here's this smartass Winder snooping around the animal lab in the middle of the night.

Mr. X. was right about the guy. Now that he was fired, he might go hog-wild. Start talking crazy shit all over the place.

"You look inspired," Kingsbury said.

Pedro Luz smiled crookedly. "Let's just say I got some ideas."

When Molly McNamara opened her eyes, she was surprised to see Bud Schwartz and Danny Pogue at her bedside.

"I thought you boys would be long gone."

"No way," said Danny Pogue. His eyes were large and intent, like a retriever's. His chin was in his hands, and he was sitting very close to the bed. He patted Molly's brow with a damp washcloth.

"Thank you," she said. "I'm very thirsty."

Danny Pogue bolted to the kitchen to get her a glass of

ginger ale. Bud Schwartz took a step closer. He said, "What happened? Can you remember anything?"

"My glasses," she said, pointing to the nightstand.

"They got busted," said Bud Schwartz. "I used some Scotch tape on the nose part."

Molly McNamara put them on, and said, "Two men. Only one did the hitting."

"Why? What'd they want—money?"

Molly shook her head slowly. Danny Pogue came back with the ginger ale, and she took two small sips. "Thank you," she said. "No, they didn't want money."

Danny Pogue said, "Who?"

"The men who came. They said it was a warning."

"Oh Christ."

"It's none of your concern," said Molly.

Grimly Bud Schwartz said, "They were after the files."

"No. They never mentioned that."

Bud Schwartz was relieved; he had worried that Francis X. Kingsbury had somehow identified them, connected them to Molly and sent goons to avenge the burglary. It was an irrational fear, he knew, because even the powerful Kingsbury couldn't have done it so quickly after their blackmail visit.

Still, it was discouraging to see how they had battered Molly McNamara. These were extremely bad men, and Bud Schwartz doubted they would have allowed him and Danny Pogue to survive the encounter.

"I think we ought to get out of here," he said to Molly. "Take you back to the big house."

"That's a sensible plan," Molly agreed, "but you boys don't have to stay."

"Like hell," Danny Pogue declared. "Look at you, all busted up. You'll be needing some help."

"You got some bad bruises," agreed Bud Schwartz. "Your

224

right knee's twisted, too, but I don't think it's broke. Plus they knocked out a couple teeth."

Molly ran her tongue around her gums and said, "I was the only one in this building who still had their own."

Danny Pogue paced with a limp. "I wanted to call an ambulance or somebody, only Bud said we better not."

Molly said that was a smart decision, considering what the three of them had been up to lately. She removed the damp cloth from her forehead and folded it on the nightstand.

Danny Pogue wanted to know all about the attackers—how big they were, what they looked like. "I bet they was niggers," he said.

Molly raised herself off the pillow, cocked her arm and slapped him across the face. Incredulous, Danny Pogue rubbed his cheek.

She said, "Don't you ever again use that word in my presence."

"Christ, I didn't mean nothin'."

"Well, it just so happens these men were white. White Hispanic males. The one who beat me up was very large and muscular."

"My question," said Bud Schwartz, "is how they slipped past that crack security guard. What's his name, Andrews, the ace with the flashlight."

Molly said: "You won't believe it. The big one had a badge. A police badge, City of Miami."

"Wonderful," Bud Schwartz said.

"I saw it myself," Molly said. "Why do you think I even opened the door? He said they were plainclothes detectives. Once they had me down, I couldn't get to my purse."

Danny Pogue looked at his partner with the usual mix of confusion and concern. Bud Schwartz said, "It sounds like some serious shitkickers. You say they were Cubans?"

"Hispanics," Molly said.

"Did they speak American?" asked Danny Pogue.

"The big one did all the talking, and his English was quite competent. Especially his use of four-letter slang."

Danny Pogue rocked on his good leg, and slammed a fist against the wall. "I'll murder the sumbitch!"

"Sure you will," said his partner. "You're a killer and I'm the next quarterback for the Dolphins."

"I mean it, Bud. Look what he done to her."

"I see, believe me." Bud Schwartz gave Molly McNamara two Percodans and said it would help her sleep. She swallowed the pills in one gulp and thanked the burglars once again. "It's very kind of you to look after me," she said.

"Only till you're feeling better," said Bud Schwartz. "We got some business that requires our full attention."

"Of course, I understand."

"We made five grand tonight!" said Danny Pogue. Quickly he withered under his partner's glare.

"Five thousand is very good," Molly said. "Add the money I still owe you, and that's quite a handsome nest egg." She slid deeper into the sheets, and pulled the blanket to her chin.

"Get some rest," Bud Schwartz said. "We'll take you to the house in the morning."

"Yeah, get some sleep." Danny Pogue gazed at her dolorously. Bud Schwartz wondered if he was about to cry.

"Bud?" Molly spoke in a fog.

"Yeah."

"Did you boys happen to find a piece of finger on the floor?"

"No," said Bud Schwartz. "Why?"

"Would you check in the kitchen, please?"

"No problem." He wondered how the pills could mess her up so quickly. "You mean, like a human finger?"

But Molly's eyes were already closed.

Nineteen

Charles Chelsea worked feverishly all morning. By half past eleven the parade was organized. The gateway to the Amazing Kingdom of Thrills was festooned with multicolored streamers and hundreds of Mylar balloons. Cheerleaders practiced cartwheels over the turnstiles while the Tavernier High School band rehearsed the theme from *Exodus*. Several of the most popular animal characters—Robbie Raccoon, Petey Possum and Barney the Bison—were summoned from desultory lunch breaks in The Catacombs to greet and be photographed with the big winner. Above a hastily constructed stage, a billowy hand-painted banner welcomed "OUR FIVE-MILLIONTH SPECIAL GUEST!!!"

And there, parked in the courtyard, was a newly restored 1966 Chevrolet Corvair, one of Detroit's most venerated deathtraps. Charles Chelsea had been unable to locate a mint condition Falcon, and the vintage Mustangs were beyond Francis Kingsbury's budget. The Corvair was Chelsea's next choice as the giveaway car because it was a genuine curiosity, and because it was cheap. The one purchased by Chelsea had been rear-ended by a dairy tanker in 1972, and the resulting explosion had wiped out a quartet of home-appliance sales-men. The rebuilt Corvair was seven inches shorter from bumper to bumper than the day it had rolled off the assembly line, but Charles Chelsea was certain no one would notice. Two extra coats of cherry paint and the Corvair shouted classic. It was exactly the sort of campy junk-mobile that some dumb Yuppie would love.

The scene was set for the coronation of the alleged five-millionth visitor to the Amazing Kingdom. The only thing missing from the festive tableau, Chelsea noted lugubriously, was customers. The park had opened more than two hours ago, yet not a single carload of tourists had arrived. The trams were empty, the cash registers mute; no one had passed through the ticket gates. Chelsea couldn't understand it—the place had not experienced such a catastrophic attendance drop since salmonella had felled a visiting contingent of Rotarians at Sally's Cimarron Saloon.

Chelsea prayed with all his heart that some tourists would show up before the television vans. He did not know, and could not have envisioned, that an eighteen-wheeler loaded with the decomposing remains of Orky the Whale had flipped on Card Sound Road and paralyzed all traffic heading toward the Amazing Kingdom. The highway patrol diligently had set up a roadblock at the junction near Florida City, where troopers were advising all buses, campers and rental cars filled with Francis X. Kingsbury's customers to turn around and return to Miami. The beleaguered troopers did not consider it their sworn duty to educate the tourists about an alternate route to the Amazing Kingdom—taking Highway 1 south past Jewfish Creek, then backtracking up County Road 905 to the park. The feeling among the troopers (based on years of experience) was that no matter how simple and explicit they made the directions, many of the tourists would manage to get lost, run out of gas and become the victims of some nasty roadside crime. A more sensible option was simply to tell them to go back, there'd been a bad accident.

Consequently Charles Chelsea stood in eery solitude on the makeshift stage, the cheery banner flapping over his head as he stared at the empty parking lot and wondered how in the hell he would break the news to Francis X. Kingsbury. Today there would be no celebration, no parade, no five-millionth visitor. There were no visitors at all.

Joe Winder felt like a damn redneck—he hadn't been to a firing range in ten or twelve years, and that was to shoot his father's revolver, an old Smith. The gun Skink had given him was a thin foreign-made semiautomatic. It didn't have much weight, but Skink promised it would do the job, whatever job needed doing. Winder had decided to keep it for ornamental purposes. It lay under the front seat as he drove south on County Road 905.

He stopped at a pay phone, dialed the sex-talk number and billed it to his home. Miriam answered and started in with a new routine, something about riding bareback on a pony. When Winder broke in and asked for Nina, Miriam told him she wasn't there.

"Tell her to call me, please."

"Hokay, Joe."

"On second thought, never mind."

"Whatever chew say. You like the horsey business?"

"Yes, Miriam, it's very good."

"Nina wrote it. Want me do the end?"

"No thank you."

"Is hot stuff, Joe. Cheese got some mansionation."

"She sure does."

Joe Winder drove until he reached the Falcon Trace construction site. He parked on the side of the road and watched

229

a pair of mustard-colored bulldozers plow a fresh section of hammock, creating a tangled knoll of uprooted tamarinds, buttonwoods, pigeon plums and rouge-berry. Each day a few more acres were being destroyed in the name of championship golf.

A team of surveyors worked the distant end of the property, near Winder's fishing spot. He assumed they were marking off the lots where the most expensive homes would be built—the more ocean frontage, the higher the price. This was how Francis X. Kingsbury would make his money—the golf course itself was never meant to profit; it was a real-estate tease, plain and simple. The links would be pieced together in the middle of the development on whatever parcels couldn't be peddled as residential waterfront. Soon, Winder knew, they'd start blasting with dynamite to dig fairway lakes in the ancient reef rock.

He saw that both bulldozers had stopped, and that the drivers had gotten down from the cabs to look at something in the trees. Joe Winder stepped out of the car and started running. He remembered what Skink had told him about the baby eagles. He shouted at the men and saw them turn. One folded his arms and slouched against his dozer.

Winder covered the two hundred yards in a minute. When he reached the men, he was panting too hard to speak.

One of them said: "What's your problem?"

Winder flashed his Amazing Kingdom identification badge, which he had purposely neglected to turn in upon termination of employment. The lazy bulldozer driver, the one leaning against his machine, studied the badge and began to laugh. "What the hell is this?"

When Joe Winder caught his breath, he said: "I work for Mr. Kingsbury. He owns this land."

"Ain't the name on the permit. The permit says Ramex Global."

The other driver spoke up: "Anyway, who gives a shit about some goddamn wolves?"

"Yeah," the first driver said. "Bury 'em."

"No," said Joe Winder. They weren't wolves, they were gray foxes—six of them, no larger than kittens. The bulldozers had uprooted the den tree. Half-blind, the little ones were crawling all over each other, squeaking and yapping in toothless panic.

Winder said, "If we leave them alone, the mother will probably come back."

"What is this, 'Wild Kingdom'?"

"At least help me move them out of the way."

"Forget it," the smartass driver said. "I ain't in the mood for rabies. Come on, Bobby, let's roll it."

The men climbed back in the dozers and seized the gear sticks. Instinctively Joe Winder positioned himself between the large machines and the baby foxes. The drivers began to holler and curse. The smartass lowered the blade of his bulldozer and inched forward, pushing a ridge of moist dirt over the tops of Joe Winder's shoes. The driver grinned and whooped at his own cleverness until he noticed the gun pointed up at his head.

He quickly turned off the engine and raised his hands. The other driver did the same. In a scratchy whine he said, "Geez, what's your problem?"

Winder held the semiautomatic steady. He was surprised at how natural it felt. He said, "Is this what it takes to have a civilized conversation with you shitheads?"

Quickly he checked over his shoulder to make sure the kits hadn't crawled from the den. The outlandishness of the situation was apparent, but he'd committed himself to melodrama. With the gun on display, he was already deep into felony territory.

The smartass driver apologized profusely for burying Winder's shoes. "I'll buy you some new ones," he offered.

"Oh, that's not necessary." Winder yearned to shoot the bulldozers but he didn't know where to begin; the heavy steel thoraxes looked impervious to cannon fire.

The lazy driver said: "You want us to get down?"

"Not just yet," said Joe Winder, "I'm thinking."

"Hey, there's no need to shoot. Jut tell us what the hell you want."

"I want you to help me fuck up these machines."

It was nine o'clock when the knock came. Joe Winder was sitting in the dark on the floor of the apartment. He had the clip out of the gun, and the bullets out of the clip. A full load, too, sixteen rounds; he had lined up the little rascals side by side on a windowsill, a neat row of identical copper-headed soldiers.

The knocking wouldn't go away. Winder picked up the empty gun. He went to the door and peeked out of the peep-hole. He saw an orb of glistening blond; not Nina-style blond, this was lighter. When the woman turned around, Winder flung open the door and pulled her inside.

In the darkness Carrie Lanier took a deep breath and said: "I hope that's you."

"It's me," Joe Winder said.

"Was that a gun I saw?"

"I'm afraid so. My situation has taken a turn for the worse." Carrie said, "That's why I came."

Winder led her back to the living room, where they sat between two large cardboard boxes. The only light was the amber glow from the stereo receiver; Carrie Lanier could barely hear the music from the speakers.

"Where's your girlfriend?" she asked.

"Moved out."

"I'm sorry." She paused; then, peering at him: "Is that a beret?"

"Panties," Joe Winder said. "Can you believe it—that's all she left me. Cheap ones, too. The mail-order crap she sold over the phone." He pulled the underwear off his head to show her the shoddy stitching.

"You've had a rough time," said Carrie Lanier. "I didn't know she'd moved out."

"Yeah, well, I'm doing just fine. Adjusting beautifully to the single life. Sitting here in a dark apartment with a gun in my lap and underpants on my head."

Carrie squeezed his arm. "Joe, are you on drugs?"

"Nope," he said. "Pretty amazing, isn't it?"

"I think you should come home with me."

"Why?"

"Because bad things will happen if you stay here."

"Ah." Winder scooped the bullets off the windowsill and fed them into the gun clip. "You must be talking about Pedro Luz."

"It's all over the Magic Kingdom," Carrie said, "about the reasons you were fired."

"Mr. X doesn't kill all his former employees, does he?"

She leaned closer. "It's no joke. The word is, you're number one on Pedro's list."

"So that's the word."

"Joe, I get around. Spend the day in a raccoon suit, people forget there's a real person inside. I might as well be invisible—the stuff I pick up, you wouldn't believe."

"The spy wore a tail! And now you hear Pedro's irritated."

"I got it from two of the other guards on lunch break. They were doing blow behind the Magic Mansion."

Winder was struck by how wonderful Carrie looked, her eyes all serious in the amber light. Impulsively he kissed her on the cheek. "Don't worry about me," he said. "You can go home."

"You aren't listening."

233

"Yes, I—"

"No, you aren't." Her tone was one of motherly disapproval. "I warned you about this before. About sticking your nose where it doesn't belong."

"You did, yes."

"Last time you were lucky. You truly were."

"I suppose so." Joe Winder felt oppressively tired. Suddenly the handgun weighed a ton. He slid it across the carpet so forcefully that it banged into the baseboard of the opposite wall.

Carrie Lanier told him to hurry and pack some clothes.

"I can't leave," he said. "Nina might call."

"Joe, it's not just Pedro you've got to worry about. It's the police."

Winder's chin dropped to his chest. "Already?"

"Mr. X swore out a warrant this afternoon," Carrie said. "I heard it from his secretary."

Francis Kingsbury's secretary was a regular visitor to The Catacombs, where she was conducting an athletic love affair with the actor who portrayed Bartholomew, the most shy and bookish of Uncle Ely's Elves.

Carrie said, "She mentioned something about destruction of private property."

"There was an incident," Joe Winder acknowledged, "but no shots were fired."

Under his supervision, the two bulldozers had torn down the three-dimensional billboard that proclaimed the future home of the Falcon Trace Golf and Country Club. The bulldozers also had demolished the air-conditioned double-wide trailer (complete with beer cooler and billiard table) that served as an on-site office for the construction company. They had even wrecked the Port-O-Lets, trapping one of the foremen with his anniversary issue of *Hustler* magazine.

Afterwards Joe Winder had encouraged the bulldozer

operators to remove their clothing, which he'd wadded in the neck of the gas tanks. Then—after borrowing the smartass driver's cigarette lighter—Joe Winder had suggested that the men aim their powerful machines toward the Atlantic Ocean, engage the forward gear and swiftly exit the cabs. Later he had proposed a friendly wager on which of the dozers would blow first.

"They spotted the flames all the way from Homestead Air Base," Carrie Lanier reported. "Channel 7 showed up in a helicopter, so Kingsbury made Chelsea write up a press release."

"A freak construction accident, no doubt."

"Good guess. I've got a Xerox in my purse."

"No thanks." Joe Winder wasn't in the mood for Chelsea's golden lies. He stood up and stretched; joints and sockets popped in protest. Lights began to flash blue, green and red on the bare wall, and Winder assumed it was fatigue playing tricks with his vision.

He squinted strenuously, and the lights disappeared. When he opened his eyes, the lights were still strobing. "Shit, here we go." Winder went to the window and peeked through the curtain.

"How many?" Carrie asked.

"Two cops, one car."

"Is there another way out?"

"Sure," he said.

They heard the tired footsteps on the front walk, the deep murmur of conversation, the crinkle of paper. In the crack beneath the door they saw the yellow flicker of flashlight as the policemen examined the warrant one more time, probably double-checking the address.

Winder picked up the semiautomatic and arranged it in his waistband. Carrie Lanier followed him to the kitchen, where they slipped out the back door just as the cops got serious with

235

their knocking. Once outside, in the pale blue moonlight, she deftly grabbed the gun from Joe Winder's trousers and put it in her handbag.

"In case you go stupid on me," she whispered. "No chance of that," he said. "None at all."

Twenty

A thin coil of copper dangled by a string from Carrie Lanier's rearview mirror. Joe Winder asked if it was some type of hieroglyphic emblem.

"It's an IUD," said Carrie, without taking her eyes off the road. "A reminder of my ex-husband."

"I like it." Winder tried to beef up the compliment. "It's better than fuzzy dice."

"He wanted to have babies," Carrie explained, shooting into the left lane and passing a cement truck. "A baby boy and a baby girl. House with a white picket fence and a big backyard. Snapper riding mower. Golden retriever named Champ. He had it all planned."

Joe Winder said, "Sounds pretty good, except for the golden. Give me a Lab any day."

"Well, he wanted to get me pregnant," Carrie went on. "Every night, it was like a big routine. So I'd say sure, Roddy, whatever you want, let's make a baby. I never told him about wearing the loop. And every month he'd want to know. 'Did we do it, sweetie? Is there a zygote?' And I'd say 'Sorry, honey, guess we'd better try harder.'"

"Roddy was his name? That's a bad sign right there."

"He was a screamer, all right."

"What happened?" Winder asked. "Is he still around?"

"No, he's not." Carrie hit the intersection at Highway 1 without touching the brakes, and merged neatly into the northbound traffic. She said, "Roddy's up at Eglin doing a little time."

"Which means he's either a drug dealer or a crooked lawyer."

"Both," she said. "Last month he sent a Polaroid of him with a tennis trophy. He said he can't wait to get out and start trying for a family again."

"The boy's not well."

"It's all Oedipal, that's my theory." Carrie nodded at the IUD and said, "I keep it there to remind myself that you can't be too careful when it comes to men. Here's Roddy with his Stanford diploma and his fancy European car and his heavy downtown law firm, everything in the whole world going for him. Turns out he's nothing but a dipshit, and a dumb dipshit to boot."

Winder said she'd been smart to take precautions.

"Yeah, well, I had my career to consider." Carrie turned a corner into a trailer park, and coasted the car to the end of a narrow gravel lane. "Home sweet home," she said. "Be sure to lock your door. This is not a wonderful neighborhood."

Joe Winder said, "Why are you doing this for me?"

"I'm not sure. I'm really not." She tossed him the keys and asked him to get the raccoon costume from the trunk of the car.

Bud Schwartz and Danny Pogue helped Molly McNamara up the steps of the old house in South Miami. They eased her into the rocker in the living room, and opened the front windows to air the place out. Bud Schwartz's hand still throbbed from the gunshot wound, but his fingers seemed to be functioning.

Danny Pogue said, "Ain't it good to be home?"

"Indeed it is," said Molly. "Could you boys fix me some tea?"

Bud Schwartz looked hard at his partner. "I'll do it," said Danny Pogue. "It don't bother me." Cheerfully he hobbled toward the kitchen.

"He's not a bad young man," Molly McNamara said. "Neither of you are."

"Model citizens," said Bud Schwartz. "That's us."

He lowered himself into a walnut captain's chair but stood again quickly, as if the seat were hot. He'd forgotten about the damn thing in his pocket until it touched him in the right testicle. Irritably he removed it from his pants and placed it on an end table. He had wrapped it in a blue lace doily.

He said, "Can we do something with this, please?"

"There's a Mason jar in the cupboard over the stove," Molly said, "and some pickle juice in the refrigerator."

"You're kidding."

"This is important, Bud. It's evidence."

In the hall he passed Danny Pogue carrying a teapot on a silver tray. "You believe this shit?" Bud Schwartz said. He held up the doily.

"What now?"

"She wants me to pickle the goddamn thing!"

Danny Pogue made a squeamish face. "What for?" When he returned to the living room, Molly was rocking tranquilly in the chair. He poured the tea and said, "You must be feeling better."

"Better than I look." She drank carefully, watching Danny Pogue over the rim of the cup. In a tender voice she said: "You don't know what this means to me, the fact that you stayed to help."

"It wasn't just me. It was Bud, too."

"He's not a bad person," Molly McNamara allowed. "I suspect he's a man of principle, deep down."

Danny Pogue had never thought of his partner as a man of

239

principle, but maybe Molly had spotted something. While Bud was an incorrigible thief, he played by a strict set of rules. No guns, no violence, no hard drugs—Danny Pogue supposed that these could be called principles. He hoped that Molly recognized that he, too, had his limits—moral borders he would not cross. Later on, when she was asleep, he would make a list.

He said, "So what are you gonna do now? Stay at it?"

"To tell the truth, I'm not certain." She put down the teacup and dabbed her swollen lips with a napkin. "I've had some experts go over Kingsbury's files. Lawyers, accountants, people sympathetic to the cause. They made up a cashflow chart, ran the numbers up and down and sideways. They say it's all very interesting, these foreign companies, but it would probably take months for the IRS and Customs to sort it out; another year for an indictment. We simply don't have that kind of time."

"Shoot," said Danny Pogue. He hadn't said "shoot" since the third grade, but he'd been trying to clean up his language in Molly's presence.

"I'm a little discouraged," she went on. "I guess I'd gotten my hopes up prematurely."

Danny Pogue felt so lousy that he almost told her about the other files, about the blackmail scam that he and Bud Schwartz were running on the great Francis X. Kingsbury.

He said, "There's nothing we can do? Just let him go ahead and murder off them butterflies and snails?" Molly had given him a magazine clipping about the rare tropical snails of Key Largo.

She said, "I didn't say we're giving up—"

"Because we should talk to Bud. He'll think a something."

"Every day we lose precious time," Molly said. "Every day they're that much closer to pouring the concrete."

Danny Pogue nodded. "Let's talk to Bud. Bud's sharp as a tack about stuff like this—"

Molly stopped rocking and raised a hand. "I heard something, didn't you?"

From the kitchen came muffled percussions of a struggle—men grunting, something heavy hitting a wall, a jar breaking.

Danny Pogue was shaking when he stood up. The bum foot made him think twice about running.

"Hand me the purse," Molly said. "I'll need my gun."

But Danny Pogue was frozen to the pine floor. His eyelids fluttered and his arms stiffened at his side. All he could think was: *Somebody's killing Bud!*

"Danny, did you hear me? Get me my purse!"

A block of orange appeared in the hallway. It was a tall man in a bright rainsuit and a moldy-looking shower cap. He had a damp silvery beard and black wraparound sunglasses and something red fastened to his neck. The man carried Bud Schwartz in a casual way, one arm around the midsection. Bud Schwartz was limp, gasping, flushed in the face.

Danny Pogue's tongue was as dry as plaster when the stranger stepped out of the shadow.

"Oh, it's you," Molly McNamara said. "Now be careful, don't hurt that young man."

The stranger dropped Bud Schwartz butt-first on the pine and said, "I caught him putting somebody's fingertip in a Mason jar."

"I'm the one who told him to," said Molly. "Now, Governor, you just settle down."

"What happened to you?" the stranger demanded. "Who did this to you, Miss McNamara?"

He took off the sunglasses and glared accusingly at Danny Pogue, who emitted a pitiful hissing noise as he shook his head. Bud Schwartz, struggling to his feet, said: "It wasn't us, it was some damn Cuban."

"Tell me a name," said the stranger.

"I don't know," said Molly McNamara, "but I got a good bite out of him."

"The finger," Bud Schwartz explained, still gathering his breath.

The stranger knelt beside the rocking chair and gently examined the raw-looking cuts and bruises on Molly's face. "This is ... intolerable." He was whispering to himself and no one else. "This is barbarism."

Molly touched the visitor's arm and said, "I'll be all right. Really."

Bud Schwartz and Danny Pogue had seen men like this only in prison, and not many. Wild was the only way to describe the face ... wild and driven and fearless, but not necessarily insane. It would be foolish, perhaps even fatal, to assume the guy was spaced.

He turned to Bud Schwartz and said, "How about giving me that Cuban's nub."

"I dropped it on the floor." Bud Schwartz thought: Christ, he's *not* going to make me go pick it up, is he?

Danny Pogue said, "No sweat, I'll find it."

"No," said the man in the orange rainsuit. "I'll grab it on the way out." He squeezed Molly's hand and stood up. "Will you be all right?"

"Yes, they're taking good care of me."

The stranger nodded at Bud Schwartz, who couldn't help but notice that one of the man's eyes was slipping out of the socket. The man calmly reinserted it.

"I didn't mean to hurt you," he said to Bud Schwartz. "Well, actually, I *did* mean to hurt you."

Molly explained: "He didn't know you fellows were my guests, that's all."

"I'll be in touch," said the stranger. He kissed Molly on the cheek and said he would check on her in a day or two. Then he was gone.

Bud Schwartz waited until he heard the door slam. Then he said: "What the hell was that?"

242

"A friend," Molly replied. They had known each other a long time. She had worked as a volunteer in his gubernatorial campaign, whipping up both the senior-citizen vote and the environmental coalitions. Later, when he quit office and vanished, Molly was one of the few who knew what happened, and one of the few who understood. Over the years he had kept in touch in his own peculiar way—sometimes a spectral glimpse, sometimes a sensational entrance; jarring cameos that were as hair-raising as they were poignant.

"Guy's big," said Danny Pogue. "Geez, he looks like—did he do time? What's his story?"

"We don't want to know," Bud Schwartz said. "Am I right?"

"You're absolutely right," said Molly McNamara.

Shortly before midnight on July 23, Jim Tile received a radio call that an unknown individual was shooting at automobiles on Card Sound Road. The trooper told the dispatcher he was en route, and that he'd notify the Monroe County Sheriff's Office if he needed backups—which he knew he wouldn't.

The cars were lined up on the shoulder of the road a half-mile east of the big bridge. Jim Tile took inventory from the stickers on the bumpers: two Alamos, a Hertz, a National and an Avis. The rental firms had started putting bumper plates on all their automobiles, which served not only as advertisement but as a warning to local drivers that a disoriented tourist was nearby. On this night, though, the bright stickers had betrayed their unsuspecting drivers. Each of the vehicles bore a single .45-caliber bullet hole in the left-front fender panel.

Jim Tile knew exactly what had happened. He took brief statements from the motorists, who seemed agitated by the suggestion that anyone would fire at them simply because they were tourists. Jim Tile assured them that this sort of thing didn't happen every day. Then he called Homestead for tow trucks to get the three rental cars whose engine blocks had been mortally wounded by the sniper in the mangroves.

One of the drivers, a French-Canadian textile executive, used a cellular phone to call the Alamo desk at Miami International Airport and explain the situation. Soon new cars were on the way.

It took Jim Tile several hours to clear the scene. A pair of Monroe County deputies stopped by and helped search for shell casings until the mosquitoes drove them away. After the officers had fled, and after the tourists had motored north in a wary caravan of Thunderbirds, Skylarks and Zephyrs, Jim Tile got in his patrol car and mashed on the horn with both fists. Then he rolled up the windows, turned up the air conditioner and waited for his sad old friend to come out of the swamp.

"I'm sorry," Skink offered the trooper a stick of EDTIAR insect repellent.

"You promised to behave," said Jim Tile. "Now you've put me in a tough position."

"Had to blow off some steam," Skink said. "Anyway, I didn't hurt anybody." He took off his sunglasses and tinkered unabashedly with the fake eyeball. "Haven't you ever had days like this? Days when you just had to go out and shoot the shit out of something, didn't matter what?"

Jim Tile sighed. "Rental cars?"

"Why the hell not."

The tension dissolved into weary silence. The men had talked of such things before. When Clinton Tyree was the governor of Florida, Jim Tile had been his chief bodyguard—an unusually prestigious assignment for a black state trooper. After Clinton Tyree resigned, Jim Tile immediately lost his job on the elite security detail. The new governor, it was explained, felt more comfortable around peckerwoods. By the end of that fateful week, Jim Tile had found himself back on road patrol; Harney County, night shifts.

Over the years he had stayed close to Clinton Tyree, partly out of friendship, partly out of admiration and partly out of certitude that the man would need police assistance now and then, which he did. Whenever Skink got restless and moved his hermitage to deeper wilderness, Jim Tile would quietly put in for a transfer and move, too. This meant more rural two-lanes, more night duty and more ignorant mean-eyed crackers—but the trooper knew that his friend would have done the same for him, had fortunes been reversed. Besides, Jim Tile was confident of his own abilities and believed that one day he'd be in charge of the entire highway patrol—dishing out a few special night shifts himself.

Usually Skink kept to himself, except for the occasional public sighting when he dashed out of the pines to retrieve a fresh opossum or squirrel off the road. Once in a while, though, something triggered him in a tumultuous way and the results were highly visible. Standing on the crowded Fort Lauderdale beach, he'd once put four rounds into the belly of an inbound Eastern 727. Another time he'd crashed the Miss Florida pageant and tearfully heaved a dead baby manatee on stage to dramatize the results of waterfront development. It was fortunate, in such instances, that no one had recognized the hoary cyclopic madman as Clinton Tyree; it was even more fortunate that Jim Tile had been around to help the ex-governor slip away safely and collect what was left of his senses.

Now, sitting in the trooper's patrol car, Skink polished his glass eye with a bandanna and apologized for causing his friend so much inconvenience. "If you've got to arrest me," he said, "I'll understand."

"Wouldn't do a damn bit of good," said Jim Tile. "But I tell you what—I'd appreciate it if you'd let me know what's going on down here."

"The usual," Skink said. "The bad guys are kicking our collective ass."

"We got a dead body off the bridge, a guy named Angel Gaviria. You know about that, right?" The trooper didn't wait for an answer. "The coroner is saying suicide or accident, but I was there and I don't think it's either one. The deceased was a well-known scumbucket and they don't usually have the decency to kill themselves. Usually someone else does the honor."

"Jim, we live in troubled times."

"The other day I pulled over a blue Ford sedan doing eighty-six down the bridge. Turns out to be a Feeb."

"FBI?" Skink perked up. "All the way down here?"

"Hawkins was his name. He badges me, we get to chatting. Turns out he's working a case at the Amazing Kingdom. Something to do with militant bunny huggers and missing blue-tongued rats." Jim Tile gave a lazy laugh. "Now this is the FBI, interviewing elves and cowboys and fairy princesses. I don't suppose you can fill me in."

Skink was pleased that the feds had taken notice of events in North Key Largo. He said, "All I know is bits and pieces."

"Speaking of which, what can you tell me about killer whales? This morning a semi rolls over and I got stinking gobs of dead whale all over my nice clean blacktop. I'm talking tonnage."

Skink said, "That would explain the buzzard shit on this state vehicle." Secretly he wished he would have been there to witness the spectacle.

"You think it's funny?"

"I think," said Skink, "you should prepare for the worst."

Jim Tile took off his Stetson and lowered his face in front of the dashboard vents; the cool air felt good on his cheeks. A gumdrop-shaped sports car blew by doing ninety-plus, and the trooper barely glanced up. He radioed the dispatcher in

Miami and announced he was going off duty. "I'm tired," he said to Skink.

"Me too. You haven't seen anybody from Game and Fish, have you?"

"The panther patrol? No, I haven't." Jim Tile sat up. "I haven't seen the plane in at least a month."

Skink said, "Must've broken down. Else they're working the Fakahatchee."

"Listen," the trooper said, "I won't ask about the dead guy on the bridge, and I won't ask about the whale—"

"I had nothing whatsoever to do with the whale."

"Fair enough," said Jim Tile, "but what about torching those bulldozers up on 905? Were you in on that?"

Skink looked at him blankly. The trooper described what had happened that very afternoon at the Falcon Trace construction project. "They're looking for a guy who used to work at the Kingdom. They say he's gone nuts. They say he's got a gun."

"Is that right?" Skink tugged pensively at his beard.

"Do you know this person?"

"Possibly."

"Then could you *possibly* get him a message to stop this shit before it gets out of hand?"

"It's already out of hand," Skink said. "The sons-of-bitches are beating up little old ladies."

"Damn." The trooper stared out the window of the car. A trio of mosquitoes bounced off the glass and circled his head. Skink reached over and snatched the insects out of the air. Then he opened the window and let them buzz away into the thick fragrant night.

Jim Tile said, "I'm worried about you."

Skink grinned. "That's a good one."

"Maybe I should haul you in after all."

"Wouldn't stick. No one saw me do it, and no one found the gun. Hell, they wouldn't even hold me overnight."

"Yeah, they would," Jim Tile said, "on my word."

Skink's smile went away.

The trooper said, "The charge wouldn't stick, that's true. But I could take you out of circulation for a month or two. Let the situation simmer down."

"Why?" Skink demanded. "You know I'm right. You know what I'm doing is right."

"Not shooting rental cars."

"A lapse of judgment," Skink admitted. "I said I was sorry, for God's sake."

Jim Tile put a hand on his friend's shoulder. "I know you think it's the right thing, and the cause is good. But I'm afraid you're gonna lose."

"Maybe not," Skink said. "I think the Mojo's rising."

The trooper always got lost when Skink started quoting old rock-and-roll songs; someday he was going to sit Skink's shiny ass down and make him listen to Aretha. Put some soul in his system. Jim Tile said, "I've got a life, too. Can't spend the rest of it looking after you."

Skink sagged against the car door. "Jim, they're paving the goddamn island."

"Not the whole thing—"

"But this is how it begins," Skink said. "Jesus Christ, you ought to know. This is how it begins!"

There was no point in pushing it. The state had bought up nearly all North Key Largo for preservation; the Amazing Kingdom and the Falcon Trace property were essentially all that remained in private hands. Still, Skink was not celebrating.

Jim Tile said, "This guy you recruited—"

"I didn't recruit him."

"Whatever. He's in it, that's the main thing."

"Apparently so," Skink said. "Apparently he's serious."

"So locking you up won't do any good, will it? Not with

him still out there." The trooper put on his hat and adjusted it out of habit. In the darkness of the car, Skink couldn't read the expression on his friend's face. Jim Tile said, "Promise me one thing, all right? Talk some sense to the boy. He's new at it, Governor, and he could get hurt. That stunt with the bulldozers, it's not cool."

"I know," said Skink, "but it's got a certain flair."

"Listen to me," Jim Tile said sternly. "Already he's got some serious people after his ass, you understand? There's things I can help with, and things I can't."

Skink nodded. "I'll talk to him, I promise. And thanks."

Then he was gone. Jim Tile reached across to shut the door and his arm instantly was enveloped by an influx of mosquitoes. Frenzied humming filled the car.

He stomped the accelerator and the big Crown Victoria sprayed a fusillade of gravel into the mangroves. Westbound at a hundred fifteen miles an hour, the trooper rolled down the windows to let the wind suck the bugs from the car.

"Two of them." His words were swallowed in the roar of the open night. "Now I got two of the crazy bastards."

Twenty-one

Carrie Lanier's place was furnished as exquisitely as any mobile home. It had a microwave, an electric can opener, a stove, a nineteen-inch color TV, two paddle fans and a Naugahyde convertible sofa where Joe Winder slept. But there was no music, so on his third day as a fugitive Winder borrowed Carrie's car and went back to the apartment to retrieve his stereo system and rock tapes. He was not totally surprised to find that his place had been broken, entered and ransacked; judging by the viciousness of the search, Pedro Luz was the likely intruder. The inventory of losses included the portable television, three champagne glasses, a tape recorder, the plumbing fixtures, the mattress, a small Matisse print and the toaster. One of Nina's pink bras, which she had forgotten, had been desecrated ominously with cigarette burns, and hung from a Tiffany lamp. Also, the freshwater aquarium had been shattered, and the twin Siamese fighting fish had been killed. It appeared to Joe Winder that their heads were pinched off.

The stereo tuner and tape deck escaped harm, though the turntable was in pieces. A pair of hedge clippers protruded from one of the speakers; the other, fortunately, was undamaged.

"It's better than nothing," Joe Winder said when he got back to the trailer. "Low fidelity is better than no fidelity."

While he reassembled the components, Carrie Lanier explored the box of cassettes. Every now and then she would smile or go "Hmmm" in an amused tone.

Finally Winder looked up from the nest of colored wires and said, "You don't like my music?"

"I like it just fine," she said. "I'm learning a lot about you. We've got The Kinks. Seeger live at Cobo Hall. Mick and the boys."

"Living in the past, I know."

"Oh, baloney." She began to stack the tapes alphabetically on a shelf made from raw plywood and cinder blocks.

"Do you have a typewriter?" he asked.

"In the closet," Carrie said. "Are you going to start writing again?"

"I wouldn't call it writing."

She got out the typewriter, an old Olivetti manual, and made a place for it on the dinette. "This is a good idea," she said to Joe Winder. "You'll feel much better. No more shooting at heavy machinery."

He reminded her that he hadn't actually pulled the trigger on the bulldozers. Then he said, "I stopped writing a long time ago. Stopped being a journalist, anyway."

"But you didn't burn out, you sold out."

"Thanks," Winder said, "for the reminder."

It was his fault for staggering down memory lane in the first place. Two nights earlier, Carrie had quizzed him about the newspaper business, wanted to know what kind of stories he'd written. So he'd told her about the ones that had stuck with him. The murder trial of a thirteen-year-old boy who'd shot his little sister because she had borrowed his Aerosmith album without asking. The marijuana-smuggling ring led by a fugitive former justice of the Florida Supreme Court. The bribery

251

scandal in which dim-witted Dade County building inspectors were caught soliciting Lotto tickets as payoffs. The construction of a $47 million superhighway by a Mafia contractor whose formula for high-grade asphalt included human body parts.

Joe Winder did not mention the story that had ended his career. He offered nothing about his father. When Carrie Lanier had asked why he'd left the newspaper for public relations, he simply said, "Because of the money." She had seemed only mildly interested in his short time as a Disney World flack, but was impressed by the reckless sexual behavior that had gotten him fired. She said it was a healthy sign that he had not become a corporate drone, that the spark of rebellion still glowed in his soul.

"Maybe in my pants," Winder said, "not in my soul."

Carrie repeated what she had told him the first night: "You could always go back to being a reporter."

"No, I'm afraid not."

"So what is it you want to type—love letters? Maybe a confession?" Mischievously she tapped the keys of the Olivetti; two at a time, as if she were playing "Chopsticks."

The trailer was getting smaller and smaller. Joe Winder felt the heat lick at his eardrums. He said, "There's a reason you've hidden that gun."

"Because it's not your style." Carrie slapped the carriage and made the typewriter ring. "God gave you a talent for expression, a gift with the language."

Winder moaned desolately. "Have you ever read a single word I've written?"

"No," she admitted.

"So my alleged talent for expression, this gift—"

"I'm giving you the benefit of the doubt," she said. "The fact is, I don't trust you with a firearm. Now come help me open the wine."

*

Every evening at nine sharp, visitors to the Amazing Kingdom of Thrills gathered on both sides of Kingsbury Lane, the park's main thoroughfare, to buy overpriced junk food and await the rollicking pageant that was the climax of the day's festivities. All the characters in the Kingdom were expected to participate, from the gunslingers to the porpoise trainers to the elves. Sometimes a real marching band would accompany the procession, but in the slow months of summer the music was usually canned, piped in through the garbage chutes. Ten brightly colored floats comprised the heart of the parade, although mechanical problems frequently reduced the number of entries by half. These were organized in a story line based loosely on the settlement of Florida, going back to the days of the Spaniards. The plundering, genocide, defoliation and gang rape that typified the peninsula's past had been toned down for the sake of Francis X. Kingsbury's younger, more impressionable customers; also, it would have been difficult to find a musical score suitable to accompany a mass disemboweling of French Huguenots.

For the feel-good purposes of the Amazing Kingdom's nightly pageant, the sordid history of Florida was compressed into a series of amiable and bloodless encounters. Floats celebrated such fabricated milestones as the first beachfront Thanksgiving, when friendly settlers and gentle Tequesta Indians shared wild turkey and fresh coconut milk under the palms. It was a testament to Charles Chelsea's imagination (and mortal fear of Kingsbury) that even the most shameful episodes were reinterpreted with a positive commercial spin. A float titled "Migrants on a Mission" depicted a dozen cheery, healthful farm workers singing Jamaican folk songs and swinging their machetes in a precisely choreographed break-dance through the cane fields. Tourists loved it. So did the Okeechobee Sugar Federation, which had bankrolled the production in order to improve its image.

One of the highlights of the pageant was the arrival of "the legendary Seminole maiden" known as Princess Golden Sun. No such woman and no such lore ever existed; Charles Chelsea had invented her basically as an excuse to show tits and ass, and pass it off as ethnic culture. Traditional Seminole garb was deemed too dowdy for the parade, so Princess Golden Sun appeared in a micro-bikini made of simulated deerskin. The authentic Green Corn Dance, a sacred Seminole rite, was politely discarded as too solemn and repetitious; instead Golden Sun danced the *lambada*, a pelvic-intensive Latin step. Surrounded by ersatz Indian warriors wearing bright Brazilian slingshots, the princess proclaimed in song and mime her passionate love for the famous Seminole chieftain Osceola. At the news of his death, she broke into tears and vowed to haunt the Everglades forever in search of his spirit. The peak of the drama, and the parade, was the moment when Golden Sun mounted a wild panther (in this case, a heavily drugged African lioness) and disappeared from sight in a rising fog of dry ice.

It was the role most coveted among the female actors employed at the Amazing Kingdom, and for six months it had belonged to Annette Fury, a dancer of mountainous dimensions whose previous job was as a waitress at a topless doughnut shop in Fort Lauderdale. A competent singer, Miss Fury had done so well with the role of Princess Golden Sun that the newspaper in Key Largo had done a nice write-up, including a photograph of Miss Fury straddling the bleary-eyed cat. The reporter had been careful to explain that the spavined animal was not actually a Florida panther, since real panthers were all but extinct. Given Princess Golden Sun's appearance, it was doubtful that a single reader even noticed the lion in the picture. Miss Fury's pose—head flung back, eyes closed, tongue between the teeth—was suggestive enough to provoke indignant outcries from a fundamentalist church in Big Pine Key, as well as the entire Seminole Nation, or what was left of it. At the first whiff of controversy, Charles Chelsea swiftly purchased the negatives from the newspaper and converted the most provocative one to a color postcard, which went on sale for $1.95 in all gift shops in the Amazing Kingdom of Thrills. As far as Chelsea was concerned, a star had been born.

On the night of July 25, however, Annette Fury's stint as Princess Golden Sun ended abruptly in a scandal that defied even Chelsea's talents for cosmetic counter-publicity. Shortly before the pageant, the dancer had ingested what were probably the last three Quaalude tablets in the entire continental United States. She had scrounged the dusty pills from the stale linty recesses of her purse, and washed them down with a warm bottle of Squirt. They had kicked in just as the float made the wide horseshoe turn onto Kingsbury Lane. By the time it rolled past the Cimarron Saloon, Annette Fury was bottomless, having surrendered her deerskin costume to a retired postal worker who had brought his wife and family all the way from Providence, Rhode Island. By the time the float reached the Wet Willy, the stone-faced Indian entourage of Princess Golden Sun had been augmented by nine rowdy Florida State fraternity men, who were taking turns balancing the drowsy young maiden on their noses, or so it must have appeared to the children in the audience. Afterwards, several parents threatened to file criminal obscenity charges against the park. They were appeased by a prompt written apology signed by Francis X. Kingsbury, and a gift of laminated lifetime passes to the Amazing Kingdom. Reluctantly, Charles Chelsea advised the Talent Manager to inform Annette Fury that her services were no longer required. The following day, Carrie Lanier was told that the role of Princess Golden Sun was hers if she wanted it. This was after they'd asked for her measurements.

So tonight she'd splurged on a bottle of Mondavi.

"To the late Robbie Raccoon," Carrie said, raising her glass.

"No one did him better," said Joe Winder.

He put on a tape of Dire Straits and they both agreed that it sounded pretty darn good, even with only one speaker. The wine was tolerable, as well.

Carrie said, "I told them I want a new costume."

"Something in beads and grass would be authentic."

"Also, no lip-synching," she said. "I don't care if the music's canned, but I want to do my own singing."

"What about the lion?" Joe Winder asked.

"They swear she's harmless."

"Tranked out of her mind is more like it. I'd be concerned, if I were you."

"If she didn't maul Annette, I can't imagine why she'd go after me."

A police siren penetrated the aluminum husk of the trailer; Joe Winder could hear it even over the guitar music and the tubercular groan of the ancient air conditioner. Parting the drapes, he watched one Metro squad car, and then another, enter the trailer park at high speed. Throwing dust, they sped past the turnoff to Carrie's place.

"Another domestic," Winder surmised.

"We average about four a week." Carrie refilled the wine-glasses. "People who take love too damn seriously."

"Which reminds me." He opened his wallet and removed twelve dollars and placed it on a wicker table. "I was a very bad boy. I called her three times."

"You shmuck."

The Nina Situation. Every time he picked up the phone, it added four bucks to Carrie Lanier's bill. Worse, Nina pretended not to recognize his voice—stuck to the script to the bitter end, no matter how much he pleaded for her to shut up and listen.

"It is pathetic," Winder conceded.

"No other word for it."

"Haven't you ever been like this?" Obsessed is what he meant.

"Nope." Carrie shrugged. "I've got to be honest."

"So what's the matter with me?"

"You're just having a bad week."

She went to the bedroom and changed into a lavender nightshirt that came down to the knees—actually, a good four inches above the knees. Her hair was pulled back in a loose, sandy-colored ponytail.

Winder said, "You look sixteen years old." Only about three dozen other guys must have told her the same thing. His heart was pounding a little harder than he expected. "Tomorrow I'll get a motel room," he said.

"No, you're staying here."

"I appreciate it but—"

"Please," Carrie said. "Please stay."

"I've got serious plans. You won't approve."

"How do you know? Besides, I'm a little nervous about this new job. It's nice to have someone here at the end of the day, someone to talk with."

Gazing at her, Winder thought: God, don't do this to me. Don't make me say it.

But he did: "You just want to keep an eye on me. You're afraid I'll screw everything up."

"You're off to a pretty good start."

"It's only fair to warn you: I'm going after Kingsbury."

"That's what I figured, Joe. Call it a wild hunch." She took his hand and led him toward the bedroom.

I'm not ready for this, Winder thought. Sweat broke out in a linear pattern on the nape of his neck. He felt as if he were back in high school, the day the prettiest cheerleader winked at him in biology class; at the time, he'd been examining frog sperm under a microscope, and the wink from Pamela Shaugnessy had fractured his concentration. It had taken a month or two for Joe Winder to recover, and by then Pamela was knocked up by the co-captain of the junior wrestling squad. The teacher said that's what she got for not paying attention in class.

The sheets in Carrie Lanier's bedroom were rose, the blanket was plum. A novel by Anne Tyler was open on the bedstand, next to a bottle of nose drops.

A fuzzy stuffed animal sat propped on the pillow: shoebutton eyes, round ears and short whiskers. Protruding slightly from its upturned, bucktoothed mouth was a patch of turquoise cotton that could only be a tongue.

"Violet the Vole," Carrie explained. "Note the sexy eyelashes."

"For Christ's sake," Joe Winder said.

"The Vance model comes with a tiny cigar."

"How much?" Winder asked.

"Eighteen ninety-five, plus tax. Mr. X ordered a shipment of three thousand." Carrie stroked his arm. "Come on, I feel like cuddling."

Wordlessly, Winder moved the toy mango vole off the bed. The tag said it was manufactured in the People's Republic of China. What must they think of us on the assembly line? Winder wondered. Stuffed rats with cigars!

Carrie Lanier said, "I've got the jitters about singing in the parade. I don't look much like a Seminole."

Winder assured her she would do just fine. "Listen, I need to ask a favor. If you say no, I'll understand."

"Shoot."

"I need you to steal something for me," he said.

"Sure."

"Just like that?"

Carrie said, "I trust you. I want to help."

"Do you see the possibilities?"

"Surprise me," she said.

258

"Don't worry, it won't be dangerous. A very modest effort, as larcenies go."

"Sure. First thing tomorrow."

"Why are you doing this?" he asked.

"Because it's a fraud, the whole damn place. But mainly because an innocent man is dead. I liked Will Koocher." She paused. "I like his wife, too."

She didn't have to add the last part, but Winder was glad she did. He said, "You might lose your job."

Carrie smiled. "There's always dinner theater."

It seemed a good time to break the ice, so he tried—a brotherly peck on the cheek.

"Joe," she murmured, "you kiss like a parakeet."

"I'm slightly nervous myself."

Slowly she levered him to the bed, pinning his arms. "Why," she said, giggling, "why are you so nervous, little boy?"

"I really don't know." Her breasts pressed against his ribs, a truly wonderful sensation. Winder decided he could spend the remainder of his life in that position.

Carrie said, "Lesson Number one: How to smooch an Indian maiden."

"Go ahead," said Winder, "I'm all lips."

"Now do as I say."

"Anything," he agreed. "Anything at all."

As they kissed, an unrelated thought sprouted like a mushroom in the only dim crevice of Joe Winder's brain that was not fogged with lust.

The thought was: If I play this right, we won't need the gun after all.

Twenty-two

Pedro Luz was in Francis Kingsbury's den when the blackmailers called. He listened to Kingsbury's half of the conversation, a series of impatient grunts, and said to Churrito, "Looks like we're in business."

Kingsbury put down the phone and said, "All set. Monkey Mountain at four sharp. In front of the baboons."

Monkey Mountain was a small animal park off Krome Avenue, a cut-rate imitation of the venerable Monkey Jungle. To Pedro Luz, it didn't sound like an ideal place to kill a couple of burglars.

With a snort, Kingsbury said, "These assholes, who knows where they get these cute ideas. Watching television, maybe."

"What is this monkey place?" Churrito asked.

"For Christ's sake, like the name says, it's basically monkeys. Two thousand of the damn things running all over creation." Kingsbury disliked monkeys and had summarily vetoed plans for a Primate Pavilion at the Amazing Kingdom of Thrills. He felt that apes had limited commercial appeal; Disney had steered clear of them, too, for what that was worth.

"For one thing, they bite. And, two, they shit like a sewer pipe." Kingsbury put the issue to rest. "If they're so damn smart, how come they don't hold it. Like people."

"They tasty good," Churrito remarked, licking his lips. "Squirrel monkey is best, where I come from."

Pedro Luz sucked noisily on the open end of the IV tube. He had purchased a dozen clear bags of five-percent dextrose solution from a wholesale medical shop in Perrine. The steroid pills he pulverized with the butt of his Colt, and funneled the powder into the bags. No one at the gym had ever heard of getting stoked by this method; Pedro Luz boasted that it was all his idea, he'd never even checked with a doctor. The only part that bothered him was using the needle—a problematic endeavor, since anabolic steroids were usually injected into muscle, not veins. Whenever Pedro Luz was having second thoughts, he'd yank out the tube and insert it directly in his mouth.

Sitting in Kingsbury's house, it gave him great comfort to feel again these magnificent potent chemicals flooding his system. With nourishment came strength, and with strength came confidence. Pedro Luz was afraid of nothing. He felt like stepping in front of a speeding bus, just to prove it.

Churrito pointed at the intravenous rig and said: "Even monkeys aren't that stupid."

"Put a lid on it," Pedro growled. He thought: No wonder these dorks lost the war.

"Stuff make you bulls shrink up. Dick get leetle tiny." Churrito seemed unconcerned by the volcanic mood changes that swept over Pedro Luz every few hours. To Francis Kingsbury he said, "Should see the zits on his cholders."

"Some other time," Kingsbury said. "You guys, now, don't get into it. There's work to do—I want these assholes off my back, these fucking burglars, and I want the files. So don't start up with each other, I mean, save your energy for the job."

Pedro Luz said, "Don't worry."

The phone rang and Kingsbury snatched it. The call obviously was long-distance because Kingsbury began to shout.

Something about a truck accident ruining an important shipment of fish. The caller kept cutting in on Kingsbury, and Kingsbury kept making half-assed excuses, meaning some serious money already had changed hands.

When Kingsbury hung up, he said, "That was Hong Kong. Some cat-food outfit, I set up this deal and it didn't work out. What the hell, they'll get their dough back."

"My uncle had a fish market," remarked Pedro Luz. "It's a very hard business."

Without warning Mrs. Kingsbury came into the room. She wore terry-cloth tennis shorts and the top half of a lime-colored bikini. She nodded at Churrito, who emitted a low tomcat rumble. Pedro Luz glowered at him.

She said, "Frankie, I need some money for my lessons."

Under his breath, Churrito said, "I give her some lessons. Chew bet I will."

Kingsbury said, "I just gave you—was it yesterday?—like two hundred bucks."

"That was yesterday." Mrs. Kingsbury's eyes shifted to Pedro Luz, and the bottle of fluid on the hanger. "What's the matter with him?" she asked.

"One of them crash diets," said her husband.

Churrito said, "Yeah, make your muscles get big and your dick shrivel up like a noodle."

Pedro Luz reddened. "It's vitamins, that's all." He gnawed anxiously on the end of the tube, as if it were a piece of beef jerky.

"What kind of vitamins?" asked Kingsbury's wife.

"For men," said Pedro Luz. "Men-only vitamins."

As always, it was a test to be in the same room with Mrs. Kingsbury and her phenomenal breasts. Pedro Luz had given up sex three years earlier in the misinformed belief that ejaculation was a waste of precious hormones. Somehow, Pedro Luz had acquired the false notion that

262

semen was one-hundred-percent pure testosterone, and consequently he was distraught when a popular weightlifter magazine reported that the average sexually active male would squirt approximately 19.6 gallons in a lifetime. For a fitness fiend such as Pedro Luz, the jism statistic was a shocker. To expend a single pearly drop of masculine fuel on a recreational pleasure was frivolous and harmful and plainly against God's plan; how could it do anything but weaken the body?

As it happened, Pedro Luz's fruit-and-steroid diet had taken the edge off his sex drive anyway. Abstinence had not proved to be difficult, except when Mrs. Kingsbury was around.

"I don't like needles," she announced. "I don't like the way they prick."

Again Churrito began to growl lasciviously. Pedro Luz said, "After a while, you don't even notice." He showed Mrs. Kingsbury how the IV rig moved on wheels.

"Like a shopping cart," she said gaily. Her husband handed her a hundred-dollar bill and she waved goodbye.

"There she goes," Kingsbury said. "Pedro, did you show your little buddy the golf painting? The one we did at Biltmore?"

"I saw," Churrito said. "In the living room."

"Those are the real McCoys," said Kingsbury.

Churrito looked perplexed. "McCoys?"

"Her tits, I mean. How you say, *hoot-aires*?" Kingsbury cackled. "Now, about this afternoon, these assholes—I'm not interested in details. Not at all interested."

That was fine with Pedro Luz. He'd skipped the details the last time, too, when they had roughed up the old lady at the condo. Although Churrito had nagged him to lighten up, the beating had been therapeutic for Pedro, a venting of toxic brain fumes. Like the rush he got while pinching the heads off Joe Winder's twin siamese fighting fish.

"I doubt this monkey place will be crowded," Kingsbury was saying, "except for the baboons."

"We'll be careful," Pedro Luz assured him.

"You get caught, no offense, but I don't know you. Never seen you bastards before in my life."

"We won't get caught."

Kingsbury snapped his fingers. "The files, I'll give you a list. Don't do anything till you get my files back. After that, it's your call."

Pedro Luz looked at his wristwatch and said it was time to go. The wheels on the IV rig twittered as it followed him to the door.

"I wanted to ask," Churrito said, "is it okay I look at the pitcher again? The one with your wife and those real McCoys."

"Be my guest," said Kingsbury, beaming. "That's what it's there for."

One problem, Bud Schwartz realized, was that he and his partner had never done a blackmail before. In fact, he wasn't sure if it was blackmail or extortion, technically speaking.

"Call it a trade," said Danny Pogue.

Bud Schwartz smiled. Not bad, he thought. A trade it is.

They were waiting in the rented Cutlass in the parking lot of Monkey Mountain. Mrs. Kingsbury's chrome-plated pistol lay on the seat between them. Neither of them wanted to handle it.

"Christ, I hate guns," said Bud Schwartz.

"How's your hand?"

"Getting there. How's your foot?"

"Pretty good." Danny Pogue opened a bag of Burger King and the oily smell of hot fries filled the car. Bud Schwartz rolled down the window and was counter-assailed by the overpowering odor of monkeys.

Chewing, Danny Pogue said, "I can't get over that guy in the house, Molly's friend. Just come right in."

"Bigfoot," said Bud Schwartz, "without the manners."

"I just hope he don't come back."

"You and me both."

Bud Schwartz was watching out for Saabs. Over the phone Kingsbury had told him he'd be driving a navy Saab with tinted windows; so far, no sign of the car.

He asked his partner: "You ever done a Saab?"

"No, they all got alarms," said Danny Pogue. "Like radar is what I heard. Just look at 'em funny, and they go off. Same with the Porsches, I fucking whisper just walkin' by the damn things."

At two minutes after four, Bud Schwartz said it was time to get ready. Gingerly he put the gun in his pocket. "Leave the files under the seat," he said. "We'll make the trade after we got the money."

At the ticket window they got a map of Monkey Mountain. It wasn't exactly a sprawling layout.

"Hey, they even got a gorilla," said Danny Pogue, "name of Brutus. From the picture it looks like an African silver-back."

"Fascinating," Bud Schwartz said. He'd had about enough of animal lore. Lately Danny Pogue had been spending too many hours watching wildlife documentaries on the Discovery Channel. It was all he talked about, he and Molly, and it was driving Bud Schwartz up the wall. One night, instead of the Cubs game, he had to sit through ninety minutes of goddamn hummingbirds. To Bud Schwartz they resembled moths with beaks; he got dizzy watching the damn things, even the slow-motion parts. Danny Pogue, on the other hand, had been enthralled. The fact that hummingbirds also inhabited North Key Largo heightened his sense of mission against Francis X. Kingsbury.

As they set out for the Baboon Tree, Danny Pogue said, "Why'd you pick this place, Bud?"

"'Cause it's out in public. That's how you do these things, extortions."

"Are you sure?"

The visitor paths through Monkey Mountain were enclosed by chicken wire, giving the effect that it was the humans who were encaged while the wild beasts roamed free. Bud Schwartz was uncomfortable with this arrangement. Above his head, screeching monkeys loped along the mesh, begging for peanuts and crackers that Bud Schwartz had neglected to purchase at the concession stand. The impatient animals—howlers, gibbons, rhesus and spider monkeys—got angrier by the second. They bared yellow teeth and spit maliciously and shook the chicken wire. When Danny Pogue reached up to give one of them a shiny dime, it defecated in his hair.

"You happy now?" said Bud Schwartz.

"Damn, I can't believe it." Danny Pogue stopped to stick his head under a water fountain. "Don't they ever feed these goddamn things?" he said.

Above them, the gang of furry, shrieking, incontinent beggars had swollen to three dozen. Bud Schwartz and Danny Pogue shielded their heads and jogged the rest of the way to the Baboon Tree, an ancient ficus in the hub of a small plaza. Bud Schwartz was relieved to escape the yammering din and the rain of monkey feces. With a sigh he sat next to a Japanese family on a concrete bench. A moat of filmy brown water separated them from the bustling baboon colony in the big tree.

Danny Pogue said: "Know why they don't let the other monkeys together with the baboons?"

"Why not?"

"Because the baboons'd eat 'em."

"What a loss that would be."

"Let's go see Brutus."

"Danny, we're here on business. Now shut the fuck up, if you don't mind."

The Japanese husband apparently understood at least one word of English, because he gave Bud Schwartz a sharp look.

The Japanese wife, who hadn't heard the profane remark, signaled that she would like a photograph of the whole family in front of the moat. Bud Schwartz motioned that his partner would do the honors; Danny Pogue had stolen many Nikons, but he'd never gotten a chance to use one. He arranged the Japanese in a neat row according to height, and snapped several pictures. In the background were many wild-eyed baboons, including a young male gleefully abusing itself.

Bud Schwartz was glad the children weren't watching. After the Japanese had moved on, Danny Pogue said: "That was two hundred bucks right there, a Nikon with autofocus. I got a guy in Carol City fences nothing but cameras."

"I told you," said Bud Schwartz, "we're through with that. We got a new career." He didn't sound as confident as he would've liked. Where the hell was Kingsbury?

Danny Pogue joined him on the concrete bench. "So how much is he gonna bring?"

"Fifty is what I told him." Bud Schwartz couldn't get the tremor out of his voice. "Fifty thousand, if he ever shows up."

In the parking lot, Pedro Luz and Churrito got into a heated discussion about bringing the IV rack. Churrito prevailed on the grounds that it would attract too much attention.

The first thing they noticed about Monkey Mountain was the stink, which Churrito likened to that of a mass grave. Next came the insistent clamor of the creatures themselves, clinging to the chicken wire and extending miniature brown hands in hopes of food. Churrito lit up a Marlboro and handed it to a rhesus, who took a sniff and hurled it back at him. Pedro Luz didn't think it was the least bit funny; he was sinking into one of his spells— every heartbeat sent cymbals crashing against his brainpan. An act of irrational violence was needed to calm the mood. It was fortunate, then, that the monkeys were safely on the other side of the chicken wire. Every time one appeared on the mesh over his head, Pedro Luz would jump up and smash at it savagely with his knuckles. This exercise was repeated every few seconds, all the way to the Baboon Tree.

The burglars—and it *had* to be them, greasy-looking red-necks—were sitting on a bench. Nobody else was around.

Pedro Luz whispered to Churrito: "Remember to get their car keys. They left the damn files in the car."

"What if they dint?"

"They did. Now be quiet."

Danny Pogue wasn't paying attention. He was talking about a TV program that showed a male baboon killing a zebra, that's how strong they were. A monkey that could kill something as big as a horse! Bud Schwartz was tuned out entirely; he was sizing up the two new men. The tall one, God Almighty, he was trouble. Built like a grizzly but that wasn't the worst of it; the worst was the eyes. Bud Schwartz could spot a doper two miles away; this guy was buzzing like a yellowjacket. The other one was no prize, dull-eyed and cold, but at least he was of normal dimensions. What caught Bud Schwartz's eye was the Cordovan briefcase that the smaller man was carrying.

"Get ready," he said to Danny Pogue.

"But that ain't Kingsbury."

"You don't miss a trick."

"Bud, I don't like this."

"Really? I'm having the time of my life." Bud Schwartz stood up and approached the two strangers. "Where's the old man?"

"Where's the files?" asked Pedro Luz.

"Where's the money?"

Churrito held up the briefcase. It was plainly stuffed with something, possibly fifty thousand in cash.

"Now," said Pedro Luz, "where's the damn files?"

"We give 'em to the old man and nobody else."

Pedro Luz checked over both shoulders to make sure there were no tourists around. In the same motion his right hand casually fished into the waistband of his trousers for the Colt. Before he could get to it, something dug into his right ear. It was another gun. *A burglar with a gun!* Pedro Luz was consumed with fury.

Bud Schwartz said, "Don't move." The words fluttered out. Danny Pogue gaped painfully.

Churrito laughed. "Good work," he said to Pedro Luz. "Excellent."

"I'm gonna be straight about this," said Bud Schwartz, "I don't know shit about guns."

The veins in Pedro Luz's neck throbbed like a tangle of snakes. He was seething, percolating in hormones, waiting for the moment. The gun barrel cut into his earlobe but he didn't feel a thing. Trying not to snarl, he said, "Don't push it, *chico.*"

"I ain't kidding," Bud Schwartz said in a voice so high he didn't recognize it as his own. "You even fart, I may blow your brains out. Explain that to your friend."

Churrito seemed indifferent to the idea. He shrugged and handed the briefcase to Danny Pogue.

"Open it," Bud Schwartz told him.

Again Pedro Luz asked, "Where are the files?" He anticipated that the burglars would soon be unable to answer the question, since he intended to kill them. And possibly Churrito while he was in the mood.

Even the baboons sensed trouble, for they had fallen silent in the boughs of the ficus. Danny Pogue opened the Cordovan briefcase and showed Bud Schwartz what was inside: sanitary napkins. "Too bad," said Bud Schwartz. And it was too bad. He had no clue what to do next. Danny Pogue took one of the maxi-pads out of the briefcase and examined it, as if searching for insight.

Pedro Luz's steroid-marinated glands were starting to cook. Infused with the strength of a thousand warriors, he announced that he wouldn't let a mere bullet spoil Mr. Kingsbury's plan. He told Bud Schwartz to go ahead and fire, and went so far as to reach up and seize the burglar's arm.

As they struggled, Pedro Luz said, "Shoot me, you pussy! Shoot me now!"

Out of the corner of his eye, Bud Schwartz spotted Danny Pogue running away in the general direction of the gorilla compound—moving impressively for someone fresh off crutches.

Just as Pedro Luz was preparing to snap Bud Schwartz's arm like a matchstick, Mrs. Kingsbury's chrome-plated pistol shook loose from the burglar's fingers and flew over the moat. The gun landed in a pile of dead leaves at the foot of the ficus tree, where it was retrieved by a laconic baboon with vermilion buttocks. Bud Schwartz wasn't paying attention, what with Pedro Luz hurling him to the ground and kneeling on his neck and trying to twist his head off. Meanwhile the other man was going through Bud Schwartz's trousers in search of the car keys.

When Bud Schwartz tried to shout for help, Pedro Luz slapped a large moist hand over his mouth. It was then that Bud Schwartz spotted the bandaged nub of the right index finger, and assimilated in his dying deoxygenated consciousness the probability that this was the same goon who had brutalized Molly McNamara. The burglar decided, in the hastening gray twilight behind his eyeballs, that the indignity of being found mugged and dead in a monkey park might be mitigated by a final courageous deed, such as disfiguring a murderous steroid freak—which Bud Schwartz attempted to do by sucking Pedro Luz's hand into his jaws and chomping down with heedless ferocity.

The wailing of Pedro Luz brought the baboon colony

to life, and a hellish chorus enveloped the three men as they fought on the ground. A gunshot was heard, and the monkeys scattered adroitly to the highest branches of the graceful old tree.

Pedro Luz rolled off Bud Schwartz and groped with his bloody paw for the Colt. It was still in his waistband. Only two things prevented him from shooting the burglar: the sight of fifty chattering children skipping toward him down the monkey trail, and the sight of Churrito lying dead with a grape-sized purple hole beneath his left eye.

Pedro Luz pushed himself to his feet, stepped over the body and ran. Bud Schwartz did the same—much more slowly and in the opposite direction—but not before pausing to contemplate the visage of the dead Nicaraguan. Judging by the ironic expression on Churrito's face, he knew exactly what had happened to him.

Now the killer was halfway up the ficus tree, barking and slobbering and shaking the branches. Mrs. Kingsbury's gun glinted harmlessly in the brackish shallows, where the startled baboon had dropped it.

The oxygen returning to Bud Schwartz's head brought a chilling notion that maybe the monkey had been aiming the damn thing. Maybe he'd even done it before. Stranger things had occurred in Miami.

Bud Schwartz lifted the keys to the Cutlass from the dead man's hand and jogged away just as Miss Juanita Pedrosa's kindergarten class marched into the plaza.

Twenty-three

Francis X. Kingsbury was on the thirteenth green at the Ocean Reef Club when Charles Chelsea caught up with him and related the problem.

"Holy piss," said Kingsbury as Jake Harp was about to putt. "If it's not one thing, it's—hell, you deal with it, Charlie. Isn't that what I pay you for, to deal with this shit?"

Jake Harp pushed the putt to the right. He looked up stonily and said, "Thank you both very much."

"Sorry," Chelsea said. "We've got a little emergency here."

Kingsbury said, "If you're gonna be a crybaby, Jake, then do it over. Take another putt. And you, Charlie, what emergency? This is nothing, a goddamn prank."

Charles Chelsea suggested that it was considerably more serious than a prank. "Every television station in South Florida received a copy, Mr. Kingsbury. Plus the *Herald* and the *New York Times*. We'll be getting calls all day, I expect."

He followed Kingsbury and Jake Harp to the fourteenth tee. "The reason I say it's serious, we've got less than a week until the Summerfest Jubilee." It was set for August 6, the day Kingsbury had rescheduled the arrival of the phony five-millionth visitor to the Amazing Kingdom of Thrills. The postponement caused by the truck accident had been a blessing in one way—it had given Charles Chelsea time to scout for a flashy new giveaway car. The "classic" Corvair had been junked in favor of a jet-black 300-Z, which had been purchased at bargain prices from the estate of a murdered amphetamine dealer. Chelsea was further buoyed by the news that NBC weather-man Willard Scott had tentatively agreed to do a live broadcast from the Kingdom on Jubilee morning, as long as Risk Management cleared it with the network.

Overall, the publicity chief had been feeling fairly positive about Summerfest until some worm from the *Herald* called up to bust his hump about the press release.

What press release? Chelsea had asked.

The one about hepatitis, said the guy from the newspaper. The hepatitis epidemic among Uncle Ely's Elves.

In his smoothest, most controlled tone, Chelsea had asked the newspaper guy to please fax him a copy. The sight of it creeping off the machine had sent a prickle down the ridge of his spine.

As Jake Harp prepared to tee off, Chelsea showed the press release to Francis X. Kingsbury and said, "It's ours."

"What the hell you—I don't get it. Ours?"

"Meaning it's the real thing. The stationery is authentic."

Kingsbury frowned at the letterhead. "Jesus Christ, then we got some kinda mole. That what you're saying? Somebody on the inside trying to screw with our plans?"

"Not necessarily," Chelsea said.

Jake Harp hooked his drive into a fairway bunker. He said, "Don't you boys know when to shut up."

This time Charles Chelsea didn't bother to apologize. He itched to remind Jake Harp that dead silence hadn't helped him one bit in the '78 Masters, when he'd four-putted the third hole at Augusta and let Nicklaus, Floyd, everybody and their mothers blow right past him.

Kingsbury said, "Probably it's some bastard from Disney.

273

A ringer, hell, I should've known. Somebody they sent just to screw me up for the summer."

"It's nobody on the inside," said Chelsea. "It wasn't done on one of our typewriters."

"Who then? I mean, why in the name of fuck?"

Jack Harp marveled at the inventive construction of Kingsbury's profanity. He imagined how fine it would feel to take a two-iron and pulverize the man's skull into melon rind. Instead he said, "You're up, Frank."

Charles Chelsea stood back while Kingsbury took a practice swing. It was not a thing of beauty. From the safety of the cart path, Chelsea said, "I think it's Joe Winder. The fellow we fired last week. The one we've had some trouble with."

"What makes you so sure—wait, Christ, didn't he used to work for The Rat?"

"Yes, briefly. Anyway, there's some stationery missing from Publicity. I thought you ought to know."

"How much?"

"Two full boxes," Chelsea replied. Enough to do one fake press release every day for about three years. Or one hundred a day until the Summerfest Jubilee.

Kingsbury knocked his drive down the left side of the fairway and grunted in approval. He plopped his butt in the golf cart and said to Chelsea: "Let me see it one more time."

Chelsea gave him the paper and climbed on the back of the cart, wedging himself between the two golf bags. He wondered if this was how the Secret Service rode when the President was playing.

Pointing over Kingsbury's shoulder, Chelsea said, "It's definitely Winder's style. I recognize some of the dry touches."

The press release said:

Medical authorities at the Amazing Kingdom of Thrills announced today that the outbreak of viral hepatitis that struck the popular theme park this week is "practically under control."

Visitors to the Amazing Kingdom are no longer in immediate danger of infection, according to specialists who flew in from the National Centers for Disease Control in Atlanta. So far, five cases of hepatitis have been positively diagnosed. All the victims were actors who portray Uncle Ely's Elves, a troupe of mischievous trolls who frolic and dance in daily performances throughout the park.

Experts say there is no reason to suspect that the highly contagious disease is being transmitted in the food and beverages being served at the Amazing Kingdom. A more likely source is the vending machine located in a dressing room often used by Uncle Ely's Elves and several other performers.

Charles Chelsea, vice president in charge of publicity, said: "We know that the candy machine down there hadn't been serviced for about seven months. There are serious questions regarding the freshness and edibility of some of the chocolate products, as well as the breath mints. All items have been removed from the machine and are presently being tested for contamination."

Although no cases of hepatitis have been reported among visitors to the Amazing Kingdom, Monroe County health officials advise testing for anyone who has had recent contact with any of Uncle Ely's Elves—or food products handled by the elves. This advisory applies to all persons who might have posed for photographs or danced with one of the little people during the Nightly Pageant of Tropics.

Moe Strickland, the veteran character actor who popularized the role of Uncle Ely, said the stricken performers are resting quietly at Baptist Hospital in Miami, and are expected to recover. He added, "I'm worried about what the kids will think when they don't see us around the park for a few weeks. I guess we'll have to tell them that Uncle Ely took the elves on a summer vacation to Ireland, or wherever it is that elves go."

Chelsea said there are no plans to close the Amazing Kingdom to the public. "This was a freakish incident, and we are confident that the worst is over," he said. "From now on, we get back to the business of having fun."

Beginning tonight, the Amazing Kingdom of Thrills will present a multi-media tribute to Vance and Violet, the last surviving blue-tongued mango voles. The gentle animals were stolen from the park ten days ago in a daring daylight robbery, and later died tragically.

The show will be presented at 8 P.M. in the Rare Animal Pavilion, and will feature color slides, videotapes, rare outdoor film footage and a Claymation exhibit. Admission is $4 for adults, $2.50 for children.

Kingsbury reread the press release as they jolted down the cart path with Jake Harp at the wheel. When they stopped next to his golf ball, Kingsbury shoved the paper back at Chelsea. "It sounds awfully damn ... what's the word?"

"Authentic, sir. This is what we're up against."

"I mean, hell, it sure puts me off the candy machines."

"It's fooling the reporters, too," Chelsea said.

"You say this maniac's got—what, two goddamn boxes?"

"That's what's missing."

Jake Harp said, "If you're not going to play that lie, pick the damn thing up."

Kingsbury paid no attention. "I guess we'll need—obviously, what am I saying!—get a new letterhead for Publicity."

"I ordered it this morning," Chelsea reported. "I'm afraid it won't be ready for two weeks."

"Don't tell me—God, two weeks. So what do we do if your theory's right? If it's Winder, I mean." Kingsbury took his stance and rifled a six-iron dead into the heart of a tea-colored pond.

"See what happens when you run your mouth," said Jake Harp.

"The options are limited," Chelsea told Kingsbury. "Do we come right out and admit it's a fake? A disgruntled former employee, blah, blah, blah. Or do we roll with it? Take the hit and hope it's over."

"Is that your advice? Roll with it?"

"For now, yes."

"Me too," Francis Kingsbury said. "Besides, Pedro's on the case." A brand-new golf ball appeared in Kingsbury's right hand, and he dropped it with a flourish on the fairway. This time he nailed the six-iron to the center of the green, fifteen feet from the flag.

Jake Harp blinked sullenly and said nothing.

A duel.

That's how Charles Chelsea saw it. The ultimate test of skills. He warmed up the word processor and began to write:

The outbreak of viral hepatitis among performers at the Amazing Kingdom of Thrills was not as serious as first believed, according to a respected epidemiologist who visited the popular tourist attraction Friday.

The disease was confined to only four persons, none of whom became seriously ill, according to Dr. Neil Shulman, an international expert on liver pathology.

"Visitors to the Amazing Kingdom are in absolutely no danger," Dr. Shulman declared. "There's no evidence that the disease originated here. The food and beverages I've sampled are perfectly safe—and tasty, too!"

Initially it was believed that five persons were infected with hepatitis. Later, however, it was determined that one of the ill employees was actually suffering from gallstones, a common and nontransmittable disorder.

The four men who were diagnosed with hepatitis all began showing symptoms on Wednesday morning. Contrary to earlier reports, however, the victims did not contract the virus from contaminated candy purchased at a vending machine in the Amazing Kingdom. It is now believed that the men—all of whom portray members of Uncle Ely's Elves—became infected during a recent promotional trip to the Caribbean aboard a Nassau-based cruise ship.

Moe Strickland, the crusty character actor who immortalized the character of Uncle Ely, recalled how some of his troupe had complained of "funky-tasting lobster" during the four-day excursion. Viral hepatitis has an incubation period of 15 to 45 days.

Those who were stricken spent only one night in the hospital, and are now resting comfortably at home. Although their conditions are good, they will not return to work until doctors are sure that they are not contagious.

Dr. Shulman, who has written extensively for national medical journals, said he is certain that the disease has been contained, and that no other employees or visitors to the Amazing Kingdom are in jeopardy. "It's as safe as can be," he said. "In fact, I'm staying over the weekend myself so I can ride the new porpoise!"

Skimming the text, Charles Chelsea changed the word "outbreak" to "incidence." Then, with uncharacteristic fire, he punched the Send button.

To an invisible enemy he snarled, "All right, Joey. It's go time."

The queasy feeling that always accompanied the prospect

of bad publicity had given way to a fresh sense of challenge; Chelsea felt he'd been training his whole professional life for such a test. He was up against an opponent who was talented, ruthless and quite possibly insane.

As much as Chelsea feared and distrusted Winder, he respected his creative skills: the vocabulary, so rich in adjectives; the glib turn of an alliterative phrase—and, of course, the speed. Joe Winder was the fastest writer that Chelsea had ever seen.

Now it was just the two of them: Winder, holed up God knows where, hammering out inflammatory libels as fast as his fingers could fly. And on the other end, Chelsea himself, waiting to catch these malicious grenades and smother them. The alternative—meaning, to tell the truth—was unthinkable. To admit a hoaxster was loose, forging demented fantasies on Amazing Kingdom letterhead ... what a story *that* would make. In their excitement the media would come all over themselves. Even worse, each publicity announcement from the theme park would be scrutinized severely by reporters and editors, whose careers are seldom enhanced by getting duped into print. One thing that Charles Chelsea (or any PR flack) didn't need was a more toxic level of skepticism and suspicion among the journalists he was supposed to manipulate.

So telling the truth about Joe Winder was out of the question. Whatever revolting fable Winder concocted next, Chelsea would be ready to extinguish it with press releases that were both calm and plausible. One pack of lies softening another.

It was going to be one roaring hell of a battle.

As the Publicity Department's fax machines were launching Chelsea's counterattack against the hepatitis scare, Moe Strickland arrived to bitch about sick pay and what the almighty Screen Actors Guild would say.

He lit up a cigar and said, "The union would go nuts."

"We don't recognize the union," Chelsea said coolly. "I really don't understand your objections, Moe. Most people would kill for two weeks off."

Moe Strickland protested with a wet cough. "You're docking us sick days, that's the objection. Because we're not really sick."

"That's something to be taken up with Personnel. It's simply not my bailiwick." Charles Chelsea waved his hands to clear the rancid smoke. The office was starting to smell like dead mice.

"I don't see why they can't just give us two weeks paid," said Moe Strickland, "and leave us our sick days. Whatever happened, it's sure not our fault."

"No, it's not," Chelsea agreed. "Listen to me, Moe. Uncle Ely and the Elves are on vacation, all right? They went to Ireland. That's the official story."

"For Christ's sake—Ireland? Does Ely sound like an Irish name?" Moe Strickland sneered in contempt.

"I'm not here to argue," Chelsea said. "But I do wish to caution you against speaking to the media. All interview requests are to be routed through me, understand?"

"You mean like the newspapers."

"Newspapers, television, anybody asking questions about a cruise. You tell them to call me. And make sure the elves do the same."

"What, now you don't trust us?"

"No interviews, Moe. The order comes straight from Mr. X."

"Figures," said Moe Strickland. "What's the name of that disease? Tell me again."

"Viral hepatitis."

"Sounds terrible."

"It's a nasty one," Chelsea conceded.

"Who in hell would make up a story like that?" The actor

smacked on the soggy stump of cigar. "What kind of sick bastard would say such a thing?"

Chelsea did not reply. He was watching a string of brown drool make its way down Moe Strickland's snowy beard.

"I feel like suing the sonofabitch," Moe Strickland remarked.

Chelsea said, "Don't take it personally. It's got nothing to do with you."

"I never had hepatitis. Is it some kind of dick disease? Because if it is, we're definitely suing the bastard. The boys're as clean as a whistle down there and they can sure prove it."

"Moe," said Chelsea, "please settle down."

"Does this mean we can't march in the Jubilee?"

"Not as Uncle Ely and the elves. We'll get you some other costumes—gunslingers, how about that?"

"Oh great, midget gunslingers. No thanks." On his way out the door, Moe Strickland spit something heavy into Charles Chelsea's wastebasket.

That night, Channel 7 devoted forty seconds to the hepatitis scare, closing the piece with a sound-bite from Charles Chelsea, cool in a crisp blue oxford shirt and tortoiseshell eyeglasses. The glasses were a new touch.

Not bad, thought Joe Winder, if you like the George Will look.

He was watching the news with a notebook on his lap. He called toward the kitchen: "He got the number of victims down from five to four. Plus he's planted the idea that the disease was picked up in the Caribbean, not at the Amazing Kingdom. Pretty damn slick on short notice!"

Carrie Lanier was fixing popcorn. "So they're toughing it out," she said.

"Looks that way."

She came out and placed the bowl on the sofa between them. "They've got to be worried."

"I hope so." Joe Winder thanked her again for stealing the letterhead paper from the stockroom in the Publicity Department. "And for renting the fax," he added. "I'll pay you back."

"Not necessary, sir. Hey, I heard somebody shot up some rental cars on Card Sound Road."

"Yeah, it was on the news."

"Did they catch the guy?"

"No," he said, "and they won't." He wondered if Skink's sniper attack was the beginning of a major offensive.

Carrie pointed at the television. "Hey, look, it's Monkey Mountain!"

A blue body bag was being carried out of the amusement park. A florid middle-aged schoolteacher, a Miss Pedrosa, was being interviewed about what happened. She said her students thought the man was merely sleeping, not dead. The news reporter said the victim was believed to be a recent immigrant, a Latin male in his mid-thirties. A police detective at the scene of the shooting said it appeared to be a suicide. The detective's voice was nearly drowned out by the jabbering of angry baboons in a tree behind him.

Carrie said, "Well, Mr. X ought to be happy. Finally someplace else is getting bad press."

"Strange place for a suicide," observed Joe Winder.

Carrie Lanier stuffed a handful of popcorn into his mouth. "They gave me my new costume today. You're gonna die."

"Let's see."

It was a white fishnet tank suit. Carrie put it on and struck a Madonna pose. "Isn't it awful?" she said.

Joe Winder said she looked irresistibly slutty. "The Indians aren't going to like it, though."

"I've got a headband, too. And a black wig."

"The Seminoles didn't wear fishnets; they used them on bass. By the way, are those your nipples?"

"Who else's would they be?"

"What I mean is, isn't there supposed to be something underneath?"

"A tan body stocking," Carrie said. "I must've forgot to put it on."

Winder told her not to bother. Exuberantly she positioned herself on his lap and fastened her bare legs around his waist. "Before we make love," Carrie said, "you've got to hear the song."

It was a bastardized version of the famous production number in *Evita*. They both burst out laughing when she did the refrain. "I can't believe it," Joe Winder said.

Carrie kept singing, "Don't Cry for Me, Osceola!" Winder buried his face in her breasts. Unconsciously he began nibbling through the fishnet suit.

"Now stop." Carrie clutched the back of his head. "I've forgotten the rest of the words."

Still gnawing, Winder said, "I feel like a shark."

"You do indeed." She pulled him even closer. "I know a little boy who forgot to shave this morning, didn't he?"

"I was busy writing." A muffled voice rising out of her cleavage.

Carrie smiled. "I know you were writing, and I'm proud of you. What's the big news at the Kingdom tomorrow—typhoid? Trichinosis?"

He lifted his head. "No more diseases. From now on, it's the heavy artillery."

She kissed him on the nose. "You're a very sick man. Why do I like you so much?"

"Because I'm full of surprises."

"Oh, like this?" Carrie grabbed him and gave a little tug. "Is this for me?"

"If you're not careful."

"Hold still," she told him.

"Aren't you going to take off that outfit?"

"What for? Look at all these convenient holes. We've just got to get you lined up."

"It's a good thing," Joe Winder said, "it doesn't have gills."

He held his breath as Carrie Lanier worked on the delicate alignment. Then she adjusted the Naugahyde sofa cushion behind his head, and braced her hands on the windowsill. The lights from the highway skipped in her eyes, until she closed them. Slowly she started rocking and said, "Tonight we're shooting for four big ones."

"Excuse me?"

"I told you, Joe, I'm a very goal-oriented person."

"I think I'm tangled."

"You're doing fine," she said.

He was still hanging on, minutes later, when Carrie stopped moving.

"What is it?"

"Joe, did you go back to the apartment tonight?" She was whispering.

"Just for a minute. I needed some clothes."

"Oh boy."

"What's the matter?"

Carrie said, "Somebody's watching us. Somebody followed you here." She lowered herself until she was flat against him, so she couldn't be seen from the window. "It's a man," she said. "He's just standing out there."

"What's he look like?"

"Very large."

"Guess I'd better do something."

"Such as?"

"I'm not exactly sure," Joe Winder said. "I need to refocus here."

"In other words, you want me to climb off."

"Well, I think the mood has been broken."

"The thing is—"

"I know. We'll need a scissors." His fingers, his chin, everything was tangled in the netting.

Outside the trailer, something moved. A shadow flickering across the windowpane. Footsteps crunching on the gravel. Then a hand on the doorknob, testing the lock.

Carrie's muscles tightened. She put her lips to his ear. "Joe, are we going to die like this?"

"There are worse ways," he said.

And then the door buckled.

Twenty-four

Skink said he was sorry, and turned away. Joe Winder and Carrie Lanier scrambled to disengage, tearing the fishnet suit to strings.

"I heard noises," said Skink. "Thought there might be trouble."

The adrenaline ebbed in a cold tingle from Winder's veins. Breathlessly he said, "How'd you know I was here?"

"Followed you from the apartment."

"In what—the bookmobile?"

"I've got friends," Skink said.

While Joe Winder fastened his trousers, Carrie Lanier dived into a University of Miami football jersey. Skink turned to face them, and Carrie gamely shook his hand. She said, "I didn't catch your name."

"Jim Morrison," said Skink. "*The* Jim Morrison."

"No, he's not," Winder said irritably.

Carrie smiled. "Nice to meet you, Mr. Morrison." Winder considered her cordiality amazing in view of Skink's menacing appearance.

Skink said, "I suppose he told you all about me."

"No," Carrie replied. "He didn't say a word."

Skink seemed impressed by Joe Winder's discretion. To Carrie he said: "Feel free to stare."

"I am staring, Mr. Morrison. Is that a snake you're eating?"

"A mud snake, yes. Medium-rare." He took a crackling bite and moved through the trailer, turning off the television and all the lights. "A precaution," he explained, peeking out a window.

In the darkness Carrie found Joe Winder's hand and squeezed it. Winder said, "This is the man who saved my life a couple weeks ago—the night I got beaten up, and you gave me a lift."

"I live in the hammocks," Skink interjected. "The heavy rains have brought out the snakes."

Winder wondered when he would get to the point.

Carrie said, "Can I ask about the red collar? Is it some sort of neck brace?"

"No, it isn't." Skink crouched on his haunches in front of them, beneath the open window. The highway lights twinkled in his sunglasses.

"Events are moving haphazardly," he said, gnawing a piece of the cooked reptile. "There needs to be a meeting. A confluence, if you will."

"Of whom?" Winder asked.

"There are others," Skink said. "They don't know about you, and you don't know about them." He paused, cocking an ear toward the ceiling. "Hear that? It's the plane. They've been tracking me all damn day."

Carrie gave Joe Winder a puzzled look. He said, "The rangers from Game and Fish—it's a long story."

"Government," Skink said. "A belated pang of conscience, at taxpayer expense. But Nature won't be fooled, the damage is already done."

Sensing trouble, Winder lurched in to change the subject. "So who are these mysterious others?"

"Remember that afternoon at the Amazing Kingdom, when a stranger gave you something?"

"Yeah, some old lady at the Rare Animal Pavilion. She handed me a note and then I got my lights punched out."

Skink said, "That was me who slugged you."

"What an odd relationship," Carrie remarked.

"My specialty," Joe Winder said. Then to Skink: "Can I ask why you knocked the door down tonight? Your timing stinks, by the way."

Skink was at the window again, lurking on the edge of the shadow. "Do you know anyone who drives a blue Saab?"

"No—"

"Because he was waiting at your apartment this morning. Big Cuban meathead who works at the park. He saw you arrive." Skink dropped down again. He said to Winder, "You were driving the young lady's car, right?"

"She loaned it to me. So what?"

"So it's got a parking sticker on the rear bumper."

"Oh shit, you're right." Joe Winder had completely forgotten: employees of the Amazing Kingdom were issued Petey Possum parking permits. Each decal bore an identification number. It was a simple matter to trace the car to Carrie Lanier.

"I need to go to fugitive school," Winder said. "This was really stupid."

Carrie asked Skink about the man in the blue Saab. "Did he follow Joe, too? Is he out there now?"

"He was diverted," Skink said, "but I'm sure he'll be here eventually. That's why we're leaving."

"No," Winder said, "I can't."

Skink asked Carrie Lanier for a paper napkin. Carefully he wrapped the uneaten segment of mud snake and placed it in a pocket of his blaze rainsuit.

He said, "There'll be trouble if we stay."

"I can't go," Winder insisted. "Look, the fax lines are already set up. Everything's in place right here."

"So you've got something more in mind?"

"You know I do. In fact, you've given me a splendid inspiration."

"All right, we'll wait until daybreak. Can you type in the dark?"

"It's been a while, but sure." Back in the glory days, Winder had once written forty inches in the blackness of a Gulfport motel bathroom—a Royal manual typewriter balanced on his lap. This was during Hurricane Frederic.

Skink said, "Get busy, genius. I'll watch the window."

"What can I do to help?" Carrie asked.

"Put on some Stones," said Skink.

"And some panties," Winder whispered.

She told him to hush and quit acting like an old prude.

While the tow truck hooked up the Saab, Pedro Luz forced himself to reflect on events.

There he was, waiting for Winder to come out of the apartment when here comes this big spade highway patrolman knocking on the window of the car.

"Hey, there," he says from behind those damn reflector shades.

"Hey," says Pedro Luz, giving him the slight macho nod that says, I'm one of you, brother.

But the spade doesn't go for it. Asks for Pedro's driver's license and also for the registration of the Saab. Looks over the papers and says, "So who's Ramex Global?"

"Oh, you know," Pedro says, flashing his old Miami PD badge.

Trooper goes "Hmmm." Just plain "Hmmm." And then the fucker jots down the badge number, like he's going to check it out!

Pedro resists the urge to reach under the seat for his gun. Instead he says, "Man, you're burning me. I'm sitting on a dude out here."

"Yeah? What's his name?"

Pedro Luz says, "Smith. José Smith." It's the best he can do on short notice, with his brain twitching all crazy inside his skull. "Man, you and that marked unit are burning me bad."

Trooper doesn't act too damn concerned. "So you're a police officer, is that right?"

"Hell," Pedro says, "you saw the badge."

"Yes, I sure did. You're a long way from the city."

"Hey, *chico*, we're in a war, remember."

"Narcotics?" The trooper sounds positively intrigued. "This man Smith, he's some big-time dope smuggler, eh?"

"Was," Pedro says. "He sees your car sitting out here, he's back in wholesale footwear."

"Hmmm," the spade trooper says again. Meanwhile Pedro's fantasizing about grabbing him around the middle and squeezing his guts out both ends, like a very large tube of licorice toothpaste.

"Don't tell me you're gonna run my tag," Pedro says.

"Nah." But the trooper's still leaning his thick black arms against the door of the Saab, his face not a foot from Pedro's, so that Pedro can see himself twice in the mirrored sunglasses. Now the trooper says: "What happened to your finger?"

"Cat bite."

"Looks like it took the whole top joint."

"That's right," says Pedro, aching all over, wishing he'd brought his intravenous bag of Winstrol-V. Talking high-octane. Same stuff they use on horses. One thousand dollars a vial, and worth every penny.

Trooper says, "Must've been some cat to give you a bite like that."

"Yeah, I ought to put the damn thing to sleep."

"Sounds like a smart idea," says the trooper, "before he bites you someplace else."

And then the sonofabitch touches the brim of his Stetson and says so long. Like John Fucking Wayne.

And here comes Winder, cruising out of the apartment with an armful of clothes. Gets in the car—not his car, somebody else's; somebody with an employee sticker from the Kingdom—and drives off with the radio blasting.

Pedro Luz lays back cool and sly, maybe half a mile, waiting until the cocky bastard reaches that long empty stretch on Card Sound Road, south of the Carysfort Marina. That's where Pedro aims to make the big move.

Until the Saab dies. Grinds to a miserable wheezing halt. A *Saab*!

Pedro Luz is so pissed he yanks the steering wheel off its column and heaves it into a tamarind tree. Only afterwards does it dawn on him that Mr. X isn't going to appreciate having a $35,000 automobile and no way to steer it.

An hour later, here comes Pascual's Wrecker Service. Guy lifts the hood, can't find a thing. Slides underneath, zero. Then he says maybe Pedro ran out of gas, and Pedro says don't be an asshole. Guy pulls off the gas cap, closes one eye and looks inside, like he can actually *see* something.

Then he sniffs real hard, rubs his nose, sniffs again. Then he starts laughing like a fruit.

"Your friends fucked you up real good," he says.

"What are you talking about?"

"Come here and take a whiff."

"No thanks," Pedro says.

Guy hoots. "Now I seen everything."

Pedro's trying to figure out when it happened. Figures somebody snuck up and did it while he was talking to that hardass trooper. Which means the trooper was in on it.

"Did a number on your engine," says the tow-truck man, chuckling way too much.

Pedro Luz grabs him by the arm until his fingers lock on

291

bone. He says, "So tell me. What exactly's in the gas tank?"

"Jack Daniel's," the guy says. "I know that smell anywhere."

So now Pedro's watching him put the hook to Mr. Kingsbury's Saab and wondering what else could go wrong. Thinking about the monkeys and shithead burglars and what happened to Churrito. Thinking about the black state trooper busting his balls for no reason, and how somebody managed to pour booze in the tank without Pedro even knowing it.

Pedro thinks he'd better shoot some horse juice in his arms as soon as possible, and get tight on Joe Winder's ass.

In one of his pockets he finds the scrap of paper where he wrote the decal number off the car Winder was driving. It's not much, but it's the only thing he's got to show for a long sorry morning.

So Pedro tells the tow-truck guy he's going to ride in the busted Saab on the way to the shop. Use Kingsbury's car phone to make a few calls.

Guy says no way, it's against company policy. Gotta sit up front in the truck.

Which is not what Pedro wants to hear after such a shitty day. So he tackles the guy and yanks his arms out of the sockets one at a time, pop-pop. Leaves him thrashing in the grass by the side of the road.

Jumps in the tow truck and heads for the Amazing Kingdom of Thrills.

The Mothers of Wilderness listened solemnly as Molly McNamara recounted the brutal assault. They were gathered in the Florida room of Molly's old house, where a potluck supper had been arranged on a calico tablecloth. Normally a hungry bunch, the Mothers scarcely touched the food; a huge bacon-cheese ball lay undisturbed on a sterling silver platter—a sure sign that the group was distracted.

And no wonder: Molly's story was appalling. No one dream-ed that the battle against Falcon Trace would ever come to violence. That Molly had been attacked by thugs in her own apartment was horrifying; equally unsettling was her lurid description of the finger-biting episode. In disbelief, several of the older members fiddled frenetically with the controls to their hearing aids.

"Obviously we've struck a nerve with Kingsbury," Molly was saying. "Finally he considers us a serious threat."

One of the Mothers asked why Molly had not called the police.

"Because I couldn't prove he was behind it," she replied. "They'd think I was daffy."

The members seemed unsatisfied by this explanation. They clucked and whispered among themselves until Molly cut in and asked for order. The lawyer, Spacci, stood up and said it was a mistake not to notify the authorities.

"You're talking about a felony," he said. "Aggravated assault, possibly even attempted murder."

One of the Mothers piped up: "It's not worth dying for, Molly. They're already clearing the land."

Molly's gray eyes flashed angrily. "It is not too late!" She wheeled on Spacci. "Did you file in federal court?"

"These things take time."

"Can you get an injunction?"

"No," said the lawyer. "You mean, to stop construction? No, I can't."

Molly drummed her fingers on the portable podium. Spacci was preparing to sit down when she jolted him back to atten-tion: "Give us a report on the blind trust."

"Yes, well, I talked to a fellow over in Dallas. He tells me the paperwork comes back to a company called Ramex Global, which is really Francis Kingsbury—"

"We *know*."

"—but the bulk of the money isn't his. It's from some S & L types. Former S & L types, I should say. Apparently they were in a hurry to invest."

"I'll bet," said one of the Mothers in the front row.

"They moved the funds through Nassau," Spacci said. "Not very original, but effective."

Molly folded her arms. "Perfect," she said. "Falcon Trace is being built with stolen savings accounts. And you people are ready to give up!"

"Our options," the lawyer noted, "are extremely limited."

"No, they're not. We're going to kill this project."

A worried murmuring swept through the Mothers. "How?" one asked. "How can we stop it now?"

"Sabotage," Molly McNamara answered. "Don't you people have any imagination?"

Immediately Spacci began waving his arms and whining about the ramifications of criminal misconduct.

Molly said: "If it makes you feel better, Mr. Spacci, get yourself a plate of the chicken Stroganoff and go out on the patio. And take your precious ethics with you."

Once the lawyer was gone, Molly asked if anyone else was having doubts about the Falcon Trace campaign. One board member, a devout Quaker, fluttered his hand and said yes, he was afraid of more bloodshed. Then he made a motion (quickly seconded) that the Mothers telephone the police to report the two men who had attacked Molly.

"We don't need the police," she said. "In fact, I've already retained the services of two experienced security men." With both hands she motioned to the back of the room, where Bud Schwartz and Danny Pogue stood near an open door. Danny Pogue flushed at the introduction and puffed his chest, trying to look like a tough customer. Bud Schwartz focused sullenly on an invisible tarantula, dangling directly over Molly McNamara's hair.

Eventually the Mothers of Wilderness quit staring at the burglars-turned-bodyguards, and Molly resumed her pep talk. Danny Pogue picked up a spoon and sidled over to the cheese ball. Bud Schwartz slipped out the door.

In a butcher shop near Howard Beach, Queens, a man known as The Salamander picked up the telephone and said: "Talk."

"Jimmy gave me the number. Jimmy Noodles."

"I'm listening," said The Salamander, whose real name was Salvatore Delicato.

"I got Jimmy's number from Gino Ricci's brother."

The Salamander said, "Fine. Didn't I already say I was listening? So talk."

"In case you wanna check it out—I'm calling from Florida. I did time with Gino's brother."

"How thrilling for you. Now I'm hangin' up, asshole."

"Wait," said the voice. "You been lookin' for a certain rat. I know where he is. The man who did the Zubonis."

The Salamander slammed down his cleaver. "Gimme a number I can call you back," he said. "Don't say another word, just tell me a number."

The caller from Florida repeated it twice. Sal Delicato used a finger to write the numerals in pig blood on a butcher block. Then he untied his apron, washed his hands, combed his hair, snatched a roll of quarters from the cash register and walked three blocks to a pay phone.

"All right, smart guy," he said when the man answered in Florida. "First off, I don't know any Zuboni brothers."

"I never said they was brothers."

"You didn't?" Shit, thought The Salamander. I gotta pay closer attention. "Look, never mind. Just hurry up and tell me what's so important."

"There's this creep in the Witness Relocation Program, you know who I'm talking about. He testified against the

295

Zuboni brothers, the ones you never heard of. Anyway, they gave this creep a new name, new Social Security, the whole nine yards. He's doing real nice for himself. In fact, he's worth a couple million bucks is what I hear."

Sal Delicato said, "You're a dreamer."

"Well, maybe I got the wrong man. Maybe I got some bad information. I was under the impression you people were looking for Frankie King, am I wrong?"

"I don't know no Frankie King."

"Fine. Nice talkin' with you—"

"Hold on," said The Salamander. "I probably know somebody who might be interested. What'd you say your name was?"

"Schwartz. Buddy Schwartz. I was with Gino's brother at Lake Butler, Florida. You can check it out."

"I will."

"In the meantime, you oughta talk to Mr. Gotti."

"I don't know no Gotti," said The Salamander. "I definitely don't know no fucking Gotti."

"Whatever."

Over the phone Bud Schwartz heard the din of automobile horns and hydraulic bus brakes and jackhammers and police sirens. He felt glad he was in Miami instead of on a street corner in Queens. At the other end, Sal Delicato cleared his throat with a series of porcine grunts. "You said they gave him a new name, right? This Frankie King."

"Yep," said Bud Schwartz.

"Well, what name does he got at the moment?"

"See, this is what I wanna talk about."

"Sounds like you're playin' games, huh?"

Bud Schwartz said, "No, sir. This ain't no game."

"All right, all right. Tell you what to do: First off, you might already got some problems. The phone lines to my shop aren't so clean, understand?"

Bud Schwartz said, "I'll be gone from here in a few days."

"Be that as it may," said The Salamander, "next time you call me at the shop, do it from a pay booth—they got pay booths in Florida, right? And don't say shit, either. Just say you want five dozen lamb chops, all right. That's how I know it's you—five dozen lamb chops."

"No problem," said Bud Schwartz.

"Thirdly, it don't matter what phones we're on, don't ever mention that fucking name."

"Frankie King?"

"No, the other one. The one starts with 'G.'"

"The one you never heard of?"

"Right," said Salvatore (The Salamander) Delicato. "That's the one."

Later, drinking a beer on the porch, Danny Pogue said, "I can't believe you done that."

"Why not?" said Bud Schwartz. "The asshole double-crossed us. Tried to rip us off."

"Plus what he done to Molly."

"Yeah, there's that."

Danny Pogue said, "Do you think they'll kill him?"

"Something like that. Maybe worse."

"Jesus, Bud, I wouldn't know how to call up the Mafia, my life depended on it. The Mafia!"

"It wasn't easy finding the right people. They're not in the Yellow Pages, that's for sure."

Danny Pogue laughed uproariously, exposing cheese-spackled teeth. "You're a piece of work," he said.

"Yeah, well." Bud Schwartz had surprised himself with the phone call. He had remained cool and composed even with a surly mob heavyweight on the other end of the line. Bud Schwartz felt he had braved a higher and more serious realm of criminality; what's more, he had single-handedly set in motion a major event.

Danny Pogue said, "How much'll they give us for turning the bastard in?"

"Don't know," said Bud Schwartz. "The man's checking it out."

Danny Pogue drained his beer and stared at his dirty tennis shoes. In a small voice he said, "Bud, I'm really sorry I ran away at the monkey place."

"Yeah, what a surprise. You taking off and leaving me alone to get my brains knocked out. Imagine that."

"I got scared is all."

"Obviously." What the hell could he expect? Like all thieves, Danny Pogue was low on valor and high on self-preservation.

He said, "It's okay if you killed that guy. I mean, it was definitely self-defense. No jury in the world would send you up on that one."

Great, Bud Schwartz thought, now he's Perry Mason. "Danny, I'm gonna tell you one more time: it wasn't me, it was a damn baboon."

Here was something Danny Pogue admired about his partner; most dirtbags would have lied about what happened so they could take credit for the shooting. Not Bud—even if a monkey was involved. That was Danny Pogue's idea of class.

"I got a feeling they meant to kill us," Bud Schwartz said. He had replayed the scene a hundred times in his head, and it always added up to a murderous rip-off. It made him furious to think that Francis Kingsbury would try it . . . so furious that he'd tracked down his old cellmate Mario, who steered him to Jimmy Noodles, who gave him the number of the butcher shop in Queens.

Noting but revenge was on Bud Schwartz's mind. "I want them to know," he said to Danny Pogue, "that they can't screw with us just 'cause we're burglars."

The screen door squeaked open and Molly McNamara joined the men on the porch. Her eyes looked puffy and tired. She asked Danny Pogue to fix her a glass of lemonade, and he dashed to the kitchen. She adjusted her new dentures and said, "The meeting went poorly. There's not much support for my ideas."

One hand moved to her chest, and she took a raspy, labored breath.

Bud Schwartz said, "You ain't feeling so good, huh?"

"Not tonight, no." She placed a tiny pill under her tongue and closed her eyes. A flash of distant lightning announced a thunderstorm sweeping in from the Everglades. Bud Schwartz spotted a mosquito on Molly's cheek, and he brushed it away.

She blinked her eyes and said, "You boys have been up to something, I can tell."

"It's going to be a surprise."

"I'm too old for surprises," said Molly.

"This one you'll like."

"Be careful, please." She leaned forward and dropped her voice. "For Danny's sake, be careful. He's not as sharp as you are."

Bud Schwartz said, "We look out for each other." Unless there's trouble, then the little dork runs for the hills.

"There's a reason I can't spill everything," Bud Schwartz said to Molly, "but don't you worry." She was in a mood, all right. He'd never seen her so worn out and gloomy.

Danny Pogue returned with a pitcher of lemonade. Molly thanked him and held her glass with both hands as she drank. "I'm afraid we won't be able to count on the Mothers of Wilderness," she said. "I sensed an alarming lack of resolve in the meeting tonight."

"You mean, they wimped out."

"Oh, they offered to picket Falcon Trace. And sign a

petition, of course. They're very big on petitions." Molly sighed and tilted her head. The oncoming thunder made the pine planks rumble beneath their feet.

"Maybe it's me. Maybe I'm just a batty old woman."

Danny Pogue said, "No, you're not!"

Yes, she is, thought Bud Schwartz. But that was all right. She was entitled.

Molly gripped the arms of the chair and pulled herself up. "We'll probably get a visitor soon," she said. "The tall fellow with the collar on his neck."

"Swell," Bud Schwartz muttered. His ribs still throbbed from last time.

"He's not to be feared," Molly McNamara said. "We should hear what he has to say."

This ought to be good, thought Bud Schwartz. This ought to be priceless.

Twenty-five

Early on the morning of July 29, a Sunday, the fax machine in the wire room of the *Miami Herald* received the following transmission:

REPTILE SCARE CLOSES THEME PARK; HIGH WATER BLAMED

The Amazing Kingdom of Thrills will be closed Sunday, July 29, due to an infestation of poisonous snakes caused by heavy summer rains and flooding. Cottonmouth moccasins numbering "in the low hundreds" swarmed the popular South Florida theme park over the weekend, according to Charles Chelsea, vice president of publicity.

Several workers and visitors were bitten Saturday, but no deaths were reported. "Our medical-emergency personnel responded to the crisis with heroic efficiency," Chelsea stated.

Reptile experts say snakes become more active in times of heavy rainfall, and travel great distances to seek higher ground. Even the so-called water moccasin, which thrives in canals and brackish lagoons, becomes uncommonly restless and aggressive during flood-type conditions.

The cottonmouth is a pit viper known for its large curved fangs and whitish mouth. While extremely painful, the bite of the snake is seldom fatal if medical treatment is administered quickly. However, permanent damage to muscle and soft tissue often occurs.

The moccasin is prevalent throughout South Florida, although it is rare to find more than two or three snakes together at a time. Cluster migrations are a rarity in nature. "They appeared to be hunting for toads," Chelsea explained.

Officials ordered the theme park to be closed temporarily while teams of armed hunters captured and removed the wild reptiles, some of which were nearly six feet in length.

Chelsea said that the Amazing Kingdom will reopen Tuesday morning with a full schedule of events. He added: "While we are confident that the grounds will be perfectly safe and secure, we are also suggesting, as a precaution, that our visitors wear heavy rubber boots. These will be available in all sizes, for a nominal rental fee."

Reporters began calling before eight o'clock. Charles Chelsea was summoned from home; he arrived bleary-eyed and tieless. Clutching a Styrofoam cup of black coffee, he hunched over the desk to examine Joe Winder's newest atrocity.

"Wicked bastard," he said after reading the last line.

A secretary told him about the TV helicopters. "We've counted five so far," she reported. "They're trying to get an aerial shot of the snakes."

"The snakes!" Chelsea laughed dismally.

To ignite his competitive spirit, the secretary said, "I can't believe they'd fall for a dumb story like this."

"Are you kidding?" Chelsea buried his hands in his hair.

"Snakes are dynamite copy. Anything with a snake, the media eats it up." A law of journalism of which Joe Winder, the ruthless sonofabitch, was well aware.

Chelsea sucked down the dregs of the coffee and picked up the phone. Francis X. Kingsbury answered on the seventeenth ring.

"I've got some extremely bad news," Chelsea said.

"Horseshit, Charlie, if you get my drift." It sounded as if Kingsbury's hay fever was acting up. "Calling me at home, Christ, what's your job description anyway—*professional pussy*? Is that what I hired you for?"

"No, sir." The publicity man gritted his teeth and told Kingsbury what had happened. There was a long unpleasant silence, followed by the sound of a toilet being flushed.

"I'm in the can," Kingsbury said. "That's what you get for calling me at home."

"Sir, did you hear what I said? About the snake story that Winder put out?"

"Yes, hell, I'm not deaf. Hold on." Chelsea heard the toilet flush again. Grimly he motioned for his secretary to get him another cup of coffee.

On the other end, Kingsbury said, "All right, so on this snake thing, what do you think?"

"Close the park for a day."

"Don't be an idiot."

"There's no choice, Mr. Kingsbury. Even if we came clean and admitted the press release was fake, nobody's going to believe it. They'll think we're covering up." That was the insidious genius of Joe Winder's strategy.

Kingsbury said: "Close the goddamn park, are you kidding? What about business?"

"Business is shot," Chelsea replied. "Nobody but reptile freaks would show up today. We're better off closing the Kingdom and taking our lumps."

"Un-fucking-real, this is."

"I forgot to mention, we'll also need to purchase some boots. Several hundred pairs." Chelsea's fingers began to cramp on the telephone receiver. He said, "Don't worry, I'll put something out on the wires right away."

"Everything's under control, blah, blah, blah."

"Right," said Chelsea. Now he could hear the water running in Francis Kingsbury's sink.

"I bruffing my teef," Kingsbury gargled.

Chelsea waited for the sound of spitting. Then he said, "I'll call a press conference for noon. We'll get somebody, some scientist, to say the snakes are almost gone. Then we'll reopen tomorrow."

Kingsbury said, "Four hundred grand is what this fucking clown is costing me, you realize? A whole day's receipts."

"Sir, it could get worse."

"Don't say that, Charlie."

In a monotone Chelsea read the phony press release to Francis Kingsbury, who said: "Christ Almighty, they get six feet long! These poison cottonheads do?"

"I don't know. I don't know how big they get." Chelsea wanted to tell Kingsbury that it really didn't matter if the imaginary snakes were two feet or twenty feet, the effect on tourists was the same.

Over the buzz of his electric razor, Kingsbury shouted, "What does he want—this prick Winder—what's he after?"

"Nothing we can give him," Chelsea said.

"It's got to stop or he'll kill our business."

"Yes, I know."

"And I'll tell you what else," Francis Kingsbury said. "I'm very disappointed in that fucking Pedro."

Molly McNamara was writing a letter to her daughter in Minneapolis when Danny Pogue rushed into the den.

Excitedly he said, "I just saw on the news about all them snakes!" His Adam's apple juked up and down.

"Yes," Molly said, "it's very odd."

"Maybe you could get your people together. The Mothers of Wilderness. Maybe go down to Key Largo and demonstrate."

"Against what?"

"Well, it said on the news they're killing 'em all. The snakes, I mean. That don't seem right—it ain't their fault about the high water." Danny Pogue was rigid with indignation, and Molly hated to dampen the fervor.

Gently she said, "I don't know that they're actually killing the snakes. The radio said something about capture teams."

"No, unh-uh, I just saw on the TV. A man from the Amazing Kingdom said they were killing the ones they couldn't catch. Especially the preggy ones." He meant "pregnant." "It's that Kingsbury asshole, pardon my French."

Molly McNamara capped her fountain pen and turned the chair toward Danny Pogue. She told him she understood how he felt. "But we've got to choose our battles carefully," she said, "if we hope to get the public on our side."

"So?"

"So there's not much sympathy for poisonous snakes."

Danny Pogue looked discouraged. Molly said, "I'm sorry, Danny, but it's true. Nobody's going to care if they use flame-throwers, as long as they get rid of the cottonmouths."

"But it ain't right."

Molly patted his knee. "There's plenty of snakes out there. Not like the mango voles, where there were only two left in the entire world."

With those words she could have hammered an icepick into Danny Pogue's heart. Morosely he bowed his head. As his environmental consciousness had been awakened, the vole theft had begun to weigh like a bleak ballast on his soul; he'd come to feel personally responsible for the

305

extinction of the voles, and had inwardly promised to avenge his crime.

He said to Molly: "What's the word you used before—'atome'?"

"Atone, Danny. A-t-o-n-e. It means making amends."

"Yeah, well, that's me."

Molly smiled and removed her reading glasses. "Don't worry, we've all made mistakes in our lives. We've all committed errors of judgment."

"Like when you shot me and Bud. Before you got to know us better."

"No, Danny, that wasn't a mistake. I'd do the same thing all over again, if it became necessary."

"You would?"

"Oh, now, don't take it the wrong way. Come here." Molly reached out and took him by the shoulders. Firmly she pulled his greasy head to her breast. The heavy jasmine scent brought the tickle of a sneeze to Danny Pogue's nostrils.

Molly gave him a hug and said, "Both you boys mean so much to me." Danny Pogue might have been moved to tears, except for the familiar bluish glint of the pistol tucked in the folds of Molly's housedress.

He said, "You want some tea?"

"That would be lovely."

As soon as Carrie Lanier left for work, Skink curled up in the shower, turned on the cold water and went to sleep.

Joe Winder kept writing for thirty minutes, until his will dissolved and he could no longer concentrate. He dialed Miriam's house and asked for Nina.

"It's six-dirty inna morning," Miriam complained.

"I know what time it is. May I speak to her, please?"

"What if chee no here?"

"Miriam, I swear to God—"

"All rye, Joe. Chew wait."

When Nina came on the line, she sounded wide awake. "This is very rude of you," she said crossly, "waking Miriam."

"What about you?"

"I was writing."

"Me too," Joe Winder said. "You were working on your phone fantasies?"

"My stories, yes."

"That's the main reason for the call. I had an idea for you." Nina said, "I've got some good news, Joe. I'm getting syndicated."

"Hey, that's great." Syndicated? What the hell was she talking about. Ann Landers was *syndicated*. Ellen Goodman was syndicated. Not women who write about bondage on Olympic diving boards.

"There's a company called Hot Talk," Nina said. "They own, like, two hundred of these adult phone services. They're going to buy my scripts and market them all over. Chicago, Denver, even Los Angeles."

"That's really something."

"Yeah, in a few months I'll be able to get off the phones and write full-time. It's like a dream come true."

She asked about Joe's idea for a fantasy and he described it. "Not bad," Nina admitted. "It just might work."

"Oh, it'll work," Winder said, but Nina didn't take the bait. She expressed no curiosity. "Remember," he added, "it has to be a fishnet suit with absolutely nothing underneath."

"Joe, please. I understand the principle."

He was hoping she would ask how he was doing, what he'd been up to, and so on. Instead she told him she'd better go because she didn't want to keep Miriam awake.

Winder fought for more time. "Basically, I called to see how you're doing. I admit it."

"Well, I'm doing fine."

"Things might get crazy in the next week or so. I didn't want you to worry."

"I'll try not to." Her tone was disconcertingly sincere. Winder waited for a follow-up question, but none came.

He blurted: "Are you seeing anybody?"

"Not exactly."

"Oh?"

"What I mean is, there's a man."

"Oh, ho!" A hot stab in the sternum.

"But we're not exactly seeing each other," Nina said. "He calls up and we talk."

"He calls on the 976 number? You mean he's a customer!"

"It's not like the others. We talk about deep things, personal things—I can't describe it, you wouldn't understand."

"And you've never actually met him?"

"Not face-to-face, no. But you can tell a lot from the way a person talks. I think he must be very special."

"What if he's a hunchback? What if he's got pubic lice?" Joe Winder was reeling. "Nina, don't you see how sick this is? You're falling in love with a stranger's voice!"

"He's very sensual, Joe. I can tell."

"For God's sake, the man's calling on the come line. What does that tell you?"

"I don't want to get into it," Nina said. "You asked if I was interested in anyone, and I told you. I should've known you'd react this way."

"Just tell me, is he paying for the telephone calls?"

"We've agreed to split the cost."

"Sweet Jesus."

"And we're meeting for dinner Tuesday up in the Gables."

"Wonderful," said Joe Winder. "What color trench coat did he say he'd be wearing?"

"I hate you," Nina remarked.

They hung up on each other at precisely the same instant.

Pedro Luz slithered beneath Carrie's mobile home. Lying on his back in the cool dirt, he listened to the shower running and laughed giddily. He placed both hands on a wooden floor beam and pushed with all his strength; he was certain that he felt the double-wide rise above him, if only a few millimeters. With a bullish snort, he tried again. To bench-press a mobile home! Pedro Luz grimaced in ecstasy.

He was proud of himself for tracing the car, even if the detective work entailed only the pushing of three lousy buttons on a computer. He was equally proud of himself for locating the address in the dark and remaining invisible to the occupants of the trailer. At dawn he had watched the woman drive off to work, leaving him alone with that crazy doomed bastard, Joe Winder.

Pedro Luz had spent a long time fueling himself for the task. He had strung the intravenous rigs in the storage room of the Security Department at the Amazing Kingdom of Thrills. There, stretched on a cot, he had dripped large quantities of horse steroids into both arms. Afterwards, Pedro Luz had guzzled nine Heinekens and studied himself naked in a full-length mirror.

The mirror examination had become a ritual to make sure that his penis and testicles were not shrinking, as Churrito had warned they would. Pedro Luz had become worried when his security-guard uniform had gotten baggy in the crotch, so every night he took a measuring tape and checked his equipment. Then he would leaf through some pornographic magazines to make sure he could still get a hard-on; on some evenings, when he was particularly anxious, he would even measure the angle of his erection.

On the night he went after Joe Winder, the angle was exactly zero degrees. Pedro Luz blamed it on the beer.

*

Inside the trailer, Winder finished typing another counterfeit press release, which said:

The widow of a young scientist killed at the Amazing Kingdom of Thrills has been offered a settlement of $2.8 million, officials of the popular amusement park have announced.

The payment would be made in a single installment to Deborah Koocher, age 31, of New York. Her husband, Dr. William Bennett Koocher, was a noted wildlife biologist who helped supervise the Endangered Species Program at the Amazing Kingdom. Dr. Koocher died two weeks ago in a tragic drowning at the park's outdoor whale tank. That incident is still under investigation.

Charles Chelsea, vice president of publicity, said the cash offer to Mrs. Koocher "demonstrates our sense of loss and sorrow over the untimely death of her husband."

Added Chelsea: "Will was instrumental in our rare-animal programs, and his heroic efforts to save the blue-tongued mango vole won international acclaim."

In a statement released Sunday morning, Francis X. Kingsbury, founder and chairman of the Amazing Kingdom, said that Dr. Koocher's death "was a tragedy for all of us at the park. We had come to love and admire Will, who was as much a part of our family as Robbie Raccoon or Petey Possum."

The $2.8 million settlement offer is "a gesture not only of compassion, but fairness," Mr. Kingsbury added. "If Dr. Koocher's family isn't satisfied, we would certainly consider increasing the payment."

Joe Winder reread the announcement, inserted the word "completely" before "satisfied," and fed the paper into the fax machine. He considered phoning Nina again, but decided it was no use; the woman was groping recklessly for male companionship. What else could explain her irrational attraction to a disembodied masculine voice?

Besides, Joe had Carrie now—or she had him. The dynamics of the relationship had yet to be calibrated.

Winder was in the mood for acoustic guitar, so he put on some Neil Young and fixed himself four eggs, scrambled, and two English muffins with tangerine marmalade. Glancing out the kitchen window, he noticed a tow truck parked crookedly on the shoulder of the dirt lane. He didn't see a driver.

The shower had been running for some time. Winder cracked the door and saw Skink curled in a fetal snooze, cold water slapping on the blaze weather suit. Winder decided not to wake him.

Suddenly he heard a pop like a car backfiring, and a hole the size of a nickel appeared in the tile six inches above Skink's face. Then came another bang, another hole.

Joe Winder yelled and dived out of the doorway.

In a way, Carrie Lanier was glad that the Amazing Kingdom was closed. It meant an extra day to work on her singing, which was still rusty, and to design a new costume for Princess Golden Sun.

Driving back toward the mainland, she couldn't wait to tell Joe about all the TV trucks and helicopters at the park's main gate. A reporter from Channel 10 had approached the car and thrust a microphone in her face and asked if she had seen any snakes. Quickly Carrie had improvised a story about a teeming herd— she wasn't sure it was the right term—slithering across County Road 905 near Carysfort. The fellow from Channel 10 had marshaled his camera crew and sprinted off toward the van.

Carrie was impressed by the immediate and dramatic effect of Joe Winder's hoax: everyone was wearing sturdy rubber hip boots.

311

On the way home, she practiced another song from the show:

You took our whole Indian nation,
Stuck us on this reservation.
Took away our way of life,
The garfish gig and the gator knife.
Seminole people! Seminole tribe!

It was a variation of a song called "Indian Reservation," which was recorded by Paul Revere and the Raiders, a band not generally remembered for its biting social commentary. Carrie Lanier thought the new lyrics were insipid, but she liked the simple tune and tom-tom rhythms. She was singing the third verse when she turned into the trailer park and spotted a bloated bodybuilder firing a pistol into the side of her double-wide.

Without hesitating, without even honking the horn, Carrie Lanier took aim.

Pedro Luz was so thoroughly engrossed in assassinating Joe Winder in the shower that he didn't hear the 1979 Buick Electra until it mowed a row of garbage cans ten feet behind him. Pedro Luz started to run but tripped over a garden hose and pitched forward, arms outstretched; it seemed as if he were tumbling in slow motion. When he stopped, the Buick was parked squarely on his left foot.

He lay there for a full minute, bracing for agony that never came. Each of the twenty-six bones in Pedro Luz's foot had been pulverized, yet the only sensation was a mildly annoying throb. Four thousand pounds of ugly Detroit steel on his toes and not even a twinge of pain. Incredible, Pedro thought; the ultimate result of supreme physical conditioning! Or possibly the drugs.

Apparently the driver had abandoned the Buick with the engine running. Steroids and all, Pedro Luz could not budge the sedan by himself. Meanwhile, the gunfire and crash had awakened other denizens of the trailer park; bulldogs yapped, doors slammed, babies wailed, a rooster cackled. Probably somebody had phoned the police.

Pedro Luz probed at the bloody burrito that was now his left foot, protruding beneath a Goodyear whitewall, and made a fateful decision.

What the hell, he mused. Long as I'm feeling no pain.

Dr. Richard Rafferty's assistant called him at home to say there was an emergency, he'd better come right away. When he arrived at the office, the doctor sourly observed a tow truck parked in the handicapped zone. Inside the examining room, a husky one-eyed man with a radio collar lay prone on the steel table.

Dr. Rafferty said: "Is this some kind of joke?"

The couple who had brought the injured man said he had been shot at least twice.

"Then he's got a big problem," said Dr. Rafferty, "because I'm a veterinarian."

The couple seemed to know this already. "He won't go to a regular doctor," Joe Winder explained.

Carrie Lanier added, "We took him to the hospital but he refused to get out of the truck."

Dr. Rafferty's assistant pulled him aside. "I believe I saw a gun," he whispered.

Skink opened his good eye and turned toward the vet. "Richard, you remember me?"

"I'm not sure."

"The night that panther got nailed by the liquor truck."

Dr. Rafferty leaned closer and studied the face. "Lord, yes," he said. "I do remember." It was the same fellow who'd charged into the office with a hundred-pound wildcat in his bare arms. The doctor remembered how the dying panther had clawed bloody striations on the man's neck and shoulders.

Skink said, "You did a fine job, even though we lost the animal."

"We gave it our best."

"How about another try?"

"Look, I don't work on humans."

"I won't tell a soul," Skink said.

"Please," Joe Winder cut in, "you're the only one he'll trust." Skink's chest heaved, and he let out a groan.

"He's lost some blood," Carrie said.

Dr. Rafferty slipped out of his jacket and told the assistant to prepare a surgical tray. "Oh, we've got plenty of blood," the doctor said, "but unless you're a schnauzer, it won't do you much good."

"Whatever," Skink mumbled, drifting light-headedly. "If you can't fix me up, then put me to sleep. Like you would any old sick dog."

Twenty-six

Charles Chelsea decided that "dapper" was too strong a word for Francis X. Kingsbury's appearance; "presentable" was more like it.

Kingsbury wore a gray silk necktie, and a long-sleeved shirt to conceal the lewd mouse tattoo. The reason for the sartorial extravagance was an invitation to address the Tri-County Chamber of Commerce luncheon; Kingsbury intended to use the occasion to unveil a model of the Falcon Trace Golf and Country Club Resort Community.

Impatiently he pointed at Charles Chelsea's belly and said: "So? The damn snake situation—let's hear it."

"The worst is over," said Chelsea, with genuine confidence. He had countered Joe Winder's moccasin attack with a publicity blurb announcing that most of the reptiles had turned out to be harmless banded water snakes that only *looked* like deadly cottonmouths. For reinforcement Chelsea had released videotape of a staged capture, peppered with reassuring comments from a local zoologist.

"By the end of the week, we can send back all those boots," Chelsea said in conclusion.

"All right, that's fine." Kingsbury swiveled toward the

window, then back again. Restlessly he kneaded the folds of his neck. "Item Number Two," he said. "This shit with the doctor's widow, is that cleared up yet?"

Here Chelsea faltered, for Joe Winder had stymied him with the Koocher gambit. The publicity man was at a loss for remedies. There was no clever or graceful way to recant a $2.8 million settlement offer for a wrongful death.

Anxiety manifested itself in a clammy deluge from Chelsea's armpits. "Sir, this one's a stumper," he said.

"I don't want to hear it!" Kingsbury clasped his hands in a manner suggesting that he was trying to control a homicidal rage. "What was it, two-point-eight? There's no fucking way—what, do I look like Onassis?"

Chelsea's jaws ached from nervous clenching. He pushed onward: "To rescind the offer could have very grave consequences, publicity-wise. The fallout could be ugly."

"Grave consequences? I'll give you grave, Charlie. Two million simoleons outta my goddamn pocket, how's that for grave?"

"Perhaps you should talk to the insurance company."

"Ha!" Kingsbury tossed back his head and snorted insanely. "They just jack the rates, those assholes, every time some putz from Boise stubs his little toe. No way, Charlie, am I talking to those damn insurance people."

In recent years the insurance company had tripled its liability premium for the Amazing Kingdom of Thrills. This was due to the unusually high incidence of accidents and injuries on the main attractions; the Wet Willy water slide alone had generated seventeen lawsuits, and out-of-court settlements totaling nearly three-quarters of a million dollars. Even more costly was the freakish malfunction of a mechanical bull at the Wild Bill Hiccup Corral—an elderly British tourist had been hospitalized with a 90-degree crimp in his plastic penile implant. The jury's seven-figure verdict had surprised no one.

There was no point rehashing these sad episodes with Francis Kingsbury, for it would only appear that Charles Chelsea was trying to defend the insurance company.

"I think you should be aware," he said, "Mrs. Koocher has retained an attorney."

"Good for her," Kingsbury rumbled. "Let her explain to a judge what the hell her old man was doing, swimming with a damn killer whale in the middle of the night."

Chelsea was now on the precipice of anger himself. "If we drag this out, the *Herald* and the TV will be all over us. Do we really want a pack of reporters investigating the doctor's death?"

Kingsbury squinted suspiciously. "What are you getting at?"

"I'm simply advising you to take time and think about this. Let me stall the media."

The swiveling started again, back and forth, Kingsbury fidgeting like a hyperactive child. "Two-point-eight-million dollars! Where the hell did that crazy number come from? I guess he couldn't of made it a hundred grand, something doable."

"Winder? No, sir, he tends to think big."

"He's trying to put me out of business, isn't he?" Francis Kingsbury stopped spinning the chair. He planted his elbows on the desk and dug his polished fingernails into his jowls. "The fucker, this is my theory, the fucker's trying to put me under."

"You might be right," Chelsea admitted.

"What's his—you hired him, Charlie—what's his angle?"

"I couldn't begin to tell you. For now, my advice is to get the insurance company in touch with Mrs. Koocher's lawyer. Before it blows up even worse."

Kingsbury gave an anguished moan. "Worse? How is that possible?"

"Anything's possible." Chelsea was alarmed by the weariness in his own voice. He wondered if the tempest of bad news would ever abate.

The phone buzzed and Kingsbury plucked it off the hook. He listened, grunted affirmatively and hung up. "Pedro's on his way in," he said. "And it better be good news or I'm gonna can his fat ass."

Pedro Luz did not look like a cheery bundle of good tidings. The wheelchair was one clue. The missing foot was another.

Kingsbury sighed. "Christ, now what?" He saw a whopper of a worker's comp claim coming down the pike.

"An accident," Pedro Luz said, wheeling to a stop in front of Kingsbury's desk. "Hey, it's not so bad."

Chelsea noticed that the security man's face was swollen and mottled like a rotten melon, and that his massive arms had exploded in fresh acne sores.

Kingsbury drummed on a marble paperweight. "So? Let's hear it."

Pedro Luz said, "I shot the bastard."

"Yeah?"

"You better believe it."

Charles Chelsea deftly excused himself; talk of felonies made him uncomfortable. He closed the door softly and nearly sprinted down the hall. He was thinking: Thank God it's finally over. No more dueling flacks.

Kingsbury grilled Pedro Luz on the details of the Joe Winder murder, but the security man edited selectively.

"He was in the shower. I fired eleven times, so I know damn well I hit him. Besides, I heard the shouts."

Kingsbury asked, "How do you know he's dead?"

"There was lots of blood," said Pedro Luz. "And like I told you, I fired almost a dozen goddamn rounds. Later I set the place on fire."

"Yeah?" Kingsbury had seen footage of a trailer blaze on Channel 4; there had been no mention of bodies.

Pedro Luz said, "It went up like a damn torch. One of them cheap mobile homes."

"You're sure the bastard was inside?"

"Far as I know. And the bitch, too."

Francis Kingsbury said, "Which bitch? You're losing me here."

"The dumb bitch he was staying with. The one who ran me over." Pedro Luz gestured at the bandaged stump on the end of his leg. "That's what she did to me."

The puffy slits made it difficult to read the expression in Pedro Luz's eyes. Kingsbury said, "She hit you with a car?"

"More than that, she ran me down. Parked right on top of me."

"On your foot? Jesus Christ." Kingsbury winced sympathetically.

Pedro Luz said: "Good thing I'm in shape." Self-consciously he folded his bulging arms and spread his hands in a way that covered the pimples.

Kingsbury said, "So what happened?"

"What do you mean? I told you what happened."

"No, I mean with the car on your foot. How'd you get free?"

"Oh, I chewed it off," said Pedro Luz, "right below the ankle."

Kingsbury stared at the stump. He couldn't think of anything to say.

"Animals do it all the time," Pedro Luz explained, "when they get caught in traps."

Francis Kingsbury nodded unconsciously. His eyes roamed the office, searching for a convenient place to throw up.

"The hard part wasn't the pain. The hard part was the reach." Pedro Luz bent down to demonstrate.

"Oh Lord," Kingsbury muttered.

"Like I said, it's a good thing I'm in shape."

At the campsite, Joe Winder told Molly McNamara it was nice to see her again. Molly congratulated Joe for blowing up Kingsbury's bulldozers. Skink thanked Molly for the bottle of Jack Daniel's, and briefly related how it had been utilized. Carrie Lanier was introduced to the burglars, whom she instantly recognized as the scruffy vole robbers. Bud Schwartz and Danny Pogue were stunned to learn that Robbie Raccoon was a woman, and apologized for knocking Carrie down during the heist.

The heat was throbbing and the hammock steamed. No breeze stirred off the water. A high brown haze of African dust muted the hues of the broad summer sky. Skink handed out cold sodas and tended the fire; he wore cutoff jeans, the panther collar and a thick white vest of tape and bandages.

"You were lucky," Molly told him.

"Guy was aiming high," Skink said. "He assumed I'd be standing up."

As most people do in the shower, thought Joe Winder. "He also assumed that you were me," he said.

"Maybe so." Skink smeared a stick of EDTIAR bug repellent on both arms. Then he sat down under a buttonwood tree to count the mosquitoes biting his legs.

Carrie Lanier told the others about the breakneck ride to the veterinarian. "Dr. Rafferty did a great job. We're lucky he knew somebody over at the Red Cross."

Between insect frenzies, Danny Pogue struggled to follow the conversation. "You got shot?" he said to Skink. "So did me and Bud!"

Sharply, Molly cut in: "It wasn't the same."

"Like hell," mumbled Bud Schwartz miserably. The humidity made him dizzy, and his arms bled from scratching the

320

bugs. In addition, he wasn't thrilled about the lunch menu, which included fox, opossum and rabbit—Skink's road-kill bounty from the night before.

Joe Winder was in a lousy mood, too. The sight of Carrie's burned-out trailer haunted him. The fax machine, the Amazing Kingdom stationery, his stereo—all lost. Neil Young, melting in the flames. Helpless, helpless, helpless, helpless.

Skink said, "It's time to get organized. Those damn John Deeres are back." He looked at Winder. "Now they've got cops on the site."

"What can we blow up next?" Molly asked.

Skink shook his head. "Let's try to be more imaginative."

"All the building permits are in Kingsbury's name," Winder noted. "If he goes down, the project goes under."

Carrie wondered what Joe meant by "goes down."

"You mean, if he dies?"

"Or gets bankrupt," Winder said.

"Or lost," added Skink, glancing up from his mosquito census.

Danny Pogue elbowed Bud Schwartz, who kept his silence. He had spoken again to the butcher in Queens, who had relayed an offer from unnamed friends of the Zubonis: fifty thousand for the whereabouts of Frankie King. Naturally Bud Schwartz had agreed to the deal; now, sitting in the wilderness among these idealistic crusaders, he felt slightly guilty. Maybe he should've ratted on Kingsbury for free.

"Mr. X had a terrible run of luck the last few days," Carrie was saying, "thanks to Joe."

Skink got up to check the campfire. He said, "It's time for a full-court press."

"Each day is precious," agreed Molly McNamara. She dabbed her forehead with a linen handkerchief. "I think we should move against Mr. Kingsbury as soon as possible."

Bud Schwartz crumpled a soda can. "Why don't we hold off a week or so?"

"No." Skink offered him a shank of opossum on a long-handled fork. He said, "Every hour that passes, we lose more of the island."

"Kingsbury's got worse problems than all of us put together," said Bud Schwartz. "If we can just lay back a few days."

Joe Winder urged him to elaborate.

"Tell him, Bud, go on!" Danny Pogue was nearly bursting.

"I wisht I could."

Skink fingered the silvery tendrils of his beard. Towering over the burglar, he said, "Son, I'm not fond of surprises."

"This is serious shit." Bud Schwartz was pleading. "You gotta understand—heavy people from up North."

Wiping the condensation from her eyeglasses, Molly said, "Bud, what on earth are you talking about?"

Winder leaned toward Carrie and whispered: "This is getting interesting."

"No damn surprises," Skink repeated balefully. "We act in confluence, you understand?"

Reluctantly Bud Schwartz took a bite of fried opossum. He scowled as the warm juices dripped down his chin.

"Is that blood?" asked Danny Pogue.

Skink nodded and said, "Nature's gravy."

Suddenly he turned his face to the sky, peered toward the lemon sun and cursed vehemently. Then he was gone, running barefoot into the bright tangles of the hammock.

The others looked at one another in utter puzzlement.

Joe Winder was the first to stand. "When in Rome," he said, reaching for Carrie's hand.

*

Humanity's encroachment had obliterated the Florida panther so thoroughly that numerals were assigned to each of the few surviving specimens. In a desperate attempt to save the species, the Game and Fresh Water Commission had embarked on a program of monitoring the far-roaming panthers and tracking their movements by radio telemetry. Over a period of years most of the cats were treed, tranquilized and fitted with durable plastic collars that emitted a regular electronic signal on a frequency of 150 megahertz. The signals could be followed by rangers on the ground or, when the animal was deep in the swamps, by air. Using this system, biologists were able to map the territories traveled by individual cats, chart their mating habits and even locate new litters of kittens. Because the battery-operated collars were activated by motion, it was also possible for rangers to know when a numbered panther was sick or even dead; if a radio collar was inert for more than a few hours, it automatically began sending a distress signal.

No such alarm was transmitted if an animal became abnormally active, but the rangers were expected to notice any strange behavior and react accordingly. For instance, a panther that was spending too much time near populated areas was usually captured and relocated for its own safety; the cats had a long and dismal record of careless prowling along busy highways.

Sergeant Mark Dyerson had retrieved too many dead panthers that had been struck by trucks and automobiles. Recently the ranger had become certain that if something wasn't done soon, Panther 17 would end up the same way. The Game and Fish files indicated that the animal was a seven-year-old male whose original range stretched from Homestead south to Everglades National Park, and east all the way to Card Sound. Because this area was crisscrossed by high-speed roads, the rangers paid special attention to the travels of Number 17.

For months the cat had seemed content to hunker in the deep upland hammocks of North Key Largo, which made sense, considering the dicey crossing to the mainland. But Sergeant Dyerson had grown concerned when, two weeks earlier, radio readings on Number 17 began to show extraordinary, almost unbelievable movement. Intermittent flyovers had pinpointed the cat variously at Florida City, North Key Largo, Homestead, Naranja and South Miami—although Sergeant Dyerson believed the latter coordinates were a mistake, probably a malfunction of the radio tracking unit. South Miami was simply an impossible destination; not only was it well out of the panther's range, but the animal would have had to travel at a speed of sixty-five miles an hour to be there when the telemetry said it was. Unlike the cheetah, panthers prefer loping to racing. The only way Number 17 could go that far, Sergeant Dyerson joked to his pilot, is if it took a bus.

Even omitting South Miami from the readings, the cat's travels were inexplicably erratic. The rangers were concerned at the frequency with which Number 17 crossed Card Sound between Key Largo and the mainland. The only two possible routes—by water or the long bridge—were each fraught with hazards. It was Sergeant Dyerson's hope that Number 17 chose to swim the bay rather than risk the run over the steep concrete span, where the animal stood an excellent chance of getting creamed by a speeding car.

On July 29, the ranger took up the twin Piper to search for the wandering panther. The homing signal didn't come to life until the plane passed low over a trailer park on the outskirts of Homestead. It was not a safe place for humans, much less wild animals, and the panther's presence worried Sergeant Dyerson. Though the tawny cats were seldom visible from the Piper, the ranger half-expected to see Number 17 limping down the center lane of U.S. Highway 1.

Later that afternoon, Sergeant Dyerson went up again; this time he marked the strongest signal in thick cover near

Steamboat Creek, on North Key Largo. The ranger couldn't believe it— twenty-nine miles in one day! This cat was either manic, or chained to the bumper of a Greyhound.

When Sergeant Dyerson landed in Naples, he asked an electrician to double-check the antenna and receiver of the telemetry unit. Every component tested perfectly.

That night, the ranger phoned his supervisor in Tallahassee and reviewed the recent radio data on Number 17. The supervisor agreed that he'd never heard of a panther moving such a great distance, so fast.

"Send me a capture team as soon as possible," Sergeant Dyerson said. "I'm gonna dart this sonofabitch and find out what's what."

The twin Piper made three dives over the campsite. Joe Winder and Carrie Lanier watched from the bank of Steamboat Creek.

"Game and Fish," Winder said, "just what we need."

"What do we do?" Carrie asked.

"Follow the water."

They didn't get far. A tall uniformed man materialized at the edge of the tree line. He carried an odd small-bore rifle that looked like a toy. When he motioned to Joe and Carrie, they obediently followed him through the hammock out to the road. Molly McNamara and the two burglars already had been rounded up; another ranger, with a clipboard, was questioning them. There was no sign of Skink.

Sergeant Mark Dyerson introduced himself and asked to see some identification. Joe Winder and Carrie Lanier showed him their driver's licenses. The ranger was copying down their names when a gaunt old cracker, pulled by three lean hounds, came out of the woods.

"Any luck?" Sergeant Dyerson asked.

"Nope," said the tracker. "And I lost me a dog."

"Maybe the panther got him."

"They ain't no panther out there."

"Hell, Jackson, the radio don't lie." The ranger turned back to Joe Winder and Carrie Lanier. "And I suppose you're birdwatchers, too. Just like Mrs. McNamara and her friends."

Beautiful, thought Winder. We're bird-watchers now.

Playing along, Carrie informed the ranger they were following a pair of nesting kestrels.

"No kidding?" Sergeant Dyerson said. "I've never met a birder who didn't carry binoculars—and here I get five of 'em, all at one time."

"We're thinking of forming a club," said Carrie. Joe Winder bit his lip and looked away. Molly's Cadillac took off, eastbound—a crown of white hair behind the wheel, the burglars slouched in the back seat.

"I'll give you this much," the ranger said, "you sure don't look like poachers." A Florida Highway Patrol car pulled up and parked beside Sergeant Dyerson's Jeep. A muscular black trooper got out and tipped his Stetson at the ranger.

"Whatcha know?" the trooper said affably.

"Tracking a panther. These folks got in the way."

"A panther? You *got* to be kidding." The trooper's laughter boomed. "I've been driving this stretch for three years and never saw a bobcat, much less a panther."

"They're very secretive," Sergeant Dyerson said. "You wouldn't necessarily spot them." He wasn't in the mood for a nature lesson. He turned to the old tracker and told him to run the frigging dogs one more time.

"Ain't no point."

"Humor me," said Sergeant Dyerson. "Come on, let's go find your other hound."

Once the wildlife officers were gone, the trooper's easygoing smile dissolved. "You folks need a lift."

"No thanks," Joe Winder said.

"It wasn't a question, friend." The trooper opened the back door of the cruiser, and motioned them inside.

Twenty-seven

The trooper took them to lunch at the Ocean Reef Club. The clientele seemed ruffled by the sight of a tall black man with a sidearm.

"You're making the folks nervous," Joe Winder observed.

"Must be the uniform."

Carrie popped a shrimp into her mouth. "Are we under arrest?"

"I'd be doing all three of us a favor," Jim Tile said, "but no, unfortunately, you're not under arrest."

Winder was working on a grouper sandwich. Jim Tile had ordered the fried dolphin and conch fritters. The dining room was populated by rich Republican golfers with florid cheeks and candy-colored Izod shirts. The men shot anxious squinty-eyed glances toward the black trooper's table.

Jim Tile motioned for iced tea. "I can't imagine why I've never gotten a membership application. Maybe it got lost in the mail."

"What's the point of all this?" Winder asked.

"To have a friendly chat."

"About what?"

Jim Tile shrugged. "Flaming bulldozers. Dead whales. One-eyed woodsmen. You pick the subject."

"So we've got a mutual friend."

"Yes, we do." The trooper was enjoying the fish platter immensely; despite the stares, he seemed in no hurry to finish. He said, "The plane scared him off, right?"

"It doesn't make sense," Winder said. "They're not after him, they're after a cat. Why does he run?"

Jim Tile put down the fork and wiped his mouth. "My own opinion—he feels a duty to hide because that's what the panther would've done. He wears that damn collar like a sacred obligation."

"To the extreme."

"Yeah," the trooper said. "I don't expect they'll find that missing dog. You understand?"

Carrie said, "He's a very interesting person."

"A man to be admired but not imitated." Jim Tile paused. "I say that with no disrespect."

Winder chose not to acknowledge the warning. "Where do you think he went?" he asked the trooper.

"I'm not sure, but it's a matter of concern."

The manager of the restaurant appeared at the table. He was a slender young man with bleached hair and pointy shoulders and brand-new teeth. In a chilly tone he asked Jim Tile if he were a member of the club, and the trooper said no, not yet. The manager started to say something else but changed his mind. Jim Tile requested a membership application, and the manager said he'd be back in a jiffy.

"That's the last we'll see of him," the trooper predicted.

Joe Winder wanted to learn more about Skink. He decided it was safe to tell Jim Tile what the group had been doing in the hammock before the airplane came: "We were hatching quite a plot."

"I figured as much," the trooper said. "You know much about rock and roll?"

Carrie pointed at Winder and said, "Hard core."

329

"Good," said Jim Tile. "Maybe you can tell me what's a Mojo? The other day he was talking about a Mojo flying."

"*Rising*," Winder said. "Mojo rising. It's a line from The Doors—I believe it's got phallic connotations."

"No," Carrie jumped in. "I think it's about drugs."

The trooper looked exasperated. "White people's music, I swear to God. Sinatra's all right, but you can keep the rest of it."

"Shall we discuss rap?" Joe Winder said sharply. "Shall we examine the lyrical genius of, say, 2 Live Crew?" He could be very defensive when it came to rock. Carrie reached under the table and pinched his thigh. She told him to lighten up.

"Rikers Island," Jim Tile said. "Is there a song about Rikers Island?"

Winder couldn't think of one. "You sure it's not Thunder Island?"

"No." Jim Tile shook his head firmly. "Our friend said he'd be leaving Florida one day. Go up to Rikers Island and see to some business."

"But that's a prison," Carrie said.

"Yeah. A prison in New York City."

Joe Winder remembered something Skink had told him the first day at the campsite. If it was a clue, it foreshadowed a crime of undiluted madness.

Winder said, "Rikers is where they keep that idiot who shot John Lennon." He cocked an eyebrow at Jim Tile. "You *do* know who John Lennon was?"

"Yes, I do." The trooper's shoulders sagged. "This could be trouble," he added emptily.

"Our mutual friend never got over it," Winder said. "The other night, he asked me about the Dakota."

"Wait a minute." Carrie Lanier made a time-out signal with her hands. "You guys aren't serious."

Gloomily Jim Tile stirred the ice in his tea. "The man gets

his mind set on things. And these days, I've been noticing he doesn't handle stress all that well."

Joe Winder said, "Christ, it was only an airplane. It's gone now, he'll calm down."

"Let's hope." The trooper called for the check.

Carrie looked sadly at Winder. "And here I thought *you* were bonkers," she said.

Agent Billy Hawkins told Molly McNamara that the house was simply beautiful. Old-time Florida, you don't see pine floors like this anymore. Dade County pine.

Molly said, "I've got carpenter ants in the attic. All this wet weather's got 'em riled."

"You'd better get that seen to, and soon. They can be murder on the beams."

"Yes, I know. How about some more lemonade?"

"No, thank you," said Agent Hawkins. "We really need to talk about this telephone call."

Molly began to rock slowly. "I'm completely stumped. As I told you before, I don't know a living soul in Queens."

Hawkins held a notebook on his lap, a blue Flair pen in his right hand. He said, "Salvatore Delicato is an associate of the John Gotti crime family."

"Goodness!" Molly exclaimed.

"Prior arrests for racketeering, extortion and income-tax evasion. The phone call to his number was made from here. It lasted less than a minute."

"There must be some mistake. Did you check with Southern Bell?"

"Miss McNamara," Hawkins said, "can we please cut the crap."

Molly's grandmotherly expression turned glacial. "Watch your language, young man."

Flushing slightly, the agent continued: "Have you ever

331

met a Jimmy Nardoni, otherwise known as Jimmy Noodles? Or a man named Gino Ricci, otherwise known as Gino The Blade?"

"Such colorful names," Molly remarked. "No, I've never heard of them. Do you have my telephone bugged, Agent Hawkins?"

He resisted the impulse to tell her that Sal Delicato's telephone was tapped by a squadron of eavesdroppers—not only the FBI, but the New York State Police, the U.S. Drug Enforcement Administration, the Tri-State Task Force on Organized Crime and the Bureau of Alcohol, Tobacco and Firearms. The New York Telephone box on the utility pole behind The Salamander's butcher shop sprouted so many extra wires, it looked like a pigeon's nest.

"Let me give you a scenario," Agent Hawkins said to Molly. "A man used your phone to call Sal Delicato for the purpose of revealing the whereabouts of a federally protected witness now living in Monroe County, Florida."

"That's outlandish," Molly said. "Who is this federal witness?"

"I imagine you already know." Hawkins jotted something in the notebook. "The man who made the phone call, we believe, was Buddy Michael Schwartz. I showed you his photograph the last time we visited. You said he looked familiar."

"I vaguely remember."

"He has other names," Hawkins said. "As I told you before, Schwartz is wanted in connection with the animal theft from the Amazing Kingdom."

"Wanted?"

"For questioning," the agent said. "Anyway, we believe the events are connected." The ominous wiretap conversation had elevated the vole investigation from zero-priority to high-priority. Billy Hawkins had been yanked off a bank-robbery case and ordered to find out why anyone would be setting up Francis X. Kingsbury, aka Frankie King. The Justice Department had pretty much forgotten about Frankie The Ferret until the phone call to Sal Delicato. The renewed interest in Washington was not a concern for Frankie's well-being so much as fear of a potential publicity nightmare; the murder of a protected government informant would not enhance the reputation of the Witness Relocation Program. It could, in fact, have a profoundly discouraging effect on other snitches. Agent Hawkins was told to track down Buddy Michael Schwartz and then call for backup.

Molly McNamara said, "You think this man might have broken into my house to use the phone!"

"Not exactly," Hawkins said.

She peered at him skeptically. "How do you know it was he on the line? Did you use one of those voice-analyzing machines?"

The FBI man chuckled. "No, we didn't need a machine. The caller identified himself."

"By name?" The blockhead! Molly thought.

"No, not by name. He told Mr. Delicato that he was an acquaintance of Gino Ricci's brother. It just so happens that Buddy Michael Schwartz served time with Mario Ricci at the Lake Butler Correctional Institute."

Molly McNamara said, "Could be a coincidence."

"They shared a cell. Buddy and Gino's brother."

"But still—"

"Would you have a problem," the agent said, "if I asked you to come downtown and take a polygraph examination?"

Molly stopped rocking and fixed him with an indignant glare. "Are you saying you don't believe me?"

"Call it a hunch."

"Agent Hawkins, I'm offended."

"And I'm tired of this baloney." He closed the notebook and capped the pen. "Where is he?"

"I don't know what you're talking about."

Hawkins stood up, pocketed his notebook, straightened his tie. "Let's go for a ride," he said. "Come on."

"No!"

"Don't make it worse for yourself."

"You're not paying attention," Molly said. "I thought G-men were trained to be observant."

Billy Hawkins laughed. "G-men? I haven't heard that one in a long—"

It was then he noticed the pistol. The old lady held it impassively, with both hands. She was pointing it directly at his crotch.

"This is amazing," said the agent. "The stuff of legends." Wait till the tough guys at Quantico hear about it.

Molly asked Billy Hawkins to raise his hands.

"No, ma'am."

"And why not?"

"Because you're going to give me the gun now."

"No," said Molly, "I'm going to shoot you."

"Lady, gimme the goddamn gun!"

Calmly she shot him in the thigh, two and one-quarter inches below the left hip. The FBI man went down with a howl, clawing at the burning hole in his pants.

"I told you to watch your language," Molly said.

The pop of the pistol brought Danny Pogue and Buddy Schwartz scrambling down the stairs. From a living-room window they cautiously surveyed the scene on the porch: Molly rocking placidly, a man in a gray suit thrashing on the floor.

Danny Pogue cried, "She done it again!"

"Christ on a bike," said Bud Schwartz, "it's that dick from the FBI."

The burglars cracked the door and peeked out. Molly assured them the situation was under control.

"Flesh wound," she reported. "Keep an eye on this fellow while I get some ice and bandages." She confiscated Billy Hawkins's Smith & Wesson and gave it to Bud Schwartz, who took it squeamishly, like a dog turd, in his hands.

"It works best when you aim it," Molly chided.

Danny Pogue reached for the barrel. "I'll do it!"

"Like hell," said Bud Schwartz, spinning away. He sat in the rocker and braced the pistol on his knee. The air smelled pungently of gunpowder; it brought back the memory of Monkey Mountain and the trigger-happy baboon.

Watching the gray-suited man squirm in pain, Bud Schwartz fought the urge to get up and run. What was the old bat thinking this time? Nothing good could come of shooting an FBI man. Surely she understood the consequences.

Danny Pogue opened the front door for Molly, who disappeared into the house with a pleasant wave. Danny Pogue sat down, straddling an iron patio chair. "Take it easy," he told the agent. "You ain't hurt so bad."

Billy Hawkins grunted up at him. "What's your name?"

"Marcus Welby," Bud Schwartz cut in. "Don't he look like a doctor?"

"I know who *you* are," the agent said. It felt as if a giant wasp were boring into his thigh. Billy Hawkins unbuckled his trousers and grimaced at the sight of his Jockey shorts soaked crimson.

"You assholes are going to jail," he said, pinching the pale flesh around the bullet wound.

"We're just burglars," said Danny Pogue.

"Not anymore." Hawkins attempted to rise to his feet, but Bud Schwartz wiggled the gun and told him to stay where he was. The agent's forehead was sprinkled with sweat, and his lips were gray. "Hey, Bud," he said, "I've seen your jacket, and this isn't your style. Assault on a federal officer, man, you're looking at Atlanta."

Bud Schwartz was deeply depressed to hear the FBI man call him by name. "You don't know shit about me," he snapped.

"Suppose you tell me what the hell's going on out here. What's your beef with Frankie King?"

Bud Schwartz said, "I don't know who you're talkin' about." Miraculously, Danny Pogue caught on before saying something disastrous. He flashed a checkerboard grin and said, "Yeah, who's Frankie King? We never heard a no Frankie King."

"Bullshit," Agent Billy Hawkins growled. "Go ahead and play stupid. You're all going to prison, anyhow. You and that crazy old lady."

"If it makes you feel any better," said Danny Pogue, "she shot us, too."

The campsite was . . . gone.

"I'm not surprised," Joe Winder said. He took Carrie's hand and kept walking. A light rain was falling, and the woods smelled cool.

Carrie asked, "What do we do if he's really gone?"

"I don't know."

Ten minutes later she asked if they were lost.

"I got turned around," Winder admitted. "It can't be too far."

"Joe, where are we going?"

The rain came down harder, and the sky blackened. From the west came a roll of thunder that shook the leaves. The birds fell silent; then the wind began to race across the island, and Joe Winder could taste the storm. He dropped Carrie's hand and started to jog, slapping out a trail with his arms. He called over his shoulder, urging Carrie to keep up.

It took fifteen minutes to find the junkyard where the ancient Plymouth station wagon sat on rusty bumpers. The yellow beach umbrella—still stuck in the dashboard—fluttered furiously in the gale.

Joe Winder pulled Carrie inside the car, and hugged her so tightly she let out a cry. "My arms are tingling," she said. "The little hairs on my arms."

He covered her ears. "Hold on, it's lightning."

It struck with a white flash and a deafening rip. Twenty yards away, a dead mahogany tree split up the middle and dropped a huge leafless branch. "God," Carrie whispered. "That was close."

Raindrops hammered on the roof. Joe Winder turned around in the seat and looked in the back of the car. "They're gone," he said.

"What, Joe?"

"The books. This is where he kept all his books."

She turned to see. Except for several dead roaches and a yellowed copy of the *New Republic*, the station wagon had been cleaned out.

Winder was vexed. "I don't know how he did it. You should've seen—there were hundreds in here. Steinbeck, Hemingway. Jesus, Carrie, he had García Márquez in Spanish. First editions! Some of the greatest books ever written."

"Then he's actually gone."

"It would appear to be so."

"Think we should call somebody?"

"What?"

"Somebody up in New York," Carrie said, "at the prison. I mean, just in case."

"Let me think about this."

"I can't believe he'd try it."

The thunderstorm moved quickly over the island and out to sea. Soon the lightning stopped and the downpour softened to a drizzle. Carrie said, "The breeze felt nice, didn't it?"

Joe Winder wasn't listening. He was trying to decide if

337

they should keep looking or not. Without Skink, new choices lay ahead: bold and serious decisions. Winder suddenly felt responsible for the entire operation.

Carrie turned to kiss him and her knee hit the glove compartment, which popped open. Curiously she poked through the contents—a flashlight, a tire gauge, three D-sized batteries and what appeared to be the dried tail of a squirrel.

And one brown envelope with Joe Winder's name printed in small block letters.

He tore it open. Reading the note, he broke into a broad smile. "Short and to the point," he said.

Carrie read it:

Dear Joe,
You make one hell of an oracle.
Don't worry about me, just keep up the fight.
We all shine on!

Carrie folded the note and returned it to the envelope. "I assume this means something."

"Like the moon and the stars and the sun," Joe Winder said. He felt truly inspired.

Twenty-eight

The Amazing Kingdom of Thrills reopened with only a minimal drop in attendance, thanks to a three-for-one ticket promotion that included a free ride on Dickie the Dolphin, whose amorous behavior was now inhibited by four trainers armed with electric stun guns. Francis X. Kingsbury was delighted by the crowds, and emboldened by the fact that many customers actually complained about the absence of wild snakes. Kingsbury regarded it as proof that closing the Amazing Kingdom had been unnecessary, a costly overestimation of the average tourist's brainpower. Obviously the yahoos were more curious than afraid of lethal reptiles. A thrill is a thrill, Kingsbury said.

The two persons forced to sit through this speech were Pedro Luz and Special Agent Ron Donner of the U.S. Marshal Service. Agent Donner had come to notify Francis X. Kingsbury of a possible threat against his life.

"Ho! From who?"

"Elements of organized crime," the marshal said. "Well, fuck 'em."

"Excuse me?"

"This is just, I mean really, the word is horseshit!" Kingsbury flapped his arms like a tangerine-colored buzzard.

He was dressed for serious golf; even his cleats were orange.

Agent Donner said: "We think it would be wise if you left town for a few weeks."

"Oh, you do? Leave town, like hell I will."

Pedro Luz spun his wheelchair slightly toward the marshal. "Organized crime," he said. "You mean the Mafia?"

"We're taking it very seriously," said Agent Donner, thinking: Who's the freak with the IV bag?

With the proud sweep of a hand, Francis Kingsbury introduced his chief of Security. "He handles everything for the park and so on. Personal affairs, as well. You can say anything in front of him, understand? He's thoroughly reliable."

Pedro Luz casually adjusted the drip valve on the intravenous tube.

The marshal asked, "What happened to your foot?"

"Never mind!" blurted Kingsbury.

"Car accident," Pedro Luz volunteered affably. "I had to chew the damn thing off." He pointed with a swathed, fore-shortened index finger. "Right there above the anklebone, see?"

"Tough luck," said Agent Donner, thinking: Psycho City.

"It's what animals do," Pedro Luz added, "when they get caught in traps."

Kingsbury clapped his hands nervously. "Hey, hey! Can we get back to the issue, please, this Godfather thing. For the record, I'm not going anyplace."

The marshal said, "We can have you safely in Bozeman, Montana, by tomorrow afternoon."

"What, do I look like fucking Grizzly Adams? Listen to me— *Montana*, don't even joke about something like that."

Pedro Luz said, "Why would the Mafia want to kill Mr. Kingsbury? I don't exactly make the connection." Then his chin dropped, and he appeared to drift off.

Agent Donner said, "I wish you'd consider the offer."

"Two words," Kingsbury held up two fingers as if playing charades. "Summerfest Jubilee. One of our biggest days, receipt-wise, of the whole damn year. Parades, clowns, prizes. We're giving away . . . I forget, some kinda car."

"And I suppose you need to be here."

"Yeah, damn right. It's my park and my show. And know what else? You can't make me go anywhere. I kept my end of the deal. I'm free and clear of you people."

"You're still on probation," said the marshal. "But you're right, we can't force you to go anyplace. This visit is a courtesy—"

"And I appreciate the information. I just don't happen to believe it." But a part of Francis Kingsbury did believe it. What if the men who stole his files had given up on the idea of blackmail? What if the damn burglars had somehow made touch with the Gotti organization? It strained Kingsbury's imagination because they'd seemed like such jittery putzes that night at the house. Yet perhaps he'd misjudged them.

"Where'd you get the tip?" he demanded.

Agent Donner was briefly distracted by the cartoon depiction of rodent fellatio that adorned Kingsbury's forearm. Eventually the marshal looked up and said, "It surfaced during another investigation. I can't go into details."

"But, really, you guys think it's on the level? You think some guineas are coming after me?" Kingsbury struggled to maintain an air of amused skepticism.

Soberly the marshal said, "The FBI is checking it out."

"Well, regardless, I'm not going to Montana. Just thinking about it hurts my mucous membranes—I got the world's worst hay fever."

"So your mind is made up."

"Yep," said Kingsbury. "I'm staying put."

"Then let us provide you with protection here at the park. A couple of men, at least."

"Thanks, but no thanks. I got Pedro."

At the mention of his name, Pedro Luz's swollen eyelids parted. He reached up and squeezed the IV bag. Then he tugged the tube out of the needle in his arm, and fitted the end into the corner of his mouth. The sound of energetic sucking filled Francis Kingsbury's office.

Agent Donner was dumbfounded. In a brittle voice he assured Kingsbury that the marshals would be extremely discreet, and would in no way interfere with the Summerfest Jubilee events. Kingsbury, in a tone approaching politeness, declined the offer of bodyguards. The last thing he needed was federal dicks nosing around the Amazing Kingdom.

"Besides, like I mentioned, there's Pedro. He's as tough as they come."

"All right," said Agent Donner, casting his eyes once again on the distended, scarified, cataleptic, polyp-headed mass that was Pedro Luz.

Kingsbury said, "I know what you're thinking but, hell, he's worth ten of yours. Twenty of yours! Any son-of abitch that would bite off his own damn leg—you tell me, is that tough or what?"

The marshal rose stiffly to leave. "Tough isn't the word for it," he said.

The trailer fire had left Carrie Lanier with only three possessions: her Buick Electra, the gun she had taken from Joe Winder and the newly retired raccoon suit. The costume and the gun had been stowed in the trunk of the car. Everything else had been destroyed in the blaze.

Molly McNamara offered her a bedroom on the second floor of the old house. "I'd loan you the condo but the cleaners are in this week," Molly said. "It's hard to rent out a place with bloodstains in the carpet."

"What about Joe?" Carrie said, "I'd like him to stay with

me." Molly clucked. "Young lady, I really can't approve. Two unmarried people—"

"But under the circumstances," Carrie persisted, "with all that's happened."

"Oh ... I suppose it's all right." Molly had a sparkle in her eyes. "I was teasing, darling. Besides, you act as if you're in love."

Carrie said it was a long shot. "We're both very goal-oriented, and very stubborn. I'm not sure we're heading in the same direction." She paused and looked away. "He doesn't seem to fit anywhere."

"You wouldn't want him if he did," Molly said. "The world is full of nice boring young men. The crazy ones are hard to find and harder to keep, but it's worth it."

"Your husband was like that?"

"Yes. My lovers, too."

"But crazy isn't the word for it, is it?"

Molly smiled pensively. "You're a smart cookie."

"Did you know that Joe's father built Seashell Estates?"

"Oh dear," Molly said. A dreadful project: six thousand units on eight hundred acres, plus a golf course. Wiped out an egret rookery. A mangrove estuary. And too late it was discovered that the fairways were leaching fertilizer and pesticides directly into the waters of Biscayne Bay.

Molly McNamara said, "Those were the bad old days."

"Joe's still upset."

"But it certainly wasn't his fault. He must've been barely a teenager when Seashell was developed."

"He's got a thing about his father," Carrie said.

"Is that what this is all about?"

"He hears bulldozers in his sleep."

Molly said, "It's not as strange as you might imagine. The question is, can you take it? Is this the kind of fellow you want?"

343

"That's a tough one," Carrie said. "He could easily get himself killed this week."

"Take the blue bedroom at the end of the hall."

"Thank you, Miss McNamara."

"Just one favor," Molly said. "The headboard—it's an antique. I found it at a shop in Williamsburg."

"We'll be careful," Carrie promised.

That night they made love on the bare pine floor. Drenched in sweat, they slid like ice cubes across the slick varnished planks. Eventually they wound up wedged headfirst in a corner, where Carrie fell asleep with Joe Winder's earlobe clenched tenderly in her teeth. He was starting to doze himself when he heard Molly's voice in the adjoining bedroom. She was talking sternly to a man who didn't sound like either Skink or the two redneck burglars.

When Winder heard the other door close, he delicately extricated himself from Carrie's bite and lifted her to the bed. Then he wrapped himself in an old quilt and crept into the hall to see who was in the next room.

The last person he expected to find was Agent Billy Hawkins of the Federal Bureau of Investigation. Trussed to a straight-backed chair, Hawkins wore someone else's boxer shorts and black nylon socks. A bandage was wadded around one bare thigh, and two strips of hurricane tape crisscrossed his mouth. He reeked of antiseptic.

Joe Winder slipped into the room and twisted the lock behind him. Gingerly he peeled the heavy tape from the agent's face.

"Fancy meeting you here."

"Nice getup," Bill Hawkins remarked. "Would you please untie me?"

"First tell me what happened."

"What does it look like? The old bird shot me."

"Any particular reason?"

"Just get me loose, goddammit."

Winder said, "Not until I hear the story."

Reluctantly, Hawkins told him about Bud Schwartz and the long-distance phone call to Queens and the possible exposure of a federally protected witness.

"Who's the flip?"

"I can't tell you *that*."

Joe Winder pressed the hurricane tape over Hawkins's lips— then fiercely yanked it away. Hawkins yelped. Tears of pain sprang to his eyes. In colorful expletives he offered the opinion that Winder had gone insane.

The excruciating procedure was repeated on one of Billy Hawkins's bare nipples and nearly uprooted a cluster of curly black hairs. "I can do this all night," Winder said. "I'm way past the point of caring."

The agent took a long bitter moment to compose himself. "You could go to prison," he mumbled.

"For assaulting you with adhesive tape? I don't think so." Winder placed one gummy strip along the line of soft hair that trailed southward from Billy Hawkins's navel. The agent gaped helplessly as Winder jerked hard; the tape came off with a sibilant rip.

"You—you're a goddamn lunatic!"

"But I'm your only hope. Who's going to believe you were shot and abducted by an elderly widow? And if they should believe it, what would that do to your career?" Joe Winder spread the quilt on the floor and sat cross-legged in front of the hog-tied agent.

"Blaine, Washington," Winder said. "Isn't that the FBI's equivalent of Siberia?"

Hawkins conceded the point silently. The political cost of prosecuting a grandmother and a pair of candyass burglars would be high. The Bureau was hypersensitive to incidents

345

incongruous with the lantern-jawed crime-buster image promoted by J. Edgar Hoover; for an FBI agent to be overpowered by a dottering senior citizen was a disgrace. An immediate transfer to some godforsaken cowtown would be a certainty.

"So what can *you* do?" Hawkins asked Winder sourly.

"Maybe nothing. Maybe save your skin. Did Molly make you call the office?"

The agent nodded. "At gunpoint. I told them I was taking a couple of sick days."

"They ask about this Mafia thing?"

"I told them it wasn't panning out. Looked like a bullshit shakedown." Hawkins sounded embarrassed. "That's what she made me say. Threatened to shoot me again if I didn't go along with the routine—and it didn't sound like a bluff."

"You did the right thing," Joe Winder said. "No sense chancing it." He stood up and rewrapped himself in the quilt. "You'll have to stay like this a while," he told the agent. "It's the only way."

"I don't get it. What's your connection to these crackpots?"

"Long story."

"Winder, don't be a jackass. This isn't a game." Hawkins spoke sternly for a man in his ridiculous predicament. "Somebody could get killed. That's not what you want, is it?"

"Depends. Tell me the name of this precious witness."

"Frankie King."

Joe Winder shrugged. "Never heard of him."

"Moved down from New York after he snitched on some of Gotti's crowd. This was a few years back."

"Swift move. What's he calling himself these days?"

"That I can't possibly tell you."

"Then you're on your own, Billy. Think about it. Your word against Grandma Moses. Picture the headlines: 'Sharpshooter Widow Gunned Me Down, Nude G-Man Claims.'"

Hawkins sagged dispiritedly. He said, "The flip's name is Francis Kingsbury. You happy now?"

"Kingsbury?" Joe Winder raised his eyes to the heavens and crackled raucously. "The Mafia is coming down here to whack Mr. X!"

"Hey," Billy Hawkins said, "it's not funny."

But it was very funny to Joe Winder. "Francis X. Kingsbury. Millionaire theme-park developer and real-estate mogul, darling of the Chamber of Commerce, 1988 Rotarian Citizen of the Year. And you're telling me he's really a two-bit jizzbag on the run from the mob?"

Ecstatically, Joe Winder hopped from foot to foot, spinning in a circle and twirling Molly's quilt like a calico cape.

"Oh, Billy boy," he sang, "isn't this a great country!"

They were thirty minutes late to the airport because Danny Pogue insisted on watching the end of a *National Geographic* television documentary about rhinoceros poachers in Africa.

In the car he couldn't stop talking about the program. "The only reason they kill 'em, see, what they're after is the horns. Just the horns!" He put his fist on his nose to simulate a rhinoceros snout. "In some places they use 'em for sex potions."

"Get off it," said Bud Schwartz.

"No shit. They grind the horns into powder and put it in their tea."

"Does it work?"

"I don't know," Danny Pogue said. "The TV didn't say."

"Like, it gives you a super big boner or what?"

"I don't know, Bud, the TV didn't say. They just talked about how much the powder goes for in Hong Kong, stuff like that. Thousands of bucks."

Bud Schwartz said, "You ask me, they left out the most important part of the show. Does it work or not?"

He drove into one of the airport garages and snatched a

ticket from the machine. He parked on Level M, as always. "M" for Mother; it was the only way Bud Schwartz could remember how to find his car. He was annoyed that his partner wasn't sharing in the excitement of the moment: they were about to be rich.

"After today, you can retire," Bud Schwartz said. "No more b-and-e's. Man, we should throw us a party tonight."

Danny Pogue said, "I ain't in the mood."

They stepped onto the moving sidewalk and rode in silence to the Delta Airlines concourse. The plane had arrived on time, so the visitor already was waiting outside the gate. As promised, he was carrying a blue umbrella; otherwise Bud Schwartz would never have known that he was the hit man. He stood barely five feet tall and weighed at least two hundred pounds. He had thinning brown hair, small black eyes and skin that was the color of day-old lard. Under a herringbone sport coat he wore a striped polyester shirt, open at the neck, with a braided gold chain. The hit man seemed fond of gold; a bracelet rattled on his wrist when he shook Bud Schwartz's hand.

"Hello," said the burglar.

"You call me Lou." The hit man spoke in a granite baritone that didn't match the soft roly-polyness of his figure.

"Hi, Lou," said Danny Pogue. "I'm Bud's partner."

"How nice for you. Where's the car?" He pointed to a Macy's shopping bag near his feet. "That's yours. Now, where's the car?"

On the drive south, Danny Pogue peeked in the Macy's bag and saw that it was full of cash. Lou was up in the front seat next to Bud Schwartz.

"I wanna do this tomorrow," he was saying. "I gotta get home for my wife's birthday. She's forty." Then he farted loudly and pretended not to hear it.

"Forty? No kidding?" said Bud Schwartz. He had been

expecting something quite different in the way of a mob assassin. Perhaps it wasn't fair, but Bud Schwartz was disappointed in Lou's appearance. For Francis Kingsbury's killer, he had envisioned someone taut, snake-eyed and menacing—not fat, balding and flatulent.

Just goes to show, thought Bud Schwartz, these days everything's hype. Even the damn Mafia.

From the back seat, Danny Pogue asked: "How're you gonna do it? What kinda gun?"

Lou puffed out his cheeks and said, "Brand X. The fuck do you care, what kinda gun?"

"Danny," Bud Schwartz said, "let's stay out of the man's private business, okay?"

"I didn't mean nothin'."

"You usually don't."

The man named Lou said, "This is the neighborhood?"

"We're almost there," said Bud Schwartz.

"I can't get over all these trees," Lou said. "Parts a Jersey look like this. My wife's mother lives in Jersey, a terrific old lady. Seventy-seven years old, she bowls twice a week! In a league!"

Bud Schwartz smiled weakly. Perfect. A hit man who loves his mother-in-law. What next—he collects for the United Way?

The burglar said to Lou: "Maybe it's better if you rent a car. For tomorrow, I mean."

"Sure. Usually I do my own driving."

Danny Pogue tapped his partner on the shoulder and said, "Slow down, Bud, it's up here on the right."

Kingsbury's estate was bathed in pale orange lights. Gray sedans with green bubble lights were parked to block both ends of the driveway. Three men sat in each sedan; two more, in security-guard uniforms, were posted at the front door. It was, essentially, the complete private security force

349

of the Amazing Kingdom of Thrills—except for Pedro Luz, who was inside the house, his wheelchair parked vigilantly at Francis Kingsbury's bedroom door.

Bud Schwartz drove by slowly. "Look at this shit," he muttered. Once they had passed the house, he put some muscle into the accelerator.

"An army," Lou said, "that's what it was."

Danny Pogue sank low in the back seat. With both hands he clutched the Macy's bag to his chest. "Let's just go," he said. "Bud, let's just haul ass."

Twenty-nine

On the morning of August 2, Jake Harp crawled into the back of a white limousine and rode in a dismal gin-soaked stupor to the construction site on North Key Largo. There he was met by Charles Chelsea, Francis X. Kingsbury and a phalanx of armed security men whose crisp blue uniforms failed to mitigate their shifty felonious smirks. The entourage moved briskly across a recently bulldozed plateau, barren except for a bright green hillock that was cordoned with rope and ringed by reporters, photographers and television cameramen. Kingsbury took Jake Harp by the elbow and, ascending the grassy knob, waved mechanically; it reminded Charles Chelsea of the rigidly determined way that Richard Nixon had saluted before boarding the presidential chopper for the final time. Except that, compared to Francis Kingsbury, Nixon was about as tense as Pee Wee Herman.

Jake Harp heard himself pleading for coffee, please God, even decaf, but Kingsbury seemed not to hear him. Jake Harp blinked amphibiously and struggled to focus on the scene. It was early. He was outdoors. The sun was intensely bright. The Atlantic Ocean murmured at his back. And somebody had dressed him: Izod shirt, Sansibelt slacks, tasseled Footjoy golf shoes. What could this be! Then he heard the scratchy click of a portable microphone and the oily voice of Charles Chelsea.

"Welcome, everybody. We're standing on what will soon by the first tee of the Falcon Trace Championship Golf Course. As you can see, we've got a little work ahead of us ..."

Laughter. These numbnuts are laughing, thought Jake Harp. He squinted at the white upturned faces and recognized one or two as sportswriters.

More from Chelsea: "... and we thought it would be fun to inaugurate the construction of this magnificent golfing layout with a hitting clinic."

Jake Harp's stomach clenched as somebody folded a three-wood into his fingers. The golf pro stared in disgust: a graphite head. They expect me to hit with metal!

Charles Chelsea's well-tanned paw settled amiably on Jake Harp's shoulder; the stench of Old Spice was overpowering.

"This familiar fellow needs no introduction," Chelsea was saying. "He's graciously agreed to christen the new course by hitting a few balls into the ocean—since we don't actually have a fairway yet."

Laughter again. Mysterious, inexplicable laughter. Jake Harp swayed, bracing himself with the three-wood. What had he been drinking last night? Vodka sours? Tanqueray martinis? Possibly both. He remembered dancing with a banker's wife. He remembered telling her how he'd triple-bogeyed the Road Hole and missed the cut at the British Open; missed the damn cut, all because some fat Scotsman booted the ball. ...

Jake Harp also remembered the banker's wife whispering something about a blowjob—but did it happen? He hoped so, but he truly couldn't recall. One thing was certain: today he was physically incapable of swinging a golf club. It was simply out of the question. He wondered how he would break the news to Francis Kingsbury, who was bowing to

352

the photographers in acknowledgment of Charles Chelsea's effusive introduction.

"Frank," said Jake Harp. "Where am I?"

With a frozen smile, Kingsbury remarked that Jake Harp looked about as healthy as dog barf.

"A bad night," the golfer rasped. "I'd like to go home and lie down."

Then came an acrid gust of cologne as Chelsea leaned in: "Hit a few, Jake, okay? No interviews, just a photo op."

"But I can't use a fucking graphite wood. This is Jap voodoo, Frank, I need my MacGregors."

Francis Kingsbury gripped Jake Harp by the shoulders and turned him toward the ocean. "And would you please, for Christ's sake, try not to miss the goddamn ball?"

Chelsea cautioned Kingsbury to keep his voice down. The sportswriters were picking up on the fact that Jake Harp was seriously under the weather.

"Coffee's on the way," Chelsea chirped lightly.

"You want me to hit it in the ocean?" Jake Harp said. "This is nuts."

One of the news photographers shouted for the security officers to get out of the way, they were blocking the picture. Kingsbury commanded the troops of Pedro Luz to move to one side; Pedro Luz himself was not present, having refused with vague mutterings to exit the storage room and join the phony golf clinic at Falcon Trace. His men, however, embraced with gusto and amusement the task of guarding Francis X. Kingsbury from assailants unknown.

Having cleared the security force to make an opening for Jake Harp, Kingsbury ordered the golfer to swing away.

"I can't, Frank."

"What?"

"I'm hung over. I can't lift the bloody club."

"Assume the position, Jake. You're starting to piss me off."

Tottering slightly, Jake Harp slowly arranged himself in the familiar stance that *Golf Digest* once hailed as "part Hogan, part Nicklaus, part Baryshnikov"—chin down, feet apart, shoulders square, left arm straight, hands interlocked loosely on the shaft of the club.

"There," Jake Harp said gamely.

Charles Chelsea cleared his throat. Francis Kingsbury said, "A golf ball would help, Jake."

"Oh Jesus, you're right."

"You got everything but a goddamn ball."

Under his breath, Jake Harp said, "Frank, would you do me a favor? Tee it up?"

"What?"

"I can't bend down. I'm too hung over, Frank. If I try to bend, I'll fall on my face. I swear to God."

Francis Kingsbury dug in his pocket and pulled out a scuffed Maxfli and a plastic tee that was shaped like a naked woman. "You're quite an athlete, Jake. A regular Jim Fucking Thorpe."

Gratefully Jake Harp watched Kingsbury drop to one knee and plant the tee. Then suddenly the sun exploded, and a molten splinter tore a hole in the golfer's belly, spinning him like a tenpin and knocking him flat. A darkening puddle formed as he lay there and floundered, gulping for breath through a mouthful of fresh Bermuda sod. Jake Harp was not too hung over to realize he could be dying, and it bitterly occurred to him that he would rather leave his mortal guts on the fairways of Augusta or Muirfield or Pebble Beach.

Anywhere but here.

Bud Schwartz and Danny Pogue had driven up to Kendall to break into a house. The house belonged to FBI Agent Billy Hawkins, who was still tied up as Molly McNamara's prisoner.

"Think he's got a dog?" said Danny Pogue.

Bud Schwartz said probably not. "Guys like that, they think dogs are for pussies. It's a cop mentality."

But Bud Schwartz was wrong. Bill Hawkins owned a German shepherd. The burglars could see the animal prowling the fence in the backyard.

"Guess we gotta do the front-door routine," said Bud Schwartz. What a way to end a career: breaking into an FBI man's house in broad daylight. "I thought we retired," Bud Schwartz complained. "All that dough we got, tell me what's the point if we're still pullin' these jobs."

Danny Pogue said, "Just this one more. And besides, what if Lou takes the money back?"

"No way."

"If he can't get to the guy, he might. Already he thinks we tipped Kingsbury off, on account of all those rent-a-cops."

Bud Schwartz said he wasn't worried about Lou going back on the deal. "These people are pros, Danny. Now gimme the scroogie." They were poised at Billy Hawkins's front door. Danny Pogue checked the street for cars or pedestrians; then he handed Bud Schwartz a nine-inch screwdriver.

Skeptically Danny Pogue said, "Guy's gotta have a dead-bolt. Anybody works for the FBI, probably he's got an alarm, too. Maybe even lasers."

But there was no alarm system. Bud Schwartz pried the doorjamb easily. He put his shoulder to the wood and pushed it open. "You believe that?" he said to his partner. "See what I mean about cop mentality. They think they're immune."

"Yeah," said Danny Pogue. "Immune." Later he'd ask Molly McNamara what it meant.

They closed the door and entered the empty house. Bud Schwartz would never have guessed that a federal agent lived there. It was a typical suburban Miami home: three bedrooms, two baths, nothing special. Once they got used to the idea, the burglars moved through the rooms with casual confidence—wife at work, kids at school, no sweat.

"Too bad we're not stealin' anything," Bud Schwartz mused. "Want to?" said his partner. "Just for old times' sake."

"What's the point?"

"I saw one of the kids has a CD player."

"Wow," said Bud Schwartz acidly. "What's that, like, thirty bucks. Maybe forty?"

"No, man, it's a Sony."

"Forget it. Now gimme the papers."

In captivity Billy Hawkins had agreed to notify his family that he was out of town on a top-secret assignment. However, the agent had displayed a growing reluctance to call the FBI office and lie about being sick. To motivate him, Molly McNamara had composed a series of cryptic notes and murky correspondence suggesting that Hawkins was not the most loyal of government servants. Prominently included in the odd jottings were the telephone numbers of the Soviet Embassy and the Cuban Special Interest Section in Washington, D.C. For good measure, Molly had included a bank slip showing a suspicious $25,000 deposit to Agent Billy Hawkins's personal savings account—a deposit that Molly herself had made at the South Miami branch of Unity National Savings & Loan. The purpose of these maneuvers was to create a shady portfolio that, despite its sloppiness, Billy Hawkins would not wish to try to explain to his colleagues at the FBI.

Who would definitely come to the house in search of clues, if Agent Hawkins failed to check in.

Molly McNamara had entrusted the bank receipt, phone numbers and other manufactured evidence to Bud Schwartz and Danny Pogue, whose mission was to conceal the material in a semi-obvious location in Billy Hawkins's bedroom.

Bud Schwartz chose the second drawer of the night-stand. He placed the envelope under two unopened boxes of condoms. "Raspberry-colored," he marveled. "FBI man uses raspberry rubbers" Another stereotype shattered.

Danny Pogue was admiring a twelve-inch portable television as if it were a rare artifact. "Jesus, Bud, you won't believe this."

"Don't tell me it's a black-and-white."

"Yep. You know the last time I saw one?"

"Little Havana," said Bud Schwartz, "that duplex off Twelfth Avenue. I remember."

"Remember what we got for it."

"Yeah. Thirteen goddamn dollars." The fence was a man named Fat Jack on Seventy-ninth Street, near the Boulevard. Bud Schwartz couldn't stand Fat Jack, not only because he was cheap but because he smelled like dirty socks. One day Bud Schwartz had boosted a case of Ban Extra Dry Roll-on Deodorant sticks from the back of a Publix truck, and given it to Fat Jack as a hint. Fat Jack had handed him eight bucks and said that nobody should ever use roll-ons because they cause cancer of the armpits.

"I don't get it," said Danny Pogue. "I thought the FBI paid big bucks—what's a baby Magnavox go for, two hundred retail? You'd think he could spring for color."

"Who knows, maybe he spends it all on clothes. Come on, let's take off." Bud Schwartz wanted to be long gone before the mailman arrived and noticed what had happened to the front door.

Danny Pogue turned on the portable TV and said, "That's not a bad picture." The noon news was just starting.

"I said let's go, Danny."

"Wait, look at this!"

A video clip showed a heavyset man in golf shoes being hoisted on a stretcher. The man's shirt was drenched in blood, but his eyelids were half open. A plastic oxygen mask covered the man's face and nose, but the jaw moved as if he were trying to speak. The newscaster reported that the shooting had taken place at a new resort development called Falcon Trace, near Key Largo.

"Lou! He did it!" exclaimed Danny Pogue. "You were right."

"Only trouble is, that ain't Mr. Kingsbury."

"You sure?"

Bud Schwartz sat down in front of the television. The anchorman had tossed the sniper story to a sportscaster, who was somberly recounting the stellar career of Jake Harp. The golfer's photograph, taken in happier times, popped up on a wide green mat behind the sports desk.

Danny Pogue said, "Who the hell's that?"

"Not Kingsbury," grunted Bud Schwartz. The mishap confirmed his worst doubts about Lou's qualifications as a hit man. It was unbelievable. The asshole had managed to shoot the wrong guy.

"Know what?" said Danny Pogue. "There's a Jake Harp Cadillac in Boca Raton where I swiped a bunch of tape decks once. Is that the same guy? This golfer?"

Bud Schwartz said, "I got no earthly idea." What was all this crap the TV guy was yakking about—career earnings, number of Top Ten finishes, average strokes per round, percentage of greens hit in regulation. To Bud Schwartz, golf was as foreign as polo. Except you didn't see so many fat guys playing polo.

"The main thing is, did they catch the shooter?"

"Nuh-huh." Danny Pogue had his nose to the tube. "They said he got away in a boat. No arrests, no motives is what they said."

Bud Schwartz was trying to picture Lou from Queens at the helm of a speedboat, racing for the ocean's horizon.

"He's gonna be pissed," Danny Pogue said.

"Yeah, well, I don't guess his boss up North is gonna be too damn thrilled, either. Whackin' the wrong man."

"He ain't dead yet. Serious but stable is what they said."

Bud Schwartz said it didn't really matter. "Point is, it's still a fuckup. A major *major* fuckup."

The Mafia had gunned down a life member of the Professional Golfers Association.

Pedro Luz finally emerged from the storage room, where he had been measuring his penis. He rolled the wheelchair out to Kingsbury Lane for the morning rehearsal of the Summerfest Jubilee, a greatly embellished version of the nightly musical pageant. Pedro Luz needed something to lift his spirits. His leg had begun to throb in an excruciating way; no combination of steroids and analgesics put a dent in the pain. To add psychic misery to the physical, Pedro Luz had now documented the fact that his sexual wand was indeed shrinking as a result of prolonged steroid abuse. At first, Pedro Luz had assured himself that it was only an optical illusion; the more swollen his face and limbs became, the smaller everything else appeared to be. But weeks of meticulous calibrations had produced conclusive evidence: His wee-wee had withered from 10.4 centimeters to 7.9 centimeters in its flaccid state. Worse, it seemed to Pedro Luz (although there was no painless way to measure) that his testicles had also become smaller—not yet as tiny as BBs, as Churrito had predicted, but more like gumballs.

These matters weighed heavily on his mind as Pedro Luz sat in the broiling sun and watched the floats rumble by. He was hoping that the sight of Annette Fury's regal bosom would buoy his mood, and was disappointed to see that she had been replaced as Princess Golden Sun. The new actress looked familiar, but Pedro Luz couldn't place the face. She was a very pretty girl, but the black wig needed some work, as did the costume—buckskin culottes and a fringed halter top. Her singing was quite lovely, much better than Annette's, but Pedro Luz would've preferred larger breasts. The lioness that shared the Seminole float was in no condition to rehearse; panting miserably in the humidity, the animal sprawled half-conscious on one side, thus thwarting the catstraddling exit that culminated the princess's dramatic performance.

As the parade disbanded, Pedro Luz eased the wheelchair off the curb and approached the Seminole float. The pretty young singer was not to be seen; there was only the driver of the float and Dr. Kukor, the park veterinarian, who had climbed aboard to revive the heatstruck lioness. Dr. Kukor was plainly flabbergasted by the sight of Pedro Luz.

"I lost my foot in an accident," the security chief explained.

Dr. Kukor hadn't noticed the missing foot. It was the condition of Pedro Luz's face, so grossly inflated, that had generated the horror. The man looked like a blowfish: puffed cheeks, bulging lips, teeny eyes wedged deep under a pimpled, protuberant brow.

To Pedro Luz, Dr. Kukor directed the most inane inquiry of a long and distinguished career: "Are you all right?"

"Just fine. Where's the young lady?"

Dr. Kukor pointed, and Pedro Luz spun the wheelchair to see: Princess Golden Sun stood behind him. She was zipping a black Miami Heat warm-up jacket over the halter.

Pedro Luz introduced himself and said, "I've seen you before, right?"

"It's possible," said Carrie Lanier, who recognized him instantly as the goon who shot up her double-wide, the creep she'd run over with the car. She noticed the bandaged trunk of his leg, and felt a pang of guilt. It passed quickly.

"You sing pretty nice," Pedro Luz said, "but you could use a couple three inches up top. If you get my meaning."

"Thanks for the advice."

"I know a doctor who specializes in that sort of thing. Maybe I could get you a discount."

"Actually," said Carrie, patting her chest, "I kind of like the little fellas just the way they are."

"Suit yourself." Pedro Luz scratched brutally at a raw patch on his scalp. "I'm trying to figure where I saw you before. Take off the wig for a second, okay?"

Carrie Lanier pressed her hands to her eyes and began to cry— plaintive, racking sobs that attracted the concern of tourists and the other pageant performers.

Pedro Luz said, "Hey, what's the matter?"

"It's not a wig!" Carrie cried. "It's my real hair." She turned and scampered down a stairwell into The Catacombs.

"Geez, I'm sorry," said Pedro Luz, to no one. Flustered, he rolled full tilt toward the security office. Speeding downhill past the Wet Willy, he chafed his knuckles trying to brake the wheelchair. When he reached the chilled privacy of the storage room, he slammed the door and drove the bolt. In the blackness Pedro Luz probed for the string that turned on the ceiling's bare bulb; he found it and jerked hard.

The white light revealed a shocking scene. Someone had entered Pedro's sanctuary and destroyed the delicate web of sustenance. Sewing shears had snipped the intravenous tubes into worthless inch-long segments, which littered the floor like plastic rice. The same person had sliced open every one of Pedro's unused IV bags; the wheelchair rested, literally, in a pond of liquid dextrose.

But by far the worst thing to greet Pedro Luz was the desolate sight of brown pill bottles, perhaps a half-dozen, open and empty on the floor. Whoever he was, the sonofabitch had flushed Pedro's anabolic steroids down the john. The ceramic pestle with which he had so lovingly powdered his Winstrols lay shattered beneath the toilet tank.

And, on the wall, a message in coral lipstick. Pedro Luz groaned and backed the wheelchair so he could read it easier. A wild rage heaved through his chest and he began to snatch items from the storage shelves and hurl them against the cinder block: nightsticks, gas masks, flashlights, handcuffs, cans of Mace, pistol grips, boxes of bullets.

Only when there was nothing left to throw did Pedro Luz stop to read the words on the wall again. Written in a loopy flamboyant script, the message said:

Good morning, Dipshit!
Just wanted you to know I'm not dead.
Have a nice day, and don't forget your Wheaties!

It was signed, "Yours truly, J. Winder."

Pedro Luz emitted a feral cry and aimed himself toward the executive gym, where he spent the next two hours alone on the bench press, purging the demons and praying for his testicles to grow back.

Thirty

Somehow Charles Chelsea summoned the creative energy necessary for fabrication:

> Golf legend Jake Harp was accidentally shot Thursday during groundbreaking ceremonies for the new Falcon Trace Golf and Country Club Resort on North Key Largo.
>
> The incident occurred as Mr. Harp was preparing to hit a ball off what will be the first tee of the 6,970-yard championship golf course, which Mr. Harp designed himself. The golfer apparently was struck by a stray bullet from an unidentified boater, who may have been shooting at nearby sea gulls.
>
> Mr. Harp was listed in serious but stable condition after undergoing surgery at South Miami Hospital.
>
> "This is a tragedy for the entire golfing world, professionals and amateurs alike," said Francis X. Kingsbury, the developer of Falcon Trace, and a close personal friend of Mr. Harp.
>
> "We're all praying for Jake to pull through," added Kingsbury, who is also the founder and chairman of the Amazing Kingdom of Thrills, the popular family theme park adjacent to the sprawling Falcon Trace project.

By mid-afternoon Thursday, police had not yet arrested any suspects in the shooting. Charles Chelsea, vice president of publicity for Falcon Trace Ltd., disputed accounts by some reporters on the scene who claimed that Mr. Harp was the victim of a deliberate sniper attack.

"There's no reason to believe that this terrible event was anything but a freak accident," Chelsea said.

Kingsbury approved the press release with a disgusted flick of his hand. He drained his third martini and asked Chelsea if he had ever before witnessed a man being shot.

"Not that I can recall, sir."

"Close up, I mean," Kingsbury said. "Dead bodies are one thing—car wrecks, heart attacks—I'm not counting those. What I mean is, *bang*!"

Chelsea said, "It happened so damn fast."

"Well, you know who they were aiming at? *Moi*, that's who. How about that!" Kingsbury pursed his lips and drummed his knuckles.

"You?" Chelsea said. "Who would try to kill you?" He instantly thought of Joe Winder.

But Kingsbury smiled drunkenly and began to hum the theme from *The Godfather*.

Chelsea said, "There's something you're not telling me."

"Of course there's something I'm not telling you. There's tons of shit I'm not telling you. What, I look like a total moron?"

Watching Francis Kingsbury pour another martini, Chelsea felt like seizing the bottle and guzzling himself into a Tanqueray coma. The time had come to look for another job; the fun had leaked out of this one. A malevolent force, unseen and uncontrollable, had perverted Chelsea's role from cheery town crier to conniving propagandist. Reflecting on the past weeks, he realized he should've quit on the day the blue-tongued voles were stolen, the day innocence was lost.

We are all no longer children, Chelsea thought sadly. We are potential co-defendants.

"No offense," Kingsbury was saying, "but you're just a flack. I only tell you what I've absolutely got to tell you. Which is precious damned little."

"That's the way it should be," Chelsea said lifelessly.

"Right! Loose dicks sink ships. Or whatever." Kingsbury slurped at the gin like a thirsty mutt. "Anyhow, don't worry about me. I'm taking—well, let's just say, the necessary precautions. You can be goddamn sure."

"That's wise of you."

"Meanwhile, sharpen your pencil. I ordered us more animals." Kingsbury wistfully studied his drink. "Who's the guy in the Bible, the one with the ark. Was it Moses?"

"Noah," Chelsea said. Boy, was the old man smashed.

"Yeah, Noah, that's who I feel like. Me and these fucking critters. Anyhow, we're back in the endangered-species business, saving the animals. There oughta be some publicity when they get here. You see to it."

The woman named Rachel Lark had phoned all the way from New Zealand. She said she'd done her best on such short notice, and said Kingsbury would be pleased when he saw the new attractions for the Rare Animal Pavilion. I hope so, he'd told her, because we could damn sure use some good news.

Fearing the worst, Charles Chelsea said, "What kind of animals are we talking about?"

"Cute is what I ordered. Thirty-seven hundred dollars' worth of cute." Kingsbury snorted. "Could be anything. The point is, we've got to rebound, Charlie. We got a fucking void to fill."

"Right."

"Speaking of which, we also need another golfer. In case Jake croaks, God forbid."

Chelsea recoiled at the cold-bloodedness of the assignment. "It won't look good, sir, not with what happened this morning. It's best if we stick by Jake."

"Sympathy's all fine and dandy, Charlie, but we got more than golf at stake here. We got waterfront to sell. We got patio homes. We got club memberships. Can Jake Harp—don't get me wrong—but in his present situation can Jake do promotional appearances? TV commercials? Celebrity programs? We don't even know if Jake can still breathe, much less swing a fucking five-iron."

For once Francis Kingsbury expressed himself in nearly cogent syntax. It must be excellent gin, Chelsea thought.

"I want you to call Nicklaus," Kingsbury went on. "Tell him money is no problem."

"Jack Nicklaus," the publicity man repeated numbly.

"No, *Irving* Nicklaus. Who the hell do you think! And if you can't get the Bear, try Palmer. And if you can't get Arnie, you try Trevino. And if you can't get the Mex, try the Shark. And so on. The bigger the better, but make it quick."

Knowing it would do no good, Chelsea reminded Kingsbury that he had tried to recruit the top golfing names when he was first planning Falcon Trace, and that they'd all said no. Only Jake Harp had the stomach to work for him.

"I don't care what they said before," Kingsbury growled, "you call 'em again. Money is no problem, all right?"

"Again, I'd just like to caution you about how this might appear to people—"

"I need a hotshot golfer, Charlie. The hell do you guys call it— a media personality?" Kingsbury raised one plump fist and let it fall heavily on the desk. "I can't sell a golf resort when my star golfer's on a goddamn respirator. Don't you understand? Don't you know a goddamn thing about Florida real estate?"

*

366

They rode to the airport in edgy silence. Danny Pogue was waiting for Lou to say something. Like it was all *their* fault. Like the people in Queens wanted their money back.

Earlier Bud Schwartz had pulled his partner aside and said, look, they want the dough, we give it back. This is the mob, he said, and we're not playing games with the mob. But it's damned important, Bud Schwartz had said, that Lou and his Mafia people know that we didn't tip off Kingsbury. How the hell he found out about the hit, it don't matter. It wasn't us and we gotta make that clear, okay? Danny Pogue agreed wholeheartedly. Like Bud Schwartz, he didn't want to go through the rest of life having somebody else start his car every morning. Or peeking around corners, watching out for inconspicuous fat guys like Lou.

So when they got to the Delta Airlines terminal, Danny Pogue shook Lou's hand and said he was very sorry about what had happened. "Honest to God, we didn't tell nobody."

"That's the truth," said Bud Schwartz.

Lou shrugged. "Probably a wire. Don't sweat it."

"Thanks," said Danny Pogue, flushed with relief. He pumped Lou's pudgy arm vigorously. "Thanks for—well, just thanks is all."

Lou nodded. His nose and cheeks were splashed pink with raw sunburn. He wore the same herringbone coat and striped shirt that he had when he'd gotten off the airplane. There was still no sign of the gun, but the burglars knew he was carrying it somewhere on his corpulent profile.

Lou said, "Since I know you're dyin' to ask, what happened was this: the asshole bent over. Don't ask me why, but he bent over just as I pulled the trigger."

"Bud thought you probably got the two guys mixed up—"

"I didn't get nobody mixed up." Lou's upper lip curled when he directed this bulletin toward Bud Schwartz. "The guy leaned over is all. Otherwise he'd be dead right now, trust me."

Despite his doubts about Lou's marksmanship, Bud Schwartz didn't want him to leave Miami with hard feelings. He didn't want any hit man, even a clumsy one, to be sore at him.

"Could've happened to anybody," Bud Schwartz said supportively. "Sounds like one hell of a tough shot from the water, anyway."

A voice on the intercom announced that the Delta flight to LaGuardia was boarding at Gate 7. Lou said, "The guy that got hit, I heard he's hanging on."

"Yeah, some golfer named Harp," said Danny Pogue. "Serious but stable."

"Maybe he'll make it," Lou said. "That would be good."

Bud Schwartz asked what would happen when Lou returned to Queens.

"Have a sitdown with my people. Find out what they want to do next. Then I got this big birthday party for my wife's fortieth. I bought her one a them electric woks—she really likes Jap food, don't ask me why."

Danny Pogue said, "Are you in big trouble?"

Lou's chest bounced when he laughed. "With my wife or the boys? Ask me which is worse."

He picked up his carry-on and the blue umbrella, and waddled for the gate.

Bud Schwartz waved. "Sorry it got so screwed up."

"What the hell," said Lou, still laughing. "I got me a nice boat ride outta the deal."

Joe Winder and Carrie Lanier met Trooper Jim Tile at the Snapper Creek Plaza on the Turnpike extension. They took a booth at the Roy Rogers and ordered burgers and shakes. Winder found the atmosphere more pleasant than it had been at Ocean Reef. Carrie asked Jim Tile if he had phoned Rikers Island.

"Yeah, I called," the trooper said. "They thought it was crazy, but they said they'd watch for anything out of the ordinary."

"Out of the ordinary hardly begins to describe him."

"New Yorkers," said Jim Tile, "think they've cornered the market on psychopaths. They don't know Florida."

Joe Winder said, "I don't think he's going to Rikers Island. I think he's still here."

"I heard about Harp," said Jim Tile, "and my opinion is no, it wasn't the governor. I'll put money on it."

"How can you be so sure?" asked Carrie.

"Because (a) it's not his style, and (b) he wouldn't have missed."

Winder said, "Mr. X was the target."

"Had to be," agreed Jim Tile. "Who'd waste a perfectly good bullet on a golfer?"

Carrie speculated that it could have been a disgruntled fan. Joe Winder threw an arm around her and gave her a hug. He'd been in a fine mood since trashing Pedro Luz's steroid den.

The trooper was saying Skink might've headed upstate. "This morning somebody shot up a Greyhound on the interstate outside Orlando. Sixty-seven Junior Realtors on their way to Epcot."

Panic at Disney World! Winder thought. Kingsbury will come in his pants.

"Nobody was hurt," Jim Tile said, "which leads me to believe it was you-know-who." He pried the plastic cap off his milkshake and spooned out the ice cream. "Eight rounds into a speeding bus and nobody even gets nicked. That's one hell of a decent shot."

Carrie said, "I'm assuming they didn't catch the culprit."

"Vanished without a trace," said the trooper. "If it's him, they'll never even find a footprint. He knows that area of the state very well."

Winder said it was a long way to go for a man with two fresh gunshot wounds.

Jim Tile shrugged. "I called Game and Fish. The panther plane hasn't picked up the radio signal for days."

"So he's really gone," Carrie said.

"Or hiding in a bomb shelter."

"Joe thinks we should go ahead and make a move. He's got a plan all worked out."

Jim Tile raised a hand. "Don't tell me, please. I don't want to hear it."

"Fair enough," Winder said, "but I've got to ask a small favor."

"The answer is no."

"But it's nothing illegal."

The trooper used the corner of a paper napkin to polish the lenses of his sunglasses. "This falls into the general category of pressing your luck. Just because the governor gets away, don't think it's easy. Or even right."

"Please," said Carrie, "just listen."

"What is it you want me to do?"

"Your job," Joe Winder replied. "That's all."

Later, in the rental boat, Joe Winder said he almost felt sorry for Charles Chelsea. "Getting your sports celebrity shot with the press watching, that's tough."

Carrie Lanier agreed that Chelsea was earning his salary. She was at the helm of the outboard, expertly steering a course toward the ocean shore of North Key Largo. A young man named Oscar sat shirtless on the bow, dangling his brown legs and drinking a root beer.

Carrie told Joe he had some strange friends.

"Oscar thinks he owes me a favor, that's all. Years ago I left his name out of a newspaper article and it wound up saving his life."

Carrie looked doubtful, but said nothing. Her hair was tied

back in a ponytail. She wore amber sunglasses with green Day-Glo frames and a silver one-piece bathing suit. Oscar didn't stare, not even once. His mind was on business, and the soccer game he was missing on television. Most Thursdays he was on his way to Belize, only this morning there'd been a minor problem with Customs, and the flight was canceled. When Joe Winder called him at the warehouse, Oscar felt honorbound to lend a hand.

"He thinks I cut him a break," Winder whispered to Carrie, "but the fact is, I *did* use his name in the story. It just got edited out for lack of space."

"What was the article about?"

"Gunrunning."

From the bow, Oscar turned and signaled that they were close enough now. Kneeling on the deck, he opened a canvas duffel and began to arrange odd steel parts on a chamois cloth. The first piece that Carrie saw was a long gray tube.

"Oscar's from Colombia," Joe Winder explained. "His brother's in the M-19. They're leftist rebels."

"Thank you, Doctor Kissinger." Carrie smeared the bridge of her nose with mauve-colored zinc oxide. It was clear from her attitude that she had reservations about this phase of the plan.

She said, "What makes you think Kingsbury needs another warning? I mean, he's got the mob after him, Joe. Why should he care about a couple of John Deeres?"

"He's a developer. He'll care." Winder leaned back and squinted at the sun. "Keep the pressure on, that's the key."

Carrie admired the swiftness with which Oscar went about his task. She said to Winder: "Tell me again what they call that."

"An RPG. Rocket-propelled grenade."

"And you're positive no one's going to get hurt?"

"It's lunch hour, Carrie. You heard the whistle." He took out a pair of waterproof Zeiss binoculars and scanned the shoreline until he found the stand of pigeon plums that Molly

McNamara had told him about. The dreaded bulldozers had multiplied from two to five: they were parked in a semicircle, poised for the mission against the plum trees.

"Everybody's on their break," Winder reported. "Even the deputies." At the other end of the boat, Oscar assembled the grenade launcher in well-practiced silence.

Carrie cut the twin Evinrudes and let the currents nudge the boat over the grassy shallows. She took the field glasses and tried to spot the bird nest that Molly had mentioned. She couldn't see anything, the hardwoods were so dense.

"I'm not sure I understand the significance of this gesture," she said. "Mockingbirds aren't exactly endangered."

"These ones are." Winder peeled off his T-shirt and tied it around his forehead like a bandanna. The air stuck to his chest like a hot rag; the temperature on the water was ninety-four degrees, and no breeze. "You don't approve," he said to Carrie. "I can tell."

"What bothers me is the lack of imagination, Joe. You could be blowing up bulldozers the rest of your life."

The words stung, but she was right. Clever this was not, merely loud. "I'm sorry," he said, "but there wasn't time to come up with something more creative. The old lady said they were taking out the plum trees this afternoon, and it looks like she was right."

Oscar gave the okay sign from the bow. The boat had drifted close enough so they could hear the voices and lunchtime banter of the Falcon Trace construction crew.

"Which dozer you want?" Oscar inquired, raising the weapon to his shoulder.

"Take your pick."

"Joe, wait!" Carrie handed him the binoculars. "Over there, check it out."

Winder beamed when he spotted it. "Looks like they're pouring the slab for the clubhouse."

"That's a large cement mixer," Carrie noted.

"Sure is. A *very* large cement mixer." Joe Winder snapped his fingers and motioned to Oscar. Spying the new target, the young Colombian smiled broadly and readjusted his aim.

In a low voice Carrie said, "I take it he's done this sort of thing before."

"I believe so, yes."

Oscar grunted something in Spanish, then pulled the trigger. The RPG took out the cement truck quite nicely. An orange gout of flame shot forty feet in the sky, and warm gray gobs of cement rained down on the construction workers as they sprinted for their cars.

"See," Carrie said. "A little variety's always nice."

Joe Winder savored the smoky scent of chaos and wondered what his father would have thought.

We all shine on.

That night Carrie banished him from the bedroom while she practiced her songs for the Jubilee. At first he listened in dreamy amazement at the door, her voice was crystalline, delicate, soothing. After a while Bud Schwartz and Danny Pogue joined him in the hallway, and Carrie's singing seemed to soften their rough convict features. Danny Pogue lowered his eyes and began to hum along; Bud Schwartz lay on the wooden floor with hands behind his head and gazed at the high pine beams. Molly McNamara even unlocked the door to the adjoining bedroom so that Agent Billy Hawkins, gagged but alert, could enjoy the beautiful musical interlude.

Eventually Joe Winder excused himself and slipped downstairs to make a call. He went through three telephone temptresses before they switched him to Nina's line.

"I'm glad it's you," she said. "There's something you've got to hear."

"I'm honestly not in the mood—"

"This is different, Joe. It took three nights to write."

What could he possibly say? "Go ahead, Nina."

"Ready?" She was so excited. He heard the rustle of paper. Then she took a breath and began to read:

> *"Your hands find me in the night, burrow for my warmth.*
> *Lift me, turn me, move me apart.*
> *The language of blind insistence,*
> *You speak with a slow tongue on my belly,*
> *An eyelash fluttering against my nipple.*
> *This is the moment of raw cries and murmurs when*
> *Nothing matters in the vacuum of passion*
> *But passion itself."*

He wasn't sure if she had finished. It sounded like a big ending, but he wasn't sure.

"Nina?"

"What do you think?"

"It's . . . vivid."

"Poetry. A brand-new concept in phone sex."

"Interesting." God, she's making a career of this.

"Did it arouse you?"

"Definitely," he said. "My loins surge in wild tumescence inside my jeans."

"Stop it, Joe!"

"I'm sorry. Really it's quite good." And maybe it was. He knew next to nothing about poetry.

"I wanted to try something different," Nina said, "something literate. A few of the girls complained—Miriam, of course. She's more comfortable with the old sucky-fucky."

"Well," Winder said, "it's all in the reading."

"My editor wants to see more."

"You have an editor?"

"For the syndication deal, Joe. What'd you think of the

last part? *Nothing matters in the vacuum of passion but passion itself.*"

He said, "'Abyss' is better than 'vacuum.'"

"The abyss of passion! You're right, Joe, that's much better."

"It's a long way from dry-humping on the Amtrak."

Nina laughed. He'd almost forgotten how wonderful it sounded.

"So how was your hot date with The Voice?"

"It was very enjoyable. He's an exceptional man."

"What does he do?"

Without skipping a beat: "He markets General Motors products."

"Cars? He sells cars! That *is* exceptional."

Nina said, "I don't want to talk about this."

"Buicks? Pontiacs? Oldsmobiles? Or perhaps all three?"

"He is a surprisingly cultured man," Nina said. "An educated man. And it's Chevrolets, for your information. The light-truck division."

"Boy." Winder felt exhausted. First the poetry, now this. "Nina, I've got to ask. Does the face match the voice?"

"There's nothing wrong with the way he looks."

"Say no more."

"You can be such a prick," she observed.

"You're right. I'm sorry—again."

"He wants to marry me."

"Showing excellent taste," Winder said. "He'd be nuts if he didn't."

There was a brief pause, then Nina asked: "Are you the one who shot the golfer?"

"Nope. But I don't blame you for wondering."

"Please don't kill anybody, Joe. I know how strongly you feel about these issues, but please don't murder anyone."

"I'll try not to."

"Better sign off," she said. "I'm tying up the phone."

"Hey, I'm a paying customer."

"You really liked the poem?"

"It was terrific, Nina. I'm very proud."

He could tell she was pleased. "Any more suggestions?" she said.

"Well, the line about the nipple."

"Yes. *An eyelash fluttering against my nipple.*"

"The imagery is nice," Winder said, "but it makes it sound like you've got just one. Nipple, I mean."

"Hmm," said Nina. "That's a good point."

"Otherwise it's great."

"Thanks, Joe," she said. "Thanks for everything."

Thirty-one

Joe Winder held Carrie in his arms and wondered why the women he loved were always a step or two ahead of him.

"So what are you planning?" he asked.

She stirred but didn't answer. Her cheek felt silky and warm against his chest. When would he ever learn to shut up and enjoy the moment?

"Carrie, I know you're not asleep."

Her eyes opened. Even in the darkness he could feel the liquid stare. "You're the only man I've ever been with," she said, "who insists on talking afterward."

"You inspire me, that's all."

"Aren't you exhausted?" She raised her head. "Was I hallucinating, or did we just fuck our brains out?"

Winder said, "I'm nervous as hell. I've been rehearsing it all in my head."

She told him to stop worrying and go to sleep. "What's the worst thing that could happen?"

"Jail is a distinct possibility. Death is another."

Carrie turned on her belly and slid between his legs. Then she propped her elbows on his rib cage, and rested her chin on her hands.

"What are you smiling at?" Winder said.

"It's all going to work out. I've got faith in you."

"But you're planning something, just the same."

"Joe, it might be my only chance."

"At what?"

"Singing. I mean really singing. Am I hurting you?"

"Oh, no, you're light as a feather."

"You asshole," she giggled, and began to tickle him ferociously. Winder locked his legs around her thighs and flipped her over in the sheets.

They were kissing when he felt compelled to pull back and say, "I'm sorry I dragged you into this mess."

"What mess? And, besides, you're doing the honest thing. Even if it's slightly mad."

"You're speaking of the major felonies."

"Of course," Carrie said. "But your motives are absolutely pure and unassailable. I'll be cheering for you, Joe."

"Clinical insanity isn't out of the question," he said. "Just thinking about Kingsbury and that damn golf course, I get noises inside my skull."

"What kind of noises?"

"Hydraulic-type noises. Like the crusher on a garbage truck."

Carrie looked concerned, and he couldn't blame her. "It goes back to my old man," he said.

"Don't think about it so much, Joe."

"I'd feel better if the governor were here. Just knowing I wasn't the only lunatic—"

"I had a dream about him," she said quietly. "I dreamed he broke into prison and killed that guy—what's his name?"

"Mark Chapman," said Winder. "Mark David Chapman."

She heard sadness in the reply, sadness because she didn't remember the details. "Joe, I was only fourteen when it happened."

"You're right."

378

"Besides, I've always been lousy with names. Oswald, Sirhan, Hinkley—it's easy to lose track of these idiots."

"Sure is," Winder agreed.

Carrie tenderly laced her hands on the back of his neck. "Everything's going to be fine. And no, you're not crazy. A little zealous is all."

"It's not a bad plan," he said.

"Joe, it's a terrific plan."

"And if all goes well, you'll still have your job."

"No, I don't think so. I'm not much of a Seminole go-go dancer."

Now it was his turn to smile. "I take it there may be some last-minute changes in the musical program."

"Quite possibly," Carrie said.

He kissed her softly on the forehead. "I'll be cheering for you, too."

"I know you will, Joe."

As far as Bud Schwartz was concerned, he'd rather be in jail than in a hospital. Practically everyone he ever knew who died—his mother, his brother, his uncles, his first probation officer—had died in hospital beds. In fact, Bud Schwartz couldn't think of a single person who'd come out of a hospital in better shape than when they'd gone in.

"What about babies?" Danny Pogue said.

"Babies don't count."

"What about your boy? Mike Jr., wasn't he borned in a hospital?"

"Matter of fact, no. It was the back of a Bronco. And his name is *Bud* Jr., like I told you." Bud Schwartz rolled down the window and tried to spit the toothpick from the corner of his mouth. It landed on his arm. "A hospital's the last place for a sick person to go," he said.

"You think she'll die there?"

"No. I don't wanna set foot in the place is all."

"Jesus, you're a cold shit."

Bud Schwartz was startled by his partner's anger. Out of pure guilt he relented and agreed to go, but only for a few minutes. Danny Pogue seemed satisfied. "Let's get some roses on the way."

"Fine. A lovely gesture."

"Hey, it'll mean a lot to her."

"Danny, this is the same woman who shot us. And you're talking flowers."

Molly McNamara had driven herself to Baptist Hospital after experiencing mild chest pains. She had a private room with a gorgeous view of a parking deck.

When he saw her shriveled in the bed, Danny Pogue gulped desperately to suppress the tears. Bud Schwartz also was jarred by the sight—she looked strikingly pallid and frail. And small. He'd never thought of Molly McNamara as a small woman, but that's how she appeared in the hospital: small and caved-in. Maybe because all that glorious white hair was stuffed under a paper cap.

"The flowers are splendid," she said, lifting the thin plastic tube that fed extra oxygen to her nostrils.

Danny Pogue positioned the vase on the bedstand, next to the telephone. "American Beauty roses," he said.

"So I see."

The burglars stood on opposite sides of the bed. Molly reached out and held their hands.

She said, "A touch of angina, that's all. I'll be as good as new in a few days."

Danny Pogue wondered if angina was contagious; it sounded fairly sexual. "The house is fine," he said. "The disposal jammed this morning, but I fixed it myself."

"A spatula got stuck," Bud Schwartz added. "Don't ask how."

Molly said, "How is Agent Hawkins?"

"Same as ever."

"Are you feeding him?"

"Three times a day, just like you told us."

"Are his spirits improved?"

"Hard to tell," Bud Schwartz said. "He don't talk much with all that tape on his face."

"I heard about the golfer being shot," said Molly. "Mr. Kingsbury's had quite a run of bad luck, wouldn't you say?" She asked the question with a trace of a smile. Danny Pogue glanced down at his shoes.

To change the subject, Bud Schwartz asked if there was a cafeteria in the hospital. "I could sure use a Coke."

"Make that two," said Danny Pogue. "And a lemonade for Molly."

"Yes, that would hit the spot. Or maybe a ginger ale, something carbonated." She patted Danny Pogue's hand. Again he looked as if he were about to weep.

In the elevator Bud Schwartz couldn't shake the vision of the old woman sunken in bed. It was all Kingsbury's fault—Molly hadn't felt right since those bastards beat her up at the condo. That one of them had been gunned down later by a baboon was only a partial consolation; the other goon, the one with nine fingertips, was still loose. Joe Winder had said don't worry, they'll all pay—but what did Winder know about the law of the street? He was a writer, for Chrissakes. A goddamn dreamer. Bud Schwartz had agreed to help but he couldn't pretend to share Winder's optimism. As a lifelong criminal, he knew for a fact that the bad guys seldom get what they deserve. More often they just plain get away, even assholes who beat up old ladies.

Bud Schwartz was so preoccupied that he got off on the wrong floor and found himself standing amidst throngs of cooing relatives at the window of the nursery. He couldn't believe the number of newborn babies—it baffled him, left him muttering while others clucked and pointed and sighed. In a world turning to shit, why were so many people still having children? Maybe it was a fad, like CB radios and Cabbage Patch dolls. Or maybe these men and women didn't understand the full implications of reproduction.

More victims, thought Bud Schwartz, the last damn thing we need. He gazed at the rows of sleeping infants—crinkly and squinty-eyed and blissfully innocent—and silently foretold their future. They would grow up to have automobiles and houses and apartments that would all, eventually, be burglarized by lowlifes such as himself.

When Bud Schwartz returned to Molly McNamara's room, he sensed he was interrupting something private. Danny Pogue, who had been talking in a low voice, became silent at the sight of his partner.

Molly thanked Bud Schwartz for the cup of ginger ale. "Danny's got something to tell you," she said.

"Yeah?"

"I must admit," Molly said, "he left me speechless."

"So let's hear it already."

Danny Pogue lifted his chin and thrust out his bony chest. "I decided to give my share of the money to Molly."

"Not to me personally," she interjected. "To the Mothers of Wilderness."

"And the Wildlife Rescue Corps!"

"Unofficially, yes," she said.

"The mob money," Danny Pogue explained.

Bud Schwartz didn't know whether to laugh or scream. "Twenty-five grand? You're just givin' it away?"

Molly beamed. "Isn't that a magnificent gesture?"

"Oh, magnificent," said Bud Schwartz. Magnificently stupid.

Danny Pogue picked up on his partner's sarcasm and tried to mount a defense. He said, "It's just somethin' I wanted to do, okay?"

"Fine by me."

Molly said, "It automatically makes him a Golden Lifetime Charter Member!"

"It also automatically makes him broke."

"Come on," Danny Pogue said, "it's for a good cause."

Bud Schwartz's eyes narrowed. "Don't even think about asking."

"Danny, he's right," said Molly. "It's not fair to pressure a friend."

Warily Bud Schwartz scanned Molly's bed sheets for any lumps that might reveal the outline of a pistol. He said, "Look, I wanna go straight. That money's my future."

Danny Pogue rolled his eyes and snorted. "Cut the bull—I mean, don't kid yourself. All we're ever gonna be is thieves."

"Now there's a happy thought. That's what I mean about you and your fucking attitude."

To Danny Pogue's relief, Molly barely flinched at the profane adjective. She said, "Bud, I respect your ambitions. I really do."

But Danny Pogue wasn't finished whining. "Man, at least can't you spare *some*thing?"

For several moments the only sound was the muted whistle of Molly's oxygen machine. Finally she said, in a voice creaky with fatigue, "Even a small donation would be appreciated."

Bud Schwartz ground his molars. "How does a grand sound? Is that all right?" Christ, he must be insane. One thousand dollars to a bunch of blue-haired bunny huggers!

Molly McNamara smiled kindly. Danny Pogue exuberantly chucked him on the shoulder.

Bud Schwartz said, "Why don't I feel wonderful about this?"

"You will," Molly replied, "someday."

Among the men hired by Pedro Luz as security officers was Diamond J. Love, Diamond being his given name and the

"J" standing for Jesus. As was true with most of the guards at the Amazing Kingdom of Thrills, Diamond J. Love's personal history was investigated with only enough diligence to determine the absence of outstanding felony warrants. It was a foregone conclusion that Diamond J. Love's career in law enforcement had been derailed by unpleasant circumstances; there was no other logical reason for applying as a private security guard at a theme park.

Initially, Diamond J. Love was apprehensive about his employment chances at the Amazing Kingdom. He knew that Disney World and other family resorts were scrupulous about hiring clean-cut, enthusiastic, All-American types; Diamond J. Love was worried because in all ways he defied the image, but he need not have worried. Nobody from the Amazing Kingdom bothered to check with previous employers, such as the New York City Police Department, to inquire about allegations of bribery, moral turpitude, substance abuse, witness tampering and the unnecessary use of deadly force, to wit, the pistol-whipping of a young man suspected of shoplifting a bag of cheese-flavored Doritos.

Diamond J. Love was elated to be hired for the security force at the Amazing Kingdom, and pleased to find himself surrounded with colleagues of similarly checkered backgrounds. On slow days, when they weren't breaking into the RVs of tourists, they'd sit around and swap stories about the old police days—tales of stacking the civil-service boards to beat a brutality rap; perjuring themselves silly before grand juries; rounding up hookers on phony vice sweeps just to cop a free hummer; switching kilos of baking soda for cocaine in the evidence rooms. Diamond J. Love enjoyed these bull sessions, and he enjoyed his job. For the most part.

The only area of concern was the boss himself, a monster steroid freak whose combustible mood swings had prompted several of his own officers to leave their holsters permanently unsnapped, just in case. Some days Pedro Luz was reasonable and coherent, other days he was a drooling psycho. The news that he had chewed off his own foot only heightened the anxiety level on the security squad; even the potheads were getting jumpy.

Which is why Diamond J. Love did not wish to be late for work on this very important morning, and why he reacted with exceptionally scathing impudence to the mild-mannered inquiry of a black state trooper who had pulled over his car on County Road 905.

"May I see your driver's license, please?"

"Get serious, Uncle Ben."

From there it went downhill. The trooper was singularly unimpressed by Diamond J. Love's expired NYPD police badge; nor was he particularly understanding on the issue of Diamond J. Love's outdated New York driver's license. Or the fact that, according to some computer, the serial numbers on Diamond J. Love's Camaro matched precisely those of a Camaro stolen eight months earlier in New Smyrna Beach.

"That's bullshit," suggested Diamond J. Love.

"Please get out of the car," the trooper said.

At which point Diamond J. Love attempted to speed away, and instead felt himself dragged by the collar through the window and deposited face-first on the macadam. Upon regaining consciousness, Diamond J. Love discovered Plasticuffs cinched painfully to his wrists and ankles. He further was surprised to see that he shared his predicament with several other security guards, who had apparently encountered the highway patrol on the pre-dawn journey to the Amazing Kingdom of Thrills. There sat Ossie Cano, former Seattle robbery detective-turned-fence; William Z. Ames, former Orlando patrolman-turned-pornographer; Neal "Bart" Bartkowski, former sergeant with the Atlanta police, currently appealing a federal conviction for tax evasion.

"The hell's going on here?" demanded Diamond J. Love.

"Roadblock," Cano replied.

"A one-man roadblock?"

"I heard him radio for backup."

"But still," said Diamond J. Love. "One guy?"

By sunrise there were nine of them handcuffed or otherwise detained, a row of sullen penguins lined up along County Road 905. Basically it was the Amazing Kingdom's entire security force, except for Pedro Luz and one other guard, who had spent the night at the amusement park.

Trooper Jim Tile was impressed by the accuracy of Joe Winder's intelligence, particularly the makes and license numbers of the guards' personal cars—information pilfered by Carrie Lanier from the files of the Personnel Department. Jim Tile was also impressed that not a single one of the guards had a clean record; to a man there arose problems with driver's licenses, expired registration stickers, doctored title certificates or unpaid traffic tickets. Each of the nine attempted to slide out of the road check by flashing outdated police ID—"badging," in cop vernacular. Two of the nine had offered Jim Tile a whispered inducement of either cash or narcotics; three others had sealed their fate by making racial remarks. All had been disarmed and handcuffed so swiftly, and with such force, that physical resistance had been impossible.

When the van from the Monroe County Sheriff's Office arrived, the deputy's eyes swept from Jim Tile to the cursing horde of prisoners and back again.

The deputy said, "Jimmy, you do this all by yourself?"

"One at a time," the trooper answered. "A road check, that's all."

"I know some of these boys."

"Figured you might."

"We lookin' at anything serious?"

"We're considering it."

From the end of the line came an outcry from Diamond J. Love: "Dwight, you gonna let this nigger get away with it?"

Jim Tile gave no indication of hearing the remark. The deputy named Dwight did, however. "Damndest thing," he said in a hearty voice. "The air-conditioning broke down in the paddy wagon. Just now happened."

The trooper said, "What a shame."

"Gonna be a long trip back to the substation."

"Probably gets hot as hell inside that van."

"Like an oven," Dwight agreed with a wink.

"Fuck you!" shouted Diamond J. Love. "Fuck the both of you."

The phone bleeped in Charles Chelsea's apartment at seven-fifteen. It might as well have been a bomb.

"That fucking Pedro, I can't find him!" Who else but Francis X. Kingsbury.

"Have you tried the gym?" Chelsea said foggily.

"I tried everywhere, hell, you name it. And there's no guards! I waited and waited, finally said fuck it and drove myself to work." He was on the speaker phone, hollering as he stormed around the office.

"The security men never showed up?"

"Wake up, dicklick! I'm alone, *comprende*? No Pedro, no guards, *nada*."

Dicklick? Charles Chelsea sat up in bed and shook his head like a spaniel. Do I really deserve to be called a dicklick? Is that what I get for all my loyalty?

Kingsbury continued to fulminate: "So where in the name of Christ Almighty is everybody? Today of all days—is there something you're not telling me, Charlie?"

"I haven't heard a thing, sir. Let me check into it."

"You do that!" And he was gone.

Chelsea dragged himself to the kitchen and fine-tuned the coffeemaker. In less than two hours, some lucky customer would breach the turnstiles at the Amazing Kingdom of Thrills and be proclaimed the Five-Millionth Visitor. Officially, at least. Chelsea was fairly certain that at least one enterprising journalist would take the time to add up the park's true attendance figures and expose the promotion for the hoax that it was. The scene was set for a historic publicity disaster; already the national newsmagazines and out-of-state papers were snooping around, waiting for poor Jake Harp to expire. In recent days Chelsea's office had been deluged with applications for media credentials from publications that previously had displayed no interest in covering the Amazing Kingdom's Summerfest Jubilee. Chelsea wasn't naive enough to believe that the New York *Daily News* was seriously interested in a feature profile of the engineer who'd designed the Wet Willy water slide; no, their presence was explained by pure rampant bloodlust. The kidnapped mango voles, the dead scientist, the dead Orky, the nearly dead Jake Harp, flaming bulldozers, phony snake invasions, exploding cement trucks—an irresistible convergence of violence, mayhem and mortality!

Charles Chelsea understood that the dispatches soon to be filed from the Amazing Kingdom of Thrills wouldn't be bright or warm or fluffy. They would be dark and ominous and chilling. They would describe a screaming rupture of the civil order, a culture in terminal moral hemorrhage.

And this would almost certainly have a negative effect on tourism.

Oh well, Chelsea thought, I gave it my best.

He foraged in the refrigerator, unearthed a stale bagel and began gnawing dauntlessly. Hearing a knock at the door, he assumed that the pathologically impatient Kingsbury had sent a car for him.

"Just a second!" Chelsea called, and went to put on a robe.

When he opened the door, he faced the immutable, bewhiskered grin of Robbie Raccoon.

Who was holding, in his three-fingered polyester paw, a gun.

Which was pointed at Charles Chelsea's throat.

"What's this?" croaked the publicity man.

"Show time," said Joe Winder.

Thirty-two

The raccoon suit was musty and stifling, but it smelled reassuringly of Carrie's hair and perfume. Even the lint seemed familiar. Through slits in the cheeks Joe Winder was able to see the procession: Bud Schwartz, Danny Pogue and the captive Charles Chelsea, entering the gates of the Amazing Kingdom of Thrills.

To affect Robbie Raccoon's most recognizable mannerisms, Winder took floppy exaggerated steps (the way Carrie had showed him) and jauntily twirled the bushy tail. In spite of the serious circumstances, he felt a bolt of childlike excitement as the amusement park prepared to open for the Summerfest Jubilee. Outside, the trams were delivering waves of eager tourists—the children stampeding rabidly toward the locked turnstiles; the women bravely toting infants and designer baby bags; the men with shoulder-mounted Camcorders aimed at anything that moved. Fruity-colored balloons decorated every lamppost, every shrubbery, every concession; Broadway show tunes blasted through tinny public-address speakers. Mimes and jugglers and musicians rehearsed on street corners while desultory maintenance crews collected cigarette butts, Popsicle sticks and gum wrappers off the pavement. A cowboy from the Wild Bill Hiccup show tested his six-shooter by firing blanks at Peter Possum's scraggly bottom.

"Show business," said Joe Winder, "is my life." The words echoed inside the plaster animal head.

If the costume had a serious flaw (besides the nonfunctioning air conditioner), it was a crucial lack of peripheral vision. The slits, located several inches below Robbie Raccoon's large plastic eyes, were much too narrow. Had the openings been wider, Winder would have spotted the fleshy pale hand in time to evade it.

It was the hand of famed TV weatherman Willard Scott, and it dragged Joe Winder in front of a camera belonging to the National Broadcasting Company. Danny Pogue, Bud Schwartz and Charles Chelsea stopped in their tracks: Robbie Raccoon was on the "Today Show." *Live.* Willard flung one meaty arm around Winder's shoulders, and the other around a grandmother from Hialeah who said she was 107 years old. The old woman was telling a story about riding Henry Flagler's railroad all the way to Key West.

"A hunnert and seven!" marveled Danny Pogue.

Charles Chelsea shifted uneasily. Bud Schwartz shot him a look. "What, she's lying?"

Morosely the publicity man confessed. "She's a complete fake. A ringer. I arranged the whole thing." The burglars stared as if he were speaking another language. Chelsea lowered his voice: "I *had* to do it. Willard wanted somebody over a hundred years old, they told me he might not come, otherwise. But I couldn't find anyone over a hundred—ninety-one was the best I could do, and the poor guy was completely spaced. Thought he was Rommel."

Danny Pogue whispered, "So who's she?"

"A local actress," Chelsea said. "Age thirty-eight. The makeup is remarkable."

"Christ, this is what you do for a living?" Bud Schwartz turned to his partner. "And I thought *we* were scumballs."

To the actress, Willard Scott was saying: "You're here to win that 300-Z, aren't you, sweetheart? In a few minutes the park opens and the first lucky customer through the gate will be Visitor Number Five Million. They'll get the new sports car and all kinds of great prizes!"

"I'm so excited!" the actress proclaimed.

"You run along now, but be careful getting in line. The folks are getting pretty worked up out there. Good luck, sweetheart!" Then Willard Scott gave the bogus 107-year-old grandmother a slurpy smooch on the ear. As he released his grip on the woman, he tightened his hug on Joe Winder.

And an awakening nation heard the famous weatherman say: "This ring-tailed rascal is one of the most popular characters here at the Amazing Kingdom of Thrills. Go ahead, tell us your name."

And in a high squeaky voice, Joe Winder gamely replied: "Hi, Willard! My name is Robbie Raccoon."

"You're certainly a big fella, Robbie. Judging by the size of that tummy, I'd say you've been snooping through a few garbage cans!"

To which Robbie Raccoon responded: "Look who's talking, lardass."

Briefly the smile disappeared from Willard's face, and his eyes searched desperately off-camera for the director. A few feet away, Charles Chelsea tasted bile creeping up his throat. The burglars seemed pleased to be standing so close to a genuine TV star.

A young woman wearing earphones and a jogging suit held up a cue card, and valiantly the weatherman attempted to polish off the segment: "Well, spirits are obviously running high for the big Summerfest Jubilee, so pack up the family and come down to"— here Willard paused to find his place on the card—"Key Largo, Florida, and enjoy the fun! You can swim with a real dolphin, or go sliding headfirst down the Wet

Willy or bust some broncos with Wild Bill Hiccup. And you kids can get your picture taken with all your favorite animal characters, even Robbie Raccoon."

Obligingly Joe Winder cocked his head and twirled his tail. Willard appeared to regain his jolly demeanor. He prodded at something concealed under one of the fuzzy raccoon arms. "It looks like our ole pal Robbie's got a surprise for Uncle Willard, am I right?"

From Winder came a strained chirp: "'Fraid not, Mr. Scott."

"Aw, come on. Whatcha got in that paw?"

"*Nothing.*"

"Let's see it, you little scamp. Is it candy? A toy? Whatcha got there?"

And seventeen million Americans heard Robbie Raccoon say: "That would be a gun, Willard."

Chelsea's ankles got rubbery and he began to sway. The burglars each grabbed an elbow.

"My, oh, my," Willard Scott said with a nervous chuckle. "It even *looks* like a real gun."

"Doesn't it, though," said the giant raccoon.

Please, thought Bud Schwartz, not on national TV. Not with little kids watching.

But before anything terrible could happen, Willard Scott adroitly steered the conversation from firearms to a tropical depression brewing in the eastern Caribbean. Joe Winder was able to slip away when the weatherman launched into a laxative commercial.

On the path to the Cimarron Saloon, Charles Chelsea and the burglars heard howling behind them; a rollicking if muffled cry that emanated from deep inside the globular raccoon head.

"Aaaahhh-oooooooooo," Joe Winder sang. "We're the werewolves of Florida! Aaaahhh-oooooooooo!"

*

The smoke from Moe Strickland's cigar hung like a purple shroud in The Catacombs. Uncle Ely's Elves had voted unanimously to boycott the Jubilee, and Uncle Ely would honor their decision.

"The cowboy getups look stupid," he agreed.

The actor who played the elf Jeremiah, and sometimes Dumpling, lit a joint to counteract the stogie fumes. He declared, "We're not clowns, we're actors. So fuck Kingsbury."

"That's right," said another elf. "Fuck Mr. X."

Morale in the troupe had been frightfully low since the newspapers had picked up the phony story about a hepatitis outbreak. Several of the actor-elves had advocated changing the name of the act to escape the stigma. Others wanted to hire a Miami attorney and file a lawsuit.

Moe Strickland said, "I heard they're auditioning up at Six Flags."

"Fuck Six Flags," said Jeremiah-Dumpling elf. "Probably another damn midget routine."

"Our options are somewhat limited," Moe Strickland said, trying to put it as delicately as possible.

"So fuck our options."

The mood began to simmer after they'd passed the joint around about four times. Moe Strickland eventually stubbed out the cigar and began to enjoy himself. On the street above, a high-school marching band practiced the theme from *2001: A Space Odyssey*. Filtered through six feet of stone, it didn't sound half bad.

One of the actor-elves said, "Did I mention there's a guy living in our dumpster?"

"You're kidding," said Moe Strickland.

"No, Uncle Ely, it's true. We met him yesterday."

"In the Dumpster?"

"He fixed it up nice like you wouldn't believe. We gave him a beer."

Moe Strickland wondered how a homeless person could've

found a way into The Catacombs, or why he'd want to stay where it was so musty and humid and bleak.

"A nice guy," said the actor-elf. "A real gentleman."

"We played poker," added Jeremiah-Dumpling. "Cleaned his fucking clock."

"But he was a sport about it. A gentleman, like I said."

Again Moe Strickland raised the subject of Six Flags. "Atlanta's a great town," he said. "Lots of pretty women."

"We'll need some new songs."

"That's okay," said Moe Strickland. "Some new songs would be good. We'll have the whole bus ride to work on the arrangements. Luther can bring his guitar."

"Why not?" said Jeremiah-Dumpling. "Fuck Kingsbury anyhow."

"That's the spirit," Moe Strickland said.

From the end of the tunnel came the sound of boots on brick. A man bellowed furiously.

"Damn," said one of the actor-elves. He dropped the nub of the joint and ground it to ash under a long, curly-toed, foam-rubber foot.

The boots and the bellowing belonged to a jittery Spence Mooher, who was Pedro Luz's right-hand man. Mooher was agitated because none of the other security guards had shown up for work on this, the busiest day of the summer. Mooher had been up all night patrolling the Amazing Kingdom, and now it looked as if he'd be up all day.

"I smell weed," he said to Moe Strickland.

In this field Mooher could honestly boast of expertise; he had served six years with the U.S. Drug Enforcement Administration until he was involuntarily relieved of duty. There had been vague accusations of unprofessional conduct in Puerto Rico—something about a missing flash roll, twenty or thirty thousand dollars. As Spence Mooher was quick to point out, no charges were ever filed.

He shared his new boss's affinity for anabolic steroids, but he strongly disapproved of recreational drugs. Steroids hardened the body, but pot and cocaine softened the mind.

"Who's got the weed?" he demanded of Uncle Ely's Elves.

"Lighten up, Spence," sighed Moe Strickland.

"Why aren't you shitheads up top in rehearsal? Everybody's supposed to be there."

"Because we're boycotting," said Jeremiah-Dumpling. "We're not going to be in the damn show."

Mooher's mouth twisted. "Yes, you are," he said. "This is the Summerfest Jubilee!"

"I don't care if it's the second coming of Christ," said Jeremiah-Dumpling. "We're not performing."

Moe Strickland added. "It's a labor action, Spence. Nothing you can do."

"No?" With one hand Mooher grabbed the veteran character actor by the throat and slammed him against a row of tall lockers. The actor-elves could only cry out helplessly as the muscular security officer banged Uncle Ely's head again and again, until blood began to trickle from his ears. The racket of bone against metal was harrowing, amplified in the bare tunnel.

Finally Spence Mooher stopped. He held Moe Strickland at arm's length, three feet off the ground; the actor kicked spasmodically.

"Have you reconsidered?" Mooher asked. Moe Strickland's eyelids drooped, but he managed a nod.

A deep voice down the passageway said, "Let him go."

Spence Mooher released Uncle Ely and wheeled to face . . . a bum. An extremely tall bum, but a bum nonetheless. It took the security guard a few moments to make a complete appraisal: the damp silver beard, braided on one cheek only; the flowered plastic rain hat pulled taut over the scalp; the broad tan chest wrapped in heavy copper-stained bandages;

a red plastic collar around the neck; one dead eye steamed with condensation, the other alive and dark with anger; the mouthful of shiny white teeth.

Here, thought Spence Mooher, was a bum to be reckoned with. He reached this conclusion approximately one second too late, for the man had already seized Mooher's testicles and twisted with such forcefulness that all strength emptied from Mooher's powerful limbs; quivering, he felt a rush of heat down his legs as he soiled himself. When he tried to talk, a weak croaking noise came out of his mouth.

"Time to go night-night," said the bum, twisting harder. Spence Mooher fell down unconscious.

With a slapping of many oversized feet, the actor-elves scurried toward the slack figure of Moe Strickland, who was awake but in considerable pain. Jeremiah-Dumpling lifted Moe's bloody head and said, "This is the guy we told you about. The one in the Dumpster."

Skink bent down and said, "Pleased to meet you, Uncle Ely. I think your buddies better get you to the vet."

Charles Chelsea tested the door to Francis X. Kingsbury's office and found it locked. He tapped lightly but received no reply.

"I know he's in there," Chelsea said.

Danny Pogue said, "Allow us." He produced a small screwdriver and easily popped the doorjamb.

"Like ridin' a bicycle," said Bud Schwartz.

From inside the raccoon costume came a hollow command. The others stood back while Joe Winder opened the door. Upon viewing the scene, he clapped his paws and said: "Perfect."

Francis X. Kingsbury was energetically fondling himself in front of a television set. On the screen, a dark young man in a torn soccer jersey was copulating with a wild-haired brunette woman, who was moaning encouragement in Spanish. Other video cassettes were fanned out like a poker hand on the desk.

Kingsbury halted mid-pump and wheeled to confront the intruders. The boxer shorts around his ankles greatly diminished his ability to menace. Today's hairpiece was a silver Kenny Rogers model.

"Get out," Kingsbury snarled. He fumbled for the remote control and turned off the VCR. He seemed unaware that the Amazing Kingdom's stalwart mascot, Robbie Raccoon, was pointing a loaded semiautomatic at him. Joe Winder tucked the gun under one arm while he unzipped his head and removed it.

"So you're alive," Kingsbury hissed. "I had a feeling, goddammit."

Bud Schwartz laughed and pointed at Kingsbury, who shielded his receding genitals. The burglar said, "The asshole's wearing golf shoes!"

"For traction," Joe Winder theorized.

Charles Chelsea looked disgusted. Danny Pogue tossed a package on the desk. "Here," he said to Kingsbury, "even though you tried to kill us."

"What's this?"

"The files we swiped. Ramex, Gotti, it's all there."

Kingsbury was confused. Why would they return the files now? Bud Schwartz read his expression and said, "You were right. It was out of our league."

Which was baloney. The true reason for returning the files was to ensure that no one would come searching for them later. Like the police or the FBI.

"I suppose you want, what, a great big thank-you or some such goddamn thing." Francis X. Kingsbury tugged the boxer shorts high on his gelatinous waist. The indignity of the moment finally had sunk in. "Get out or I'm calling Security!"

"You've got no Security," Winder informed him.

"Charlie?"

"I'm afraid that's right, sir. I'll explain later."

Bud Schwartz said to his partner, "This is pathetic. Let's go."

"Wait." Danny Pogue stepped up to Kingsbury and said: "Beating up an old lady, what's the matter with you?"

"What the hell do you care." By now Kingsbury had more or less focused on Joe Winder's gun, so he spoke to Danny Pogue without looking at him. "That fucking Pedro, he gets carried away. Not a damn thing I can do."

"She's a sick old woman, for Chrissake."

"What's your point, Jethro?"

"My point is this," said Danny Pogue, and ferociously punched Francis Kingsbury on the chin. Kingsbury's golf cleats snagged on the carpet as he toppled.

Surveying the messy scene, Charles Chelsea felt refreshingly detached. He truly didn't care anymore. Outside, a roar of thousands swept the Amazing Kingdom, followed by gay cheers and applause. Chelsea went to the window and parted the blinds. "What do you know," he said. "Our five-millionth customer just walked through the gate."

With gray hands Kingsbury clutched the corner of the desk and pulled himself to his feet. In this fashion he was also able to depress a concealed alarm button that rang in the Security Office.

Bud Schwartz said, "We'll be saying good-bye now."

"You're welcome to stay," offered Joe Winder.

"No thanks." Danny Pogue examined his knuckles for bruises and abrasions. He said, "Molly's having surgery this afternoon. We promised to be at the hospital."

"I understand," Winder said. "You guys want to take anything?" He motioned with his gun paw around the lavish office. "The VCR? Some tapes? How about a cellular phone for the car?"

"The phone might be good," said Danny Pogue. "What'd you think, Bud? You could call your little boy from the road, wouldn't that be cool?"

"Let's roll," Bud Schwartz said.

Later they were driving on Card Sound Road, halfway back to the mainland, when Bud Schwartz motioned with a thumb and said: "Right about here's where it all started, Danny. Me throwin' that damn rat in the convertible."

"It was a vole," said Danny Pogue. "A blue-tongued mango vole. *Microtus mango.* That's the Latin name."

Bud Schwartz laughed. "Whatever you say." There was no denying he was impressed. How many burglars knew Latin?

A few more miles down the road, Danny Pogue again brought up the topic of portable phones. "If we had us one right now, we could call the hospital and see how she's doin'."

"You know the problem with cellulars," said Bud Schwartz. "The reception?"

"Besides the reception," Bud Schwartz said. "The problem with cellulars is, people always steal the damn things."

"Yeah," said his partner. "I hadn't thought about that."

The emergency buzzer awakens Pedro Luz in the storage room. He sits up and blinks. Blinks at the bare light bulb. Blinks at the pitted walls. Blinks at the empty intravenous bags on the hangers. He thinks, What the hell was it this time? Stanozolol, yeah. He'd pilfered a half-dozen tabs from Spence Mooher's locker. Ground them up with the toe of a boot, stirred it in the bag with the dextrose.

Feeling good. Feeling just fine. The beer sure helped.

Then comes Kingsbury's alarm and it sounds like a dental drill. Better get up now. Better get moving.

Pedro Luz pulls the tubes from his arms and tries to stand. Whoa, hoss! He forgot all about his foot, the fact that it was missing.

He grabs a wooden crutch and steadies himself. Facing the mirror, Pedro notices he's buck naked from the waist down. The image shocks him; his legs are as thick as oaks, but his penis is no larger than a peanut. Hastily he scrambles into the trousers of his guard uniform, the gun belt, one sock, one shoe.

Time to go to work. It's the Summerfest Jubilee and Mr. Kingsbury's in some kind of trouble.

And the damn door won't open.

Pedro can't fucking believe it. Okay, now somebody's either locked the damn thing from the outside, which don't make sense, or maybe welded it shut, which is even crazier. Pedro lowers one shoulder and hits the door like a tackle dummy. *Nada*. Now he's getting pissed. Through the steel he yells for Cano or Spence or Diamond J. Love, and gets no answer. "Where the hell *is* everybody?" hollers Pedro Luz.

Next logical step is using his skull as a battering ram. Wedging the crutch against the baseboard, he uses it to vault himself headfirst at the door. Amazing thing is, it don't hurt after a while. Tense the neck muscles just before impact and it acts like a spring. Boom, boom, boom. Boing, boing, boing.

No more door! Flattened.

What a fine feeling, to be free again.

The Security Office is empty, which is a mystery. Pedro checks the time cards and sees that none of the other guards have clocked in; something's going on here. Outside, the morning sun burns through a milky August haze, and the park is crawling with customers. There's a middle-aged lady at the security window complaining how somebody swiped her pocketbook off the tram. Behind her is some guy from Wisconsin, red hair and freckles, says he locked his keys in the rental car. And behind him is some bony old man with a shnoz that could cut glass. Claims one of the animals is walking around the park with a gun. Which one? Pedro asks. The possum? The raccoon? We got bunches of animals, says Pedro Luz. And the old guy scratches his big nose and says he don't know the difference from animals. Was Wally Wolverine for all he knows, but it damn sure was a gun in its paw. Sure, says Pedro, whatever you say. Here's a form to fill out. I'll be back in a few minutes.

Between the whiny tourists and all that banging with his head, Pedro's finally waking up. On the floor near the broken door he spots something shiny, and checks it out: a new Master padlock, still fastened to the broken hasp.

Pedro never would've imagined it was the lovely Princess Golden Sun who'd locked him in the storage room with his drugs and beer. He figured it was Spence Mooher or one of the other security guards, playing a joke.

He could deal with those jerk-offs later. Now it was time to haul ass over to Mr. Kingsbury's office and see what was wrong. For a moment Pedro Luz thought he heard the alarm go off again, but then he realized no, it was just the regular buzzing in his eardrums. Only it seemed to be getting louder.

Thirty-three

"First things first," Joe Winder said. "Who killed Will Koocher?"

Francis X. Kingsbury was rolling a shiny new Titleist from hand to hand across the top of his desk. The brassy strains of a marching band rose from the street below; the Summerfest Jubilee was in full swing.

"This Koocher," Kingsbury said, "he was threatening to go public about the voles. Pangs of conscience, whatever. So what I did, I told that fucking Pedro to go talk sense with the boy. See, it would've been a disaster—and Charlie'll back me up on this—a goddamn mess if it came out the voles were fake. Especially after the stupid things got stolen—talk about embarrassing."

Winder said, "So the answer to the question is Pedro. That's who committed the murder."

Kingsbury smothered his nose with a handkerchief and snuffled like a boar. "Damn hay fever!" The handkerchief puckered with each breath. "Far as I'm concerned, Koocher drowned in the Orky tank. Plain and simple. Case closed."

"But everyone knew the truth."

"No!" Chelsea protested. "I swear to God, Joey."

"Tell me about the blue-tongued mango voles," said Joe Winder. "Whose clever idea was that?"

From behind the veil of the soggy hanky, Kingsbury said: "I figured wouldn't it be fantastic if the Amazing Kingdom had an animal we could save. Like Disney tried to do with the dusky sparrow, only I was thinking in terms of a panda bear. People, I've seen this, they go fucking nuts for pandas. Only come to find out it's too hot down here, they'd probably croak in the sun.

"So I call this connection I got, this old friend, and I ask her what's endangered in Florida and she says all the good ones are taken—the panthers and manatees and so forth. She says it'd be better to come up with an animal nobody else had or even knew about. She says we might even get a government grant, which it turns out we did. Two hundred grand!"

Chelsea tried to act appalled; he even made a sound like a gasp. Impatiently, Winder said, "Charlie, this might come as a shock, but I don't care how much you knew and how much you didn't. For the purposes of settling this matter, you've become superfluous. Now show Mr. Kingsbury what we've prepared."

From an inside pocket Chelsea withdrew a folded sheet of Amazing Kingdom stationery. He handed it across the desk to Francis X. Kingsbury, who set aside both the handkerchief and the golf ball in order to read.

"It's a press release," Chelsea said.

"I see what it is. Horseshit is what it is." Kingsbury scanned it several times, including once from the bottom up. His mouth moved in twitchy circles, like a mule chewing a carrot.

"You ought to consider it," Winder advised him, "if you want to stay out of jail."

"Oh, so now it's blackmail?"

"No, sir, it's the cold fucking hand of fate."

Nervously Kingsbury fingered the bridge of his nose. "The hell is your angle, son?"

"You arranged an elaborate scientific fraud for the purposes of profit. An ingenious fraud, to be sure, but a felony nonetheless. Two hundred thousand is just about enough to interest the U.S. Attorney's Office."

Kingsbury shrugged in mockery. "Is that, what, like the end of the world?"

"I forgot," Winder said, "you're an expert on indictments. Aren't you, Frankie?"

Kingsbury turned color.

"Frankie King," said Winder. "That's your real name, in case you don't remember."

Kingsbury shrank into the chair. Winder turned to Charles Chelsea and said, "I think somebody's finally in the mood to talk."

"Can I leave?"

"Certainly, Charlie. And thanks for a terrific job on the publicity release."

"Yeah, right."

"I mean it," Winder said. "It's seamless."

Chelsea eyed him warily. "You're just being sarcastic."

"No, it was perfect. You've got a definite flair."

"Thanks, Joe. And I mean it, too."

The rescue of Francis Kingsbury was further delayed when a disturbance broke out near the front gate of the Amazing Kingdom; a tense and potentially violent dispute over the distribution of prizes, specifically a Nissan 300-Z.

The security-guard uniform is what gave Pedro Luz away. As he crutched toward Kingsbury's office, he was spotted and intercepted by a flying wedge of disgruntled customers. Something about the Summerfest contest being rigged. Pedro Luz insisted he didn't know about any damn contest, but the customers were loud and insistent. They led the security man back to the stage, where a short plump tourist named Rossiter had just been presented the keys to the sleek new sports car.

Draped around Mr. Rossiter's neck was a shiny streamer that said: "OUR FIVE-MILLIONTH SPECIAL GUEST!" In response to questions from a tuxedoed emcee, Mr. Rossiter said he was visiting the Amazing Kingdom with his wife and mother-in-law. He said it was only his second trip to Florida.

Mr. Rossiter gave the car keys to his wife, who squeezed her torso into the driver's seat and happily posed for pictures. Several persons in the crowd began to hiss and boo. Somebody threw a cup of frozen yogurt, which splattered against one of the car's wire wheels.

This was too much for Pedro Luz's jangled, hormone-flooded sensory receptors. He grabbed the microphone from the emcee and said, "Next person that throws food, I break their fucking spine."

Instantly a lull came over the mob. Pedro Luz said, "Now somebody explain what's going on."

At first no one spoke up, but there was a good bit of whispering about the bloody purple knots on the security chief's forehead. Finally a man in the crowd pointed at the Rossiters and shouted, "They cheated, that's what!"

Another male voice: "He cut in line!"

Pedro Luz said, "Jesus, I can't believe you people." He turned to the Rossiters. "Is it true? Did you cut in line?"

"No, Officer," Mr. Rossiter answered. "We got here first, fair and square."

Mrs. Rossiter popped her head from the car and said, "They're just a bunch of sore losers." Mrs. Rossiter's mother, a stubby woman wearing sandals and a Petey Possum T-shirt, said she'd never seen such rude people in all her life.

Pedro Luz didn't know what to do next; for one pleasantly deranged moment, he considered throwing the Rossiters off the stage and claiming the 300-Z for himself. *Daring* anyone to try to take it away from him. Then Charles Chelsea materialized and Pedro Luz gratefully surrendered the microphone. His ears buzzed and his head clanged and all he really wanted to do was limp to the gymnasium and pump some iron.

"Ladies and gentlemen," Chelsea intoned, "please settle down." He looked smooth and confident in a crisp blue oxford shirt and a wine-colored tie. He looked as if he could talk his way out of practically anything.

"I've reviewed the tapes from our security cameras," Chelsea told the crowd, "and whether you like it or not, Mr. Rossiter and his family were clearly the first ones through the turnstiles this morning—"

"But he threatened me!" yelled a teenager in the crowd. "I was here first but he said he'd kill me!"

A middle-aged woman in a straw Orky hat hollered: "Me too! And I was ahead of that kid—"

The crowd surged toward the stage until Pedro Luz drew his revolver and aimed it toward the sky. Seeing the gun, the tourists grew quiet and rippled back a few steps.

"Thank you," Chelsea said to Pedro Luz.

"I got an emergency."

"You can go now. I'll be fine."

"You need a gun?"

"No," said Chelsea, "but thanks just the same."

"You got something against fun."

Francis Kingsbury made it an indictment. "What, you got something against little children? Little cutey pies having a good time?"

Joe Winder said: "You can keep the park, Frankie. The park is already built. It's the golf resort that's eighty-sixed, as of today."

"Oh, ho," said Kingsbury. "So you got something against golf?"

"That's the deal. Take it or leave it."

"You think you can scare me? Hell, I got gangsters shooting at me. Professionals." Kingsbury cut loose an enormous sneeze, and promptly plugged his nostrils with the handkerchief.

Winder said, "I was hoping to appeal to the pragmatic side of your nature."

"Listen, I know how to handle this situation from up North. The way to handle it is, I cut the wop bastards in. The Zubonis, I'm talking about. I cut 'em in on Falcon Trace, you'd be surprised how fast they let bygones be bygones. You watch what good friends we are, once I start using Zuboni roofers, Zuboni drywall, Zuboni plumbing." Kingsbury looked positively triumphant. "Blackmail, my ass. The fuck are you going to blackmail me with now?"

"I believe you misunderstood the offer," Joe Winder said. "I'm not planning to go to the mob. I'm planning to go to the media."

Defiantly Kingsbury snatched the hanky from his nose. "Jesus, you're pissing me off." He picked up the phone and commanded the operator to connect him with Security. Joe Winder took two steps toward the desk, raised his paw and shot the telephone console to pieces.

Impressed, Kingsbury probed at the tangle of wires and broken plastic. "Goddamn lunatic," he said.

Winder sat down and tucked the gun into the furry folds of the costume. "Think in terms of headlines," he said. "Imagine what'll happen when the newspapers find out the Amazing Kingdom of Thrills is run by a Mafia snitch. You'll be famous, Frankie. Wouldn't you love to be interviewed by Connie Chung?"

"Let me just say, fuck you."

Winder frowned. "Don't make me shoot up more office equipment. Stop and consider the facts. You obtained the bank notes and financing for Falcon Trace under false pretenses; to wit, using a false name and phony credit references. Ditto on your construction permits. Ditto on your performance bond. Once the money boys find out who you really are, once they read about it on the front page of the *Wall Street Journal*, not only is Falcon Trace dead, you can look forward to spending the rest of your natural life at the courthouse, getting your ass sued off. Everybody'll want a piece, Frankie. We're talking clusterfuck."

He now had Francis X. Kingsbury's undivided attention. "And last but not least," Winder said, "is the criminal situation. If I'm not mistaken, you're still on probation."

"Yeah, so?"

"So the terms of probation strictly prohibit consorting with known felons and other unsavory dirtbags. However, a review of your Security Department indicates you're not only consorting with known criminals, you've surrounded yourself with them."

"This isn't Orlando," Kingsbury said. "Down here it's not so easy to get good help. If I was as strict as Disney, I'd have nobody working for me. What, maybe altar boys? Mormons and Brownie Scouts? This is Miami, for Chrissakes, I got a serious recruiting problem here."

"Nonetheless," Joe Winder said, "you've gone out of your way to dredge up extremely primitive life-forms."

"What's wrong with giving a guy a second chance?" Kingsbury paused for a second, then said, "I'm the first to admit, hell, Pedro was a bad choice. I didn't know about the damn drugs." Speaking of Pedro, he thought, where the hell is he?

"What's done is done," Winder said. He fanned himself with his spare paw; it was wretchedly hot inside the costume. "Frankie, this is a matter for you and the probation bureau. Between us boys, I wouldn't be surprised if they packed you off to Eglin for six or eight months. You do play tennis, don't you?"

The haughtiness ebbed from Kingsbury's face. Pensively he traced a pudgy finger along the lines of his infamous rodent tattoo. "Winder, what exactly is your problem?"

"The problem is you're mutilating a fine chunk of island so a bunch of rich people have a warm place to park their butts in the winter. You couldn't have picked a worse location, Frankie, the last green patch of the Keys. You're bulldozing next door to a national wildlife refuge. And offshore, in that magnificent ocean, is the only living coral reef in North America. I believe that's where you intended to flush your toilets—"

"No!" Kingsbury snapped. "We'll have deep-well sewage injection. High-tech facilities—no runoff, no outfall."

"Imagine," Winder mused, "the shit of millionaires dappling our azure waters."

Kingsbury reddened and clenched his fists. "If I go along with this deal, what, it's some major victory for the environment? You think the ghost of Henry Fucking Thoreau is gonna pin a medal or some such goddamn thing on your chest?"

Joe Winder smiled at the thought. "I've got no illusions," he said. "One less golf course is one less golf course. I'll settle for that."

"The lots, Jesus, they're worth millions. That's what this goddamn piece of paper'll cost me."

"I'll settle for that, too."

Kingsbury was still stymied. He glared furiously at Charles Chelsea's final publicity release.

"You'll never understand," Winder said, "because you weren't born here. Compared to where you came from, this is always going to look like paradise. Hell, you could wipe out every last bird and butterfly, and it's still better than Toledo in the dead of winter."

With a dark chuckle, Kingsbury said, "No kidding."

"Don't read too much into this operation, Frankie. I'm just sick of asshole carpetbaggers coming down here and fucking up the place. Nothing personal."

It came out of the blue, Kingsbury saying, "There was a guy named Jack Winder. Big-time land developer, this goes back a few years, before I was selling waterfront. Winder Planned Communities was the company."

"My father."

"What?" said Kingsbury. "Quit whispering."

"Jack Winder was my father."

"Then what the hell are you doing? Biting the hand is what I'd call it. Dishonoring the family name."

"Depends on your point of view."

Kingsbury sneered. "I hear this line of bullshit all the time: 'We got our slice of sunshine, fine, now it's time to close the borders.' Selfish is what you are."

"Maybe so," Winder said. "I'd like to fish that shoreline again, that's for sure. I'd like to see some tarpon out there next spring."

Dramatically, Francis Kingsbury straightened in the chair. He began talking with his eyes and hands, unmistakably a sales pitch: "People come to the Amazing Kingdom, they might like to play some golf. Mommy takes the kids to the theme park, Daddy hits the fairways. So what?"

Winder said nothing. Kingsbury began to knead his jowls in exasperation. "What the hell's so wrong with that picture? Eighteen lousy holes, I just don't see the crime. It's what Disney did. It's what everybody does with prime acreage. This is Florida, for Chrissakes."

"Not the way it ought to be, Frankie."

"Then you're living in what they call a dreamworld. This ain't Oz, son, and there's no fairy wizard to make things right again. Down here the brick road's not yellow, it's green. Plain and simple. Case closed."

But Joe Winder wasn't changing his mind. "I hope the papers get your name right," he said.

Bleakly Kingsbury thought of front-page headlines and multimillion-dollar lawsuits and minimum-security prisons with no driving range. "All right," he said to Winder, "let's talk."

"You've got my offer. Read the press release, it's all tied up with a pretty ribbon. You shut down Falcon Trace for the noblest of reasons and you're a hero, Frankie. Isn't that what you want?"

"I'd rather have my oceanfront lots."

Then the door flew open and there, bug-eyed and seething, was Pedro Luz. He aimed a large blue handgun at Joe Winder and grunted something unintelligible.

"Nice of you to put in an appearance," Kingsbury remarked. His eyes flooded with a mixture of rage and relief. "This asshole, get him out of my sight! For good this time."

"Drop the gun," Pedro Luz told Winder. "And put on your goddamn head."

Winder did as he was told. Zipping himself in, he felt cumbersome and helpless and feverishly short of breath.

Kingsbury said, "He doesn't leave the park alive, you understand?"

"No problem," said Pedro Luz.

"*No problem*," mimicked Kingsbury. "No problem, my ass. This is Mr. Crackerjack Bodyguard, right? Mr. Lightning Response Time."

For a moment Pedro Luz felt an overwhelming urge to turn the pistol on Francis X. Kingsbury; something told him it would be every bit as satisfying as shooting Joe Winder. Maybe another time, he decided. After payday.

A muted voice inside the raccoon head said: "This is a big mistake, Frankie."

Kingsbury laughed mordantly and blew his nose. "Pedro,

it's your last fucking chance. I hope you still got enough brain cells to do this one simple chore."

"No problem." With the crutch he roughly shoved Joe Winder toward the door.

"Hey, Pedro."

"What, Mr. Kingsbury?"

"That's a six-hundred-dollar animal costume. Try not to mess it up."

Thirty-four

Carrie Lanier was practicing a song at the mirror as she dressed for the pageant. The door opened behind her, and she saw a flash of orange.

"Hey! We thought you were headed for New York."

"I seriously considered it." Skink shut the door with his foot.

"Your friend Officer Tile mentioned Orlando. Somebody shot up a tour bus, he figured it might be you."

"Another pale imitation, that's all. Where's your boyfriend?"

Carrie described Winder's plan to confront Francis Kingsbury. "Joe's got all the bases covered."

Skink shook his head. "It'll never work."

"Where have you been, anyway?"

"Down here in the underground, away from all radio beams. I needed a break from that damn plane."

Carrie moved closer to the mirror and began to put on her makeup. "What's with the gas cans?" she asked.

Skink carried one in each hand. "Let's pretend you didn't see these," he said. "I just want to make sure you've got a way out of the park."

"When?"

"Whenever."

"What about Joe?"

"I expect he's in some trouble," Skink said. "I've got a chore to do, then I'll check around."

"Don't worry, Pedro's locked in the storage room."

"How? With what?"

When Carrie told him, Skink frowned. "I guess I'd better get going."

She said, "Can you zip me up? There's a little hook at the top."

Skink set down the gas cans and fastened the back of her gown. He wondered what had happened to the Indian theme.

"When do you go on?" he asked.

"Half an hour."

"The dress is lovely," he said, stepping back. "Half an hour it is."

"Thanks. Wish me luck."

"You'll do fine."

Carrie turned from the mirror. "Should I wait for Joe?"

"Of course," said Skink, "but not too long."

When they got to the security office, Pedro Luz ordered Joe Winder to remove the raccoon costume and hang it neatly in the uniform closet. Then Pedro Luz dragged Winder into the storage room, clubbed him to the floor and beat him seven or eight times with the crutch—Joe Winder lost count. Every time Pedro Luz struck a blow, he emitted a queer high-pitched peep that sounded like a baby sparrow. When he finally stopped to rest, he was panting heavily and his face shone with damp splotches. Spying from a fetal position on the floor, Joe Winder watched Pedro Luz swallow two handfuls of small orange tablets. Winder assumed these were not muscle relaxants.

"I can kill you with my bare hands," Pedro Luz said informatively.

Winder sat up, hugging his own chest to prevent pieces of broken ribs from snapping off like dead twigs. He couldn't figure out why Pedro Luz kept a full-length mirror in the storage room.

"It's raining outside," Pedro Luz said.

"That's what we're waiting for?"

"Yeah. Soon as it stops, I'll take you out and kill you."

Pedro Luz stripped off his shirt and began to work out with a pair of heavy dumbbells; he couldn't take his eyes off his own glorious biceps. The syncopation of Pedro's breathing and pumping put Joe Winder to sleep. When he awoke much later, still on the floor, he saw that Pedro Luz had put on a fresh uniform. The security man rose unsteadily and reached for the crutch; his hands trembled and his eyelids were mottled and puffy.

"The parade starts soon," he said. "Everyone in the park goes to watch—that's when you're gonna break into the ticket office to rip off the cashboxes."

"And you're going to catch me in the act, and shoot me."

"Yeah," Pedro Luz wheezed, "in the back."

"Pretty sloppy. The cops'll have plenty of questions."

"I'm still thinking it through." His head lolled and he shut his eyes. Joe Winder sprang for the door and regretted it instantly. Pedro Luz was on him like a mad bear; he grabbed Winder at the base of the neck and hurled him backward into the stock shelves.

"And that was one-handed," Pedro Luz bragged. "How much do you weigh?"

Winder answered, with a groan, "One seventy-five."

The security man beamed. "Light as a feather. No problem."

"I'd like to speak with your boss one more time."

"No way." Pedro Luz hoisted Winder from a tangle of intravenous tubes and set him down in a bare corner. He said, "Remember, I still got that gun you were carrying—I figure that's my throwdown. The story is, I had to shoot you because of the gun."

Winder nodded. "I'm assuming there'll be no witnesses."

"Course not. They'll all be at the parade."

"What about the rain, Pedro? What if the parade's washed out?"

"It's August, asshole. The rain don't last long." Pedro Luz hammered the heel of his hand against the side of his skull, as if trying to knock a wasp out of his ear. "God, it's loud in here."

"I don't mean to nag," Joe Winder said, "but you ought to lay off the steroids."

"Don't start with me!" Pedro Luz cracked the door and poked his head out. "See, it's stopped already. Just a drizzle." He gripped Joe Winder by the shoulder. "Let's go, smartass."

But Winder could barely walk for the pain. Outside, under a low muddy sky, the tourists rushed excitedly toward Kingsbury Lane, where a band had begun to play. Pedro Luz marched Winder against the flow of yammering, gummy-faced children and their anxious, umbrella-wielding parents. The ticket office was on the other side of the park, a long hike, and Joe Winder had planned to use the time to devise a plan for escape. Instead his thoughts meandered inanely; he noticed, for example, what a high percentage of the Amazing Kingdom's tourists were clinically overweight. Was this a valid cross-section of American society? Or did fat people travel to Florida more frequently than thin people? Three times Winder slowed to ponder the riddle, and three times Pedro Luz thwacked the back of his legs with the dreaded crutch. No one stopped to interfere; most likely they assumed that Winder was a purse snatcher or some other troublemaker being rousted by Security.

Eventually the crowds thinned and the light rain stopped. The two men were alone, crossing the walkway that spanned the dolphin tank. The swim-along attraction had closed early because the trainers were needed at the parade, in case the lion got testy. Joe Winder heard a burst of applause across the amusement park—fireworks blossoming over Kingsbury Lane. The pageant had begun!

Winder thought of Carrie Lanier, and hoped she had the good sense not to come looking for him. He felt Pedro Luz's crutch jab him between the shoulder blades. "Hold it," the security man commanded.

A hoary figure appeared at the end of the walkway ahead of them. It was a tall man carrying two red containers.

"Now what?" said Pedro Luz.

Joe Winder's heart sank. Skink didn't see them. He went down two flights of stairs and stacked the gas cans on the back of a Cushman motor cart. He ran back up the steps, disappeared through an unmarked door near the Rare Animal Pavilion and quickly emerged with two more cans of gasoline.

"The Catacombs," Pedro Luz said, mainly to himself.

Joe Winder heard him unsnap the holster. He turned and told Pedro Luz not to do anything crazy.

"Shut up, smartass."

As they watched Skink load the second pair of cans onto the Cushman, Winder realized his own mistake: he had tried too hard to be reasonable and civilized and possibly even clever. Such efforts were wasted on men such as Francis X. Kingsbury. Skink had the right idea.

Pedro Luz aimed his .45 and shouted, "Freeze right there!" Skink stopped at the top of the steps. Pedro Luz ordered him to raise his hands, but Skink acted as if he didn't hear.

"Don't I know you?" Skink said, coming closer.

Pedro Luz found it difficult to look directly at the bearded stranger because one of the man's eyeballs seemed dislodged from the socket. As Skink approached, he gave no indication of recognizing Joe Winder.

"Hello, gentlemen," he said. Casually he bent to examine

the taped stump of Pedro Luz's leg. "Son, you're dropping more parts than a Ford Pinto."

Flustered, Pedro Luz fell back on standard hardass-cop colloquy: "Lemme see some ID."

Skink reached into the blaze-orange weather suit and came out with a small kitchen jar. He handed it to the security man and said, "I believe this belongs to you."

Pedro Luz felt his stomach quake. At the bottom of the jar, drifting in pickle juice, was the tip of his right index finger. It looked like a cube of pink tofu.

"The old woman bit it off," Skink reminded him, "while you were beating her up."

Beautiful, Joe Winder thought. We're both going to die long horrible deaths.

Hoarsely, Pedro Luz said, "Who the hell are you?"

Skink gestured at the soiled bandages around his chest. "I'm the one you shot at the trailer!"

All three of them jumped as a Roman candle exploded high over Kingsbury Lane. A band was playing the theme from *2001: A Space Odyssey*. It sounded dreadful.

In the tank below, Dickie the Dolphin rolled twice and shot a light spray of water from his blowhole. A few drops sprinkled the barrel of Pedro Luz's gun, and he wiped it nervously on the front of his trousers. The circuits of his brain were becoming badly overloaded; assimilating new information had become a struggle—the drugs, the finger in the jar, the one-eyed stoner with the gas cans, the fireworks, the god-awful music. It was time to kill these sorry bastards and go to the gym.

"Who first?" he asked. "Who wants it first?"

Joe Winder saw no evidence of urgency in Skink's demeanor, so he took it upon himself to ram an elbow into the soft declivity beneath Pedro Luz's breastbone. Winder was stunned to see the bodybuilder go down, and idiotically he leapt upon him to finish the job. Winder's punching ability was hampered by the searing pain in his rib cage, and though Pedro Luz was gagging and drooling and gulping to catch his wind, it was a relatively simple exercise to lock his arms around all hundred and seventy-five pounds of Joe Winder and squeeze the breath out of him. The last thing Winder heard, before blacking out, was a splash in the tank below.

He hoped like hell it was the pistol.

Marine biologists debate the relative intelligence of the Atlantic bottle-nosed dolphin, but it is generally accepted that the graceful mammal is extremely smart; that it is able to communicate using sophisticated underwater sonics; that it sometimes appears capable of emotions, including grief and joy. Noting that the dolphin's brain is proportionally larger and more fully developed than that of human beings, some experts contend that the animals are operating in a superior cognitive realm that we simply cannot comprehend.

A more skeptical view (and one endorsed by Joe Winder) is that dolphins probably aren't quite as smart as tourist lore suggests. Otherwise why would they allow themselves to be so easily captured, subjugated, trained and put on public display? It seemed to Winder that somersaulting through Hula Hoops in exchange for a handful of sardines was not proof of high intellect. Given fins and some Milk-Bones, your average French poodle could master the same feat.

It is certainly true, however, that captive dolphins exhibit distinct and complex personalities. Some are gregarious and easily tamed, while others are aloof and belligerent; some are happy to perform stunts for cheering tourists, while others get ulcers. Because each dolphin is so sensitive and unique, curators must be extremely careful when selecting the animals for commercial aquarium shows.

When it came to jumping Hula Hoops, Dickie the Dolphin was competent if unspectacular. The same could be said for his tail-walking, his backward flips and his mastery of the beach ball. While most spectators thought he was a lovable ham, experienced dolphin trainers could see he was just going through the motions. Ever since replacing the deceased Orky as the Amazing Kingdom's aquatic star, Dickie had approached each performance with the same sullen indifference. He took a similar attitude into the swim-along sessions, where he habitually kept a large distance between himself and whatever loud pale humanoid had been suckered into entering the tank.

The exception, of course, was when Dickie the Dolphin got into one of his "moods." Then he would frolic and nuzzle and rub eagerly against the swimmer, who inevitably mistook these gestures for honest affection. Dolphin researchers have documented numerous sexual advances upon human beings of both genders, but they cannot agree on the animals' intention in these circumstances. If dolphins truly are second to people on the intelligence scale, then they most certainly would not mistake a bikini-clad legal secretary for a member of their own species. Which raises a more intriguing hypothesis: that captive male dolphins attempt these outrageous liaisons out of mischief, or perhaps even revenge. The truth is locked deep inside the dolphin's large and complicated cerebrum, but the phenomenon has been widely reported.

On the evening of August 6, Dickie the Dolphin was in a state of high agitation as he circled the darkened whale tank at the Amazing Kingdom of Thrills. Perhaps it was the percussion of the nearby fireworks that disrupted the powerful creature's peace, or perhaps it was the effect of a long and lonely confinement. Although the trained seals and pelicans could be entertaining, Dickie the Dolphin probably would have preferred the companionship of a female partner. And he would have had one if Francis X. Kingsbury had not been so cheap. In any event, the solitary dolphin was keeping a sharp and wily eye on the commotion taking place along the walkway above.

At the first splash, Dickie swiftly sounded, tracking a small steel object to the bottom of his tank. He never considered retrieving the item, as there would be no reward for his effort—the buckets of cut fish had been hauled away hours ago. So the dolphin disregarded Pedro Luz's gun, glided slowly to the surface and waited.

The second splash was different.

Pedro Luz was astonished by the strength of the one-eyed man. He took a punch as well as anyone that Pedro Luz had ever assaulted, plus he was quick. Every time Pedro Luz swung and missed, the bearded stranger hit him two or three times in the gut. It was starting to hurt immensely.

Having lost his own gun, Pedro Luz tried to retrieve the spare—Joe Winder's gun—from the pocket of his trousers. Every attempt brought a new flurry of punches from the one-eyed hobo, so Pedro Luz abandoned the plan. With a bellowing lunge, he was able to get a grip on the stranger's collar—an animal collar!—and pull him close. Pedro Luz preferred squeezing to boxing, and was confident he could end the fight (and the big freak's life) with a vigorous hug. That's when somebody grabbed Pedro Luz's hair from behind, and yanked his head back so fiercely that a popping noise came from his neck. Next thing he knew, his pants were off and he was thrashing in the warm water. Above him stood Joe Winder and the stranger, peering over the rail.

Swimming is an exercise that depends more on style than muscle, and Pedro Luz was plainly a terrible swimmer. The throbbing of his truncated leg added pain to ineptitude as he paddled the tank haplessly in search of a ladder. When the massive dolphin rolled beside him in the dark, Pedro Luz cursed and splashed his arms angrily. He was not the least bit afraid of a stupid fish; perhaps he was deceived by the dolphin's friendly smile, or misled by childhood memories of the hokey "Flipper" television series. In any event, Pedro Luz struck out at the creature with the misguided assumption that he could actually hurt it, and that it was too tame and good-natured to retaliate. Pedro's drug-inflamed brain failed to register the fact that Dickie the Dolphin was a more attuned physiological specimen than Pedro Luz himself, and about five hundred pounds larger. When the animal nudged him playfully with its snout, Pedro Luz balled his fists and slugged its silky gray flank.

"Be careful," Joe Winder advised from the walkway, but Pedro Luz paid no attention. The damn fish would not go away! Using its pectoral flippers almost as arms, it held Pedro Luz in a grasp that was gentle yet firm.

Spitting curses, he kicked the dolphin savagely and pushed away. Stroking clumsily for the wall of the tank, he saw the long sleek form rise beneath him. A fin found Pedro Luz's armpit and spun him roughly. He came up choking, but again the creature tugged him down. Once more Pedro Luz fought his way to the top, and this time Dickie the Dolphin began to nip mischievously—tiny needle-like teeth raking Pedro's neck, his shoulders, his bare thighs. Then the dolphin rolled languidly on its side and gave a soft inquisitive whistle, the same sound Flipper used to make at the end of the TV show when he waved at the camera. Pedro Luz tried not to be afraid, but he couldn't understand what this dolphin was trying to say, or do. The salt water stung his eyes and his throat, and the stump of his leg felt as if it were on fire.

Again Pedro Luz felt cool fins slide under his arms as the dolphin gradually steered him toward the deepest part of the tank. The security man tried to break free, but it did no good. Something else propelled him now—a formidable protuberance that left no doubt as to Dickie the Dolphin's true purpose.

Pedro Luz was awestruck and mortified. The long pale thing loomed from the gray water and touched him—hooking, in fact, around his buttocks. The amphibious prodding brought an unfamiliar plea to Pedro Luz's lips: "Help!"

Watching events unfold in the tank below, Skink agreed it was an extraordinary scene.

"I told you," said Joe Winder. "It's one of Nature's marvels."

Pedro Luz began to whimper. No regimen of weight training and pharmaceutical enhancement could have prepared him, or any mortal man, for an all-out sexual attack by a healthy bottle-nosed dolphin. Pedro Luz had never felt so helpless, exhausted and inadequate; desperately he punched at the prodigious inquiring tuber, only to be rebuked by a well-placed slap from Dickie's sinewy fluke.

Leaning over the rail, Joe Winder offered more advice: "Just roll with it. Don't fight him."

But the futility of resistance was already clear to Pedro Luz, who found himself—for the first time in his adult life—completely out of strength. As he was pulled underwater for the final time, terror gave way to abject humiliation: he was being fucked to death by a damn fish.

Thirty-five

Nina asked where he was calling from.

"Charlie's office," Winder said. "Here's what I'm going to do: I'll leave the phone off the hook all night. That way you can work on your poetry and still make money."

"Joe, that'll cost him a fortune. It's four bucks a minute."

"I know the rates, Nina. Don't worry about it."

"You ready for the latest?"

"Just one verse. Time's running out."

"Here goes," she said, and began to recite:

> *"You flooded me with passions*
> *Hard and lingering.*
> *You took me down again*
> *Pumping breathless, biting blind.*
> *Hot in your bloodrush, I dreamed of more."*

"Wow," Winder said. Obviously things were going gangbusters between Nina and the light-truck salesman.

"You really like it? Or are you patronizing me again?"

"Nina, you're breaking new ground."

"Guess what the moron at the phone syndicate wants.

Limericks! Sex limericks, like they publish in *Playboy*. That's his idea of erotic poetry!"

"Stick to your guns," Winder said.

"You bet I will."

"The reason I called was to say good-bye."

"So tonight's the night," she said. "Will I be seeing you on the news?"

"I hope not." He thought: What the hell. "I met a woman," he said.

"I'm very happy for you."

"Aw, Nina, don't say that."

"I *am*. I think it's great."

"Christ Almighty, aren't you the least bit jealous?"

"Not really."

God, she was a pisser. "Then lie to me," Winder said. "Have mercy on my lunatic soul and lie to me. Tell me you're mad with jealousy."

"You win, Joe. You saw through my act."

"Was that a giggle I heard?"

"No!" Nina said. The giggle burst into a full-blown laugh. "I'm dying here. I might just leap off the building. I'm so damn jealous. Who is she? Who is this tramp?"

Now Winder started laughing, too. "I'd better go," he said, "before I say something sensible."

"Call me, Joe. Whatever happens, I'd love to get a phone call."

"I know the number by heart," he said. "Me and every pervert on the Gold Coast."

"You go to hell," Nina teased. "And be careful, dammit."

He said good-bye and placed the receiver on Charles Chelsea's desk.

Skink munched a cotton candy and said, "These are excellent seats."

"They ought to be." Joe Winder assumed Francis X. Kingsbury would arrive at any moment; it was his private viewing box, after all—leather swivel chairs, air-conditioning, video monitors, a wet bar. Thirty rows up, overlooking the parade route.

"What will you do when he gets here?" Skink asked.

"I haven't decided. Maybe he'd like to go swimming with Pedro's new friend."

The grandstand was packed, and Kingsbury Lane was lined five deep with eager spectators. As the history of Florida unfolded in song and skit, Joe Winder imagined that the Stations of the Cross could be similarly adapted and set to music, if the audience would only forgive a few minor revisions. Every float in the Summerfest pageant was greeted with the blind and witless glee displayed by people who have spent way too much money and are determined to have fun. They cheered at the sight of a bootless Ponce de León, an under-aged maiden on each arm, wading bawdily into the Fountain of Youth; they roared as the pirate Black Caesar chased a concubine up the mizzenmast while his men plundered a captured galleon; they gasped as the Killer Hurricane of 1926 tore the roof off a settler's cabin and the smock off his brave young wife.

Skink said, "I never realized cleavage played such an important role in Florida history." Joe Winder told him to just wait for the break-dancing migrants.

Carrie Lanier gave a cassette of the new music to the driver, and took her place on the last float. The Talent Manager showed up and demanded to know why she wasn't wearing the Indian costume.

"That wasn't an Indian costume," Carrie said, "unless the Seminoles had streetwalkers."

The Talent Manager, a middle-aged woman with sweeping

427

peroxide hair and ropes of gold jewelry, informed Carrie that a long gown was unsuitable for the Jubilee parade.

"It's ideal for what I'm singing," Carrie replied.

"And what would that be?"

"That would be none of your business." She adjusted the microphone, which was clipped into the neck of her dress.

The Talent Manager became angry. "Paul Revere and the Raiders isn't good enough for you?"

"Go away," said Carrie.

"And where's our lion?"

"The lion is taking the night off."

"No, missy," the Talent lady said, shaking a finger. "Thousands of people out there are waiting to see Princess Golden Sun ride a wild lion through the Everglades."

"The lion has a furball. Now get lost."

"At least put on the wig," the Talent lady pleaded. "There's no such thing as a blond Seminole. For the sake of authenticity, put on the damn wig!"

"Toodle-loo," said Carrie. And the float began to roll.

At first, Sergeant Mark Dyerson thought the telemetry was on the fritz again. How could the panther get back on the island? No signal had been received for days, then suddenly there it was, beep-beep-beep. Number 17. The sneaky bastard was at it again!

Sergeant Dyerson asked the pilot to keep circling beneath the clouds until he got a more precise fix on the transmitter. The greenish darkness of the hammocks and the ocean suddenly was splayed by a vast sparkling corridor of lights—the Amazing Kingdom of Thrills. The plane banked high over a confetti of humanity.

"Damn," said the ranger. Sharply he tapped the top of the radio receiver. "This can't be right. Fly me over again."

But the telemetry signals were identical on the second pass, and the third and the fourth. Sergeant Dyerson peered out the window of the Piper and thought, He's down there. He's inside the goddamn park!

The ranger told the pilot to call Naples. "I need some backup," he said, "and I need the guy with the dogs."

"Should I say which cat we're after?"

"No, don't," Sergeant Dyerson said. The top brass of the Game and Fish Department was tired of hearing about Number 17. "Tell them we've got a panther in trouble," said Sergeant Dyerson, "that's all you need to say."

The pilot reached for the radio. "What the hell's it doing in the middle of an amusement park?"

"Going crazy," said the ranger. "That's all I can figure."

The break-dancing migrant workers were a sensation with the crowd. Skink covered his face during most of the performance; it was one of the most tasteless spectacles he had ever seen. He asked Joe Winder if he wished to help with the gasoline.

"No, I'm waiting for Kingsbury."

"What for?"

"To resolve our differences as gentlemen. And possibly pound him into dog chow."

"Forget Kingsbury," Skink advised. "There's your girl."

Carrie's float appeared at the end of the promenade; a spotlight found her in a black sequined evening gown, posed among ersatz palms and synthetic cypress. She was perfectly dazzling, although the crowd reacted with confused and hesitant applause—they'd been expecting a scantily clad Indian princess astride a snarling wildcat.

Joe Winder tried to wave, but it hurt too much to raise his arms. Carrie didn't see him. She folded her hands across her midriff and began to sing:

> *"Vissi d'arte, vissi d'amore*
> *Non feci mai male ad animal viva! Con man furtiva*
> *Quante miserie conobbi, aiutai ... "*

Winder was dazed, and he was not alone; a restless murmuring swept through the stands and rippled along the promenade.

"Magnificent!" Skink said. His good eye ablaze, he clutched Winder's shoulder: "Isn't she something!"

"What is that? What's she singing?"

Skink shook him with fierce exuberance. "My God, man, it's Puccini. It's *Tosca*!"

"I see." It was a new wrinkle: opera.

And Carrie sang beautifully; what her voice lacked in strength it made up in a flawless liquid clarity. The aria washed sorrowfully across the Amazing Kingdom and, like a chilly rain, changed the mood of the evening.

Skink put his mouth to Winder's ear and whispered: "This takes place in the second act, where Tosca has just seen her lover tortured by the ruthless police chief and sentenced to death by a firing squad. In her failed effort to save him, Tosca herself becomes a murderess. Her song is a lamentation on life's tragic ironies."

"I'd never have guessed," Winder said.

As the float passed the Magic Mansion, Carrie sang:

> *"Nell'ora del dolore*
> *Perchè, perchè, Signore,*
> *Perchè me ne rimuneri così?"*

Skink closed his eyes and swayed. "Ah, why, dear Lord," he said. "Ah, why do you reward your servant so?"

Winder said the audience seemed fidgety and disturbed.

"Disturbed?" Skink was indignant. "They ought to be distraught. Mournful. They ought to be *weeping*."

430

"They're only tourists," Joe Winder said. "They've been waiting all afternoon to see the lion."

"Cretins."

"Oh, she knew," Winder said fondly. "She knew they wouldn't like it one bit."

Skink grinned. "Bless her heart." He began to applaud rambunctiously, "Bravo! Bravo!" His clapping and shouting caught the attention of spectators in the lower rows, who looked up toward the VIP box with curious annoyance. Carrie spotted both of them in Kingsbury's booth, and waved anxiously. Then she gathered herself and, with a deep breath, began the first verse again.

"What a trouper." Joe Winder was very proud.

Skink straightened his rain cap and said, "Go get her."

"Now?"

"Right now. It's time." Skink reached out to shake Winder's hand. "You've got about an hour," he said.

Winder told him to be careful. "There's lots of kids out there."

"Don't you worry."

"What about Kingsbury?"

Skink said, "Without the park, he's finished."

"I intended to make him famous. You should've heard my plan."

"Some other time," Skink said. "Now go. And tell her how great she was. Tell her it was absolutely wonderful. Giacomo would've been proud."

"*Arrivederci!*" said Joe Winder.

From his third-floor office above Sally's Cimarron Saloon, Francis X. Kingsbury heard the parade go by. Only Princess Golden Sun's dolorous aria brought him to the window, where he parted the blinds to see what in the name of Jesus H. Christ had gone wrong. The disposition of the crowd had changed

431

from festive to impatient. Unfuckingbelievable, thought Kingsbury. It's death, this music. And what's with the evening gown, the Kitty Carlisle number. Where's the buckskin bikini? Where's the tits and ass? The tourists looked ready to bolt.

Carrie hit the final note and held it—held it forever, it seemed to Kingsbury. The girl had great pipes, he had to admit, but it wasn't the time or place for Italian caterwauling. And God, this song, when would it end?

As the float trundled by, Kingsbury was surprised to see that Princess Golden Sun wasn't singing anymore; in fact, she was drinking from a can of root beer. Yet her final melancholy note still hung in the air!

Or was it something else now?

The fire alarm, for instance.

Kingsbury thought: Please, don't let it be. He tried to call Security but no one answered—that fucking Pedro, he should've been back from his errand hours ago.

Outside, the alarm had tripped a prerecorded message on the public-address system, urging everyone to depart the Amazing Kingdom in a calm and orderly fashion. When Kingsbury peeked out the window again, he saw customers streaming like ants for the exits; the performers and concessionaires ran, as well. Baldy the Eagle ripped off his wings and sprinted from the park at Olympic speed; the animal trainers fled together in a hijacked Cushman, but not before springing the hinge on the lion's cage and shooing the wobbly, tranquilized beast toward the woods.

Kingsbury ran, too. He ran in search of Pedro Luz, the only man who knew how to turn off the fire alarm. Golf spikes clacking on the concrete, Kingsbury jogged from the security office to King Arthur's Food Court to The Catacombs, where he found Spence Mooher limping in mopey addled circles, like a dog who'd been grazed by a speeding bus.

But there was no trace of Pedro, and despair clawed at

Kingsbury's gut. People now were pouring out of the park, and taking their money with them. Even if they had wished to stop and purchase one last overpriced souvenir, no one was available to sell it to them.

Chickenshits! Kingsbury raged inwardly. All this panic, and no fire. *Can't you idiots see it's a false alarm?*

Then came the screams.

Kingsbury's throat tightened. He ducked into a photo kiosk and removed the laminated ID card from his belt. Why risk it if the crowd turned surly?

The screaming continued. In a prickly sweat, Kingsbury tracked the disturbance to the whale tank, where something had caught the attention of several families on their way out of the park. They lined the walkway, and excitedly pointed to the water. Assuming the pose of a fellow tourist, Kingsbury nonchalantly joined the others on the rail. He overheard one man tell his wife that there wasn't enough light to use the video camera; she encouraged him to try anyway. A young girl cried and clutched at her mother's leg; her older brother told her to shut up, it's just a plastic dummy.

It wasn't a dummy. It was the partially clothed body of Pedro Luz, facedown in the Orky tank. His muscular buttocks mooned the masses, and indeed it was this sight—not the fact he was dead—that had shocked customers into shrieking.

Francis X. Kingsbury glared spitefully at the corpse. Pedro's bobbing bare ass seemed to mock him—a hairy faceless smile, taunting as it floated by. So this is how it goes, thought Kingsbury. Give a man a second chance, this is how he pays you back.

Suddenly, and without warning, Dickie the Dolphin rocketed twenty feet out of the water and performed a perfect triple-reverse somersault.

The tourists, out of pure dumb reflex, broke into applause.

*

The Amazing Kingdom of Thrills emptied in forty minutes. Two hook-and-ladder rigs arrived from Homestead, followed by a small pumper truck from the main fire station in lower Key Largo. The fire fighters unrolled the hoses and wandered around the park, but found no sign of a fire. They were preparing to leave when three green Jeeps with flashing lights raced into the empty parking lot. The fire fighters weren't sure what to make of the Game and Fish officers; an amusement park seemed an unlikely hideout for gator poachers. Sergeant Mark Dyerson flagged down one of the departing fire trucks and asked the captain if it was safe to take dogs into the area. The captain said sure, be my guest. Almost immediately the hounds struck a scent, and the old tracker turned them loose. The wildlife officers loaded up the dart guns and followed.

Francis Kingsbury happened to be staring out the window when he spotted the lion loping erratically down Kingsbury Lane; a pack of dogs trailed closely, snapping at its tail. The doped-up cat attempted to climb one of the phony palm trees, but fell when its claws pulled loose from the Styrofoam bark. Swatting at the hounds, the cat rose and continued its disoriented escape.

Lunacy, thought Kingsbury.

Someone knocked twice on the office door and came in—a short round man with thin brown hair and small black eyes. A hideous polyester-blend shirt identified him as a valued customer. Pinned diagonally across the man's chest was a wrinkled streamer that said "OUR FIVE-MILLIONTH SPECIAL GUEST!" In the crook of each arm sat a stuffed toy animal with reddish fur, pipestem whiskers and a merry turquoise tongue.

Vance and Violet Vole.

"For my nieces," the man explained. "I got so much free stuff I can hardly fit it in the car."

Kingsbury smiled stiffly. "The big winner, right? That's you."

"Yeah, my wife can't fuckin' believe it."

"Didn't you hear it, the fire alarm? Everybody else, I mean, off they went."

"But I didn't see no fire," the man said. "No smoke, neither." He arranged the stuffed animals side by side on Kingsbury's sofa.

The guy's a total yutz, Kingsbury thought. Does he want my autograph or what? Maybe a snapshot with the big cheese.

"What's that you got there?" the man asked. "By the way, the name's Rossiter." He nodded toward a plaid travel bag that lay open on Kingsbury's desk. The bag was full of cash, mostly twenties and fifties.

The man said, "Looks like I wasn't the only one had a lucky day."

Kingsbury snapped the bag closed. "I'm very busy, Mr. Rossiter. What's the problem—something with the new car, right? The color doesn't match your wife's eyes or whatever."

"No, the car's great. I got no complaints about the car."

"Then what?" Kingsbury said. "The parade, I bet. That last song, I swear to Christ, I don't know where that shit came from—"

"You kiddin' me? It was beautiful. It was Puccini."

Kingsbury threw up his hands. "Whatever. Not to be rude, but what the fuck do you want?"

The man said, "I got a confession to make. I cheated a little this morning." He shrugged sheepishly. "I cut in line so we could be the first ones through the gate. That's how I won the car."

It figures, thought Kingsbury. Your basic South Florida clientele.

The man said, "I felt kinda lousy, but what the hell. Opportunity knocks, right? I mean, since I had to be here anyway—"

"Mr. Rossiter, do I look like a priest? All this stuff, I don't need to hear it—"

"Hey, call me Lou," the man said, "and I'll call *you* Frankie." From his Sansibelt slacks he withdrew a .38-caliber pistol with a silencer.

Francis Kingsbury's cheeks went from pink to gray. "Don't tell me," he said.

"Yeah," said Lou, "can you believe it?"

Thirty-six

Francis X. Kingsbury asked the hit man not to shoot.

"Save your breath," said Lou.

"But, look, a fantastic new world I built here. A place for little tykes, you saw for yourself—roller coasters and clowns and talking animals. Petey Possum and so forth. I did all this myself."

"What a guy," said Lou.

Kingsbury was unaccustomed to such bald sarcasm. "Maybe I make a little dough off the operation, so what? Look at all the fucking happiness I bring people!"

"I enjoyed myself," Lou admitted. "My wife, she's crazy about the Twirling Teacups. She and her mother both. I almost spit up on the damn thing, to be honest, but my wife's got one a them cast-iron stomachs."

Kingsbury brightened. "The Twirling Teacups, I designed those myself. The entire ride from scratch."

"No shit?"

The hit man seemed to soften, and Kingsbury sensed an opening. "Look, I got an idea about paying back the Zubonis. It's a big construction deal, we're talking millions. They'd be nuts to pass it up—can you make a phone call? Tell 'em it's once in a lifetime."

Lou said, "Naw, I don't think so."

"Florida waterfront—that's all you gotta say. Florida fucking waterfront, and they'll be on the next plane from Newark, I promise."

"You're a good salesman," said the hit man, "but I got a contract."

Kingsbury nudged the plaid travel bag across the desk. "My old lady, she wanted me to go on a trip—Europe, the whole nine yards. I was thinking why not, just for a couple months. She's never been there."

Lou nodded. "Now's a good time to go. The crowds aren't so bad."

"Anyhow, I emptied the cash registers after the parade." Kingsbury patted the travel bag. "This is just from ticket sales, not concessions, and still you're talking three hundred and forty thousand. Cash-ola."

"Yeah? That's some vacation, three hundred forty grand."

"And it's all yours if you forget about the contract."

"Hell," said Lou, "it's mine if I don't."

Outside there was a bang, followed by a hot crackling roar. When Kingsbury spun his chair toward the window, his face was bathed in flickering yellow light.

"Lord," he said.

The Wet Willy was on fire—hundreds of feet of billowed latex, squirming and thrashing like an eel on a griddle. White sparks and flaming bits of rubber hissed into the tropical sky, and came down as incendiary rain upon the Amazing Kingdom of Thrills. Smaller fires began to break out everywhere.

Francis Kingsbury shivered under his hairpiece.

Lou went to the window and watched the Wet Willy burn. "You know what it looks like?"

"Yes," Kingsbury said.

"A giant Trojan."

"I know."

"It ain't up to code, that's for sure. You must've greased some county inspectors."

"Another good guess," Kingsbury said. Why did the alarm cut off? he wondered. Where did all the firemen go?

Lou farted placidly as he walked back to the desk. "Well, I better get a move on."

Kingsbury tried to hand him the telephone. "Please," he begged, "call the Zuboni brothers."

"A deal's a deal," Lou said, checking the fit of the silencer.

"But you saw for yourself!" Kingsbury cried. "Another five years, goddamn, I'll be bigger than Disney."

Lou looked doubtful. "I wasn't gonna say anything, but what the hell. The car and the prizes are great, don't get me wrong, but the park's got a long ways to go."

Petulantly, Kingsbury said, "Fine, let's hear it."

"It's the bathrooms," said Lou. "The fuckin' Port Authority's got cleaner bathrooms."

"Is that so?"

"Yeah, and it wouldn't hurt to keep an extra roll of toilet paper in the stalls."

"Is that it? That's your big gripe?"

Lou said, "People notice them things, they really do." Then he stepped toward Francis X. Kingsbury and raised the pistol.

Joe Winder led her through the dense hammock, all the way to the ocean's edge. It took nearly an hour because Carrie wore high heels. The gown kept snagging on branches, and the insects were murder.

"I'm down two pints," she said, scratching at her ankles.

"Take off the shoes. Hurry." He held her hand and waded into the water.

"Joe!" The gown rose up around her hips; the sequins sparkled like tiny minnows.

"How deep are we going?" she asked.

At first the turtle grass tickled her toes, then it began to sting. Winder kept walking until the water was up to his chest.

"See? No more bugs."

"You're full of tricks," Carrie said, clinging to his arm. From the flats it was possible to see the entire curving shore of the island, including the naked gash made by the bulldozers at Falcon Trace. She asked if the trees would ever come back.

"Someday," Joe Winder said, "if the bastards leave it alone."

Stretching toward the horizon was a ribbon of lights from the cars sitting bumper-to-bumper on County Road 905—the exodus of tourists from the Amazing Kingdom. Winder wondered if Skink had waited long enough to make his big move.

He listened for the distant sounds of sirens as he moved through the shallows, following the shoreline south. The warm hug of the tide soothed the pain in his chest. He pointed at a pair of spotted leopard rays, pushing twin wakes.

"What else do you see?" Carrie said.

"Turtles. Jellyfish. A pretty girl with no shoes." He kissed her on the neck.

"How far can we go like this?" she asked.

"Big Pine, Little Torch, all the way to Key West if you want."

She laughed. "Joe, that's a hundred miles." She kicked playfully into the deeper water. "It feels so good."

"You sang beautifully tonight. Watch out for the coral."

When Carrie stood up, the water came to her chin. Blowing bubbles, she said, "I didn't know you liked opera."

"I hate opera," Winder said, "but you made it wonderful."

She splashed after him, but he swam away.

They didn't leave the ocean until the road was clear and the island was dark. They agreed it would be best to get out of Monroe County for a while, so they took Card Sound Road toward the mainland. The pavement felt cool under their feet.

They wanted to hold hands, but it hampered their ability to defend themselves against the swarming mosquitoes. Every few minutes Winder would stop walking and check the sky for a change in the light. One time he was sure he heard a helicopter.

Carrie said, "What's your feeling about all this?"

"Meaning Kingsbury and the whole mess."

"Exactly."

"There's thousands more where he came from."

"Oh, brother," Carrie said. "I was hoping you'd gotten it all out of your system."

"Never," said Winder, "but I'm open to suggestions."

"All right, here's one: Orlando."

"God help us."

"Now wait a second, Joe. They're shooting commercials at those new studios up there. I've got my first audition lined up for next week."

"What kind of commercials?"

"The point is, it's national exposure."

"Promise me something," Winder said. "Promise it's not one of those personal-hygiene products."

"Fabric softener. The script's not bad, all things considered."

"And will there be singing?"

"No singing," Carrie said, picking up the pace. "They've got newspapers in Orlando, don't they?"

"Oh no, you don't."

"It'd be good for you, Joe. Write about the important things, whatever pisses you off. Just write *something*. Otherwise you'll make me crazy, and I'll wind up killing you in your sleep."

The Card Sound Bridge rose steeply ahead. A handful of crabbers and snapper fishermen sleepily tended slack lines. Joe and Carrie took the sidewalk. For some reason she stopped and gave him a long kiss.

Halfway up the rise, she tugged on his hand and told him to turn around.

There it was: the eastern sky aglow, fat clouds roiling unnaturally under a pulsing halo of wild pink and orange. Baleful columns of tarry smoke rose from the Amazing Kingdom of Thrills.

Joe Winder whistled in amazement. "There's arson," he said, "and then there's arson."

Bud Schwartz and Danny Pogue were surprised to find Molly McNamara wide awake, propped up with a stack of thin hospital pillows. She was brushing her snowy hair and reading the *New Republic* when the burglars arrived.

"Pacemaker," Molly reported. "A routine procedure."

"You look so good," said Danny Pogue. "Bud, don't she look good?"

"Hush now," Molly said. "Sit down here, the news is coming on. There's a story you'll both find interesting." Without being asked, Danny Pogue switched the television to Channel 10, Molly's favorite.

Bud Schwartz marveled at the old woman in bed. Days earlier, she had seemed so weak and withered and close to death. Now the gray eyes were as sharp as a hawk's, her cheeks shone, and her voice rang strong with maternal authority.

She said, "Danny, did you get the bullets?"

"Yes, ma'am." He handed Molly the yellow box.

"These are .22-longs," she said. "I needed shorts. That's what the gun takes."

Danny Pogue looked lamely toward his partner. Bud Schwartz said, "Look, we just asked for .22s. The guy didn't say nothin' about long or short."

"It's all right," Molly McNamara said. "I'll pick up a box at the range next week."

"We don't know diddly about guns," Danny Pogue reiterated. "Neither of us do."

"I know, and I think it's precious." Molly put on her

rose-framed glasses and instructed Bud Schwartz to adjust the volume on the television. A nurse came in to check the dressing on Molly's stitches, but Molly shooed her away. She pointed at the TV and said, "Look here, boys."

The news opened with videotape of a colossal raging fire. The scene had been recorded at a great distance, and from a helicopter. When the TV reporter announced what was burning, the burglars simultaneously looked at one another and mouthed the same profane exclamation.

"Yes," Molly McNamara said rapturously. "Yes, indeed."

Danny Pogue felt mixed emotions as he watched the Amazing Kingdom burn. He recalled the gaiety of the promenade, the friendliness of the animal characters, the circus colors and brassy music, the wondrous sensation of being inundated with fun. Then he thought of Francis X. Kingsbury killing off the butterflies and crocodiles, and the conflagration seemed more like justice than tragedy.

Bud Schwartz was equally impressed by the destruction of the theme park—not as a moral lesson, but as a feat of brazen criminality. The torch artist had been swift and thorough; the place was engulfed in roaring, implacable flames, and there was no saving it. The man on TV said he had never witnessed such a fierce, fast-moving blaze. Bud Schwartz felt relieved and lucky and wise.

"And you wanted to stay," he said to Danny Pogue. "You wanted to ride the Jungle Jerry again."

Danny Pogue nodded solemnly and slid the chair close to the television. "We could be dead," he murmured.

"Fried," said his partner. "Fried clams."

"Hush now," Molly said. "There's no call for melodrama."

She announced that she wasn't going to ask why they'd gone to the Amazing Kingdom that night. "I don't like to pry," she said. "You're grown men, you've got your own lives."

Danny Pogue said, "It wasn't us who torched the place."

Molly McNamara smiled as if she already knew. "How's your foot, Danny?"

"It don't hardly hurt at all."

Then to Bud Schwartz: "And your hand? Is it better?"

"Gettin' there," he said, flexing the fingers.

Molly removed her glasses and rested her head against the pillows. "Nature is a wonder," she said. "Such power to renew, or to destroy. It's an awesome paradox."

"A what?" said Danny Pogue.

Molly told them to think of the fire as a natural purge, a cyclical scouring of the land. Bud Schwartz could hardly keep a straight face. He jerked his chin toward the flickering images on television, and said, "So maybe it's spontaneous combustion, huh? Maybe a bolt of lightning?"

"Anything's possible," Molly said with a twinkle. She asked Danny Pogue to switch to the Discovery Channel, which just happened to be showing a documentary about endangered Florida manatees. A mating scene was in progress as Danny Pogue adjusted the color tint.

Not tonight, thought Bud Schwartz, and got up to excuse himself.

Molly said, "There's a Dodgers game on ESPN. You can watch across the hall in Mr. McMillan's room—he is in what they call a nonresponsive state, so he probably won't mind."

"Swell," Bud Schwartz muttered. "Maybe we'll go halfsies on a keg."

Danny Pogue heard none of this; he was already glued to the tube. Bud Schwartz pointed at his partner and grinned. "Look what you done to him."

Molly McNamara winked. "Go on now," she said. "I think Ojeda's pitching."

Trooper Jim Tile braked sharply when he saw the three green Jeeps. The wildlife officers had parked in a precise triangle at the intersection of Card Sound Road and County 905.

"We'll be out of the way in a minute," said Sergeant Mark Dyerson.

The rangers had gathered between the trucks in the center of the makeshift triangle. Jim Tile joined them. He noticed dogs pacing in the back of one of the Jeeps.

"Look at this," Sergeant Dyerson said.

In the middle of the road, illuminated by headlights, was a battered red collar. Jim Tile crouched to get a closer look.

"Our transmitter," the ranger explained. Imprinted on the plastic was the name "Telonics MOD-500."

"What happened?" Jim Tile asked.

"The cat tore it off. Somehow."

"That's one tough animal."

"It's a first," Sergeant Dyerson said. "We've never had one that could bust the lock on the buckle."

Another officer asked, "What now?" It was the wretched plea of a man being devoured by insects.

"If the cat wants out this bad," said Sergeant Dyerson, "I figure we'll let him be."

From the south came the oscillating whine of a fire truck. Sergeant Dyerson retrieved the broken panther collar and told his men to move the Jeeps off the road. Minutes later, a hook-and-ladder rig barreled past.

Jim Tile mentioned that the theme park was on fire.

"It's breaking my heart," Sergeant Dyerson said. He handed the trooper a card. "Keep an eye out. My home number is on the back."

Jim Tile said, "All my life, I've never seen a panther."

"You probably never will," said the ranger, "and that's the crime of it." He tossed the radio collar in the back of the truck and slid behind the wheel.

"Not all the news is bad," he said. "Number Nine's got a litter of kittens over in the Fakahatchee."

"Yeah?" Jim Tile admired the wildlife officer's outlook and dedication. He was sorry his old friend had caused the man so much trouble and confusion. He said, "So this is all you do— track these animals?"

"It's all I do," Sergeant Dyerson said.

To Jim Tile it sounded like a fine job, and an honorable one. He liked the notion of spending all day in the deep outdoors, away from the homicidal masses. He wondered how difficult it would be to transfer from the highway patrol to the Game and Fish.

"Don't you worry about this cat," he told Sergeant Dyerson. "I worry about all of them."

"This one'll be all right," the trooper said. "You've got my word."

As soon as he spotted the police car, Joe told Carrie to hike up her gown and run. She followed him down the slope of the bridge and into a mangrove creek. Breathlessly they clung to the slippery roots; only their heads stayed dry.

"Don't move," Joe Winder said. "There's a june bug in your ear."

"Yes, I'm aware of that." He quietly dunked his face, and the beetle was swept away by the milky-blue current.

She said, "May I raise the subject of snakes?"

"We're fine." He wrapped his free arm around her waist, to hold her steady against the tide. "You're certainly being a good sport about all this," he said.

"Will you think about Orlando?"

"Sure." It was the least he could do.

The metronomic blink of the blue lights grew stronger, and soon tires crunched the loose gravel on the road; the siren died with a tremulous moan.

Winder chinned up on a mangrove root for a better view. He saw a highway patrol cruiser idling at an angle on the side of the road. The headlights dimmed, and the trooper honked three times. They heard a deep voice, and Winder recognized it: Jim Tile.

"We lucked out," he said to Carrie. "Come on, that's our ride." They climbed from the creek and sloshed out of the mangroves. Before reaching the road, they heard another man's voice and the slam of a door.

Then the patrol car started to roll.

Joe Winder sprinted ahead, waving both arms and shouting for the trooper to stop. Jim Tile calmly swerved around him and, by way of a farewell, flicked his brights as he drove past.

Winder clutched his aching rib cage and cursed spiritedly at the speeding police car. Carrie joined him on the centerline, and together they watched the flashing blue lights disappear over the crest of the Card Sound Bridge.

"Everyone's a comedian," Joe Winder said.

"Didn't you see who was in the back seat?"

"I didn't see a damn thing."

Carrie laughed. "Look what he threw out the window." She held up a gooey stick of insect repellent. The top-secret military formula.

"Do me first," she said. "Every square inch."

Epilogue

A team of police divers recovered the body of PEDRO LUZ from the whale tank at the Amazing Kingdom of Thrills. The Monroe County Medical Examiner ruled drowning as the official cause of death, although the autopsy revealed "minor bite marks, contusions and chafing of a sexual nature."

JAKE HARP recovered from his gunshot wound and rejoined the professional golfing circuit, although he never regained championship form. His next best finish was a tie for 37th place at the Buick Open, and subsequently he set a modern PGA record by missing the cut in twenty-two consecutive tournaments. Eventually he retired to the Seniors' Tour, where he collapsed and died of a cerebral hemorrhage on the first hole of a sudden-death play-off with Billy Casper.

With his payoff money from the mob, BUD SCHWARTZ started a private security company that specializes in high-tech burglar-alarm systems for the home, car and office. Bearing a letter of recommendation from Molly McNamara, DANNY POGUE moved to Tanzania, where he is training to be a game warden at the Serengeti National Park.

After Francis X. Kingsbury's murder, AGENT BILLY HAWKINS was docked a week's pay, and given a written reprimand for taking an unauthorized leave of absence. A month later he was transferred to the FBI office in Sioux Falls, South Dakota. He endured one winter before resigning from the Bureau and returning to Florida as an executive consultant to Schwartz International Security Services Ltd.

NINA WHITMAN quit the phone-sex syndicate after three of her poems were published in the *New Yorker*. A later collection of prose and short fiction was praised by Erica Jong as a "fresh and vigorous reassessment of the female sexual dynamic." Shortly after receiving the first royalty statement from her publisher, Nina gave up poetry and moved to Westwood, California, where she now writes motion-picture screenplays. Her husband owns the second-largest Chevrolet dealership in Los Angeles County.

The estate of FRANCIS X. KINGSBURY, aka FRANKIE KING, was sued by the Walt Disney Corporation for copyright infringement on the characters of Mickey and Minnie Mouse. The lawsuit was prompted by accounts of a pornographic tattoo on the defendant's left forearm, as described by newspaper reporters attending the open-casket funeral. After deliberating only thirty-one minutes (and reviewing a coroner's photograph of the disputed etching), an Orlando jury awarded the Disney company $1.2 million in actual and punitive damages. PENNY KINGSBURY is appealing the decision.

CHARLES CHELSEA accepted a job as executive vice president of public relations for Monkey Mountain. Four months later, disaster struck when a coked-up podiatrist from Ann Arbor, Michigan, jumped a fence and attempted to leg-wrestle a male chacma baboon. The podiatrist was swiftly killed and dismembered, and the animal park was forced to close. Chelsea retired from the public-relations business, and is now said to be working on a novel with Gothic themes.

At his own request, TROOPER JIM TILE was reassigned to Liberty County in the Florida Panhandle. With only 5.1 persons per square mile, it is the least densely populated region of the state.

DICKIE THE DOLPHIN survived the fire that destroyed the Amazing Kingdom of Thrills, and was temporarily relocated to a holding pen at an oceanfront hotel near Marathon. Seven months later, a bankruptcy judge approved the sale of the frisky mammal to a marine attraction in Hilton Head, South Carolina. No swimming is allowed in Dickie's new tank.

After the Amazing Kingdom closed, UNCLE ELY'S ELVES never worked together again. Veteran character actor MOE STRICKLAND branched into drama, taking minor roles in television soap operas before miraculously landing the part of Big Daddy in a Scranton dinner-theater production of *Cat on a Hot Tin Roof*. A freelance critic for the *Philadelphia Inquirer* described Strickland's performance as "gutsy and brooding."

Several weeks after fire swept through Francis X. Kingsbury's theme park, a piano-sized crate from Auckland, New Zealand, was discovered outside the padlocked gate. No one was certain how long the crate had been there, but it was empty by the time a security guard found it; whatever was inside had clawed its way out. Soon residents of the nearby Ocean Reef Club began reporting the disappearance of pet cats and small dogs at a rate of two per week—a mystery that remains unsolved. Meanwhile, Kingsbury's estate received a handwritten invoice from a person calling herself RACHEL LARK. The bill, excluding shipping, amounted to $3,755 for "miscellaneous wildlife."

The widow of DR. WILL KOOCHER hired a Miami lawyer and filed a wrongful-death action against the Amazing Kingdom of Thrills, Ramex Global Trust, N.A. and Bermuda Intercontinental Services, Inc. The insurance companies hastily settled the lawsuit out of court for approximately $2.8 million. The gutted ruins of the Amazing Kingdom were razed, and the land was replanted with native trees, including buttonwoods, pigeon plums, torchwoods, brittle palms, tamarinds, gumbo-limbos and mangroves. This restoration was accomplished in spite of rigid opposition from the Monroe County Commission, which had hoped to use the property as a public dump.

The surviving owners of the FALCON TRACE golf resort sold all construction permits and building rights to a consortium of Japanese investors who had never set foot in South Florida. However, the project stalled once again when environmentalists surveying the Key Largo site reported the presence of at least two blue-tongued mango voles, previously thought to be extinct. According to an unsigned press release faxed to all major newspapers and wire services, the tiny mammals were spotted at Falcon Trace during a nature hike by MOLLY MCNAMARA and the Mothers of Wilderness, who immediately reported the sighting to the U.S. Department of Interior.

Eventually the Falcon Trace and Amazing Kingdom properties were purchased from bankruptcy by the state of Florida, and became part of a preserve on NORTH KEY LARGO. In the spring of 1991, a *National Geographic* photographer set out to capture on film the last surviving pair of blue-tongued mango voles. After two months in the woods, the photographer

451

contracted mosquito-borne encephalitis and was airlifted to Jackson Memorial Hospital, where he spent three weeks on clear fluids. He never got a glimpse of the shy and nocturnal creatures, although he returned to New York with a cellophane packet of suspect rodent droppings and a pledge to keep searching.

Read more from Carl Hiaasen

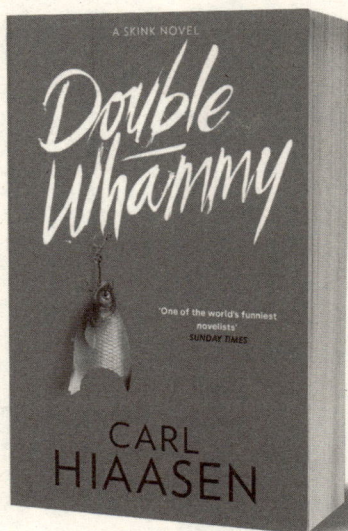

R.J. Decker, star tenant of the local trailer park and neophyte private eye is fishing for a killer. Thanks to a sportsman's scam that's anything but sportsmanlike, there's a body floating in Coon Bog, Florida – and a lot that's rotten in the murky waters of big-stakes, large-mouth bass tournaments ...

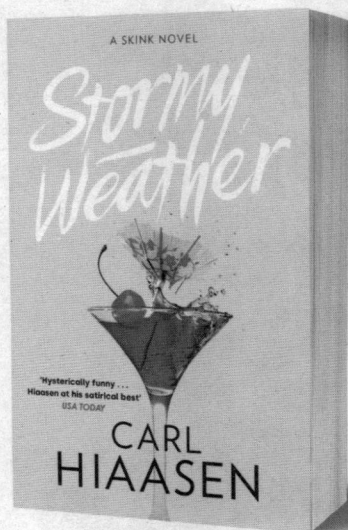

When a ferocious hurricane rips through southern Florida, insurance fraudsters, amateur occultists, and ex-cons waste no time in swarming over the disaster area. And caught in the middle are Max and Bonnie Lamb, honeymooners who abandon their Disney World plans to witness the terrible devastation. But when Max vanishes, Bonnie, aided by a mysterious young man with a tranquilizer gun and a roomful of human skulls, has to follow her only clue: a runaway monkey.

A SKINK NOVEL

Sick Puppy

'Unrelentingly hilarious.
Just dive in and have
a wonderful time'
WASHINGTON POST

CARL
HIAASEN

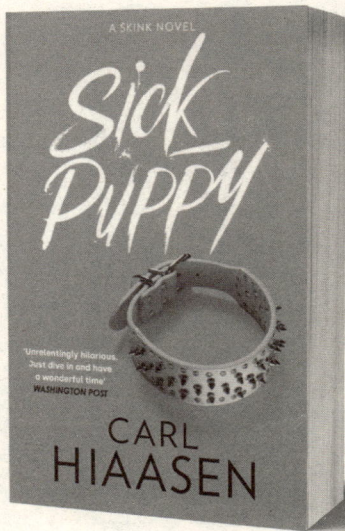

When Palmer Stoat notices the black pickup truck following him on the highway, he fears his precious Range Rover is about to be carjacked. But Twilly Spree, the man tailing Stoat, has vengeance, not sport-utility vehicles, on his mind. Idealistic, independently wealthy and pathologically short-tempered, Twilly has dedicated himself to saving Florida's wilderness from runaway destruction. After watching Stoat blithely dump a trail of fast-food litter out the window, Twilly decides to teach him a lesson . . .

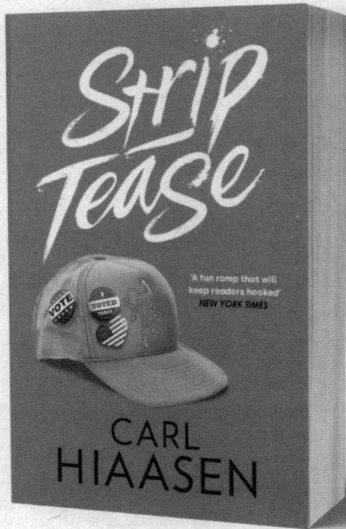

Only in America could an innocent, if drunken, guest of honor at a strip joint bachelor party become a mortal threat against Big Money and Big Government. Only in south Florida, land of roadside honky-tonks and sinister pleasure boats – not to mention blackmail and murder – would a virtuous topless dancer join forces with a cool but clueless cop.

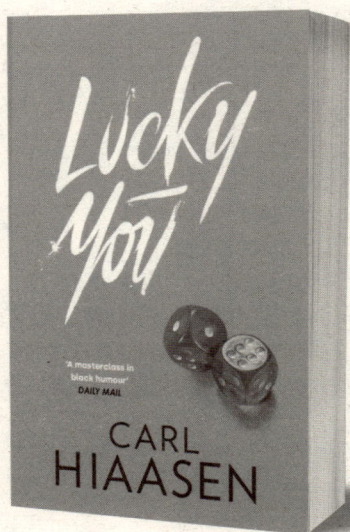

Grange, Florida is famous for its miracles – the weeping fiberglass Madonna, the Road-Stain Jesus, the stigmata man. And now it has JoLayne Lucks, unlikely winner of the state lottery. Unfortunately, JoLayne's winning ticket isn't the only one. The other belongs to Bodean Gazzer and his raunchy sidekick, Chub, who want the whole $28 million jackpot to start their own underground militia . . .